The Fever

By

Thomas Fenske

The Fever

While he hiked, he daydreamed again and brooded over the same question he asked himself every time he hiked in the quiet chill of this lonely landscape.

"Is this really worth it?"

His friends back in Austin asked him that same question every time he left town to make another long drive out west and the same rationalizations were always debated. The danger, the weather, the time and money, and most of all, the trespassing.

"Did you try asking for permission?" Sally had once innocently asked him.

"Of course I did," he answered.

Early on, it had indeed seemed reasonable enough to simply ask, "Mind if I look around?"

But then the inevitable next question would come.

"Why?"

Sam pondered the simple one-word answer to that question, the word that complicated everything. As he walked, he could only muster a coarse whispered response:

"Gold."

His friends scoffed at the word and he had found that strangers scoffed too, but with an added mixture of suspicion and skepticism. That alone gave him plenty of incentive to avoid the subject, but he knew there were other deeper undertones to a stranger's reaction. The moment one got to the heart of the matter, something came over people, as if a smoldering bit of wonderment had been ignited deep within them. It would glisten back at him through their eyes and he would know they had already begun to secretly conjure up an infinite number of "what if" scenarios. He could predict this as readily as a scientist could predict the outcome of a chemical reaction because it always happened whenever he stammered out that one simple word.

"It changes people," he said out loud, adding in a trailing tone, "...even *me*."

The Fever

By

Thomas Fenske

Mainstream Novel

Dedication

I want to thank the many people who made this novel possible. Support and suggestions came at various stages from Dennis Walker, Jessica Lutz, Carol Bonomo, Karen Ward, Debra Ferguson, Janet Fenske, Donna Elkins, and Holly Carver. Texas Parks and Wildlife biologist Misty Sumner very generously provided valuable information on the wildlife in the region and on the people and culture as well.

Most of all, I want to thank my wife Gretchen for offering tremendous insight and support. She gets extra credit for putting up with my grumpy writing moods. I dedicate this novel to her.

NOTE: This is a work of fiction, and although the Lost Ben Sublett Mine is truly a part of Texas lore, all of the speculations mentioned in this work are products of the author's imagination. Please don't burden the kind folks of Hudspeth and Culberson counties in Texas by following any information in this novel in an attempt to find gold. It really IS all private land. Trespassing is against the law and it is dangerous.

One

Sam blinked crusty remnants of the trail from his eyelids and tried to make some sense of his surroundings.

There was an electronic beeping in the darkness and each beep jabbed into his brain like a hot needle. Stars twinkled through the chill in the air. His hands were trapped by the folds of his sleeping bag, but once freed they fumbled with his watch, trying to find the tiny button hidden on the side. When he caught the edge of that small dimple with his fingernail, the night was quiet again.

He wedged an elbow under his body and rubbed his eyes with his other hand. The moon was high, providing some muted light. After a quick yawn, he fought off the impulse to lie back down and snatch a few extra minutes of sleep.

"Best get to it," he said to himself.

A pair of boots was on the ground next to him and he shook them to make sure they were empty. Scorpions tended to think boots were perfect little caves to hide in. It was the first step in a practiced routine.

After he got out of the sleeping bag, he put the boots on, then rolled the bag and secured it to his backpack. He rummaged through one of the zippered pockets and pulled out some cellophane-wrapped peanut butter crackers and a bottle of caffeine pills.

The crackers would be his breakfast and the pills would be his coffee. Sam was not hungry but he knew from experience that those pills didn't sit well on an empty stomach, so he quickly downed a pill with a mouthful of water from his canteen and ate three of the six crackers. He slipped the remaining crackers into his shirt pocket.

Sam stood over a small "V" on the ground made up of seven rocks, and followed the point, looking off into the distance where he saw two lights.

"They're still there," he muttered with relief. "If the lights are still on now, they'll probably be on all night."

Those lights had been his reference points the night before when he had set up the rocks. According to the map, his car was somewhere between those two lights. In the north he could see The Big Dipper, and that pointed him to Polaris, the North Star. If the night stayed clear, it would help keep him on course as well.

The previous afternoon, he had carefully made his way down the western face of a rocky outcrop, moving slowly in the failing light. In the past, he had tried the same thing in the dark and on one trip had fallen. He had been lucky that time but it had scared him, so after that he decided it was worth the risk to descend with a little light.

It wasn't just his decision. There had been a little prodding from his friend Godson as well.

"Sure, darkness is your friend when it works for you," he had said. "But going up in the dark is easier than coming down in the dark. Late in the afternoon nobody is going to see you. Use the light, buddy. Don't be stupid."

As Sam thought about that last statement, he chuckled to himself.

"Famous last words," he joked. He talked to himself a lot on these trips.

The tricky thing about night hiking was keeping on track. A scoutmaster from his brief stint in the Boy Scouts had schooled him in navigation.

"Making your way across open country requires constant correction with a compass and a map," he had said. "You have to note the bearing to an obvious landmark not too far away. Then when you get there, you repeat the same action with another landmark."

There was not a lot of course correction he could do in the dark, so the two lights he had chosen as his landmarks would have to do. Although it was something like seventeen miles to his car, the fact that it was across relatively flat ground worked in his favor.

"Besides, I've got to hit that ranch road at some point," he chuckled, "as long as I walk due west."

He clipped a canteen to his belt and put his knife in the sheath on the other side. The knife had been a conscious choice as his primary protection, although it would probably not be much use against a big cat and might only slightly discourage a pack of coyotes.

Godson had argued that point with him more than once.

"Why don't you carry a gun?" he had asked.

"A rifle is too heavy," Sam had responded, "and it's hard to use in an emergency. If a cat or something jumped me, I'd be fumbling with it. I just don't think it would work with the type of hiking I'm doing. It's also a red flag to someone who might spot me from a distance. Although I could conceal a pistol, well, I don't know. If I am discovered, I want to appear harmless. Out on a ranch like that, there are no rules to speak of and once they are close enough to see it, I'm back to that situation where it becomes a red flag. I think I would have a better chance of talking myself out of any trouble if I was unarmed."

"A knife is still a weapon," Godson had said.

"Yeah, and I have thought about that. If *I* see any kind of gun, I immediately get a bit alarmed. I see a knife, especially on a hiker, I figure it is just more a normal piece of camping equipment. Maybe that's just the city boy in me talking, but that's what I think."

In those conversations, he never added his other more personal reason: he really wasn't a gun person. Still, he had followed this routine six times in the past and he had yet to see a big cat and the only coyotes he had encountered had been yips in the distance.

"No, that's not true," he said out loud, interrupting those thoughts with another memory.

On one of his earlier trips, he was pretty sure something big had been close by, possibly stalking him. It could have been anything, a deer or a badger or, as he had feared at the time, it might have been a cougar. He opted to make a lot of noise for a minute or so, then he crouched down by a mesquite that would offer at least some protection from one side. He had his knife ready that time as he waited about twenty minutes for an attack that never came.

He shook off those thoughts and used a small flashlight to check his compass against his marker and his two distant landmarks, then compared the compass bearing with the North Star. Satisfied, he slipped the flashlight into his pants pocket and hoisted the pack over his shoulders. After fastening the strap around his waist, Sam headed off into the night. He had checked his watch just before stowing his flashlight ...it was 11:12 PM.

Sam Milton was twenty-eight years old and in pretty good shape, so he felt good as he walked along at a steady pace. It was chilly, but he knew he would warm up appreciably once he started walking. There was no trail, but the light from the moon helped him avoid most obvious obstacles. Although it looked flat from a distance, there were numerous dips across his path and the entire route was dotted with small clumps of vegetation, mesquite and oak trees, and rocks. He knew he would cross some dry creeks along the way and would pass a couple of jeep trails. One of those jeep trails would be his superhighway.

"Once I hit that," he reminded himself, "it will be smooth sailing, at least for a while."

He was retracing his steps from the previous Friday when he had begun this trip. He fixed his gaze and walked toward a spot between the two pinpoints of light. Polaris hovered to his right, so he knew he was walking directly west. He had a long way to go, so he let his mind wander a bit to help alleviate the boredom of the hike.

It would be an early Monday morning when he reached the car. These trips were generally four-day affairs spread over a long weekend. It meant taking two days of vacation from his job in Austin. Another confidante, his co-worker Sally, had once asked him why he did it that way.

"It takes me the better part of Friday to drive out to west Texas," he had told her. "It works out well for me because I need to start hiking after dark. I park my car in some quiet spot I've already chosen on my map. Then I head off into the wilderness and hike for a couple of hours before finding a spot to settle in for the rest of the night."

"But why do you have to do it at night?" she had asked.

"Because I am trespassing. Since I have to hike across open ground to get to the hills, getting in and out poses the greatest risk of being seen, so that is why I hike at night. I spend Saturday and Sunday carefully creeping around up in the mountains and sleeping under the stars. I don't get as much sleep Friday night but I get a long night's sleep Saturday. There's really nothing else to do after I eat. I try to get as much sleep as I can on Sunday too, but I have to wake up in the middle of the night so I can hike back to the car in the dark. After that, I always get a good breakfast and spend most of Monday driving home."

Sam smiled as he remembered this conversation, because he was proud of his well-practiced routine.

The sound of something scurrying nearby stopped him in his tracks, but the noise had been quickly absorbed by the night. He figured it was probably a badger, which could be vicious if cornered, but he had no intention of confronting one and he assumed the feeling was mutual: he had only glimpsed the distinctive stripes of a badger a couple of times on these trips, always making a hasty exit away from him.

It wasn't that difficult to pick his way through the rocks and scrubby vegetation, although he was occasionally brushed by unseen low limbs of some oak or mesquite tree. In the past, he had been skewered by cactus more than a few times. In the back of his mind, he was also very wary of the other dangers that lurked in the darkness—like snakes, coyotes, and even mountain lions. He had heard that even an occasional bear wandered through the area. The chilly autumn air probably reduced the danger of snakes, but everything else on the list was warm-blooded, so he tried to stay alert.

"Still, a big cat or a bear would not be too likely out here on the flatland," he reminded himself with a muttered whisper.

A gentle breeze rustled some nearby dry vegetation and he paused again to listen. The sound faded and he continued walking.

With so little light to help, he depended a great deal on his other senses, like hearing and especially touch. Loose rocks often shifted under his feet as he made his way through the darkness. His sense of touch also helped him adjust his pace when there were slight changes in elevation, but abrupt changes were impossible to anticipate.

Almost on cue, Sam cursed as he fell into a small depression that he had not seen in the shadows. It had not been a hard fall but time had seemed to shift into slow motion. Only a quick reaction had saved him from planting his face into the ground.

"Oops."

The sound of an indistinct gravelly voice faded into an even more indistinct chuckle.

Sam answered, "Slim?" But the young man shook his head. "No. How could it be Slim?"

Sam glanced around nervously as he stood and dusted his hands. In the shock of the fall, it had almost seemed real, but then he realized it had to have been his imagination. It was not the first time he had heard that voice on the darkest parts of his hikes, and it was really creepy out there, so why wouldn't he imagine he heard things?

"Anyway, you're long gone, aren't you, Slim?"

There was no answer.

He readjusted his pack, wincing because his hands still stung from the impact. Once he climbed out of the depression, he reoriented himself with his two landmarks and, with a quick glance at the North Star, he headed west again.

Soon, in the dim light of the moon, he could just make out the ghostly image of the jeep trail he was expecting. It stood out as more of a gash of barren ground than anything else. He stumbled over a bump of loose dirt at the edge, then paused in the middle of the rough road and looked both ways. He turned left and continued, walking at a swifter pace.

While he hiked, he daydreamed again and brooded over the same question he asked himself every time he hiked in the quiet chill of this lonely landscape.

"Is this really worth it?"

His friends back in Austin asked him that same question every time he left town to make another long drive out west and the same rationalizations were always debated. The danger, the weather, the time and money, and most of all, the trespassing.

"Did you try asking for permission?" Sally had once innocently asked him.

"Of course I did," he answered.

Early on, it had indeed seemed reasonable enough to simply ask, "Mind if I look around?"

But then the inevitable next question would come.

"Why?"

Sam pondered the simple one-word answer to that question, the word that complicated everything. As he walked, he could only muster a coarse whispered response:

"Gold."

His friends scoffed at the word and he had found that strangers scoffed too, but with an added mixture of suspicion and skepticism. That alone gave him plenty of incentive to avoid the subject, but he knew there were other deeper undertones to a stranger's reaction. The moment one got to the heart of the matter, something came over people, as if a smoldering bit of wonderment had been ignited deep within them. It would glisten back at him through their eyes and he would know they had already begun to secretly conjure up an infinite number of "what if" scenarios. He could predict this as readily as a scientist could predict the outcome of a chemical reaction, because it always happened whenever he stammered out that one simple word.

"It changes people," he said out loud, adding in a trailing tone, "...even *me*."

So he became an interloper, trespassing into the distant hills under the cover of darkness. He spent hours studying maps, preparing equipment, and stockpiling supplies. He knew it wasn't just the word "gold" that had infected him. His obsession was fueled by another secret he had carried for years.

Two

As the minutes turned into hours, he periodically paused to take a sip from his canteen. Whenever he stopped, he had a habit of readjusting his pack and belt because it felt better to move the bindings a little where they were digging into his skin. The knife sheath in particular seemed to bother him during one break and as he moved it around, it reminded him of another knife from his past. As he started walking again, his mind was immediately flooded with memories of that knife and how it had lead him directly to this place and time.

~ * ~

Ten years earlier, he had been just another college student on a wild streak in Houston during his first Christmas break. Life seemed to be an endless series of good times with no consequences, and like most eighteen-year-olds, he felt invulnerable. The most serious thing on his mind was the next party and, to Sam, school seemed to be an impediment to his lifestyle. He was considering dropping out.

It was another lively night shortly into the New Year with Vickie, Mollie, and Gary.

"I wish we could do something fun," Vickie said.

They all agreed and Mollie chimed in, "Hey, we should go to Austin and camp up at the lake."

This suggestion met with a resounding group approval.

So, at eight p.m., they all decided to head to Austin and go camping at one of the area lakes. It didn't seem to matter to any of them that they had no idea of where they were going or, really, what they were doing.

"I guess we could call Joe," Sam had said. Joe was a friend of theirs who was from Austin and had recently moved back. Joe had a wife and infant daughter and their plan hinged on a blind hope that he would point them in the right direction once they got there. They were all completely oblivious to the fact that dropping in on their friend and his family in the middle of the night, with no advance notice, was an inappropriate and completely stupid idea.

Nobody had a car, so they decided their only option was to hitchhike, something that was fairly common at that time, or at least it had seemed so to the four adventurers.

They just headed out into a dark January night with minimal supplies and no plan. Of the four, Sam probably had the most experience hitchhiking because the previous summer he had hitchhiked all around the city of Houston, but he knew that thumbing for a ride in the city was different from thumbing for a ride on the highway.

They managed to get another friend to give them a head start by dropping them off outside the city limits on the interstate highway on the western side of town. On the way, they stopped by Sam's house. He wanted to change clothes and pick up Joe's number.

His mother was trusting. "Where are you off to?"

"I'm heading to Austin to go camping with some friends," he said. As an afterthought he asked his father, "Dad, can I borrow your hunting knife? I don't know that I'll need it, but out camping it might be something good to bring along."

His father seemed a bit puzzled at first, but went into the bedroom to retrieve the knife.

"I guess it's okay," he said, adding, "be careful with it."

Their friend Murray had tried to talk them out of the trip.

"You sure you want to do this? When I drop you off, you are pretty much on your own," he said.

"Murray, why don't you just come with us?" Vickie had said.

"It's tempting," he said, "but you know I have a job. I can't just drop everything and go."

He continued to urge them to reconsider, but eventually they stopped near an exit where he could turn back.

"This is your last chance," he said. "Why don't we just go back to town and get something to eat?"

They all just laughed and assured him they would be fine, so Murray drove off, leaving them to their adventure.

Once out on the highway, the four stuck out their thumbs and tried to get a ride. It was a chilly night and they huddled against the cold. They were lucky because a car stopped in just a few minutes.

"I'm headed to San Antonio," the driver said, "but if you're going to Austin, I can drop you at the Columbus exit."

"That's great," Sam had said.

That ride was quick, and once he dropped them off, they didn't have to wait a long time for the next one, which was a relief. A guy stopped who was on his way to Austin and he took them the rest of the way. Sam knew first hand that it was a lucky break because it could sometimes take hours to get a ride, and even when someone *did* stop, not everyone was going to the same place a rider wanted to go. They were lucky on another count as well: it was usually hard enough for a single person to get a ride, but here they were trying to do it with four people. The presence of two women in their motley group probably helped them but, naïve as they were, they failed to realize what a dangerous game they were playing.

They were unfamiliar with Austin, so they talked with their host about where they needed to go.

"Your best bet will be for me to drop you on The Drag," he said. "That's the main street in front of the university. Of course, if you aren't sure where you have a place to stay, I could probably put you all up for the night."

Vickie responded, "No, that's okay, we have a friend we can stay with."

The driver hastily scribbled down a phone number and said, "Well, call me if you end up stranded."

Of course, Vickie had been referring to the loose plan they had made to connect with Joe, their Austin friend, but since they had not called beforehand and didn't even know where he lived, this did not seem to be even worthy of the word plan.

The Drag was a several block stretch of storefronts and churches that faced the large buildings of the University of Texas on the other side of the street. It was about one a.m. and once they were deposited on the street by their ride, the four friends huddled together in the brisk January night trying to figure out their next move. It was as if the warmth and comfort of the car had dulled their senses and, once they were alone out on the cold street, they were a bit paralyzed by the shock of their new surroundings.

Gary said, "Maybe we should have taken that guy up on his offer."

"Yeah," Sam agreed. "We can't very well just drop in on Joe in the middle of the night."

"Oh, it'll be okay," Mollie said, "he's used to it."

Sam scanned up and down the block and said, "I guess we had better find a phone."

He didn't see one, but he did notice some tough looking individuals who appeared to be harassing another group of people nearby. They decided to sit tight for a few minutes so they could make sure the situation was safe before they moved on to find a phone. With some concern for the nearby toughs, Sam opened his pack and took out the sheath-clad hunting knife he had brought with him and placed it on his pack. He sat on it to both hide it and to keep it ready in case he needed it.

One o'clock in the morning was apparently the time the Austin police started moving people off the streets and right then a police car stopped in front of them and two officers got out and approached them. Sam glanced to the side when the cops pulled up, but all of the nearby individuals had disappeared when the police arrived.

"You people are going to have to go home; you can't hang around here on the street," the first officer said.

One of Sam's group said, "We're waiting for someone."

The officer would have none of it. "I don't care; you can't stay here. You have to get off this street."

While this exchange was taking place, Sam realized that something more substantial was going to be required so he pulled the note with Joe's phone number out of his pocket and stood. He had intended to ask the officer where the nearest pay phone was so they could call their friend and hasten their pickup. He didn't get a chance to utter a single word because when he stood, the second officer bent over and picked up the knife and opened the sheath to examine it more closely. He then drew the other officer's attention to the knife. This took about two seconds. The next thing Sam knew, both officers grabbed him and spun him to face the wall.

"You are under arrest. Put your hands on the wall and spread your legs," said one of the officers. Sam complied with more than a little help from the officers. They frisked him, then clicked some handcuffs on his hands behind his back. With each and every one of those clicks, a chill ran down his spine. Once he was firmly shackled, they turned him back around and confronted him. His friends remained wide-eyed but mute.

"This knife is illegal," said the first officer.

"Huh? It's just a hunting knife," Sam responded.

"It has a snap across the sheath ... that makes it an offensive weapon."

Sam was mystified. It didn't make any sense to him. How could his father own something illegal? But he also began to realize it didn't have to make sense to him because the police obviously made their own sense of things. They each grabbed an arm, escorted him to the police car and deposited him in the back seat. His life was officially out of his own control. Apparently, the peril presented by his three friends being loose on the streets of Austin was forgotten in this swirl of activity because the Austin police had their man and they got in the car and drove off. From the back seat, Sam could see his friends just staring at him as the car sped away.

At the police station, he sat alone in a small room for a long time. Eventually he was greeted by a detective who seemed quite friendly and reasonable at first and as they chatted, Sam hoped the mistake would soon be realized and he would be released with some kind of warning. That naïve hope was short-lived. The detective stopped with the friendly banter and got down to business.

"The knife you were carrying is a *quarter-inch* too long and qualifies as a Bowie Knife under Texas state law," the detective said.

Sam blinked in disbelief.

"You are going to be charged with possession of an illegal weapon."

The detective explained the law on knives in some detail and was almost apologetic at times, but even at that, it was made clear that the law was the law and that charges would be pressed. Sam could not believe this was happening to him. He was soon brought before someone he assumed was some kind of judge and he was formally charged. He was doubly amazed that a "Bowie Knife" was illegal. Jim Bowie was a Texas hero and he was famous for his knife. To Sam it just didn't seem right.

He was again escorted to a police car and was soon on his way to the county jail.

The police officer driving the car explained, "Normally we would have just booked you into the city jail, but it has been a busy night and the city jail is full. The usual procedure," he said, "is to transfer several prisoners in groups to the county jail later in the day."

After he was fingerprinted and photographed at the Travis County Jail, Sam was taken up to the jail blocks. The metallic clang of the door closing behind him was one shock, but a second shock came when he surveyed his new home. In the center there was a common area and a row of several smaller enclosures extended along one side. Everything was painted in an awful color he could not identify but it hovered between orange and beige. The smaller enclosures each had three beds in tiers. The common area had two built-in stainless steel tables with benches. There were open toilets in each of the bunk areas and two other open toilets along one wall in the common area. These were also stainless steel. Obviously, this jail was overcrowded too, because all of the bunk areas were taken and there were still quite a number of people in the common area. Some of them were trying to lie down and sleep on the floor. Several were playing cards or talking while sitting at the tables. Other inmates were just sitting on the floor.

A profound din of background noise was already giving him a headache. The prevalent sound was constant chatter, intensified by the bare walls. People took turns standing at a small barred opening on the main door, yelling back and forth between neighboring jail blocks as they tried to communicate with real or imagined comrades.

Someone would yell something like, "Hey, Joe … Joe!"

A muffled response would filter through the hallway totally unintelligible by Sam.

That would be followed by a new message, "Tell Joe Mick C. is down here!"

Then another vague and distant reply could be heard.

This went on and on. Sam assumed that understanding such garbled chatter was an acquired trait he secretly hoped was a skill he would never need to master.

At first, it seemed as if the other inmates were oblivious to his existence, but it was not long before he perceived a few sidelong glances as he stood there. He felt vulnerable under such scrutiny so he sought a way to blend into the background. The air was smoky because cigarettes were apparently one of the few possessions one could retain when arrested. He glanced around and tried to find a place where he could get off his feet. He spied a small open space along the wall on the far side of the block and quickly claimed that spot as his own by leaning against the wall and sliding down to a sitting position.

He looked at his nearest neighbor, a filthy, slightly built man who was slouched over on one elbow with his eyes closed. The guy smelled of body odor and alcohol. Sam wasn't sure which was worse, but before he could decide, the man moaned ominously and then leaned down close to the floor and wheezed and coughed uncontrollably for several seconds. There was bloody spittle on the floor so he leaned over and nudged the man.

"Hey, buddy, you okay?"

The man raised his head, surprised at the question, and glared at Sam with glassy, bloodshot eyes.

"Hell no, I ain't okay," he rasped. "Damn bastids hit me in my goddam throat." He hacked and coughed again as if to emphasize the statement.

Sam's neighbor had the same ruddy complexion commonly seen on street winos, but there was also an odd tinge that just didn't look right.

"Want me to tell somebody, get you some help?"

"Won't do no good, they don't give a goddam rat's ass about me. They know I'm hurt," the old man said. "Hell, *they* hurt me." This statement was followed by more coughing and wheezing, "Damn bastid cops." Red was seeping from the edge of the man's mouth.

Sam had noticed earlier that there was a conical paper cup dispenser near one of the sinks in the common area so he got up and went over and filled one of the cups. Walking back, his heart almost skipped a beat because the guy had rolled over on his back and the prone body looked like a corpse. That spell was broken by another round of coughing. He knelt and gently lifted the man's head.

"Here, buddy," he said, "I brought you some water. Try to take a sip." He held the cup to the man's lips and the guy managed a small sip. He looked up at Sam with bloodshot eyes.

"Thanks. Name's Ted," he said, "but everybody calls me Slim. Slim Longo."

"I'm Sam."

Slim coughed and wheezed again, turned to his side and weakly raised a hand to his mouth as he continued coughing. As he gasped for breath, he held up his hand and there was bright red blood in the palm.

"See? The goddam cops hurt me. Hit me right in the goddam throat."

"Take it easy, Slim."

"The bastids killed me, Sam. I tell ya," and he coughed again, deep and hard and then moaned before wheezing out, "I'm dying, goddamit."

Sam looked around and was surprised that all of this coughing and moaning and talk of death had spurred no reaction at all from those around them, perhaps masked by the pervading racket. All the routine chatter and smoking and sleeping continued unabated; it was just another day in the jail block.

Looking at Slim, he could see that the name fit because this shell of a man was as thin as a rail. Sam guessed Slim had been thin even before he had let alcohol control his life. The old man's clothes were tattered and his shoes were well-worn. What hair he had was unkempt and he had a stubble of speckled salt and pepper beard. Sam again noted the distinctly odd pallor on Slim's face as he turned his head and coughed again, leaving another streak of blood on the grimy jail floor.

Sam got up and went to the door and attracted a patrolling guard's attention through the same paperback book-sized opening used for the attempts at inter-block communication.

"There's a guy in here that's hurt," he said, pointing over to Slim by the far wall.

"Oh, him?" The guard smiled like he was enjoying a private joke. "Don't mind him. That's just Slim, one of our regulars. I'm sure he's fine," the guard said. "Just leave him alone and let him sleep it off," he added before turning to walk away.

After the guard left his line of sight, Sam returned to Slim, first stopping at the sink to get several paper towels from a dispenser next to the paper cups. He moistened a couple and kept the others dry, then returned to his patient, who looked worse, with fresh blood at the corner of his mouth. Sam dabbed at the blood with one dry towel to wipe it away and then patted Slim's face with one of the moistened towels. This roused the old man.

"Wha ... who? Oh, yeah," Slim managed a slight smile of recognition. "I remember now, Sam. Thanks, son. What'cha here for?" he rasped.

"Illegal weapon," Sam said. "I had a knife they said was too long."

"Damn cops. Can't they just leave you kids alone? They gotta ruin your life for a stupid knife?" Slim coughed again, and more blood dribbled down his chin.

Sam mopped a damp towel across the older man's forehead and said, "Just take it easy, buddy."

Slim looked up at him with wild eyes that seemed to be looking right through him.

"Take it easy? I ...I'm dying, I know it." Slim wheezed, and struggled to get a breath, then continued in a harsh whisper, "Listen, Sam, I gotta tell ya something." The old man coughed again, so hard that Sam half expected to see a bloody lung on the floor.

Sam put his hand on Slim's shoulder. "Okay, okay, Slim," he said. "Don't work yourself up."

"I'm serious, you asshole," Slim said, then he realized what he had said and frowned, shaking his head. "Naw, I'm sorry, you ain't no asshole. You're being nicer to me than anybody's been to old Slim in a long time. I don't deserve it. I ain't lived a good life, what with the drinking and leaving my family, but maybe I can make up for some of it. I gots something for you, Sam."

Slim coughed again and turned to his side, grabbing one of the dry towels out of Sam's hand. When Slim turned back, there was deep red blood on the towel.

Sam looked around. The card games and talking and smoking continued as before. Nobody else cared what was going on over against the wall.

Slim continued with his rasping, wheezing whisper, "You gotta remember, you hear me? You gotta remember." He grabbed Sam's arm in a weak but desperate way, trying to pull their faces closer.

"Okay, okay, just take it easy." He patted the old man's shoulder again, trying to be reassuring, but deep inside he was scared to death.

Slim coughed again, then said, "Shit. Ain't much time. I need to tell you something, but first, I need a favor. Out south of the river near Oltorf Street, you know where that is?"

Sam nodded, lying because he really had no idea.

"Go up Oltorf, just past the Safeway, you need to go left up the railroad tracks. Can't drive up there, ya gotta walk. That's where my camp is. I ain't got much, but ever-thing I own is there. When you get to the camp, my buddies will ask you for the code word or they won't let you near my spot. We take care of each other out there. Tell them what happened to me and that I said 'Tesoro.' That's my code. I got me a Bible there and some papers, letters. Go get them. I need you to see if you can track down my granddaughter. I want her to have them. She was somewhere in San Antone last I heard from her." Slim coughed again. "Her mama didn't want nothing to do with me anymore. Can't say I blame her, but that little girl was the apple of my eye. Find her somehow and give them to her. Can you do that?" He wheezed deeply, trying to catch his breath.

Sam nodded again and patted the old man on the shoulder. "Sure I will."

"Now listen ...this is the real deal. Way out in west Texas ...out between Van Horn and the Carlsbad Caverns ... there's some mountains. There's..." Slim hesitated, coughed, then looked around and pulled Sam's ear close to his mouth as he rasped, " ...*gold.*"

Time seemed to stand still as the word emerged out of an invisible cloud of stale, wine-laden bad breath.

Slim held Sam's arm a little tighter, as he continued in a wheezing whisper.

"There's a gold mine out there. I ain't never seen it, but my grandpa knew about it ...he looked for it for years. My daddy looked for it too. Hell, I looked for it ...for years. We *all* knew it was there. None of us ever found it but, I tell you, it's out there somewhere. My kid, she's got no use for me, so I ain't never told her the details, but you've been good to me when nobody else woulda helped an old broken down drunk, so I'm telling you."

The old man, spent from the exertion, relaxed his grip on the younger man's arm and Sam cradled Slim's head and leaned down close to whisper, "It's all right, man. Just take it easy."

Slim coughed and any remaining color seemed to be fading from his lips and face. "I don't have no time, so listen." His voice was barely a whisper. "My grandpa knew a guy named Ben Sublett. Look him up, he's a regular legend. They was drinkin' buddies. One time they was drinkin', just the two of them, and old Ben told my grandpa all about the mine. Ben always told people it was in the Guadalupes, but that's just what he told people to throw them off ...it wasn't there. Nope. He told my grandpa it was south of there. Remember that. South! He told grandpa 'ya gotta follow the devil and look for the table, then turn around and you'll see the why of it.' That's what he told grandpa. Remember it. I know it don't make no sense, but it ain't supposed to until you get there. You just have to keep searching until it does make sense. A fortune, that's what I'm giving you, a fortune." Slim coughed for half a minute, exhausted from his exertion. Then he looked Sam right in the eyes and said, "Don't forget what I told you. You find it and it's yours."

Slim wheezed deeply, then coughed again before going totally limp in Sam's arms. He shook the old man slightly and received no response. He looked around. Nobody was paying any attention to them. He shook Slim again. Nothing. He gently lowered Slim's head to the floor and ran back up to the door and yelled through the small opening, "Hey, HEY!"

The same disinterested guard returned. "Oh, you again, look, quit bothering me."

"I think this guy's dead ...same guy, I think he just died. He isn't breathing!"

After a quick glance through the opening, Sam saw a wave of shock spread over the guard's face. The scene obviously looked too real to be a trick. The guard immediately ran down the hall to get more help.

Three

Sam broke out of his daydream and abruptly stopped walking as he realized that one of the lights he was using as a reference landmark had disappeared. He scanned the horizon and the sky. The moon was low in the western sky and Polaris was still visible and just one light remained far ahead of him.

"Shit," he muttered.

He pulled out his canteen and took a long drink, then decided to take a short break and removed the pack so he could stretch out his back as best as he could. He pulled the package of uneaten crackers out of his shirt pocket and quickly downed the three crackers. He took another drink, then verified his direction with his compass and flashlight focusing on the one remaining light. He hoisted the pack to his shoulders again, secured it and continued down the rocky jeep trail, with one eye on the trail and one eye on that light.

As he walked, he soon let his thoughts return to the events of that night in jail. The labored wheeze of that one word had changed his life, although he didn't realize it at the time.

As the years passed, it became obvious that the old man had planted a seed deep in his subconscious just as surely as he might have planted a sapling in his front yard. That damned riddle echoed through his thoughts on every trip into the mountains as he tried to make some sense of the phrase, but in the background that one word, gold, was the beacon that kept him moving forward.

"Seven trips now," he said out loud, "with nothing to show for it."

Every time he replayed those words in his mind, he would try to figure some different way to piece the puzzle together. Slim haunted his thoughts every time he hiked or scanned his maps. Sam often seemed to feel Slim's presence, looking over his shoulder. No wonder he had imagined the old man laughing at him in the dark when he fell.

No matter where he went, or how ardently he searched, the cryptic words just didn't make sense. But as this thought entered his mind, he was drawn back to the memory of the old man with the bloody spittle on his mouth whispering, "It ain't supposed to ...until you get there."

Of course, Slim had also said he hadn't found the gold after a lifetime of searching, and neither had his father and grandfather.

"Maybe it was all just some sort of cruel joke ...or a curse," he blurted to himself.

Like Slim's homeless camp. He thought that had been a joke until he actually tried to find it.

~ * ~

One of the first things he thought of when he got out of jail was fulfilling Slim's last wish. It felt something like a sacred bond. He wasn't sure about the gold mine, but he *was* sure he had to find that camp and get the Bible and letters.

His friends had found Joe, who managed to bail Sam out of jail. Surprisingly, Oltorf Street was not far from Joe's house and when he found the street, he saw that there was indeed a Safeway supermarket and nearby railroad tracks, just as Slim had said. He walked along the tracks for a couple of hundred yards and when he came across some thick brush, he could see some evidence of habitation. A tattered man emerged out of the brush to meet him.

"You looking for something, chief?"

For some reason, Sam had not expected anyone to confront him, so he stammered, "Uh, uh, I guess."

"You guess? Look here, chief, I got places to go and people to see. Why don't you just move along?"

"Uh, is this Slim's camp?"

"Slim's dead. News travels fast in our world. Now get lost."

"I know he's dead. I was with him in jail when he died. He told me to come here. Told me to give you the code, Tesoro, so I could get his Bible and some letters for his granddaughter."

The man's eyes brightened at hearing the code.

"I reckon you must be telling the truth." The man smiled. "I thought that code word was stupid but when you come up with it, I know'd it had to come from Slim. What the hell happened to him?"

"He said the cops hit him in the throat. He was coughing up a lot of blood. I tried to get them to help him, but they just ignored me."

"The cops?"

Sam nodded.

"Figures. We live outside the real world so we ain't nothing to them and to most people."

"Can I get his things? He wanted me to try to find his granddaughter."

"Yeah, we've got them. When we heard he was dead, we started to get his stuff together. I kept the Bible and letters, don't know why. We are a bit superstitious sometimes. Come on back," he said, leading Sam through the bushes.

The camp was composed of a couple of tents and some small tarps folded over ropes strung between trees. There were odd assortments of debris around, old ragged mattresses and piles of cans and bottles.

"Name's Fred," the guy said. Two other men appeared, one from one of the tents and one emerged from under one of the tarps. It was a diverse group. Fred was white, one man looked Mexican and the other was Black.

"This here's Wilton," he said, indicating the Black man, "and this here's Eliseo, but we call him Lee."

"Name's Sam." He extended a hand but nobody took it.

"Sam here knew Slim. He was with him in jail when he died. Gave me the code, so I brought him in."

At this both men extended their hands and Sam shook them.

"He came to get Slim's Bible."

The other men nodded.

"What about the bottle?" Wilton asked.

Fred laughed. "Now that's a good question." He turned to Sam, "Slim had half a bottle of hooch down in his stuff. Like I said, we're a superstitious bunch, wanted to drink it but we didn't, you know?"

All the men were staring at Sam.

"And?"

"Well, seeing as Slim gave you the rights to his belongings, I guess that makes you the executor of his estate, right?"

"Oh, so you want me to give you his bottle?"

"Well, how about this," Fred started, "how's about we all give Slim a toast with his own hooch?"

"Great idea," Wilton said. "And fittin'."

"*Si*," Lee added.

"I'll get it," Fred said, and he ducked into one of the tents and emerged carrying a half empty pint bottle of some sort of rotgut wine.

He unscrewed the cap and handed the bottle to Sam, who raised the bottle and took a sip. It burned all the way down to his stomach. He handed it to Fred, who followed suit with a deep gulp. The bottle was then passed to Lee, who drank deeply and he handed it to Wilton. Sam expected Wilton to finish it off, but he drank only enough to leave a good sip remaining, then raised the bottle.

"To Slim!" he said as he poured the rest of the wine to the ground.

They all said in unison, "To Slim!"

Wilton then broke the bottle on a nearby rock. At that moment, a church bell rang somewhere in the distance. It was ten o'clock in the morning.

Fred went back into his tent and emerged with a tattered book with some papers folded inside the cover.

"Here, Sam, these are Slim's. Do your best with them."

Sam said, "I will," as he took them, then added, "Nice meeting you gentlemen," he said.

They each in turn shook his hand and, with a final pat on his shoulder from Fred, Sam turned and made his way back to his own meager reality.

~ * ~

The moon had set while he had been daydreaming. He had been hiking for hours. Sam looked up and could see just a hint of dawn beginning to glow behind the mountain to the east, but all around him there were only vague jutting outlines of scrub, cactus, and rocks. He looked at his watch and saw it was just after five o'clock. He sighed deeply as he started walking again. Soon a distinctive clump of trees came into view up ahead on the side of the road and as he approached it, he searched for the small knot of white cord he had tied to it Friday night.

"Yep, I see it," he said.

It marked the spot where he had originally intersected the road and that meant it was time to go cross-country again. He made a right turn and continued due west, heading slightly to the left of his marker light.

As he moved forward, the faint glow of the dawn became gradually more pronounced and the dim light helped him to speed his pace. He was anxious to get back to the car because he had a long drive ahead of him. As the darkness began to slowly lift, he walked with more confidence.

He considered this to be the most precarious time of his hike. Darkness was his best cover, and as the dawn came, he knew he would be more visible, but he also assumed most ranchers would still be home at this early hour. If all went well, he would soon be safely seated in his car and driving away before they had even finished their first cup of coffee. At least that was another one of his working theories. He trudged on.

He stopped to squint into the distance and thought he could just make out a vague form that seemed out of place. He quickened his pace and soon that indistinct object began to take some shape.

After a hundred or more steps, he identified a familiar figure.

"The Clunker!"

It became a focal point for him as he made his way through the scrubby brush. He stopped about forty yards away and carefully surveyed the area. The ranch road was a dark ribbon just beyond the car, veering off into the distance to the north and south. Nothing was moving on the road this early in the morning and the only sounds he heard were a few chattering birds. He slowly inched forward, looking closely at the ground ahead of him. It was still more dark than light.

About twenty yards from the car, he dropped his pack and started to look for a particular rock that covered the place where he had buried his keys in a small plastic box. He told himself this was just in case, but in case of what, he wasn't sure. It simply seemed to be a prudent thing to do.

He found the rock and moved it aside, then pulled a small folding shovel from the outside of his pack and used it to gingerly dig through several inches of softened soil until the plastic box revealed itself. Inside were his keys and two packs of peanut butter snack crackers placed there as another contingency. He slid the keys into his pants pocket, then stuffed the small plastic box into his pack and refilled the small hole, smoothing the area around it with the toe of his boot. He imagined it might be noticeable in broad daylight but in the dimness of predawn he thought it looked pretty good. It didn't really matter to him now, anyway, because his hiding place had served its purpose.

The car was just beyond a barbed wire fence. He dropped his pack and shovel over the fence, then climbed over it. In the past, he had ruined several articles of clothing on other such fences so he took great care as he scaled the wire. As barbed wire fences went, it wasn't very impressive, but the wire was tight and the barbs were sharp. He picked up his pack and shovel and carried both over to the car.

What he called The Clunker was a dusty, white, 1974 VW Beetle. There did not seem to be any evidence of intruders or tampering. He had faith in the notion that an abandoned car might be left alone for two or three random days. Breakdowns were not uncommon, and a couple of days stretching across a weekend were not a long time in the overall scheme of things. It was yet another one of his working theories.

He unlocked and opened the passenger door and after retrieving a shirt from the top compartment of his pack, he shoved it into the back seat. He quickly changed his shirt, then popped the trunk lock using the latch in the glove compartment. After depositing the shovel in the trunk, he grabbed a gallon of water in a plastic bottle that had been nestled next to a tool box and took a long, deep drink. It was tepid and a bit stale, but after rationing the remaining water in his canteen during the night hike, it was a relief to his parched mouth and throat.

Gentle shadows were already beginning to form and he decided he had better be on his way, so he replaced the cap, returned the bottle, and closed the trunk, then shut the passenger door. When he unlocked the driver's door, he instinctively brushed himself off before sitting in the driver's seat. After he put the key in the ignition, he pulled away the note he had scratched on a sheet of notebook paper and taped to the inside of the windshield. It said simply, "Car broke down ...will return to tow."

As he reached for the key, he felt a wave of apprehension that often swept over him when he started his car, especially after it had been sitting for several days. The dread faded when the engine cranked and quickly came to life. He smiled with relief and gently tapped the gas pedal, listening to the smooth puttering of The Clunker's air-cooled engine. The car was pointed north as he pulled onto the road, so he turned to the left, executed a three-point turn and headed south.

As he drove, he twisted the dial on the AM radio but found only crackling static mingled with muted snatches of Spanish and faint glimpses of unidentifiable music. He finally settled on the scratchy signal of what was probably a distant Mexican station that played familiar-sounding rock music, but the songs were recorded by cover bands in Spanish. The announcer sounded like he was broadcasting from the bottom of a well.

The road stretched ahead of him in the growing dawn.

"I'm glad I found the car so easily this time," he said.

It was not unusual for him to spend upwards of an hour trying to find where he had left the car. Now he looked forward to getting some hot food. Breakfast was a tradition for him after one of these forays into the mountains, because as a general rule he didn't eat well in the field. He subsisted on things that didn't need cooking because he couldn't risk an open fire. Sam knew that any hint of smoke would draw attention and any attention would be bad.

As he drove south, he thought about that Bible and papers. He still had them back in his apartment. He *had* tried to find the granddaughter, but never found her or the mother. He barely glanced at the letters but they contained mostly pleas like, "why don't you get help, we'll help you" with smatterings of "I'm sorry" and "we still love you." There was something about a health crisis with the granddaughter, but it only highlighted another emotional plea. The letters were so personal he felt uncomfortable reading them and so he concentrated on looking for identification information, but there was nothing he thought he could use and there were no envelopes so there wasn't even a return address. Sam guessed Slim held the sentiments dear, but not dear enough to get sober and go home.

He drove through sleepy Sierra Blanca and intersected with Interstate 10 where he headed east. There wasn't much traffic, but the sun would soon be blinding him so he pressed the accelerator and tried to shorten the trip to Van Horn as he yawned against fatigue. He was hungry, so he pushed The Clunker harder than he liked to, but he figured a state trooper would be easy to spot out here. Soon, the Van Horn exit peeked at him in the distance and he reduced his speed because he didn't want some bored local cop to decide he was easy pickings. He looked at his watch and couldn't help but notice two days' worth of dust, dirt, and grime on his arm. He exited and pulled through town until he spied one of his usual stops, The Mossback Cafe. Some people might call it a greasy spoon, but he liked the place. He pulled into the parking lot and let the dust settle a moment before getting out of the car.

Four

The Mossback Café was nestled between two decrepit, boarded-up businesses. The clapboard siding needed paint and the molding was peeling back in places. Sam found that the restaurant's tattered appearance gave it a certain rustic appeal. Out front there was what looked like an ancient hitching post with worn and weathered wood that would have been at home in a museum or an antique store. The Mossback did have three things going for it: it was quiet, the food was good, and it was cheap. A good hot meal was his standard post-hike tradition before he started the long drive to the east.

As the door closed behind him, Sam looked around, amazed that the place always looked exactly the same. It had probably not changed much since it first opened. The linoleum floor was scratched and faded but it was clean. The walls contained an assortment of random pictures and posters and he guessed they alluded to the varied history of both the restaurant and the town.

On the wall near the register there were three calendars, two from the current year and one from several years before. The older calendar proudly proclaimed January 1971 and the third was circled but there was nothing to indicate why that date had any significance. All three advertised either food or ranch products.

There was an elderly couple sitting at a table at the far edge of the dining room, but they were the only other customers in the place. The man and woman both glanced at him as he came in and the attention made him uncomfortable. Then he remembered the dirt on his arms and decided he had better wash up a little. As he headed across the dining room toward the restrooms, the waitress, familiar from past trips, popped out of the kitchen. The swinging door flapped in her wake. She smiled at him in recognition.

"Good morning. Sit down and I'll be right with you. Coffee?"

"Uh, yeah, after the restroom," he said.

"Sure, hon," she said as she turned with a smile and a wink.

In the bathroom he looked at himself in the faded mirror. His short sandy-brown hair was mussed and his blue eyes looked weary. Grime and dust and three days of stubble on his face served to enhance the tired appearance. He sighed.

"Of course I look tired," he said, "I *am* tired."

On the wall there was a pump action soap dispenser and he pumped it once and washed his face, splashing it with cold water. He then pumped the dispenser several more times and lathered up with the water running. He proceeded to work the soap up and down his arms. The water was warm and it felt good against his dirty skin as he rinsed his arms and hands. He turned the hot water off and did a second rinse of his face with cold water. There was an old towel machine that ran a continuous roll of cloth, and he pulled the cloth down to reach a clean spot. He dried his face and his arms, leaving a darkened stain.

He checked himself in the mirror again and was satisfied with the improvement, although he needed a shave and his hair was still a bit mussed. He instinctively reached in his back pocket but remembered he had forgotten his comb on Friday. Using his fingers, he straightened and smoothed his short hair as best as he could. After one last glimpse in the mirror, he headed out the door to find a table and the promised cup of coffee.

The elderly couple eyed him again as he walked past. The woman managed a slight smile and he returned it, gently nodding. He picked a table by a window on the opposite side of the café and as he sat down, the waitress suddenly appeared with a menu, a mug of coffee, and some silverware wrapped in a napkin.

"You clean up real nice," she said. "You musta been out working really early."

Sam looked up. He guessed she was just a little older than he was, probably in her mid-thirties. She was pretty, with dark hair in a long ponytail. Her hair framed a smiling face with dark soulful eyes.

"Been camping up north at the National Park," he said. This was one of his standard lies. The park was about an hour north of Van Horn, so he thought the story was believable. He felt bad about lying, but he rationalized that it was at least almost true.

"Camping, huh? You must be ready for some *real* food," she said, smiling.

She had a soft drawl and he thought her features hinted at some Hispanic ties but she had nothing like a Spanish accent. Her name tag simply said, "Smidgeon."

He had probably seen that before but for some reason he hadn't remembered it, which he should have because it was an unusual name. She was short so the name seemed to fit. She put the coffee and silverware down and handed him the menu.

"Thanks, Smidgeon," he said, adding, "...that is an unusual name."

"Well, I was a real tiny baby and when my grandma first laid eyes on me, she said 'why she's just a smidgeon of a thing,' and my mom liked it so the name stuck."

He laughed and said, "That's a great story."

"I think I've seen you in here before," she said.

"Yeah. I love hiking in the mountains," he said, adding, "I go there a lot. This is sort of my traditional stop on the way home."

"I've driven by that park a bunch of times but I've never been up in there," she said. "But that's how it is, you know—locals don't usually do the tourist stuff and besides, I gotta work here most of the time, you know, to feed you hungry campers." She laughed, ending the brief conversation with a quick spin to return to work, her long ponytail swinging behind her.

He surveyed the menu. The Mossback had a standard coffee shop menu for the most part, with the addition of a few Mexican dishes. He sipped his coffee and tried to figure out what he wanted to eat. His stomach growled a couple of times as he looked at the menu. After two days of camp food, he was ready for something hot and satisfying. His eyes kept returning to the *"Huevos Rancheros Especial,"* which was something he had noted in the past but had never tried. The menu had this item boxed off with no description, just the name and a price.

Smidgeon returned and said, "You decided, sweetie?"

"What exactly *is* the *Huevos Rancheros Especial*?"

"Well, you know *Huevos Rancheros*, right?"

"Yeah,"

"Well, we make a stack of cheese enchiladas and then we poach some eggs in ranchero sauce. That all goes on top of the enchiladas, and then we top it with cheese and pop it for a second under the broiler to melt the cheese. You hungry?"

"Yeah, I'm pretty hungry this morning."

"Well, it's a lot of food, but it's good if you're hungry. We got the best enchiladas around here and the ranchero sauce is good too. Listen, this is the real deal, 'cause our cook used to work ranches around here, so he knows what he's doing. Oh, and there's one more thing..."

"Yes?"

"It kinda tends toward the hot end of the spectrum, if you know what I mean."

"I can handle that," he said. "You talked me into it."

Smidgeon smiled. "Okay," she said. She jotted his order on a small pad and headed back through the swinging door to the kitchen.

Sam looked out the window and could see that the morning sky was bright and blue. A rusty old jeep pickup pulled into the parking lot as he sipped his coffee. Then his thoughts turned toward the events of his trip. The previous Friday, he had driven all day from Austin and arrived shortly after dusk. The trip, roughly four hundred and fifty miles, usually took about eight and a half hours. It hadn't been that long since the speed limit had been seventy on most highways, before the oil embargo had spiked gasoline prices. Driving at seventy would take almost two hours off a trip like this. But he also knew those higher speeds took a toll on a smaller car like The Clunker.

He used to have an older VW and he had driven that car on his first trip to the Guadalupe Mountains area.

Sam sighed.

He missed that car, a 1964 model Beetle, even though it had a fault in the starting system that he sometimes had to jolt to life with a screwdriver. It was cheaper than repairing it, but that operation always scared him because he had to lie under the car to reach up behind the engine to cross the starter terminals on the solenoid, with sparks flying and the engine kicking mere inches above his face. It was probably why he still experienced starter anxiety every time he turned the key on The Clunker.

He raised his cup to take another sip of coffee just as the swinging door to the kitchen opened and Smidgeon emerged with a huge, steaming plate of food.

She beamed with pride as she put it down in front of him and said, "There, what do you think of THAT?"

He hoped the expression on his face revealed a glimmer of what he was feeling. "It looks awesome," he said.

Melted cheese ran over thick layers of green and brown gooey goodness with bright bits of yellow egg yolks peeking out in places. This was supported by a platform of classic west Texas stacked enchiladas. At this point, Sam could only imagine their own sauce-laden layers of tortillas, cheese, and onion. Generous helpings of refried beans and chunky potatoes arranged on the periphery of the plate seemed superfluous. He smiled up at the dark twinkling eyes of the still grinning Smidgeon. He hoped he was up to the task of completing the massive dish.

She laughed, "You sure were deep in thought—thinking about the election? Reagan or Carter?"

"Oh, no, wasn't thinking about the election. Still haven't decided yet," he said.

"Me either. I got too much work to do here to worry much about things like elections. Well, I better get you some more coffee to go with your feast."

Sam tentatively tasted the enchilada sauce from the bottom of the stack. It was spicy and delicious. He then tasted the ranchero sauce, which was even hotter. Smidgeon had been right about that. Both sauces hinted at a complex but subtle combination of flavors, something he had found typical of good Mexican food.

He sipped the last of his coffee and then dug into the dish. The combination of sauces so overwhelmed his palate he had to stop to catch his breath, forcing air through his mouth in an attempt to settle down his smoldering taste buds. At that moment, Smidgeon returned with the coffee pot and a glass of water.

"You must have been reading my mind," he said as he grabbed the glass and immediately took a large sip of the cold water.

"This ain't my first rodeo, sweetie," she said, laughing, and he realized that she was even prettier when she laughed.

"Yes, this is wonderful," he said as he prepared to dive in for another bite.

"Now you're getting to the best part, the eggs," she said with an air of anticipation.

Following her lead, Sam looked down and saw one of the egg yolks peeking out from the edge of his last bite. He pierced the yolk and lemon-colored goodness oozed down the side of the stacked enchiladas. He cut into the stack with his fork, trying to incorporate all of the components into one mouthful.

He paused for a few seconds to savor the flavors before chewing and eventually swallowing. Then he greedily dug back into the dish for another bite.

Smidgeon put her hand on his shoulder. "See? I told you it was good."

"It ...it is fantastic." He fumbled with the words as he tried to answer with his mouth full.

"Well just enjoy it. We aim to please," she giggled, as she turned to greet a couple of cowboys who had just entered the café.

With steady work, he quickly devoured the masterpiece, leaving an almost empty plate by the time Smidgeon returned with more coffee.

He smiled. "That is a major meal."

Smidgeon laughed. "Hah, I warned you."

After she left, he cleared his plate in three more bites and pushed the empty dish away. He picked up the check and smiled. He had just eaten a veritable feast and it was cheaper than most breakfasts he'd have ordered anywhere else.

As he got up to leave, Smidgeon hurried over to the register, gliding across the floor in a practiced dance of economy and efficiency as she maneuvered around tables and chairs with ease.

"I see a happy plate over there," she said. Her eyes sparkled, further brightening her pretty smile. A stray strand of hair had come loose from her ponytail and she tried to blow it away from her eyes but finally used her wrist to swipe it behind her ear. As she did this, her eyes never left his.

"I have to admit, that is quite a meal. I needed something like that before getting back on the road."

"Oh, where you going?" she asked.

"Austin. I have to get back by tonight. I have to go to work tomorrow," he said.

"I love Austin, but I haven't been there for years," she said.

"Well, you probably wouldn't recognize it, because it seems to be changing every day."

"Too bad. It was a fun place, a city but almost like a small town too," she said, adding, "But, Austin ... that's a long drive."

He nodded as he fumbled in his wallet and pulled out more money than was needed. He was calculating a good tip in his head. She deserved it. "There ...whatever is left is for you," he said.

"Why thank you, kind sir!" Then she added, "Wait, you want some more coffee to go?"

Sam did not need to contemplate this question. "Sure," he said, "it will mean another rest break down the road but I'll definitely need some extra caffeine after a feed like that."

Smidgeon giggled. "Okay, I'll be right back."

While waiting, he looked around the register area and noticed a small business card holder and picked up one of the cards. It read "The Mossback Café" and under that, "Smidgeon Toll, Owner" with the address and phone number. He slipped it into his shirt pocket.

When Smidgeon returned with the coffee, he pointed to the cards, "So you're the owner?"

"Yep. I inherited the place from my mom and dad. My dad, Joe Toll, was an institution around here. They even used to call me Little Jo as a nickname. Some still do. I've worked here all my life."

"Cool. You have a nice place, Smidgeon."

"Thanks. I like it. I didn't see you use any creamer—do you need sugar or something?"

"No, I just take it black," he said. He picked up the cup and as he turned to leave, Smidgeon reached out and touched his forearm.

"Hey, what's *your* name?"

He turned and extended his hand. "Sam," he said, "Sam Milton."

Smidgeon reached out and shook his hand and he relished the gentle, soft warmth of her palm and felt goose-bumps sprout as a tingle ran up and down his spine.

"Well, Sam, glad to meet you. Come back again real soon ...and you drive careful, okay? There's a lot of crazies out on that highway."

"That's for sure. And I've got at least eight hours of crazies to look forward to." He smiled and waved as he headed out the door.

Five

Outside, Sam blinked in the bright early morning sun and squinted down at his watch: ten minutes after eight. As he approached The Clunker, he heard the sound of a car door opening across the lot. He looked toward the sound and saw it had come from the rusty truck he had noticed earlier.

An older man with sparse gray hair emerged and, looking right at him, shouted, "Hey, buddy."

Sam stopped and turned toward the man, saying nothing. He was not in a position to deal with trouble, so he just stood silently and gave the man a blank questioning stare.

"Come on over here fer a second," the man said, motioning with his hand.

Sam reluctantly obliged, but it was a tough decision for him because he always tried to keep a low profile. He had even hesitated before telling Smidgeon his name, but she was so friendly and pleasant, answering her had seemed the natural thing to do. Now, he thought to himself, perhaps even that had been a mistake, because people were not only beginning to notice him, but strangers were also beckoning to him in parking lots. It was an uncomfortable feeling, but he walked over to the truck anyway.

The guy was gangly, several inches taller than Sam's five-eight, and had a grizzly salt and pepper stubble that adorned a tired face with bloodshot hazel eyes. He judged that the stranger was probably not as old as he looked, but Sam knew that many people in the country lived hard lives, so ages were difficult to gauge. The truck was an older model Jeep, with its classic grill and high fenders. A bald spare was mounted to the side of the bed behind the driver. He had always liked Jeeps but this one had definitely seen better days. The guy stood behind the open door so it served as a narrow barrier separating the two men.

Sam spoke first. "Can I help you?"

"Did you have any luck?" There was gravel in the man's voice.

Sam was perplexed. "Luck? What do you mean?"

"I seen your car out on the road north of Sierra Blanca. Broke down, was it?" The stranger let a sly smile crack across one side of his face.

"Minor problem. I got some help and got it fixed."

"Look, buddy," the guy said, "I seen you here before, I know the signs. Yer prospectin', ain't ya?"

He was shocked and couldn't help but stumble his words slightly, "I, I, d-don't know what you're talking about."

"Hell, buddy, I ain't going to blow yer cover. I wanted to warn you."

"Warn me?"

"Look, let me try again," the old man said as he stepped from behind the door and held out his hand. "Name's Loot. Loot Meldings."

"Loot?" Sam said, returning the handshake almost automatically. The stranger's palms had hard, thick calluses that scratched his hands.

"Nickname. It's all I've been called around here for so long I don't even hardly remember my given name anymore."

"Warn me about what?" He pointedly didn't return the introduction.

Loot continued, "Listen, if I noticed, others will notice. Ya gotta be more careful."

"I still don't know what you are talking about," he said.

"People 'round here think I'm a nutty old coot, and maybe I am, but I don't care what the hell they think. I prowled around them mountains as long as I could, trapping mostly, but I'd look around when I found the time. There ain't nothing out there, or I woulda found it. I sure can't blame a guy for trying, but ya gotta understand... if you draw attention to yerself, they'll kill you. Them ranchers I mean, or their hands. Some of them ranch hands are nothing more than crooks."

Sam was shocked by this unexpected turn of the conversation and didn't know what to say.

"Okay, uh, Loot. Thanks for your concern."

"Concern, hell, I'm trying to help you, you asshole!"

Sam flushed at the last word. "Okay, I get it. Watch out. Right. I'll be careful."

Loot whispered with a guttural and grave tone, "You'll be dead." Then his eyes brightened a little as he rasped, his voice obviously running out of steam, "Listen, I'm sorry, I don't mean to get yer dander up. When you coming back out here? I've seen you before. You must be coming back."

"Maybe sometime, maybe never ... I really don't know. Thanks for the warning but I need to get on the road."

"You think about what I said. When you come back, you look me up; I can give you some pointers, some help. Heck, I'm not looking for nothing from you, I just hate to see a damn fool get hisself killed."

"You have a phone?"

"Hells bells, I ain't got no phone. I just got me a shack on the edge of town," he said, "and this broken-down old beater here, and a social security check to keep me warm. You got something to write with?"

Sam had a pen in his shirt pocket, thought for a second and pulled out the Mossback card.

Loot said, "Four six five three Tesoro Road—got it?"

He wrote down the address. "Got it," he said.

"It's right down off Broadway this way," Loot said, pointing west down the main road, toward the end of town.

Sam jotted a small note to that effect. "Okay, got that too. I can't promise I'll come, or when."

Loot revealed a subtle, knowing smile and said, "Oh, you'll come. I know what you're doing and what that does to people. You'll come because the more you think about it, the more you'll wonder 'just what does old Loot know?' Wait and see; you'll come."

"Uh, right," Sam stammered, "...maybe, but I don't know when."

"I'll see ya when I see ya, that's all. When I see yer little car, I'll know it's you and we'll have a nice chat, okay?"

Loot got back in the old truck and seconds later the rusty Jeep wheezed to life and the old man gunned the engine a couple of times, then drove away in the direction he had just pointed, kicking up a cloud of dust.

A haze settled around Sam as he headed back to his car. The door to the café opened and Smidgeon poked her head out.

"Everything okay?"

"Yeah," Sam said.

"Don't pay any mind to that old coot," she said. "Loot Meldings is as crazy as a loon. Everybody around here knows he is just a nutty old drunk who's had too much sun. If I see him out here bothering my customers again, I'll call the law."

"No need to do that," he said, "I think he just wanted some work or something. He seemed harmless."

"You sure you're okay?" she asked.

"Yeah, and I'm late, so thanks again for the wonderful food, the coffee, and for your concern."

Smidgeon's face brightened with her infectious smile and she said, "Well, if you're sure everything is okay, you have a nice day and be sure to drive careful," then she waved before disappearing back into the café.

He got into The Clunker and secured the cup as best as he could in the space between the two bucket seats.

"One bad thing about a Volkswagen ... there is no place to put something like hot coffee," he reminded himself.

He put the key in the ignition and again felt a brief flash of anticipation, but the car started right up. He had to keep reminding himself that *it was the other car*. He made his way back to the interstate and headed east. He was thankful the sun had risen high enough to be covered by the visor. He had tried driving east into that sun before and the blinding orb at the end of the highway was unbearable. It was another reason a post-hike breakfast was a tradition.

As the miles flashed past, he sighed to himself and began to let his mind wander. Daydreams were what these long lonely drives were all about. Austin was four hundred and fifty miles away.

Six

Sam Milton was twenty-eight with a college degree but he had no career, and prospects for anything better had so far eluded him. Pursuing a liberal arts degree had seemed like an okay idea at the time, and for a while school had insulated him from the military draft. A person with a history degree generally became a teacher, but he had stayed in school long enough to see some former classmates who had become teachers come back completely disillusioned, seeking to get a degree in something else. So he put the option of teaching on the back burner and found what work he could.

He was single and lived month-to-month, spending any extra money he had on these trips. As far as romance went, there had been no time for any serious dating for a couple of years. In fact, he had only a few good friends. One was Godson Millet, whom he had known since college. Godson's wife Moll was a friend too, but most of the time these days, he seemed to deal with them together as a unit. Another friend was a coworker named Sally Beeman. They had shared an office for a number of years. Godson, Moll, and Sally all knew the basic facts about his secret, and all of them routinely tried to talk him out of making these trips.

Sam didn't know why those three continued to stand by him, because in his opinion, he wasn't much of a friend, especially lately. The one thing they all had in common was a bond through employment. Godson and Moll had worked with him at a bar in Houston back in their college days and a deep friendship had grown out of their work experiences. His current working relationship with Sally wasn't that different and, in the years they had shared an office, they had become quite close.

"It is either that or become mortal enemies," he joked out loud, almost shouting over the road noise.

He had grown up in Houston and his early years had been a fairly typical middle-class, post-war childhood. The youngest of three children, he grew up as the baby of the family.

The sudden blast of a truck's horn interrupted these musings and he realized he had let the car drift a little to the left. He corrected his course and readjusted his speed as the truck passed him.

"Got to pay attention," he said to himself as he took a long drink of coffee.

The plastic lid on the Styrofoam cup had no opening except for a tiny vent hole in the top, so he had torn a little flap on one side. The coffee had cooled enough to allow him to almost suck the fluid until air squeaked from the hole. After another gulp of coffee, he let his mind wander again.

Early in high school, he had been unadventurous and conforming. He was adequate as a student but he didn't study hard, and he was not involved in school beyond showing up in the morning, filling a desk, and then leaving at the end of the day. He had school friends, but they tended to be slackers like him, people who were not athletes or social climbers. He formed no serious bonds with any of them.

As he started college, he gradually drifted toward marijuana, and to him it was just a tool he was using to relax from his imagined pressures and rigors of life. At the time, he thought it was not unlike the nightly pitchers of martinis his parents drank. He began to be more adventurous and rebellious and it was that rebellious streak that had landed him in jail. As he thought about it. he marveled at the irony ...an idiotic bit of youthful indiscretion had landed him right where he was today, in this car, exhausted, with a long day's drive ahead of him.

He turned his thoughts back to the jail story but not the fact of Slim's death or the fateful confession. He began to reflect on the aftermath.

~ * ~

Once the guard had been alerted, there was quite a whirlwind of activity. A buzzer sounded and all of the prisoners were ordered into the bunk areas along one wall of the block. These were enclosures with sliding doors and when the prisoners were all crammed into those smaller spaces, the doors were shut. Slim's limp body looked pitifully alone on the floor, but it was soon joined by a swarm of guards.

The prisoners immediately began to chatter about the situation, some offering unwelcome advice and comments as the guards lifted Slim and took him to the corridor.

"Don't hurt yourself."

"One down, how many more to go?"

"Quiet over there!" a guard retorted.

"Didn't you check his pockets before you locked him up?"

"What happened to him?"

"Uh-oh, somebody's gonna get in trouble!"

Once the body had been removed and the main door was secured, the sliding doors to the bunks were opened again.

There was a lot of speculation about what had happened, but apparently nobody had noticed Sam talking to Slim, so none of the speculation included him. Jailhouse gossip was swift and inventive.

"I think he was stabbed," one prisoner said, nervously looking around.

"Naw, they'd be frisking us all by now ...he musta swallowed a lot of drugs when they arrested him."

"Died of a broken heart. I've seen it before," one guy said, laughing.

"He couldn't take it, killed himself."

"Now how would he do that?"

"Dunno, but it has to be what it was."

In a short time, everything calmed back down and the normal din of the jail resumed. The card games picked up where they had left off, and the yelling between the cell blocks started again. People slept, smoked, and endlessly chattered. Life went on.

"Well, except for poor Slim," Sam whispered to himself.

Sam found another place against the wall several yards away from the spot where he and Slim had been sitting and slid to the floor again, still in shock by what had happened. In all, he had known Slim for less than an hour. Although he felt bad about what had happened, he knew he had tried to help the old man as best as he could. In his mind, the blame fell to the jailer for ignoring his first alert and he finally resigned himself to the fact that there probably wasn't anything anyone could have done. It was simply Slim's time and he had passed away with a content look on his face, no doubt happy to be relieved of the burden of his secret. The odd parting words reverberated in Sam's mind as he leaned over to the floor and slipped into an uncomfortable and restless sleep.

While he languished in jail, the rest of his hitchhiking crew had managed to connect with their Austin friend Joe, who scraped up the money to bail him out of jail. It wasn't really that much money, but Sam was embarrassed by the favor.

Still, as Joe later said, "What am I going to do, leave you in jail?"

By the time the fee was paid and he was released, his hitchhiking buddies had already left on the rest of their trip. Nice friends, he thought to himself. He found he had just enough cash to buy a bus ticket back to Houston. Not long after Sam had completed the small side trip to collect Slim's belongings, Joe dropped him off at the bus station.

"Thanks, Joe, I promise to pay you back."

"I know, buddy, just be careful," Joe said.

When he got home, Sam had to go through the hassle of getting a lawyer. It was going to be expensive and he thought about asking his parents to help, but he dreaded what they might say, so he just skipped telling them. Parental ignorance was both a gift and a curse in that he was grateful for the blind trust but he also felt a bit guilty. They had no idea what he was going through and he was amazed that his dad never even asked him about the knife.

The case was resolved within six months but it took him a full year to pay off the lawyer. Until the case was resolved, he didn't have time to think about Slim's cryptic comments because he had to worry about his pending criminal charge. He hadn't been working at that point but he quickly got a job so he could come up with the money to pay back his friend Joe and to start paying his legal fees. On top of all of this, he had to go back to school for the spring semester because his attorney had insisted he stay in school.

"Good thing," Sam said to himself, "If I had dropped out then, I probably never would have gone back to school."

He was fortunate because, as his lawyer had told him, "Sam, this is essentially a spurious charge, a case of the police erring on the side of right, but erring nonetheless."

Like many legal cases, the entire episode had a different perspective when his attorney and the prosecutor were reviewing the details in the back room of the courthouse. The fact that he had no prior trouble with the law was a plus for him and there were a lot of more pressing matters taking up the court's time so the charges were dropped. He was free and clear of the legal problems, but the entire experience was far from over. He had been changed by the incident in ways he would gradually begin to understand in the coming years.

For a long time, he didn't dwell upon the things Slim had told him, because to him, the notion of a gold mine was preposterous. He considered those statements to be the irrational ramblings of a dying wino. The shock of being arrested and having a man die in his arms were the prevalent details in his memory. Even so, as he later found, that one word, gold, kept a quiet vigil somewhere in the deep recesses of his soul.

He eventually found that the account of the arrest was a good bar tale, usually related over a pitcher or two of beer well into a night of drinking, but he always skipped the part about the gold mine. Yet whenever he told the story, later, alone in his dark apartment, he eventually began to sit and replay the rest of the incident in his head. The name "Ben Sublett" and that oddly worded clue "ya gotta follow the devil and look for the table, then turn around and you'll see the why of it" would cycle through his thoughts again and again. These quiet secrets shared the lonely vigil with him.

He had first let Godson and Moll into his confidence after one of these drunken retellings back in college. They had met at a little dive called Trotsky's, a strange little place with a dingy storefront that would not have been out of place on a back street in 1920s Paris. Despite the tagline they used on their ads, "A Revolutionary Experience," it was basically a low budget bar catering to a college crowd who liked cheap beer and an appreciation for acoustic music. Moll worked there and one night she mentioned to them that they had just let a couple of people go.

"We had to fire them for being counter-revolutionaries," she joked. "Are you guys interested in maybe working here?"

At the time, Sam desperately needed a job and the hours were flexible, so he signed up. Godson followed suit. The three of them worked together most weekends but they alternated during the week, sometimes Sam and Godson, sometimes Godson and Moll, sometimes Moll and Sam. The three quickly became good friends because they all worked well together, enjoyed each other's company and the bar was fun most of the time. It was an eccentric little bar with catchy Russian Revolution-inspired reproductions of 20s-and 30s-era Soviet worker posters on the walls. They always played a scratchy old recording of the Communist *Internationale* for last call and if they had the right crowd, usually on Saturday nights, everyone would join in. It was quite a scene and it must have sounded extremely alarming from the outside.

Late most Saturdays, after the place was closed and they had finished cleaning up, the three of them would sit in the back to enjoy a nightcap and just talk and relax. One night, after telling the famous jail story again, Sam tipsily added to the tale. This was not long after Godson and Moll had started dating.

"There is a little more to the story," he told them and then he let the rest of the story unfold, just the same way he did when he was by himself.

He didn't know why he did that, but they were his best friends and he just felt comfortable with them. Of course, they scoffed and he let the matter drop, but later, when he began to plan his trips, they realized it wasn't just a drunken story.

Their true bonding experience took place two nights before Christmas, during one of those late-night rap sessions. On that particular night, someone decided to firebomb the building. There is nothing quite like a disaster to draw people together. The police never found out who had done it, but suspected it was the work of extreme right-wing fanatics like the ones who had bombed Houston's Pacifica radio station off the air a couple of years earlier. Although that was a plausible explanation, Sam always thought the act could have been perpetrated from the other end of the political spectrum. On more than one occasion, they had been confronted by left-wing self-styled Trotskyites who took offense to their hero's name being taken in vain.

It didn't matter. The three friends had been in the back and were just about ready to leave when they heard the crash and felt the heat of the fire. Moll had not put the cash bag in the safe yet, so she grabbed that and they unbarred the back door and rushed into the alley just as the fire swooshed into the room. It had been a narrow escape and as they huddled together in the chilly December night and watched Trotsky's burn, a deeper bond of friendship was forged. The owner took the insurance money and never reopened the bar and the three of them were out of work, but they were forever united by that flirtation with death. After that night, they called it Christmas Eve-Eve and generally celebrated it every year together.

~ * ~

Sam broke out of his daydream long enough to note that he was approaching Fort Stockton. He shook his empty coffee cup and decided he needed to pull over for more coffee and gas.

Seven

After topping off his fuel and coffee, Sam got back on the highway, and as he merged into the traffic lanes his mind returned to his previous musings. These daydreams served to counteract the monotony of the endless Texas landscape.

He ran the riddle back through his mind and played with the words the same way he had done countless times before.

"Follow the devil," he said out loud, but then repeated it as a question. "Follow the devil?"

It was a perplexing statement. Obviously, it referred to something specific, but he could also appreciate it as a metaphor because he felt as if he might have to literally sell his soul to attain the elusive prize. The final statement, "the why of it," was another conundrum.

"*Why*? Getting rich, that is the why of it, isn't it?"

And then there was the mention of a table. It seemed to be the most accessible clue but it was also the most intangible. Slim had been emphatic about these words but for Sam, they were shrouded in mystery.

He played with the words for a few more miles before his mind wandered back to the beginnings of his search.

~ * ~

Not long after Trotsky's burned, he was in the library doing research in the Texas History section of the stacks, looking for a book relating to the Mexican War. As he scanned the books looking for a particular title, another book caught his eye. *Lost Gold Mines of Texas* glowed from the shelf like the glint of a lost gem. A quiet spark fired in the back of his brain and he could not ignore the compulsion to pull the book out and thumb through the index until he suddenly stopped and, blinking in disbelief, he stared at the page. There in front of him was the same name mentioned by Slim.

"Ben Sublett," he whispered.

At the time, he had been tempted to check the book out, but he shook himself to reality because this paper was important and he had a deadline. His overriding objective that day was to get a passing grade on his research project so he managed to suppress the impulse and simply noted the details of the book in the margin of his notebook with a bold BEN SUBLETT circled in the corner of the page. Then he went on and found his other research items. He completed his paper and got a passing grade, but as he later realized, that seed, hidden deep in his soul, had finally germinated.

~ * ~

Sam laughed as he drove. "I'd never be able to put something like that off now."

~ * ~

After he graduated, he began to work at a series of dead-end jobs and eventually moved away from Houston to northeast Texas following a current love interest. That experiment only lasted a few months and ended in disaster because they both had made a sudden shift from big city to small town life, a transition that was much more difficult than either of them had anticipated. They were both desperate for diversion and one of Sam's outlets was the small local library where he found he could check out books from other libraries through an inter-library loan program. Wallowing in small-town boredom one day, he remembered the book about lost gold mines. He had a vague recollection that he had written the title down somewhere in one of his notebooks so he rummaged through boxes of his possessions and leafed through a dozen or more notebooks until he found the right one. He took the information down to the librarian and asked if she could find the book for him.

"Will this do?" he asked her when he showed her the title and author and publisher information he had jotted down.

"Oh, yes, that's all I need," she said, adding, "I need to make some inquiries, so it will probably be a few weeks."

She made her calls and found the book for him and when it finally arrived, he concentrated on the small section about Ben Sublett. He read that Ben had lived out in west Texas, and eventually settled in Odessa with a family where he pretty much kept to himself. But it was well-known that he often had gold. It was also said that for years he would periodically disappear for a few days or a few weeks and he would always return with more gold. The mine was thought to be in the Guadalupe Mountains but no one was really sure. Several people had tried to follow him to no avail. Ben's secret, the book said, died with him.

Sam ended up reading the book cover-to-cover and made a lot of notes, both on the Sublett mine and on some of the other mines in the book. The odd thing about gold mines in Texas was that, according to the geology of the state, there really shouldn't be any gold, but legends about the elusive mineral were not in short supply, probably due to the intense interest early Spanish explorers gave to the notion.

Not long after that, Sam broke up with his girlfriend and moved to Austin. Ironically, he found out Godson and Moll had just moved there as well. They all shared a duplex for a few months and Sam worked a couple of temporary jobs to pay his share of the bills. He eventually got a full-time job at the University of Texas. For him, that was a stroke of luck because it gave him full privileges at their impressive library system. He eventually found his own place: a garage apartment in South Austin. It was at the edge of a park, affording privacy and quiet. It was almost like living on the edge of a forest, except for the occasional blaring lights of the tennis court. Oddly, the place had a couple of wide crank-out windows facing the street instead of the park. A visiting friend called it *"Vista Del Camino,"* Spanish for "view of the road."

Still, despite the new job and new apartment, there was a definite void in his Austin life. For one thing, he was lonely. He had put pot behind him, but he tended to drink more, usually at home because he no longer liked to hang around in bars. Obviously, the fire at Trotsky's might have had something to do with that aversion, but Trotsky's had also shown him that a bar was not an ideal place to find a meaningful relationship anyway. Of course, there was that *other* diversion that drew increasing levels of his attention. Sam saw no way to reconcile his loneliness with his obsession. The university library became a regular stop after work and research helped fill the void in his life, along with providing a lot of useful information about the lost Sublett mine.

Slim had said "look him up" and Sam did. It was an intriguing story but there were few hard facts. According to the anecdotal evidence he read, Ben had led an almost stereotypical late nineteenth century frontier life. It was said he was befriended by an old man, either a Mexican or an Indian, the stories varied on that point, who told him the secret of a mine in the Guadalupe Mountains. Ben periodically disappeared and always returned with gold. Although that area was not considered potential gold country, Sam was intrigued to find other anecdotal evidence of such a possibility, for instance, even Geronimo had once mentioned a secret rich mine somewhere in west Texas.

Other sources mentioned the same story Sam had read before, that Ben eventually settled in the Odessa area with a family but repeated the notion that, from time-to-time, Ben would disappear and he would always return with gold. People tried to follow him but to no avail; he eluded them.

Sam marveled at the stories he read, thinking to himself that old Ben was a sly character ...once he found the gold, he just let it keep him comfortable, using it as sort of his own private nineteenth century Social Security. It was said that Ben took his young son with him one time, but the boy could never remember details of the mine or its location. Every time Sam read something new about the Sublett mine, his face flushed and an odd sensation would engulf his entire body and he began to understand that he was caught by something he was going to have to see through to the end.

"Damn," he said, breaking his train of thought as he grabbed a napkin to mop a bead of sweat that had formed on his forehead. He tried to blink away the sting of one drop that had fallen into his eye and returned to his musings.

Although he managed to go through the motions of his humdrum life, he knew he was being guided by that relentless gnawing urge. Even so, he managed to find a few diversions, but often even those diversions had secondary motives that pointed back to his obsession. At one point, he decided to take some karate classes and he kept it up for a couple of years. He justified this because he thought the skills might come in handy to him later in his quest. He liked the discipline and the camaraderie and, for a while, his karate club was the major social component of his life. The dojo was very close to the library and he was able to work in both pursuits on most days. He became moderately good at it and managed to advance to just below the black belt stage.

Ironically, he had to quit because he was injured when he joined a couple of his karate buddies on a day trip hiking in a rocky area fairly close to Austin. As usual, he had a dual motive. Although it was supposed to be fun, he also figured it would be a good chance to grab some additional hiking experience in a rugged area. Sam made a stupid move and he fell hard, injuring his thigh. He managed to limp his way back to the car, but his leg was badly bruised and tender and took a long time to fully heal. He tried to continue to work out with his club, but he soon realized it was not the sort of thing he could risk reinjuring, so he dropped out for a while. But he never went back because his free time was quickly absorbed by more research and he was soon back down to the basics, working at his job and focusing on the Sublett mine.

Eight

Sam first met Sally Beeman when he started at the university. She was a secretary upstairs and he worked in the warehouse. They had a fairly cordial working acquaintance until the day she noticed him limping after his fall and asked him about it. That led to a lunch where he explained his injuries. After that, they would regularly get lunch together and eventually they'd sometimes go out for drinks after work as well. Sam liked Sally. She was bright and funny, and they shared a lot of common interests. Normally he might have tried to take that interest further, but she made it clear she had a serious boyfriend, although the boyfriend travelled a lot for his job and that left her lonely and bored. For Sam, the friendship gave him a social outlet with none of the complications of a relationship. Many people at the office thought they were dating, and whenever that rumor popped up, which it did from time to time, they both shared a good laugh about it.

Fate intervened when Sam got a chance at a new job upstairs. At the same time, Sally found out that she was being squeezed out of her secretarial job, but was offered a position that had opened up, working with Sam.

"Hey, are you going to apply for the other job with me?" he asked her.

"I don't know," she said, "they don't seem to want me here. Maybe I'd do better going someplace else."

"Come on, it's a job. We get along real well; we'd make a great team."

She finally agreed to do it and they ended up sharing an office. Through it all, they continued to be good friends.

He kept his growing obsession a secret for a long time, but once they started working in such close quarters, she soon realized Sam seemed to have a lurking dark mystery in his life. He eventually leaked a few details to her one day when they had gone for a beer after work just before he made his first organized trip.

"I need to tell you something," he said.

"Oh, this sounds ominous. Is it about your trip?"

"Yeah, it is a little weird."

"I've noticed you thinking a lot at your desk, and I wondered what was going on."

"I guess I don't have many secrets in that tiny office. You're right, I *have* been thinking a lot. This trip might be a little dangerous."

"What? Why would it be dangerous? I thought you were just going camping or something."

"It involves a lot of tromping around on private land, that sort of thing. I've never done it before."

"Oh, my god, Sam. What are you doing?"

"Okay, we've been friends for a long time, so please, trust me, you can't tell anybody."

"You know, I had a feeling you've had some secret little something you've always kept from me. Woman's intuition, you know?"

"Did it tell you about a lost gold mine?" he whispered.

"What? Gold mine?"

"Shhh, not so loud."

Sam proceeded to let her in on a few of the general details. Without revealing the clues, he did tell her there were some specifics he was looking for.

"But you have no idea where this thing is," she said, with a bit of skepticism.

"No, and it is dangerous enough ...well, I just think someone should know where I am going in case something happens, like if I don't show up on Tuesday."

"And where *are* you going?"

"Well, I meant kind of generally. It will be along some mountains between Van Horn and the Guadalupe Mountains National Park. My car will be parked on the side of a highway and I should be in that area. I'm not a hundred percent sure where I'll go this time. But I'm worried in case ...well, in case I fall or something, or get bitten by a snake ...or worse."

"What could be worse?"

"Cougar maybe, perhaps a scared bobcat. Possibly a bear. But the most likely worse scenario is human."

"Wouldn't that just get you arrested?"

"That's a best-case scenario, I think. THEN, I'd call."

"Sam, this is stupid. I don't think you should do it." Sally was looking intently at Sam with her eyes glistening.

"Oh, that's all worst-case crap. I'll be all right. I just have to sneak around and be on my toes. Don't worry, unless I'm late."

"What do you want me to do? Call the police or something if you don't show up Tuesday?"

"More like cover for me Tuesday and call Wednesday. I might possibly just get delayed."

"You've done this before?" she asked.

"Not quite this way. This will be my first time going in after dark. I've looked around a little and scouted out the roads. Went in the National Park once, too."

"Why don't you just forget it? Stay here. Robert will be here this weekend ...let's all go do something, listen to some music somewhere or something."

Sam was steadfast. "No, I have to go do this. I really do."

Like he had done with Godson and Moll, he swore her to secrecy concerning the scarce details he shared. He had to trust that their friendship was strong enough to keep her quiet. He then told her about his one disastrous trip out west when he was still in college, long before he had met her. He had never even told Godson and Moll about that one. This trip really had been a worst-case scenario. He was unprepared, acting only on the vague notion that maybe he could look around. He was so naïve, he even ignored Slim's basic instruction to look *south* of the Guadalupe Mountains.

The trip demonstrated the fact that he didn't have the slightest idea of what he was doing. All Sam knew was that he was unfamiliar with such a distant area and it was a struggle to figure out the best way to start searching, so he blindly moved forward.

The geologic survey maps changed that. One day, Sam spotted a tiny article in the newspaper about a new toll-free ordering service for US Geologic Survey maps. Of course, he already knew about topographic maps, but he did not have the slightest idea how to find them. He called the toll-free number and found out his first step was to get a free index map, and that allowed him to make informed purchases. Once he bought a few maps, he pored over them, using a bright light and a magnifying glass.

He didn't know what he was looking for, but as he scanned the maps, he was amazed at the details he could see. The squiggly lines revealed canyons, ridges, gullies and there were other things marked on the maps, including roads, jeep trails, buildings, and even marked mines. When he saw the marked mines, he researched the geologic history as well, and found that some silver and other minerals had been mined south of the Guadalupe Mountains in his proposed search area. That excited him, despite the fact that there was no mention of gold. He still pressed on.

He bought some survey maps of the Guadalupe Mountains, too, because all the anecdotal evidence pointed there. Shortly after the jail encounter, the Guadalupe Mountains had become a National Park and this concerned Sam, but Slim had been adamant that it *wasn't* in the Guadalupe Mountains. He hoped Slim had been right, because the prospect of dealing with private property owners was one thing, but to deal with the federal government was something else entirely. As Sam studied the maps, he tried to put himself in the old prospector's shoes and he began to entertain a notion that Ben likely had a certain genius in the area of deceit.

"It makes sense," Sam had said to himself. "If a person had a gold mine, why would he tell anyone where it was? He'd naturally tell them where it *wasn't*!"

This principle was also supported by Slim's account.

As he followed this line of thought, Sam also considered an alternate theory. Nineteenth century West Texas was a wild and inhospitable place, and the maps of the time were often crude and inaccurate. The Guadalupe Mountains were a well-known landmark, especially the impressive face of El Capitan, but there were ranges stretching north and south as well.

"Back then, maybe local people just called that entire string of different mountain ranges the Guadalupe Mountains," he would tell himself.

It seemed to be a reasonable alternate theory, but he preferred to stick with his original notion. If old Ben openly gave reason to believe his gold was in the Guadalupes, it obviously *wasn't* the location of the mine.

As he pored over his maps, Sam began to look for likely canyons and gullies in the ranges south of the Guadalupe Mountains, down between the official range and Van Horn. He had no idea what 'devil' meant, so he concentrated on the 'table' part of the clue, working from the assumption that the word likely had something to do with a mesa-topped mountain or hill.

As a rule, mesas, with their flat tops, were easy to distinguish on the contour maps but there was one problem with this line of thought.

"There just aren't any mesas out there," he told himself again and again.

When he realized this, Sam thought it possible that some mesas might be visible in the distance, so he widened his search and bought more maps when he could. He also returned to his maps of the Guadalupe Mountains Park area and looked there, just in case. He found nothing.

He knew he was just going to have to get out into the field to get more ideas, so he identified what he thought might be likely areas to at least go out and take a look and he began to plan his first real trips. He did not want a repeat of his first naïve attempt several years before, so once he had done more research on backpacking and camping and assembled some equipment, he began to practice hiking with his gear at some county parks out at Lake Travis. He knew he'd have to travel light, and would have to carry water. He also began walking, sometimes walking to work instead of bicycling. He knew he had to get in shape.

On that first serious excursion to search for clues, he went south of the Guadalupe Mountains. That was also when he tried asking for permission and concocted what he thought was a reasonable cover story, saying he just wanted to hike and do some nature photography. The rancher looked him up and down. At the time he had long hair and no doubt looked quite out of place to the staid and conservative landowner.

"No, I don't want you out on my land," the rancher said.

There was a deflating tone in his voice, especially the hard emphasis the man had placed on the last two words. Despite the friendly reputation of the area, exemplified by the ever-present "wave" from passing vehicles on the lonely country roads in the area, the locals were private and quite protective of their concept of "my land."

That long trip was almost a total bust, but he did scout around quite a bit. Sam prowled up and down Highway 54, the road that runs the entire length of the mountains he was interested in. The mountains and gullies seemed to mock him as he drove between the new National Park area and the small town of Van Horn. He scouted to the west of these ranges too, finding ranch roads and smaller graded roads that crisscrossed the scrub desert to the west of these mountains. He took a lot of notes so he could remember any interesting features he saw.

On subsequent trips, he experimented a little more. He made one more inquiry, even mentioning his true intent and the rancher laughed in his face. On other trips, he drove to more distant locations like the Davis Mountains, just in case Ben Sublett might have gone farther afield. After these trips, he decided to stick with Slim's statement. It was his best evidence, the only real lead he had ... and there was another reason too.

"I just have a gut feeling about it," he told himself.

Sam flushed when he drove past those particular mountains and he didn't know if it was psychological, or logical, or if it was some sort of psychic connection. He did know that when he drove up past the prominent face of El Capitan and on past the Guadalupe Mountains proper, he didn't have the same feeling.

The feverish wave of emotion spread over him *only* when he passed the ranges to the south.

"*This* has to be the place," he once mumbled as he was driving past.

Then he followed that thought up with another, "Now all I have to do is find the darned thing."

Nine

All of these reflections kept Sam's mind busy as he drove down the interstate, zipping past the small towns like Ozona and Sonora. As he approached Junction, he decided to stop for gas and coffee and as he pulled into a truck stop near the highway, he spotted the familiar contours of an old 1963 Chevy Impala in the parking lot. He smiled because it reminded him of the car his uncle had driven years ago in Houston. Seeing the same model of car reminded him of simpler times and fun things like baseball games and trips to the beach.

It was pushing nine o'clock by the time Sam hit the outskirts of Austin. He grabbed a burger and fries at a fast-food joint and headed to his garage apartment. As he rounded the corner, he felt a wave of relief to see the light in the window of his apartment. He had a timer connected to both a lamp and his stereo and it cycled on and off at different times in the hope it would deter burglars, not that he had much to worry about.

He pulled into the alley, then angled into his short driveway and he parked his car in the garage. He started to grab his pack but decided to leave it for later and trudged up the stone and concrete steps that wrapped around an old cedar tree next to his front door. The steps were beginning to crumble because the tree had grown too large for the space, but Sam appreciated the rustic appeal their rough condition added to the place. Rock music was playing in the background as he unlocked the door, and once he was inside, he looked around. The apartment seemed just the same. He walked over to the shelf and turned the stereo off and was engulfed in a wave of quiet which was a relief after enduring hours of constant road noise.

He grabbed a beer and took a long deep swig. The apartment was basically a studio, with one big room with no couch or chairs, just big throw pillows and a bed. He'd tried to outfit the place with a table and then a recliner but there just wasn't room, so he switched to big floppy pillows. He plopped down on one of the pillows and proceeded to devour his hamburger. The fries were limp and greasy, but the burger tasted good, and was a welcome change from the endless supply of cheese crackers and candy bars he had eaten on the road. He finished his meal and sipped his beer for a few minutes before he grabbed the phone and dialed Godson's number.

"Hello?"

"Hey, buddy, it's Sam. I'm back."

"Oh, that's good." Godson sounded sleepy. "Glad you're home safe and sound. How'd it go?"

It was a standard question but Sam hesitated a bit to formulate an answer. "Okay. I guess about the same as last time."

"Nobody saw you?" Godson asked that same question after every trip.

"There's something interesting about that," he said.

71

"Wait," Godson had a level of shock in his voice. "Somebody saw you?"

"Well, no, at least not out on the land. It was some guy in town, in Van Horn. In a café parking lot. I'm not exactly sure what he was talking about, but he said he saw my car. He said he had seen my car before, too, and he knew what I was doing. He flat out asked me if I was prospecting."

"Man, that's bad. I've said it before and I'll say it again ...you can get in a lot of trouble doing what you're doing."

Sam sighed. "I know, Godson, but this guy ...well, it was weird. I swear he acted like he actually wanted to help me. He warned me, said he didn't want me to get hurt. I think he was just an old coot, you know, messing with me. Even the lady at the café told me he was a nut and to watch out for him. Still, he said he wants me to come talk to him next time I'm out there."

"You're not going to do that, are you?" Godson asked.

Sam laughed. "Probably not, but I never know exactly what I'm going to do out there. I thought I had a good angle this time, but I didn't find anything."

"Listen," Godson said, "maybe it is just time you faced facts. You should just forget about this. You've given it a good shot. What's this, your sixth time out there?"

"Seventh," Sam said.

"Seven times," Godson continued, "all the way across Texas, and for what? Not a damn thing. And you spend money for gas and food, not to mention the hours and hours of driving both ways. Then there is all this risky trespassing, hiking across dangerous ground, and for what? Nothing. It might be time to think about blowing it all off."

Sam silently drew in a deep breath. He knew his friend was only trying to help. In the beginning Godson had been cautiously supportive in ways one would expect a friend to be, but lately he always said the same things about these trips. Deep inside, Sam appreciated this sort of reaction from a friend because it helped to ground him a little, and in that moment, although he didn't agree with Godson, he did appreciate the concern.

"I know," Sam said. "But in my gut, I know I can find this thing. I know it's out there."

"Sure, sure, and what happens if you find it? What then? It isn't your land, buddy. Say you find this thing ... you'll be finding somebody else a pile of gold."

Godson had a point and it was something Sam had mulled over quite a number of times. "I don't know," he said, "but I have to find it first, right? Then I'll try to figure that out."

"Yeah, right," Godson said. "I'm just glad you're home safe and sound. Well, safe anyway," He laughed. "You need anything?"

"Naw," Sam said. "I'm just having a beer, relaxing after the long drive. I just wanted to let you know I was back."

"I don't mean to get on your case ...I just don't want you to get hurt. You know?"

He smiled, "I know, Godson, and I appreciate your concern, really I do. I'll talk to you later, okay?"

"Sure. Now go get some sleep. Bye."

As he placed the handset down, Sam thought about what Godson had said. It was nothing new. There was no way anyone else could begin to understand. They had not been there that night in jail, smelling the rancid breath of a broken little man as he whispered his secret in that fading, raspy voice. That scene was etched in his memory and the ember of those words burned right through him. He knew he'd never stop looking. He would get up in the morning and trudge back to his mindless job and then he would come home and pull out his magnifying glass and his maps and once again spend an evening poring over the scribbly lines, trying to make some sense of the riddles, trying to find something that tied to the clues.

He sipped his beer and glanced at the stack of neatly folded maps on the shelf along one wall and remembered he had two others down in his pack. Then he shook his head.

"Maybe Godson is right," he said to himself.

Here he was, sitting on the floor, alone, nursing a light buzz from the beer, exhausted from a long weekend of driving and hiking and sleeping on the hard ground. He was safe here. There was no worry of ranchers or animals or weather. The strain of the long drive, dulled by the alcohol, began to ease from his body and brain. He lifted the beer and finished the bottle, then his thoughts were interrupted by the phone.

"Hello?"

"Sam?" The voice was female. It was Sally.

"Sally, I was just going to call you," he lied. In fact, he had meant to call her too, to let her know he had safely returned but he had forgotten, the intention overshadowed by his musings.

"Are you okay?"

"Yeah. Just got back a few minutes ago. Just another long, futile trip," he said.

"I figured you'd be back about now," she said. "You going to be at work tomorrow?"

"Yup, time to get back to the old grindstone."

They both laughed. He had to give her some credit as a friend ...she put up with him day after day and yet she still talked to him.

"So there was nothing?"

"No, big surprise. I didn't find a damn thing." He laughed again.

"Well, you're back safe, that's the important thing," she said.

"Right. I'm more worried about some big rig running over me on the interstate than I am about having any trouble out in the mountains." He chose not to tell her about the encounter with Loot because of Godson's reaction.

"Oh, that's for sure. You can't make all these long trips without worrying about that. Plus you're tired—you have to be. I mean, you hike out of the mountains and then hop in your car and drive?"

"Yeah, that's the usual plan," he said.

"That's ridiculous. You should at least get a motel out there, get a good night's sleep and then drive back."

"Yeah, that's a good idea, but that's another day off I have to take and more expense. I can barely afford these junkets as it is. But I'm doing okay. I actually do sleep pretty well out there, sleeping under the stars. There's not much to do after dark, camping in the rough like that."

"I don't know how you do it," Sally said. "Well, see you at work tomorrow, okay?"

"Yeah, see you there. Thanks for calling. I'm sorry you beat me to it. I was just grabbing a bite and a beer after being on the road for so long. I'm sort of brain dead."

Sally laughed. "I'm supposed to accept that as an excuse? You were born brain dead."

He laughed too. "Geez, thanks a lot. See you tomorrow."

"Bye, Sam."

After hanging up, he felt satisfied with himself now that his two confidants had been updated. He wondered about another beer but decided against it. He looked at the clock and saw it was pushing eleven o'clock. Twenty-four hours earlier, he had been nestled along the bottom edge of a rocky outcrop, partially sheltered under a scrubby mesquite tree.

He thought about the rest of his day, his hike, that enormous breakfast, the long drive, and finally, he remembered Smidgeon and her infectious smiling eyes. He was amazed he had never really noticed her on his previous visits but just figured that was how it went with life sometimes. Maybe he had just been extra tired, or it was busy or maybe their paths had just not crossed for unknown reasons. He really liked The Mossback but he hadn't eaten there on the previous fall trip and before that it had been spring, and he didn't remember where he had eaten back then.

He got up and flicked on the TV, checked that his alarm was set and stretched out on the bed, still wearing his dusty clothes. He looked at the TV, not even listening to the sound.

The next thing he knew, his clock radio was blaring some news about the upcoming election and he got out of bed and switched it off.

"Bleh, Carter and Reagan again," he said out loud. Then, as he realized he had fallen asleep in his dirty pants he added, "Damn!"

He dragged himself into his kitchen and put some water on to boil so he could make some coffee. He looked at the pile of dishes in the sink and resolved not to leave town with the kitchen in this shape next time. Deep inside, he knew it was a hopeless expectation. He made a cup of instant coffee and was momentarily hypnotized by the curls of vapor rising from the cup. Instant coffee was not particularly good, but it was fast and that is what he wanted at that moment, a fast cup of coffee. The coffee was followed by a long, hot shower and the normal morning rituals of getting ready for work.

Ten

The aggravation of Austin's rush hour traffic spurred Sam to make a side trip on the way to work. Mrs. Johnson's was a doughnut shop that had carved a niche in the collective appetite of Austin. If he drove past the shop late at night when the hot doughnuts were being freshly glazed, the aroma would permeate the air with a sweet and luscious fragrance that was impossible to ignore without stopping.

"My car starts shaking and then automatically pulls in," he would joke to friends.

Despite its reputation, the store itself was not impressive. It was a low-slung frame building with peeling paint and a parking lot that resembled the lunar surface.

"A dozen glazed," was his order.

The clerk sauntered over to the production line and pulled his order from the warm doughnuts that were resting after being glazed. As he carried his prize back to the car, he savored the irresistible aroma and could feel a gentle warmth radiating from the box.

Sam's department was empty when he arrived, so he placed the box of doughnuts on a table, grabbed a coffee mug from his desk and walked down to the break room, where he was relieved to see a fresh pot of coffee waiting for him. He went back to his desk with a cup of coffee and sat down.

He stared at the pile of papers on his desk and appreciated the disparity that separated his exhausting weekend pursuit from his day job. He and Sally worked together in this small office managing subscription lists for a number of academic publications. Most of what they did was reduced to tiny holes punched on computer cards.

Each day they churned through a chaotic cycle of requests, orders, renewals, and complaints. The pile of papers on his desk showed him that he had a price to pay for taking two days off. He fingered through the pile and took a sip of coffee, then sighed and got up to retrieve one of the doughnuts. Sally arrived just as he was reaching into the box.

"Sam," she said, "you made it!" Then she added, "Doughnuts! You must be either really happy, or really depressed." They both laughed.

"Yeah," he said, "probably a little of both."

Back at their desks she said, "You didn't miss much around here, mostly the usual stuff. I did as much of it as I could, but," she said pointing, "*that* pile needs your special touch."

He winced because that usually meant things needed research or perhaps a creative approach to resolution. Eventually Sam and Sally started in on the day's chores. There was a certain level of drudgery about the work, but he preferred it to his previous job in the warehouse. He thought about this as he walked to the mail room.

The warehouse crew had its own ways of doing things and they delighted in being irreverent rebels, in stark contrast to the staid business-like nature of the rest of the office. He was still friendly with Manny and the others, but the relationship was never quite the same after he moved upstairs. Of course, Sam always thought the embarrassing escapade at the Christmas party a few years earlier might have changed those dynamics as well.

The door to the warehouse stairwell loomed just beyond the mailroom and almost every time he saw that door, he had embarrassing flashbacks of that fiasco.

~ * ~

The party was always on the last day before the holiday break. His original plan had been to take a day off, but at the last minute he changed his mind and just showed up for work.

When his boss, Manny, saw him, he said, "I thought you weren't coming."

Sam shrugged. "I dunno," he said, "...plans changed. That isn't a problem, is it?"

"Hell no," Manny said, smiling. "I'm glad you made it."

He handed Manny a carton of eggnog he had brought and Manny put it in the small warehouse refrigerator. On the day of the party, the warehouse crew always provided enhanced eggnog to anyone who walked through. People upstairs knew about this and many of them would make their way downstairs for a cup because it was a party day and this gave everybody a head start on the party.

Manny poured Sam a glass of eggnog and tipped in a hefty glug or two of bourbon.

"Here ya go, Merry Christmas," Manny said, smiling.

He sipped it and felt the bourbon warm its way down his throat.

"Now, go get some work done ...we need to get finished up before noon."

The party was basically a potluck dinner and was held in a big conference room upstairs. Sam had neglected to bring anything due to his change of mind, but he hoped no one would notice. He ate sparingly because he felt a little guilty, but what he *did* do was drink. He drank beer and he drank whiskey, often combining the two into a makeshift boilermaker.

He pretty much made a fool of himself toward the end of the party by knocking a few things over. Somewhere through the fog of his drunkenness, he realized he was starting to get a bit out of control and decided he should make good his escape, so he slowly weaved his way down the long hallway to the stairwell that led down to the warehouse. There were two sets of stairs, separated by a landing.

He negotiated these stairs several times every day, but this time he lost his balance and tumbled down to the landing. He was almost convinced he had been tripped or pushed and thought he heard someone faintly chuckling but he knew he was alone in the stairwell.

A concerned voice came from the top of the stairs, "Are you okay?"

As Sam stood, he made a show of dusting himself off and said, "I'm okay, I'm okay, I've got it under control."

Then he immediately fell down the second set of stairs and ended up in a heap on the warehouse floor. Manny, Chuy, and Ray were all sitting around talking in Manny's office, which was right next to the stairwell. They ran out and found his crumpled body at the base of the stairs, and they were all laughing while they tried to help him up.

After his second fall, his memory failed him, probably due more to the boilermakers than the fall. He did vaguely recall being corralled by Manny, but the fact of the matter was that all of them were drunk by this time and in general a drunk can't effectively watch a drunk. After a few minutes, he took advantage of a diversion and made his way out to his car and somehow made it home without killing himself or someone else.

There were multiple aftereffects, the worst of which was a ruined tire. He had no idea how that happened but he knew he was lucky he hadn't been stopped and arrested. Also unexplained were deep burns on his shoulder and arm, but those were secondary to the multiple aches and pains he suffered as a result of his stairway tumble. Then there was the embarrassment at work, but he hoped the long holiday break would soften the memories of most people.

~ * ~

As he walked away from the mailroom, his thoughts returned to the present. Time had healed the physical wounds and the jokes from the warehouse crew had faded, except maybe at Christmas. Still, it had seemed to him that everyone down there treated him a little differently after that day and he was relieved when he had been offered a job upstairs.

Eleven

"You want to go get some lunch?"

Sally had asked the question and it wasn't an unusual sort of thing to ask in the office, but Sam thought for just a moment before answering. He hadn't planned on going out that day because his funds were short.

"Okay," he said, "maybe something cheap?"

Sally continued, "Sure. It's a nice day, maybe someplace outside."

"Yeah, but where? The Posse?"

Sally frowned. "I don't think so."

He couldn't blame her for the negative comment. He liked the place but it was basically a beer joint with food and wasn't for everyone.

"But," Sally continued, "there aren't that many places close by to eat outside and their food isn't *that* bad. But no beer," she said. "You've been out for two days; I need you working this afternoon."

"Yeah, okay," he said with a sheepish tone. Sally knew him too well and he knew she was right. Beer at lunch meant not nearly as much work would get done in the afternoon.

"Can you drive?" Sally asked.

He said, "Sure, although my car is still a mess from my trip."

As he was cleaning up some of the flotsam from the passenger seat, Sally asked, "Where are your maps? You always seem to have maps with you."

"They're in a pocket on the pack," he said, pointing to the back seat. "I have a bunch of them at home, but the ones from this last trip are still in there."

On the way to the restaurant, Sally started in with the usual questions. "Don't you ever get tired of all this stuff? I mean, like the long drives and the hiking, stuff like that. Wouldn't somebody have found that gold mine by now if it was there?"

"You know," he said, "sometimes I do wonder if it is all worth it but deep down inside, well … it's really hard to explain. The more I do this, the more I know there is something out there waiting for me."

"But what can you do if you find it?"

"That's a really good question and I just don't have a good answer to it. That's a bridge I'll have to cross if I ever find it."

The Posse was a repurposed gas station jutting out at the point of a "Y" intersection. The stucco-like concrete exterior was painted a dark brown. A patio stretched across the driveway of the old station, littered with weathered picnic tables. The kitchen and front counter were both located where the office and storage areas of the gas station had been and the interior dining room had formerly been the garage. Most people seemed to prefer the patio if it wasn't cold or raining. It was a pleasant place to sit on a nice day if you didn't mind being close to the traffic, because the old driveway opened right onto the street, with no fence or barrier.

While they waited for their food, Sally said, "Why don't you get one of your maps and show me where you went this weekend?"

"Really?"

"Yes, I want to see," Sally repeated.

They had parked fairly close, so he retrieved his maps and once back at the table he carefully unfolded the first one.

"Look at how nicely folded you keep them," she said, adding with a laugh, "That is so unlike you."

He laughed and explained. "When you order them, they come rolled up. I lent the first maps I bought to a guy in my karate club and when he returned them, he had folded them like this. I'm not sure where he learned that but he said it helps keep them organized and it's easier than dealing with rolled up maps. I like how it clearly shows the map title."

"What does it all mean," Sally asked when she gazed at the map. "All these lines are so confusing."

"Those are contour lines. They show changes in elevation. The closer together the lines are, the steeper it is. Where the lines sort of go in parallel 'V' shapes means there is a little gully or valley, something like that."

"So where were you?"

He scanned the map and pointed to a dense line and said, "I parked over in this area, a few miles from where I wanted to go. See? There is a road there. I just pulled over and put a sign on the dash that said my car was broken down."

"And, so then you hiked ...to where?"

"I concentrated on this area," Sam said, pointing to some dense squiggles. "I purposely parked miles from where I wanted to go." He pointed back to the previous spot again and added, "That is a paved ranch road so I thought it was pretty safe."

"Aren't you afraid of someone seeing you hiking out there? I mean, it's all private land, right? And you are hiking so far."

"Yeah, trespassing is a gamble," he said. "But that's why I go in at night, and I try to sort of separate the hike from the car to throw off suspicion. At least that's the theory."

"In the dark? That's crazy. Can't you ask for permission so you could park closer?"

"Not really. I tried in the beginning but it's tough. It's still a little like the old west out there."

"But these are roads, right?" Sally asked, pointing to some obvious road lines on the map.

"Yeah, but those are mostly rough, graded private roads and some are just jeep trails. These are working ranches and the ranchers are suspicious of anybody they don't know."

"So if you find this thing..." Sally started.

"Right," he interrupted. "It's theirs, at least *if* I tell them."

"So you think you could keep it a secret if you found it?"

"Maybe ...I don't know. Like I said, that is just something I'll have to figure out but, of course, I have to find it first."

Sally scanned the map, admiring the contours and lines even after they got their food. Occasionally she asked a few questions.

"What are these dots?" she asked, pointing.

Sam squinted at the map in the sunlight. "Buildings of some sort, probably a ranch house and barn."

"So people live out there?"

"Yeah, here and there," he said, "but it's mostly just a lot of open country."

While he munched on his food, lost in thought, Sally carefully folded the first map and opened the other one.

"Some of the place names are so cool," she said as she munched her chips, still carefully looking at the map. "Like this— Diablo Rim, look how close together those squiggles are," she said pointing. She repeated it, "Diablo Rim ...scary, huh? Good place for a Halloween search, I guess," she said with a giggle.

Sam was still lost in thought and just sort of randomly glanced over and said, "Mmmm, yeah, it looks really steep there. I haven't been over in that area yet."

"It looks pretty long, going from here to here," she said, tracing a line on the map, but Sam still wasn't paying attention to her. "I wonder if there is a trail up there you could follow?"

"Hmmm? Possibly, but I doubt it. Except for the jeep trails, most other trails out there are animal trails. Don't forget, this isn't a park, it is just land ..." Sam stopped in mid-sentence and stared at the map. It was as if he had been hit in the back of his head.

Sally noticed the obvious change in demeanor and asked, "What's wrong? Are you okay? You're not choking, are you?"

"You said something about Diablo ...Diablo Rim. Is that what you said? Show me again!"

Sally pointed at the map, moving her finger along a jagged series of contour lines. This time he followed the track of her finger carefully.

"See? It goes along here, first up this way and then around and over to there..."

"Diablo Rim," Sam said, then said it again as he read the words on the map, "Diablo Rim!" Then, he muttered under his breath, "I'm such an idiot..."

"What the hell are you talking about?"

"I've looked at that map countless times and missed it. It is so simple, so obvious." He was still staring at the map.

"You're not going to tell me, are you?"

"Well, I don't want to go into details," he said, still staring at the map.

"What is it? What's the big deal with Diablo Rim?"

86

"It ...I think it might actually be one of the things I've been looking for," he said, shifting the map and eyeing it with even greater interest.

Sally sat back and sipped her tea in a definite pout. "Happy to help out," she said in an obviously offended tone.

He looked up. "I'm sorry," he said, "but it's really better if you don't know the details."

Then he could see from the look on Sally's face that this paltry explanation was not going to suffice.

"Okay," he said with a sigh, then continued in a hushed tone, "here's the deal. There is a clue I've been trying to figure out, a reference that says something about 'following the devil'.... Okay? Diablo, the devil ...it is so obvious but somehow I've missed it. That's as good as you get."

Sally smiled and seemed happy with this explanation. "So ...Diablo Rim. That's where you'll go next?"

"Maybe. I need to look at this map more closely with my magnifying glass, but maybe, just maybe, you might have opened a whole new can of worms for me. I'll have to see."

He carefully folded the maps, noting this particular map name and set them both aside.

"So this is a good thing?" Sally asked.

He smiled. "Well, at first glance this looks harder than anything I've tried before. I have a lot of analysis and planning to do. Like, I need to figure out how I can find a safe way to get over there so I can approach it without being seen. You know, that sort of thing."

"More danger, I guess." Sally frowned.

"It is always dangerous," he said, "but it ... well I think this is important. I'll just have to get out there and look around and see what I can see."

They finished their lunch and he carefully gathered his maps. Back at the car, he placed them in the special pocket in his pack.

Although he worked hard that afternoon, in the back of his mind Sam was thinking about Diablo Rim. Back at home, he spread out several maps side by side and crawled over them with a gooseneck lamp and a magnifying glass.

"Diablo Rim!" he said to himself, "how did I never make that connection?" He stared at the maps for a long time, then sat on his pillows deep in thought throughout the evening, not even bothering to eat.

Twelve

As Sam studied his maps in greater detail, he could see that a hike to Diablo Rim presented major difficulties. First, there was no easy way in. Although the area was crossed by a number of ungraded roads and jeep trails, the rim was farther from public roads than any location he had searched. He could tell from the map that it was also one of the more rugged sections of the entire range, so he knew he would be in for a tough hike. As he scanned the maps, he could still see nothing whatsoever that might solve the elusive 'table' clue. Still, since Diablo Rim was a new search area for him, he knew the only way to find something was to go out and take a look for himself.

There were always three problems with planning a trip like this. The first was the weather. In the past, he had limited his expeditions to the fall and spring because he didn't want to deal with extremes. The west Texas summer was just too brutal to consider and such heat intensified the need to carry a lot of water. Water was heavy and every gallon added another eight pounds to his load. As for the winter, although there *could* be mild weather in the west Texas winter, that situation could change in a heartbeat. If it got really cold, he knew he couldn't build a fire to keep warm because it would announce his presence like a neon sign.

Another problem was money. He had already assumed that his most recent outing was his last trip of the year, so his savings had dwindled. It took him months to scrimp and save for these trips and he simply hadn't budgeted for another trip so soon. It wasn't just gas for the car ...he also had to stock up on supplies. November and December also meant Thanksgiving and Christmas trips to Houston and he winced when he thought about Christmas.

"Christmas always means shopping too," he said out loud.

The third major problem was time, and it was a problem that had several components. First, a round trip to west Texas required two full days of driving. His active searching time was further limited by the amount of time it took him to hike into his target area, and he had to repeat this to get out again. This was no recreational camping trip where he could drive his vehicle to a prepared site and set up his tent, pull out a box of camping supplies and just kick back and enjoy nature. He had to sneak in on foot and that took hours. Once there, he could tell from the map that the ragged rim would be slow going. The only easy hiking was on jeep trails, and up in the hills, he tended to avoid those because they presented the greatest chance of being seen. He had once almost been caught that way.

In the past, he had basically just abandoned his car on the side of a road feigning a breakdown, hoping it would be ignored for two or three days. But he also knew this was not a ploy he could depend on forever, especially since a Volkswagen sort of stood out in this land of pickup trucks.

To emphasize that point, he said out loud, "Remember? That the old guy in the parking lot said he had seen the car."

He had thought about buying another vehicle as a spare and alternating them and he rationalized that a pickup truck would be the best choice because it was more likely to go unnoticed out in west Texas. Of course, that notion just returned him to the question of money and a second vehicle was simply something he could not afford.

There was also considerable time involved in preparation. If success could be measured by not getting caught, he had always attributed his past success to his preparation and planning. He assumed that if he took care of as many details as he could, he would survive.

On the last trip, he had spent two full days looking around. Of course, that was only after a long day's drive and then a lengthy hike into his search area. At the end of his search, he had another hike back to his car followed by the same long and boring journey back home. Two days of searching was the ideal, but there were times when he could only manage a single day in the mountains.

This past fall he had targeted two specific search areas. He made a three-day trip in mid-September and followed that up with a four-day trip in late October. Every trip had basically the same routine. Exhaustion was a constant through it all, especially on the return drive.

He shook his head as he continually examined the long, craggy contours of Diablo Rim. It was obvious he would never be able to search the entire rim on one trip.

"I've got to figure this out," he said, "after all this time, I finally have a solid clue!"

He knew he *had* to get out on that rocky rim to look for the other signs and the more he thought about it, the more he wanted to do it as soon as possible, but those three basic problems constantly percolated through his mind. Cold weather was a looming threat because of the season and, because of his recent trips, money was in short supply, but time was the most vexing problem.

"How can I carve out enough time to get in, get out and still explore that rim?"

It was obvious to Sam that Diablo Rim was going to require an extended hike to get in, and even more time to search. Still, the scope of these problems seemed trivial when he thought about the significance of finally uncovering a clue. He could not wait to get out there to "follow the devil" and try to make sense of the other clues.

In the past, he had depended on guesses and hunches, as he simply looked for what he thought might be a good hiding place for a lost gold mine. On one level, he knew it was silly to do it that way, really, but he sincerely felt that fate had handed him this situation and he trusted that fate would eventually intervene on his behalf and that a clue would reveal itself as he explored blindly on his own. He had tried to be methodical with his searches, and with each trip he tried to explore a different part of the same general area. The revelation of Diablo Rim gave him even more confidence and reduced his focus to basically just one clue—the table.

Sam knew he would have two days off for Thanksgiving and a longer break in December between Christmas and New Year's. Planning any trip this late in year was a definite risk, but he was out of vacation time and those were large blocks of time-off he could use. As he considered those two breaks, he realized there wasn't enough time before Thanksgiving to effectively save money and prepare for the trip, and a four-day weekend probably would not be long enough for this particular search anyway. So he decided to make the week after Christmas his tentative target date. One of his primary problems, time, would be taken care of by that break. The longer wait time would help him on the money and preparation fronts as well.

"Now all I have to really worry about is the weather, but *that* is something I will have to leave until the last minute."

Sam knew that no amount of preparation could help him survive the sudden approach of a winter storm, what people in Texas called a "Blue 'Norther." In both Austin and Houston, he had seen the temperature go from the eighties one day to the twenties the next. Cold weather could mean ice and snow as well and he knew that such bad weather might be even worse at higher elevations. He could easily abort if the weather changed before he headed out, but once he left his car and started hiking, he would be at the mercy of the elements. He would be exposed, with minimal shelter and a fire was simply out of the question. He always packed light and that meant no tents because he knew a tent would be easy to spot, just as if he had put up a huge sign. If the weather changed while he was up in the mountains, hiking back down in ice or snow would be difficult, if not downright dangerous.

"And that's not all. I'd have to deal with bad road conditions on the return trip as well," he interjected.

As for money, he would have to start saving right away. He knew how to cut corners, so he would just have to squeeze his budget as tight as he could. Christmas meant shopping and he did worry about how he could apply some money for both Christmas and this trip but it wasn't anything he hadn't done before and deep inside he knew that nobody expected much from him in the way of presents anyway. Thanksgiving usually meant a trip to his parents in Houston and that incurred some expense as well.

"Maybe I can skip that," he said to himself, then he sighed deeply.

At work, it was obvious to Sally that his attention was diverted. He hardly talked and sat staring into space a lot of the time. She had seen this before, so she knew something was up. Friday was Halloween and as they were both preparing to leave for the day, she finally mentioned it to him.

"So, Sam, are you doing anything for Halloween?"

"No," he said, "I didn't really plan anything this year."

Sally frowned, "I was afraid of that. What is it? It's not that stupid Diablo Rim thing, is it?"

He looked at her and frowned. "You know me too well," he said. "...yeah, you got me thinking."

"That's what I was afraid of," she said. Sally was familiar with his usual patterns so she added, "At least you have until next spring to plan, right?"

"I was thinking of maybe heading out there during Christmas break." He wasn't looking directly at her when he said it.

"What? You've always said no winter trips because you'd die if you got caught by a cold front out there."

"It's just an idea," he said, shifting a bit in his chair as Sally gave him the evil eye. "I know how to watch the weather and I wouldn't go if it looked bad, but there is probably a good chance for mild weather that week."

"Yeah, and sometimes it is awful. And don't forget, this isn't *our* weather. It's hundreds of miles away ...it's *their* weather. I can't believe you are even thinking of doing this. It's a really bad idea."

Sam just turned back to his desk, dropped his head, and nodded. Nothing more was said and they both went on their way.

He spent Halloween night by himself, poring over his maps. He almost always carved a pumpkin, what he liked to call a ritual disemboweling of the gourd, but he had skipped it this year, opting to save money by not buying one. In his mind it was a sacrifice to the cause, but on his way home he passed a number of glowing jack-o'-lanterns and a wave of nostalgia hit him. Sam knew it was usually this simple touch that rekindled some of the childhood delight of the day, but there was no magic for him this All Hallows Eve because something else already owned his soul.

The following Sunday he went to Godson and Moll's house for dinner. He hadn't had much of a chance to talk to Godson about his most recent trip and now that these new details had emerged, he dreaded telling them both about his newest plans. He expected the same reaction he had received from Sally. They lived on a street that bordered a big commercial bakery and as he parked outside their house, the air was permeated with the smell of baking bread and his stomach grumbled as he walked up to the door.

Just as he reached up to knock on the door, it opened and Godson offered him a bottle of beer as a greeting. "Hah! Saw you coming. How's it going?"

"Pretty good, just getting back into the groove of things," Sam said as he accepted the beer and took a sip. "Thanks, that's just what I needed. How did you know?"

Godson gave him a knowing look followed by a hearty laugh. "Silly boy!" he said, "come on in."

"Geez, the bread smell is heavy tonight."

"Is it? We don't even notice it anymore."

He had known Godson since college. It was an odd friendship that had formed out of almost nothing because they had no classes together, but after their first chance meeting they just seemed to hit it off. They both liked a good beer, and back in college they both liked a good toke as well. Their shared affinity for marijuana was probably what first brought them together, which was ironic because neither of them smoked it anymore.

"So, what's happening?" Godson asked him. "Relaxing now that you've brushed the gold dust off your jacket for the year?"

"Pretty much," he said, "but maybe not for the year."

"What?"

"Uh, I'm thinking about making another trip."

"No way," Godson said, shaking his head. "The weather will get you, buddy."

"Like I said, I'm just thinking about it, but it's a gamble, that's for sure," he said, taking another swig from his beer.

Moll came in from the kitchen. "Hi, Sam."

Sam got up and gave Moll a light hug and kissed her on the cheek. "Hey, Moll."

Godson spoke up, "Moll, Mr. Sam here says he's about to go out west again."

Moll looked surprised and even a little shocked. "I thought you always said late fall and winter were off limits."

"It's complicated. I know it's risky, but I've come across something I just HAVE to go check out."

Godson chimed in. "You just got back ...and what did you find out there?"

"Not a damned thing. You know that," he said.

"Sam, I've always sort of gone along with this little venture of yours because, well, you're my friend, but I have to tell you something as a friend. You're nuts."

"Really," Moll added. She was now visibly upset. "You've always said you had a plan and that was the main thing that protected you, sticking to the plan. This is NOT sticking to the plan, Sam!" She quickly turned away and walked back into the kitchen, first turning to glare at him again, her blue eyes almost glowing.

He just dropped his head and nodded.

"Look," Godson said. "We know this is your thing. You've got your secrets about it and we both get that. We do. We're just concerned for YOU, you understand? I know this is important to you but you need to listen to me because this is good advice. Whatever this is, it can surely wait until spring, can't it?"

"Maybe," he said, but there was an obvious condescending tone in his voice.

"Maybe?" Godson said, putting his beer down on an end table so he could lean forward and look at Sam head on. "Maybe? When were you thinking about going back out there?"

"After Christmas. I think I need more than a day or two. I have that entire week off."

Godson looked shocked. "You have got to be kidding me. Like Moll said, what about 'the plan?' You have always said 'short and sweet' was the only way you'd get away with these trips. Now you want to go out for a week? You're trespassing, buddy. Did you forget that?"

"No, I didn't forget that. I know," he said, his voice trailing off. Then he added, "But..."

"But? I don't want to know about any buts," Godson interrupted.

Sam continued, "Yeah, but, I think I can do it, if the weather cooperates."

Moll returned from the kitchen. "Okay, boys. Arguing is not going to get us anywhere right now. Dinner's ready. Godson, we have a couple of months to talk some sense into Sam. And you, Sam, you're an idiot. Okay? Now let's eat."

He looked up and Moll had her hands on her hips staring at them both like they were errant children. He smiled, "Okay, Moll. I'm not going to go off half-cocked ... I promise to think about it before I do anything."

Godson gave his friend a long hard look, as if he were trying to penetrate Sam's hard skull with his stare, then shook his head and grabbed his beer in one hand and patted Sam on the shoulder with the other as he stood. "You ARE an idiot, you know, but I love you, buddy."

Sam smiled and sheepishly picked up his near empty beer as he stood and they all went to the dinner table. The trip was not mentioned again that night.

Thirteen

November was the busiest time of the year at the office, so his life became a blur of work and maps. At home, in the quiet solitude of his apartment, Sam continued to plot and plan. After years of sweat, expense and frustration, this was the first solid clue he had ever uncovered, so of course the one thought in his mind was to head west as soon as possible. There was no way he was not going out there, no matter what season it was. As Moll had reminded him, there was safety in sticking to a plan, but he knew he had to amend that thought because every time he read the words "Diablo Rim" on his map, his soul burned with a new excitement he hadn't felt before. It was obvious to him that this was where he *had* to go and he had to figure out how he was going to do it.

"Of course, they don't understand," he said to himself. "How could they?"

So, he read his maps and the more he read his maps, the more he realized how difficult it was going to be to approach Diablo Rim undetected. He spent a lot of time trying to solve that one problem. He could see that hiking west from highway 54 was the most direct route because part of the rim seemed more accessible from that direction, but that route had major visibility problems. The "broken down car" gambit might be more natural on the highway, but there was more risk of the car being towed or wrecked or vandalized because the highway had more traffic. A week would just be too long to trust the highway route.

On the other hand, approaching the rim from the other direction meant a longer hike and it also meant that the car would more obviously be out of place. Still, he knew that if he picked the right road, it might not even be noticed at all.

More than once, Sam thought he heard something, and he imagined Slim standing behind him as he looked at his maps, saying, "Ain't no way, son, ain't, no way."

He decided to grab a bite to eat. He had been scrimping on food because that was the easiest way he could save money. To that end, he had returned to the same kind of low budget food he had eaten in his early college days to save money. At that time, he had needed the money to fund weekend exploits, but he considered his current goal to be somewhat loftier.

In the kitchen, he opened a sleeve of crackers and picked up a small can. He looked at the label.

POTTED MEAT FOOD PRODUCT.

He laughed to himself because it didn't get much more basic than that. He usually had a can or two of this in his pack when he hiked, but he rarely resorted to it in the field. The fact that manufacturers had never bothered to apply some kind of a catchy brand name to it indicated their disdain for their own product. It was the lowest of the low in the processed food chain.

He had offered a taste to a cat once but it gave him a look that bordered on "you have got to be kidding me" and turned its back on him.

He put all such considerations aside because he knew this was a means to an end. He spread the pinkish paste on a cracker and ate it. It really wasn't *that* bad, he decided. That thought stuck with him until a familiar metallic aftertaste kicked in. The best way he had found to overcome that side effect was to quickly eat another cracker. Then he repeated the cycle. He stood there in the kitchen, eating, and sipping water because he did not want to impress upon this culinary degradation the slightest chance of calling it a meal. He dropped the empty can in the trash, ate one last cracker and emptied his glass. He would have preferred a beer, but even that luxury had been deferred in the interest of saving money.

He returned to his maps, but, wearied by the research, he soon put them aside and turned on the television. Although there was a football game on the screen, the audio was lost in the background of his thoughts. The various challenges of the trip were still bothering him.

The situation with the car was bugging him the most. He ran over his meager checking account in his mind, trying to figure out how he could afford a truck, because he knew that would make this trip much easier. A Volkswagen was just too out of place on those back roads. He again thought of the old man in The Mossback parking lot who had blatantly emphasized that point. He finally sighed and surrendered the notion because his finances were too tight ... but the parking lot confrontation stuck in his head.

He had scarcely thought about it since that beat-up old truck had left him in a cloud of dust weeks before, but now he searched his memory for more details of the encounter. Sam remembered a crusty weather-beaten face with just a tinge of crazy around the bloodshot eyes. Smidgeon Toll from the café had called the guy a crazy old coot. He seemed to recall that the man had even said the same thing about himself.

"What was his name?" he asked himself. "It was something odd I should remember."

In his thoughts he realized that, crazy or not, the guy had spotted him and had followed him and seemed to know exactly what he was doing. At the time, Sam had wondered about that because it was a fairly random assumption to see a parked car and assume someone was prospecting. There was also the stern warning the old man had given him, followed by what seemed to be a sincere offer of help. He was sure he remembered writing down the man's name and address on one of the Mossback's cards. At the time he was just humoring the guy, but he *had* written it down.

He thought for a second, wondering where he had put the card and his eyes scanned the room and finally settled on top of a dresser in the corner. There was a pile of papers, the remains of items he had emptied out of his pockets when he was gathering laundry. He started picking through the papers, which were primarily receipts for gas or forgotten meals. He sighed as he rummaged through the pile, because most of it was trash. Then he spotted a business card and picked it up, glad that he had preserved this "trash."

He read out loud, "Mossback Café," and smiled, remembering he had grabbed this card at the café. He turned it over and again read out loud from the scribbles on the back, "Loot Meldings 4653 Tesoro Road."

He experienced a wave of relief.

"Loot Meldings," he repeated. "How could I have forgotten a name like Loot?"

This unleashed a new rush of memories and feelings about their brief meeting and he realized this was something important. This Loot guy *had* noticed him and at first Sam began to worry about what else Loot might know. He looked over at the maps spread out across the floor and reassessed the entirety of what he was doing. Then he began to reconsider his more immediate plans. He realized that the question of Loot needed to be considered carefully. He decided to afford himself a beer and after he got one. he stepped back over his maps and sat on one of his big pillows. The football game droned on in the background.

Sam knew he needed to know more about Loot, and he wondered to himself if maybe he could call him. The telephone was sitting near the maps on the floor and he reached over, grabbed it and dialed for information.

The operator intoned, "Which city?"

"Van Horn, Texas," he said. "I need a listing for someone named Meldings."

"First name?"

"I'm not sure," he said, "but it should be on Tesoro Road.

"No listing for that name on that street."

"Thank you," he said and hung up.

Then Loot's distinct voice echoed in his mind and he remembered the old man had said, "I ain't got no phone."

Sam sat pondering his memories of the encounter for quite a while, sipping his beer. When he emptied the bottle, he looked at his maps splayed out on the floor and sighed, then he went over and started picking them up.

In that instant, his plans had changed. He knew he was going to have to go out to Van Horn and find Loot Meldings. He hadn't shelved the idea of the Christmas trip, but in that moment, he grasped a new reality. He had to somehow work in a second, shorter trip. He got another beer and began calculating the details. It was around four hundred and fifty miles to Van

Horn and that equated to roughly fifteen gallons of gas each way. He tried to remember what he had spent on this last trip and blurted out loud, "That's at least another forty bucks in gas!"

He felt a twinge of apprehension because he knew he was already starving himself trying to save for the December trip. Squeezing in another trip was going to be yet another challenge. He had been saving money, but he was barely making ends meet as it was. His mind raced as he wondered to himself if another trip was even possible. He finally managed to convince himself he might be able to just barely swing it financially, but he also realized that the challenge wasn't just the money. His primary rule of the three problems of a trip was in effect, money, time and weather.

"This isn't that different from searching for the mine," he said out loud. "I'm just searching for another unknown here."

Then he remembered Thanksgiving was coming up. He silently shook his head. It was ideal because it was a long weekend and he had used up his vacation time for the year, but it was first and foremost a family holiday, but then he realized something. If he begged off the Houston trip he was almost halfway there ... the gas for a round trip to Houston would be almost half the money he needed anyway. He had skipped Thanksgiving once before. His mother *seemed* to accept it when he had a job where he had to work on Friday. If he could explain it in some reasonable way, he'd get away with it. Then he'd only have to come up with a little more than twenty bucks for the rest of the gas.

Loot's words, "You'll come," echoed in his memory. He smiled at that thought. The old man *knew,* and as he remembered those words, he understood that the crafty old bastard had been right. He had no choice but to work out the details and make the November trip happen.

Fourteen

As Sam continued to work hard in the following weeks, Sally knew more than ever that something else was up. Sam was more distracted than she had ever seen him. On the Monday before Thanksgiving, she decided to broach the subject.

"Sam, you've been too quiet, so I know you must be up to something else. This can't all be a trip still a month away ... you've got to be planning something. Is this still Diablo Rim or is it something else. You're not worried about Reagan winning the election, are you?"

He had been lost in thought while concentrating on his computer printouts.

"Sam!"

"Mmmm?" he said, looking up. "Huh? I'm sorry, Sally, did you ask me something?"

"Yes, you moron. I asked you about Diablo Rim. You've been so quiet the last week or so. I know you've got something on your mind. You had been talking about Christmas, have you changed it to Thanksgiving?"

"Well," he said, "yes and no."

"Oh, it's riddles now?"

He smiled. "Heh. Sorry. You're right, I'm thinking about a quick trip, but not to hike. This Diablo Rim thing is driving me crazy. It's going to be much tougher than I thought and I need to go out there to check a few things out, so I was thinking of maybe going this weekend."

"During Thanksgiving?"

"Well," he said, patting the computer printouts, "I can't take time off now, can I?"

Sally laughed. "Well, that's very considerate of you. But what do you need to check out?"

He laughed nervously. "I'm not a hundred percent sure. Just working out some hunches, I guess, but I definitely need more information."

Sally smirked. "The terms 'quick trip' and 'Van Horn' do not go together at all. What about Thanksgiving?"

"Yeah, my mom would be pissed-off if I skipped going home, but, well, uh, I've still not decided about that."

"You're certifiable. You know that, right? Nuts."

"Guess so."

"So, you would rather go on a wild goose chase than go spend time with your family?"

He sat quietly for a second, staring down at his feet and then he turned and looked Sally right in the eyes with a gaze that gave her a slight shiver.

"I think I *have* to," he said.

Sally let the matter drop. She had learned that when he wanted to talk about his business, he talked, and when he didn't want to talk about it, especially when he was in a planning stage, he kept things to himself.

She couldn't know it, but their short conversation had bolstered the notion in his mind. In truth, he had been waffling on the trip out west. With his attention diverted by work and his worries about money, he had almost managed to convince himself to skip it. A process of avoidance had replaced his usual planning, but in those few seconds of conversation, all of the issues had flooded his mind again. An image of the crusty old man invaded his mind and his fixation had switched to one thing: Loot Meldings, and he knew he *had* to go out there and talk to Loot in person. Loot's parting words once again echoed in his mind, "You'll come."

Sam had to decide about Houston.

The phone rang Wednesday night and Sam stared at it after the first ring. He knew it was his mother. Ever since he had talked to Sally, he had still been pretty firm about the idea of skipping Houston.

It rang again.

He could use work as a reason, and that would be an acceptable excuse to his mother, but right then, everyone in his family already knew he didn't have a job like that. That meant there was no justifiable pretext for him to skip the holiday at home.

It rang again.

A rush of particulars ran through his mind in a whirlwind of confusion as the phone rang again. It really was a lot to expect, driving to Houston and back *and* driving to Van Horn and back. Compounding the equation was the fact that he didn't even know what to expect in Van Horn or how long he'd need to be there.

The phone rang again and he had to ask himself the same simple question Sally had asked him two days before. Was he willing to sacrifice a traditional family holiday and possibly face his mother's wrath for some inane quest? He took a deep breath and answered the phone.

"Hello?"

"Sam? It's your mother."

He knew that, but she was always quite formal on the phone. He had always assumed it was probably a cultural vestige from an era when phones were still considered something almost magical and special.

"Hi, Mom."

"You haven't called in a couple of weeks so I thought I had better check on you. I guess you're not coming in tonight?"

"I'm really tired tonight, Mom. Work has been awful this week."

"Well," she said, "you *are* coming, aren't you? You know your grandmother hasn't been well."

He knew that and he also knew the guilt machine was shifting into high gear. Her 'mom radar' was working, because she obviously suspected something was up.

"Yes, Mom, I know but, well, I ...was thinking of skipping it this year..."

He could almost hear her frowning on the other side of the phone.

"... I'm really behind at work. I need to work Friday ... I need the extra day to catch up."

The silence was deafening. Finally, his mom spoke. "So you'll not have a Thanksgiving dinner?"

"I'll figure something out; I've got some friends I can visit," Sam lied, "I'll be okay. I just have to catch up at work."

His mother sighed. "Okay, baby. Everybody will be disappointed, but if you can't make it, you can't make it."

"I'll call again tomorrow."

"You had better. Sam, is there something going on I should know about?"

His parents did not have a clue about his interest in the Sublett mine, but they knew he had made numerous trips out to west Texas. It was something they considered to be a hobby and he had never elaborated, preferring to gloss over the details. As far as they were concerned, he was just a camping enthusiast.

"No, Mom," he said, "I've been really busy lately. Sometimes I just have to work extra to catch up."

"Okay, I love you, honey. Don't stretch yourself too thin. And you better come at Christmas!"

"I will, Mom. Bye, I love you."

"I love you too, son."

He stared at the telephone after he put the handset back in the cradle. He really hated lying to his mother, but what else could tell her? That he was traipsing off to the other side of Texas in search of lost gold? This wasn't the sort of thing she would understand and, if he started to tell her about that, he would have to go into other details of his past that he had always spent a good deal of effort avoiding. There was an unwritten rule: parents were better off not knowing about some of the things their kids did.

He smiled and said to himself, "If she only knew..." remembering episodes of his past. His mother would freak out if she had even an inkling of some of the 'adventures' he had experienced through the years, and he assumed most children were like that. Generally speaking, there was a certain amount of parental bliss in not knowing too much about their children's secret lives.

The next morning, he slept late. After some coffee, he went down and began doing some initial preparations for his trip. He checked the air in his tires. He glanced at the odometer, then pulled a small notebook out of his glove compartment. He used this to keep track of his mileage and the dates of oil changes and valve adjustments, repairs, and any other notable maintenance. He compared the odometer mileage with the entry for his last oil change.

"Oh, no!"

He saw that he was close to needing an oil change. He knew one of the keys to keeping an aging Volkswagen running was to religiously change the oil every three thousand miles. So he would have to change the oil before he proceeded to Van Horn.

He looked over in the corner of the garage and saw that he still had part of a case of oil he had bought a few months before, so he already had the oil for the change, but then he remembered he'd need an oil change gasket too. He wondered if any auto parts stores were open. He knew some grocery stores were open Thanksgiving but most other businesses were closed.

He went upstairs and grabbed the phone book and made a few calls to no avail. Nothing was open. He sat for a few seconds and wondered if this was one of the few times he could just skip changing the gasket around the oil sump plate. Ideally, after draining the oil, he'd remove that plate and clean the strainer, which was what served as an oil filter on the VW beetle. He thought for a few minutes more. Auto parts stores might be open on Friday, but that would delay his departure. He had skipped the screen and gasket before ...maybe he could do it again this time. Sam sighed and went back down.

He opened the trunk at the front of The Clunker and squinted in the dim light of the garage, looking through the jumbled assortment of tools in his toolbox. He grabbed a suitable wrench, went back to the case of oil and grabbed three quarts and a grimy, dusty flat plastic pan. He got in the car, started the engine and let it run a few minutes to warm up the oil a bit, then shut it off and proceeded to change his oil.

When he was finished, he went upstairs and cleaned up, then glanced at the clock and could see it was approaching noon. He was hungry and he imagined the wonderful aromas of comfort food he was missing at home. He washed up and decided to go get a bite to eat, opting for a Denny's just down highway.

Instead of his mother's turkey and dressing, he ordered an open-faced turkey sandwich with gravy. He thought about his coming trip as he munched. He didn't know what to expect when he got to Van Horn, but he knew he'd have to camp somewhere to avoid the expense of a motel, so he made a quick mental list of the camping supplies he wanted to take along.

He found his tent and camp stove along with a can of camp fuel in a box in the garage. He shook the can and could tell it was about one-quarter full. He smiled because that was plenty for this trip. He arranged this assortment of camping gear and supplies around his toolbox. Upstairs, he retrieved his winter sleeping bag from a closet. He also grabbed a small box from a shelf in the kitchen. It was marked "Camp Box" and it contained some beat-up pots and plates and utensils. He looked through his cupboard and grabbed a can of Wolf Brand Chili and two packages of ramen and a few other odds and ends, including another spare can of potted meat. He was thankful he had an extra jar of instant coffee. He put those things into a paper grocery bag and added it to the small pile of items next to the door. Next, he gathered up some clothes and personal items for his trip. Preparations complete, he stood in the doorway trying to remember if he needed anything else, then he took all the items downstairs and stowed them in the car. As requested, he also called his mom. Then he grabbed a beer and settled down to watch TV. He drank beer and munched on whatever he could find the rest of the afternoon and evening. He was soon dreaming of rocks and cactus.

Fifteen

Sam woke out of a dead sleep yelling to himself.

"Those damn birds!"

In the tree right outside his window, a couple of birds were having an excited exchange. He shook his head, unsettled at the sudden intrusion, then he glanced at the clock.

"Crap!"

It was eight forty-five. Usually, he'd be lured awake by the news and weather from the clock radio, but he had forgotten to set it. Although he was glad for the extra sleep, he lamented the late start. The birds continued their quarrel a few feet from his head and he silently recanted his complaint because they had done him a favor by waking him up.

He skipped any notion of making coffee or breakfast, reasoning that he could get something once he was on his way. He dressed and grabbed the items he had gathered the night before and took them down to his car. The day was bright, cool and clear.

Even though he was running late, he opted for a quick shower, ending it with a cold water rinse. *That* woke him up. He quickly got dressed and was back down and in the car by nine-fifteen. As he navigated toward highway 290, he made a couple of stops, first at his bank to cash a check for a little spending money, and then at a small Mexican bakery where he bought two potato and egg breakfast tacos and two *pan dulce*, along with a large coffee. He hoped the Mexican sweet bread would help stave off hunger down the road.

Fortified with some road food and coffee, he headed down the road into traffic that was a little heavier than he had expected, but he remembered that the day after Thanksgiving was a big shopping day and assumed he was caught up in it because of his late start. The hustle and bustle of the city was soon behind him and he was heading west.

As he drove, he reviewed his expectations of this trip. His primary goal was to find Loot Meldings, but he wanted to do a little back road investigation if he had the time. He hoped Loot could provide answers to some of the questions that were plaguing him about Diablo Rim. It was a risk to bring in an outsider, but everything he was trying to do was a risk and this time he knew he was going to need some local help and Loot was basically his only option.

As the miles drifted past, he saw gathering clouds ahead. From past experience, he knew they might indicate a weather change and he slapped his forehead as he realized he hadn't checked the weather for two days. For several miles, he thought about the clothes he had brought with him and as he considered his possessions, he realized he wasn't totally ill-prepared for a spell of colder weather if it came. He remembered he had a light coat in the space behind the back seat that had been buried there since the previous spring. He did at least bring his winter sleeping bag and, on a whim, he had included some long underwear with his clothes, along with a flannel shirt. He remembered thinking the nights might be cool and the long underwear might make him more comfortable if that were the case. He figured he could manage a couple of layers, but he had no heavy socks and no gloves.

"No, that's not right," he said out loud, remembering he had some cloth work gloves in the trunk. They were not insulated gloves, but he knew that any covering was better than nothing. As he drove on, he could see darker clouds moving in from the north.

In Fredericksburg, he spotted a small general store, the type of place that had a little of everything. He didn't have a lot of time, or much cash to spare, but he wanted to see if he could get a few extra items to fend off the cold if he had to. He saw they had gloves but most of them cost more than he wanted to spend. He found an Enchanted Rock sweatshirt on a sale rack that was a good bargain. In general, he did not like writing or pictures on his clothes, but it was the only sweatshirt in his size on sale, and at least it was from one of his favorite landmarks. Looking around some more, he found they had a variety of knit stocking hats that were reasonably priced and then, near the hats, he spotted some inexpensive knit gloves. On closer examination, they seemed small, likely made for a child or a petite woman, but they were cheap and he thought his hands might just squeeze into them. Then he saw some reasonably-priced wool blend socks. They were thicker than the socks he had brought and an extra layer might be a welcome relief if his feet got chilled.

As he approached the register, he realized his checkbook was still jutting out of his shirt pocket. He had stuck it there when he had dropped by his bank.

"Will you take an Austin check?" he asked, playing a hunch.

The clerk, an older man, looked up with some surprise. He deftly touched the bridge of his glasses, which were perched toward the end of his nose, raising them about an eighth of an inch.

He looked Sam up and down and after several seconds of this scrutiny, the man said, "Let me see your check and ID."

Sam handed them to the man, who studied both items intently, his face wrinkling as he squinted at the documents. He glanced back at Sam, then back to the driver's license. As he handed the items back, the man hesitated for a second.

"Okay," he said, "but I need your work number on your check. You do have a work number, don't you?" It was like a final test.

"Yes, I work at the University of Texas."

The guy's face brightened into a smile, "They sure beat them Aggies yesterday, didn't they?"

Although the Texas/Texas A&M game was a yearly tradition, he hadn't watched it and didn't even know Texas had won the game.

"Yeah, they sure did," he said, while finishing the check, complete with his work phone number in the memo field.

As he handed over the check to complete the transaction, the guy said, "Have a good day, sir, drive careful. I think the weather is about to change on us."

When Sam returned outside, he was glad he had made the stop because it already felt cooler than it had before he went into the store. He removed the tag from the sweatshirt and slipped it on in the parking lot. It was made of thick cotton and he was glad he had bought it because he already felt warmer.

He opened the car door to get in, but as an afterthought, he grabbed a small fast-food napkin from some trash behind the driver's seat and went to the back of the car and opened the engine compartment lid. He pulled the dipstick and cleaned it with the napkin and inserted it then pulled it out again. He inspected the stick and was satisfied that his oil level was good. He had learned the hard way that it was a good idea to double check for oil loss after any oil change. He headed the car west on 290 and was soon on Interstate 10. Van Horn was somewhere beyond the horizon.

As the miles sped past, he could feel a growing chill in the car, despite the added warmth of his new sweatshirt. He reached down between the seats and fiddled with the heater controls. The Volkswagen had an air-cooled engine and the heat for the passenger compartment was transferred directly from the engine. Water cooled engines did a similar thing, but had the advantage of a fan. In a VW, the heat depended on the same fan that also cooled the motor. For temperature control, there was a louver regulating how much hot air came into the compartment. It was relatively primitive and sometimes there was a fine line between too warm and not warm enough, but that wasn't the problem this time. He had adjusted the controls so the louvers should be wide open but when he reached down to the vents, he could tell there was very little heat coming through. It wasn't freezing outside, so he just pressed on, hoping he could cope until the weather warmed up again.

As he shivered from the chill, he remembered this wasn't the first time he had struggled with the cold. Years ago, his initial foray into the mountains of west Texas had served as a frosty false start to his quest.

~ * ~

That first trip to the Guadalupe Mountains was a near-disaster and it was a hard lesson learned in the importance of preparation and planning, because Sam had hiked into the mountains with no plan at all.

At the time, Sam's memory on the subject of the mine was still a jumbled mess of bits and pieces, so he embarked upon a spring break whim triggered by the vague memory that Slim had mentioned these mountains. Sam had read about the new Guadalupe Mountains National Park ...that news had prompted him to head west. As he drove west, he did remember–the old man had told him the mine was south of the Guadalupe range, but he decided to go there anyway just to sort of look around. The park seemed to be a more accessible option.

Of course, he had no idea of what he was doing and at that time the park was so new the rangers didn't seem to care too much what a person's plans were, as long as they registered in and registered out. Sam was outfitted with a cheap knapsack, barely suitable for even a day hike, no means of preparing food, and only minimal plans for shelter. He was out of shape, totally unprepared for the rigors of hiking up a mountain, especially alone. After a couple of hours on the trail, he found himself tired and forlorn and he became quite discouraged because the hike was already longer and more arduous than he had expected. As he walked, he would glance up, but the top always seemed to be an endlessly indistinct point high above him.

Along the trail he met up with two other hikers, Phil and Ray, who had nice frame packs and seemed well prepared. Phil was a postal worker from Baytown and he apparently knew a lot about backpacking. His buddy Ray was just along for the ride.

"Mind if I hike along with you?" Sam asked.

They both agreed. Sam didn't particularly like the idea of attaching himself to others like this, but he realized it gave him an extra margin of safety.

The small group slowly trudged up the mountainside, traversing switchback after switchback. Sam might have been out of shape, but Ray was even less prepared physically and he struggled on the hike, which caused a number of delays. Sam took full advantage of Ray's numerous rest stops, grateful that they weren't stopping because of him and in fact, this gave him an added impetus to go on. At that point, Sam was sure he would have given up if he had stayed by himself.

Then he had a breakthrough. During one of Ray's frequent breaks, Sam kept hiking and moved several switchbacks ahead of his companions. Phil was obviously in great shape, but he continued to stick with his friend. Sam looked down the trail at Phil and Ray, and then looked up again. He blinked and stared. This time the top actually looked *closer*! Energized by this revelation, he hiked up another couple of switchbacks with a quickened pace and looked up again and the top actually appeared to be looming almost within reach.

He called back down the trail to alert his trail buddies. "Hey, Ray, Phil, keep going, I think we're close to the top."

Down the trail, Phil, standing next to a red-faced and panting Ray, smiled and waved in acknowledgement. Sam turned and walked up another couple of switchbacks and his own exhaustion vanished in a wave of exhilaration as the top seemed so close, he thought he could reach out and touch it. At that point, he managed a lame sprint up several more switchbacks in quick succession until the trail stopped trending up and he halted. He was standing at the top of the trailhead.

For hours, his only view had been the trail immediately ahead of him, but when he turned around, a glorious panorama of west Texas spread below him, and beyond the slope of the mountain a dusty haze embellished the view with amazingly subtle hues in the late afternoon light. As he enjoyed the scene, he conceded that the rigors of the long hike had been worth the effort. While he stood there, he became aware of a muffled rolling crescendo not unlike the distant sound of a jet plane high overhead. He looked up but could see no contrail then he looked down and realized it was the sound of the wind blowing up the mountainside.

What he didn't realize at the time was that the wind and the distant dusty haze were warning signs of a cold front moving in. The subtle hues he had admired foretold a potentially dangerous situation.

In his ignorance, he blissfully dropped his pack and trotted back down the trail with renewed energy. He knew Phil was okay to hike on up but he wanted to help Ray, who was once again sidelined by exhaustion.

"Come on, Ray," he said, "It is really close!"

Ray nodded, unconvinced, but Sam grabbed his pack and ran back up the trail with it. Ray, relieved of his burden, slowly staggered up the final switchbacks to the top. Once they were all together at the trailhead, Sam and Phil quietly absorbed the impressive view, but Ray sat on the ground and looked indifferent to the whole thing.

Sam's plan, if one could call it a plan, was to stretch an old army-surplus blanket he had carried in his pack across a rope stretched between two trees. He also had included a light sleeping bag that had barely fit inside his pack with the blanket. He had some crackers and a can of beans and a gallon jug of water, half of which he drank on the way up. In contrast, Phil and Ray had a proper tent and down sleeping bags, a small propane stove and freeze-dried camp food.

A profound chill settled around them as the sun set. Their camps were about thirty yards apart but they all shared a meal together close to the tent. Phil and Ray enjoyed their hot freeze-dried food packets, reconstituted from hot water Phil boiled with his small stove. Sam ate his cold beans right out of the can, but after he had eaten several bites, Phil offered to heat the can on his stove. Sam decided that warm beans would be much better than cold beans and so he agreed and Phil again lit his little stove and placed the can directly over the flame.

When some vapor started to rise from the can, Sam said, "That's good, Phil, that should be warm enough."

He gingerly lifted the can by the lid and relished the improvement as he ate the remainder of the warm beans. The darkness closed around them and, because there wasn't much else to do, they all retired to their respective camps.

So began one of the most miserable nights of his life. As the lonely minutes ticked by, the wind began to really kick up and he discovered that his cheap sleeping bag was of no use against the bitter cold. Sam had naively thought a sleeping bag was a sleeping bag and it would naturally be warm in any weather. He had slipped off his boots before he climbed into the bag but it did not take long for him to realize that his feet were freezing, so he got up and put his boots on and climbed back into the bag. It barely helped.

His contrived blanket shelter was useless against the wind because it was open at both ends and there was no escape from the hard, gusting wind. Eventually he gave up on that arrangement, pulled the blanket down and wrapped it around the sleeping bag. This helped a little, but not enough. He got up at one point and spent a few minutes doing some exercises to get his blood flowing before miserably crawling back into his bag again, trying to retain a portion of the heat he had generated. He repeated this exercise routine several times and hoped he wasn't making too much noise with his jumping jacks and running in place and pushups. He did manage to drift off to sleep for short periods of time, until the throbbing pain fueled by numbing cold woke him up and spurred him to start another cycle of exercise. The night passed like that—wretched snatches of sleep punctuated by frantic exercise.

When the dawn came and he heard sounds of Phil and Ray stirring, he got up, frozen to the core. Breakfast was packaged peanut butter crackers. Phil graciously offered him a cup of instant coffee from his own supplies and Sam relished the hot drink and enjoyed the warm fluid running down to his stomach. The day had dawned clear and calm and the combination of bright sun and little to no wind was a stark contrast to the awful cold of the previous night.

As they broke camp, Phil asked him, "So, do you want to tag along with us again today? We're heading into 'The Bowl' and maybe up to Guadalupe Peak."

Sam hesitated as he considered his situation before he said, "That sounds so great, Phil, but I don't think I can take another night like that."

Phil laughed, "Heh, I guess you have a point. You should probably get some better equipment before you try this again."

The morning warmed quickly and they packed up their camps and parted ways. Phil and Ray advanced into the depths of the park and Sam headed back down the mountain.

He found that going downhill was much preferable to the alternative and as he descended it warmed up quite a bit. On the way, he passed a uniformed scoutmaster resting under a tree, surrounded by a few tired boy scouts. The scoutmaster looked even worse than Ray had looked the previous day and Sam was grateful he was in better shape than that. As he walked, he wondered how Ray was doing, hiking alongside the unstoppable Phil.

Around noon he got back to his car, surprised he had descended the mountain so quickly. The initial hike had seemed endless, but it was obvious it had not been as far as it seemed. A few scouts were prowling around the trailhead and Sam assumed they belonged to the exhausted scoutmaster. They had obviously gone ahead on their own and he wondered if he should hang around to provide some adult supervision, but he had a vision of the scoutmaster taking hours to return and he really needed to get on his way. So he loaded his car and, after checking out at the ranger station, where he did mention the unsupervised scouts, he headed back home.

The ranger asked him, "Did you climb Guadalupe Peak?"

"No," Sam told him, "I wasn't prepared enough this time and when the weather kicked up, I just got way too cold. Maybe next time."

The ranger laughed and Sam couldn't tell if the laugh was at him, or with him.

~ * ~

As he drove along, Sam smiled at the memory of how foolish he had been that first time. His naiveté could have been dangerous, but his luck had held.

"I've come a long way since then," he chuckled to himself. "Yep, a long way."

He drove on toward a cloudy western horizon.

Sixteen

Sam checked the vents again and could feel just a trickle of heat radiating from the passenger side but nothing at all was coming from the driver's side. He shivered as the bleak miles streaked past The Clunker, thankful it was not as cold as it had been that night on the mountain, at least not yet. He stopped in Fort Stockton for gas and to stretch his legs.

While pumping his gas, he realized he had no idea where he would bed down for the night and it would soon be dark.

"What an idiot!" he murmured under his breath.

It had been a stupid mistake because he always prided himself on his planning, but this time he had depended too much on his past routines, forgetting that this trip was quite different. If he continued on, he would get to Van Horn well after sunset and he did not want to try to find Loot after nightfall. A motel was no option, because he couldn't afford it, and all of his experience with camping in the Van Horn area had involved trespassing.

As he got back on the highway, he pondered his options and Balmorhea State Park popped into his head. It was ideal, just off the interstate about forty miles ahead, safe and inexpensive and only a little more than an hour from Van Horn.

"That's it," he said above the road noise.

With this decision in place, his mind returned to the weather. The temperature was in the mid-forties, according to a lighted time and temperature sign he had seen in Fort Stockton. The overcast had never developed into rain, at least so far, and even if it did rain, he had a good tent and there were likely shelters at the state park.

At the Balmorhea exit, Sam headed the short distance south to the state park, passing through the tiny town of Balmorhea. He decided to stop at a typical sort of small town store, part convenience store, part general store. It even had a fresh meat selection so he bought a small steak and bag of charcoal. He knew he had his camp stove and a few canned goods, but when he saw the meat, he realized he could take advantage of a charcoal fire to help ward off the chill for a while. Besides, a steak just sounded good to him after his long drive.

At the register he asked, "Know anything about the weather?"

The young cashier just shrugged and said, "Not really. Heard something about a cold front but I don't really know."

Balmorhea State Park was famous for its system of natural springs and it included a huge spring-fed swimming pool, so it was known as something of an oasis in arid west Texas. He paid his fee and found a campsite. He was so intent on getting his camp set up, he forgot to ask the ranger about the weather, but then again, he figured if it was dangerous or something, surely the ranger would have warned him. There were a few recreational vehicles scattered around, but he pretty much had his pick of camping spots on this chilly Thanksgiving holiday weekend. Although the springs tended to make the park a bit greener than the surrounding area, the season and the overcast conspired to make it seem quite dreary. He chose a secluded slot with a covered picnic table and a small grill, then pulled out his equipment to set up his simple camp.

Night was beginning to rise from the east, so he hurried to his dinner plans. He opened the small bag of charcoal and could immediately smell the petroleum-based fluid infused on the briquettes. He made a small pyramid of the briquettes in the bottom of the grill, then lit the pile at several places. As a general rule, he didn't like using these ready-to-go briquettes but he opted for convenience. The flames soon grew to encompass all of the briquettes and as he watched them burn, he was grateful for the small pocket of heat they provided against the blustery chill.

Sam scanned the sky again from horizon to horizon and could see that it was darkening quickly. As he contemplated the overcast and the quickly coming night, he realized another planning failure.

"I forgot my camp lantern!"

So he went back to the car and dug around in the trunk until he found an old flashlight and tested it, smiling when he saw a beam of light. It wasn't as much light as his lantern, but it worked and he didn't think he would need much light anyway because he planned to eat and immediately turn in. He went back to the small fire and warmed his hands and as he stood there another small detail popped into his head. He had forgotten to bring any seasonings.

"Damn," he said to himself.

For a man who prided himself on planning, this trip was quickly turning into a fiasco. Sam realized he had clearly focused too much on Loot Meldings, and not enough on the mechanics of this trip. Then he realized he might have a solution.

"The stupid food bags behind my seat!"

At the car, he looked through the pile of crumpled paper sacks stashed behind the driver's seat of The Clunker. These were the ruins of many fast-food meals of indeterminate age. On the third try he hit pay dirt: small packets of salt and pepper.

"Hah!"

It was not much, but it would help. He grabbed his steak and at the picnic table he opened a salt packet and seasoned one side of the steak, then added a packet of pepper to the steak. This process was repeated on the other side.

Gathering or cutting firewood at a state park was prohibited, but Sam knew people often brought their own and he also knew they sometimes left what they didn't use, so he searched around the adjoining campsites and luckily found about a half dozen pieces of wood stacked next to a grill. This stash was appropriated and brought back to his campsite. After dinner he planned to use the remaining hot coals to kindle a small fire to give him a few moments of extra heat and light.

He shivered in the chilly air as he watched the flames die down and the briquettes began glowing a dusty pastel red in the darkness. Sam hunched closer to the grill, relishing the heat for a minute as he used a smaller stick of the firewood to knock down the pyramid and spread the coals around. Using a small military-style can opener, Sam opened a can of beans, leaving a small hinge on the lid. He removed the label and carefully placed the can on the grill near the coals but not directly over them. He had done this in the past and knew that this allowed one to heat something without dirtying a pot. The trick was to not let the can get too hot.

He placed the steak directly over the coals with a sudden sizzle and Sam watched the steak cook while warming his hands over the grill. After several minutes, he carefully flipped the meat with his fingers, almost burning them because the underside of the steak was hotter than he expected.

He used his flashlight to check the can of beans and saw a slight vapor rising through the opening in the lid. Using a towel as a pot holder, he grabbed the can, opened the top a little wider with a spoon and stirred the contents, then tasted the spoon, looking more to gauge the heat than the flavor. The beans were only vaguely warm, so he returned the can to the grill, this time placing them a little closer to the coals, hoping they would be nicely heated when the steak was ready.

Although he liked recreational camping for the most part, he appreciated the fact that this was more of a utilitarian camping experience, sacrificing comfort for economy. He returned to the table to check the plate and silverware, touching them in the darkness in an attempt to magically determine their state of cleanliness. They seemed okay, but he decided to rinse them thoroughly at the small campsite faucet anyway.

When he removed the steak from the grill, it continued to sizzle for a few seconds on the plate while he carefully removed the can of beans. He cut into the steak and used the flashlight to examine the interior more closely. It glistened in the light and looked to be a perfect medium rare. The air was full of the wonderful aroma of grilled meat and he sat and quickly ate the meal while it was still hot, even finishing the remainder of the beans right out of the can.

The dishes were thoroughly rinsed at the faucet but Sam had forgotten dish soap too. This seemed to be a recurring theme for this trip and he was again internally disgusted at these planning lapses.

"I gotta do better than this. This is ridiculous..." he muttered as he tried to use his hands to clean off the dishes as best as he could.

He put a couple of pieces of the scrounged firewood on top of the coals and they began to smoke almost immediately and in a surprisingly short time, they burst into flame. He added another piece of wood and soon had a small but adequate fire. He stood in the dim firelight and enjoyed the warmth, at least with his upper body. It was better than nothing, although his feet were still cold.

When the fire began to die down, he decided against adding the remainder of the wood to it and used one stick to spread the coals out a bit more so they could more readily consume themselves. In his tent, he took off his shoes and squeezed himself into the sleeping bag, which soon captured enough body heat to warm him thoroughly.

"You'll come, you wait and see, you'll come," echoed in his mind as he lay there before he dropped into a sound sleep.

He had set his digital watch alarm for six-thirty and at the appointed time, it responded with a relentless beep and he opened his eyes. At first, he did not fully realize where he was, but then the combination of the hard ground and the constrictions of the sleeping bag sparked his memory.

"Geez," he said as he stretched and wondered if he should sleep another hour, but resetting the watch was a daunting challenge with bleary eyes and he had messed up that option several times in the past. So he reluctantly emerged from the warmth of the bag and slipped on his shoes. He opened the tent and stepped outside, where he was not particularly surprised to find that it was still chilly, about the same as the previous evening.

"At least it hasn't rained," he said.

Normally he would fire up his camp stove and boil some water to make some instant coffee, but this morning he opted for packing up immediately. The nearby town would likely provide coffee and perhaps a spot of breakfast as well. His funds were tight, to be sure, but he had budgeted for road food. Within fifteen minutes, he had stowed his camping equipment and was driving back through Balmorhea, where he stopped, bought some coffee and a packaged pastry at the same store. In his groggy state, he failed to get a weather update. Once he got back on the interstate, he tried the radio but all he found were distant music and Spanish stations. The coffee was bitter, the pastry was stale, and the car was cold, but he pushed on to Van Horn, only about ninety minutes away.

Seventeen

It was still early when Sam pulled off the interstate and drove into Van Horn. He saw that the Mossback Café was open and decided to stop for several reasons. For one thing, he was hungry, despite the stale pastry, and, of course, one cup of coffee was never enough for him, especially if it was bad coffee. He also needed some time to gather his thoughts and think about what he would do once he found Loot. Then there was the owner, Smidgeon Toll. He wanted to bask in her infectious smile again, and the last time he had stopped here, she had warned him about Loot Meldings, so he wondered if he could tactfully find out what she knew about the old man.

After parking, he took a quick look into the rear-view mirror in an effort to judge his early morning appearance and frowned. He was a mess. He dug into his back pocket, retrieved his comb and ran it through his hair, and then he realized that in his haste to break camp he hadn't even brushed his teeth, so he reached around to the back seat and, by feel, rooted around in his knapsack until he found a toothbrush with the end of it wrapped in a plastic sandwich bag. A little more rummaging produced a small tube of toothpaste. He did a quick dry-brush with a little toothpaste, which he followed up with a swish of water from a gallon plastic jug he had stashed on the floor in front of the passenger seat. The water was quite cold because it had been sitting there all night and the shock of it made his teeth ache. He had no other option so he discreetly spit into the parking lot.

The door to the Mossback creaked ominously as he entered. At the coffee station, Smidgeon Toll looked up from her busy work and her eyes brightened in recognition.

"Hey, stranger, welcome back. Sam, right?"

"You got it on the first try," he said. "Hi, Smidgeon, how are you?"

He sat at a table and Smidgeon approached him with a menu, silverware, and a cup of coffee. "I'm just fine. Lordy, I hope you aren't out camping today."

"No, just passing through. Why?"

"We're expecting a Blue 'Norther ...maybe some snow but most definitely ice. I'd hate to think about anybody out camping in weather like that. If you're heading east, you best eat and get moving."

"Really? I didn't know," he said. He hoped the alarm he was feeling didn't show on his face because something else to worry about was all he needed.

"Yep. Kind of early for that kind of weather around here, but we get all kinds of weather, so who knows what to expect?"

"Yeah," he answered. "If you don't like the weather in Texas, just wait around a few minutes, right?" It was an old joke, but they both laughed at it.

Three more customers came in the door. Smidgeon greeted them, then turned her attention momentarily back to Sam.

"I'll be right back to get your order, okay?"

"Sure," he said, opening the menu. He sipped the coffee as he read, then glanced over the top of the menu to watch her.

Smidgeon walked over to greet the new group, efficiently getting three cups of coffee. She briefly chatted with them while depositing the cups on their table. She obviously knew these people quite well, which wasn't that surprising in such a small town. She had an easy way about her, and that projected a certain earthy attraction to him. He loved her long black hair loosely tied into a ponytail. She was short and just a little plump, but she carried herself well, gliding in and out of the arrangement of tables and chairs with ease. He enjoyed watching her as she worked. She had a confident and efficient air about her, and a friendly and easy-going way with her customers. It was difficult to judge the age of some people, but he guessed she was two or three years older than he was, but he couldn't be sure because in his experience he knew country people seemed to lead a harder life than city folk, something that aged them faster than their big city counterparts. It was another one of Sam's working theories.

Smidgeon suddenly reappeared at his table and this snapped him out of this bit of speculation. He wasn't sure if she had noticed him watching her, but deep down he knew she probably had because it had always seemed to him that women had a good instinct for that sort of thing. As she looked down at him, she smiled as much with her eyes as she did with her mouth and it was a pleasant and genuine smile.

"You know what you want?"

He had been so engrossed in watching her that he hadn't even finished checking the menu. That "Especial" breakfast still lingered in his memory but it was huge and he didn't really think he was that hungry, so he opted for something smaller.

"I'll have the regular breakfast, two scrambled eggs, sausage, and hash browns," he said.

"You want biscuits or flour tortillas with that?"

"How are the biscuits?"

"I make them," she said, with one hand on her hip and an unmistakable look of pride on her face.

"Then biscuits, of course," he said. He was particularly fond of a good biscuit and he had a vague recollection of enjoying the biscuits here in his almost forgotten past visits. She jotted down his order and turned to head back to the kitchen, when one of the other customers intoned, "Jo, honey, can we get some more coffee here?"

"Sure, hon," she said as she hurried her pace.

He sipped his coffee, and mused a little on this statement, somewhat confused. Then he remembered that the last time he had been there, she had told him that "Jo" was an old nickname, something to do with her father. After she carried the pot over to the other table, she came back by his table.

"You ready for another cup?" she asked.

"Sure, you can top it off while you're here. Did he call you 'Jo?' I remember you said something about that the last time I was here. So people still call you that?"

"Well, my full name is Smidgeon Josephine Toll," she laughed. "And like I must have told you, my dad's name was Joe and this was originally his place, and I've been working here all my life. My folks called me Little Jo and for years everybody always called me that too."

"So, what do I call you?"

She leaned forward, looked right into his eyes and said in a low whispering tone, "Sam, you can call me whatever you want to call me."

She leaned back and added with a nervous laugh, "You know, after I got older, I sort of preferred Smidgeon, but all the old regulars around here still call me Jo. I answer to both. I know it might be confusing, but, hey, that's my life."

"I guess maybe I'll surprise you," he said, and they both laughed.

When Smidgeon brought his food, he risked another question.

"Can I ask you something?"

"Sure."

"It's about that old guy who talked to me in the parking lot a while back."

Smidgeon frowned slightly, "You mean old Loot. Old coot is more like it. Damn, he's been raising drunken hell around here for years. He's got no family that I know about, just lives in an old shack on the edge of town. They say he can be pretty handy but I've never hired him for anything 'cause of the drinking. I hear he still does some trapping and he works a little at some of the ranches, but mostly he's just a town character. Most people can take him or leave him. There was some kind of trouble years ago with my dad, I don't rightly know what, but I think he knows better than to come in here."

"Interesting," he said.

"I wondered why he was bothering you," she said.

Sam thought fast. "I think he saw my car on the side of the road. I must have got out to ...uh, you know..."

Smidgeon gave a slight nod and smiled knowingly.

"...and he probably thought I had some car trouble or something. I think he was maybe looking for some work."

"Well, could be, but I'd steer clear of him. I don't like him."

"Yeah, I will," he said, looking down. He felt bad about lying to her. "Thanks for the information."

"Just trying to keep you safe, sweetie." She smiled and winked at him.

He smiled back. These days he didn't notice many women flirting with him, so he didn't know quite what to make of some of Smidgeon's signals. Most likely, he thought to himself, she just has a practiced easy way with customers and is probably this friendly with everyone. He figured he might have to add that to his book of working theories.

He finished his breakfast, including the extra biscuit she offered him, which he greedily devoured as a sort of dessert, lavishing extra butter and strawberry preserves on it. He headed up to the register and the ever-vigilant Smidgeon moved over with that easy gliding way of hers to meet him there.

At the register he asked, "So what time are they expecting the weather to change?"

"They say late afternoon, but that's the weather man. If I were you, I'd head east right away."

"Sounds like a plan," he said, reaching out to take the change she was handing him. He was taken aback when she suddenly embraced his hand with hers. He was surprised at their silky warmth and this sent a silent shiver through his body.

"I mean it. You get on the road, Sam, and you drive careful, and you make sure you come back here in one piece." She picked up another one of her cards, then turned it over and jotted a number on the back, "Call me if you have trouble. That's my home number ...call that if the café is closed. Don't take chances. If the weather gets bad, you turn around and if you get stuck, call me. I know all the cops and wreckers around here for miles and miles."

He accepted the card and squeezed one of her hands gently with his. "Okay. Thanks," he said. "I appreciate it, Smidgeon, I really do."

"Bye now, and you remember what I said. Be careful." She reached out and lightly touched his shoulder. "Okay?"

Sam nodded and turned to head out the door. Outside, he glanced up at the ominous sky. The wind had picked up and it seemed colder. The Clunker complained a little in the chilly air, but it started. He hesitated for just a second before turning left out of the parking lot, secretly hoping Smidgeon wouldn't notice as he headed west, the same direction Loot had pointed weeks earlier.

About a mile down Van Horn's main road, he spied a weathered street sign for Tesoro Road and he turned right. It was a rough road and in the gloomy, muted light he wasn't sure if he was driving on crumpled pavement, graded rock, or the surface of the moon. There were hardscrabble shacks and beaten-up mobile homes and assorted scrubby outbuildings stretching along both sides of the ragged road. He did his best to dodge the many potholes as he rattled farther down the road looking for the right house. Several of the shacks didn't even have numbers. He could see that he was coming to a dead end and on the left, at the end of the road, there was a final rough-looking shack with a weather-beaten garage alongside. A faded sign proclaimed this shack as 4653. He navigated the crude turnaround just beyond the driveway and parked in front of the shack. He wanted to be on the right side of the road so he could make a quick escape if he needed to.

As he opened his car door, he was fretful because it felt even colder than it had back at the Mossback just a few minutes before. He got out and walked up to the door, wrenching up his shoulders to help block his exposed neck from the cold. He had to dodge bits and pieces of worn lawnmowers and broken washing machines and other things he couldn't even identify. The rubbish gave the impression that it was as much a junkyard as it was a residence.

The door opened before he had a chance to knock and a wrinkled face with bloodshot eyes greeted him. Loot Meldings was smiling as he stretched out his hand.

"Hah, I know'd you'd come. I know'd it. Remember?" Loot looked up at the sky as he added, "Weather's gonna get real bad, real soon, so we better make it quick. Come on in."

"Okay," he said as he accepted Loot's hand and shook it. The hand was crusty with calluses, evidence of a lifetime of hard work. As Sam stood there, the day was darkening behind him and the wind was picking up. He glanced back at his car, wondering if he should turn tail and run away, but then he remembered ... *this* was why he was here.

He crossed the threshold and entered the darkness of Loot's lair.

Eighteen

It took Sam's eyes a few seconds to adjust to the dusky shadows that stretched in front of him. Squinting in the dim light, he began to understand that the debris in the yard was just the tip of the iceberg because there was much more junk inside.

"Watch your step," Loot cackled back as he led the way.

Piles of papers and stacks of boxes competed with a wide array of assorted unidentifiable flotsam and jetsam to fill every square inch of the house, with only a narrow pathway leading back into the gloomy depths of the unknown. The layout of the shack made it seem bigger that it was, bigger than it looked from the outside, but that impression was in conflict with the claustrophobic effect created by the massive amount of clutter. There were permeating odors as well, with a solid base of stale cigarette smoke. He did not want to even speculate about any of the other subtle smells that were assaulting his nose. Somewhere in the shadows he could hear a television or radio, but amidst the confusing canyons of debris, the location was vague.

They emerged into what was once probably a den or dining room or something else he could not immediately identify. At least there was more light in this room, although a quick glance around could not identify the source. It was augmented by the glow from a small television perched precariously on the end of ... well, he could not quite make out what it was sitting on, but he assumed it most likely a table. There was a tattered recliner in front of the TV and next to that he could see a sort of depression in the debris field.

Loot turned the television off and busied himself with this spot, gathering up newspapers, bags, and other things Sam could not recognize. Loot quickly relocated the newspapers to a nearby stack of brother newspapers and stashed several sacks in a nearby garbage bag that was ironically almost empty. Other items were placed at various points in the room and Loot exercised surprising care in this rearrangement.

He saw the edge of a couch or love seat; he could not tell which. Whatever it was, it was obvious Loot was preparing a place for him to sit. As he waited, he continued to survey the room and deduced that there did seem to be some organization to the chaos. Loot apparently spent a lot of time gathering up things discarded by others, attracted by some innate value he saw in the items. Sam began to wonder about some of his own belongings as he watched Loot putter about, and he made a mental note to take a good long look at his own apartment when he got home.

Loot finished with this straightening-up and looked back at Sam, pointing down at the cleared spot. The upholstery, freed from its protective covering of debris, looked surprisingly clean in the dim light.

"There, have a seat, young fella. If I'd a known you was coming, I woulda cleaned up a little," Loot said with a laugh.

Sam chuckled at this massive bit of understatement, unsure of what Loot's idea of 'cleaning up' might be. He eased into the designated spot, taking care not to touch anything else in the room, afraid he might loosen something and start an avalanche. Loot plopped down in his ancient recliner with a distinct 'thump' and as he sat, he stared at Sam for a full minute before he spoke again. Sam returned the stare, but he was uncomfortable under the penetrating scrutiny of the old man's gaze.

Finally, Loot broke the silence. "I knowed it! I knowed you'd be coming. You're onto something, aintcha? You're onto something and you need my help. I knowed it."

Sam hesitated and said, "Maybe," then he sighed and added, "...and, you were right, I've been poking around up in the hills north of here."

"Dangerous ground," Loot said. "All them ranchers are protective of their land. 'Git off of mah land' they'll say with the business end of a rifle pointed at you." Loot mimicked the action like a child playing cowboy, adding, "And some of 'em will let the gun do the talking."

"Yeah, I'm aware of the danger."

"Oh, I seen your car out there, supposedly broke down. I seen it a bunch of times in different places. Mighta fooled some of them, but it didn't fool old Loot."

"Well, I figured maybe I didn't come out here often enough to attract too much attention."

"Figured wrong with me." Loot laughed.

"Maybe so."

"So what'cha looking for ...silver?"

"Maybe, or gold."

"Gold? Hah. Ain't no gold up there. There's a silver mine north of here, but gold? Naw. Had a buddy years ago who thought there was gold there, though. Hain't seen him in a coon's age ...good old Slim." Loot scratched his chin as he looked up in thought then continued. "Old Slim Longo. He was always prowling around up there, just like you. Got the shit kicked out of him once too. Real bad. Hospital bad."

Sam started at the name and Loot noticed Sam's reaction.

"Ha, I shoulda knowed it. Slim, he sent you. I shoulda knowed it!"

Sam stammered as he spoke, "You knew Slim Longo?"

"Old buddy of mine. I heared he ended up in Austin or San Antone."

"I met him in Austin," he said.

"How is old Slim?"

"Dead," Sam said, with a deadpan expression painted on his face by the unhappy memory. "About ten years ago. He died in my arms."

"Damn," Loot said with a distinct sadness in his voice, finally trailing off with, "Old Slim..."

Sam thought he could detect the beginnings of a tear in the old man's eyes as he recounted the general details of Slim's passing.

Once Sam finished, Loot sat deep in thought for a few seconds then exclaimed, "Shit. Slim ...well, hell, we all carried a hankering for likker from way back, but he was good people. Good people. He'd give you the shirt off his back, he would. But he had what I call 'the fever'...it gets in yer blood and you can't do nothing about it once you got that."

"The fever?" Sam was amazed that Loot had used the same term he sometimes used himself.

"Yeah. Gold fever," Loot said. "Or could be silver fever, or hell, I guess diamond fever. It's whatever gets under your skin and makes you scratch the ground looking to git rich. I reckon it musta been eatin' away at old Slim all them years even after he couldn't do nothing about it."

Loot leaned forward and stared Sam right in the eye. "You got it too, aintcha?"

Sam leaned back, instinctively retreating from Loot's penetrating gaze. This sudden movement caused something to shift in one of the piles behind him and it fell, not to the floor but to another vantage point. Loot did not waver; his bloodshot eyes were fixed on Sam.

Finally, the old man leaned back and grinned. "No matter," he said. "Now you need old Loot's help."

"Well, I have a hunch about a place I've never been. You ever heard of Diablo Rim?"

Loot whistled under his breath.

"Diablo Rim!" he said. "Hell yeah, I know it. You couldn't pick a worse place. Good name for it 'cause it's a devil of a place to get to, at least the way you have to go about it. Ain't close to nothing and the owner is a tough sonovabitch. The ranch hands are a pretty rough bunch, too, and the foreman is the meanest of the lot. Hell, even their *animals* are mean. I work around most of the local ranches from time to time, but I hain't worked for them in years.

"Ain't worth it, son. You best steer clear of that place, gold or no gold. Even if you found something up there, you'd never get it out, and the rim, well it's rough, really rough. It would be a tough hike. You'd never get your car close enough to make it worth your while for the looking."

"I know it's a tough hike. That's why I'm asking you about it."

Loot ran his fingers over the scraggly scraps of stubble on his chin while looking off in the distance and said, "Still, old Loot would love to pull one over on those assholes. Let me think on it for just a second or two."

"I have been looking at the maps ...I've got government survey maps of the whole area. I use them to figure out where I need to go ...uh, looking."

Loot slapped his knee.

"Old Slim told you something, didn't he." He howled with delight. "That old bastard. I always knowed he was working some angle he wouldn't tell me."

Loot leaned forward again, and looked closely at Sam.

"When he died, you was being nice to him ...all that water and talking and shit in jail. Him dying in yer arms; hell ...it's like something outta some old movie. He *told* you something, didn't he?"

Sam just stared back, meeting Loot's gaze halfway, but he said nothing.

Loot leaned back, realizing he had perhaps overstepped his bounds.

"Aw, it's okay. I don't want to know, not really." He then caught Sam's gaze again and said, "I'll help you, sure, but if you find anything, I want a piece. I'm mostly just a trapper and a handyman, but while tromping around I've always had my eye on the ground, looking around up there too. A man can't help but look. There's something about that land up there that just makes you *feel* something is out there. I just want me a piece. Not even a share, just a piece."

Sam wasn't sure what this meant, but he nodded slightly and Loot grinned back.

"When you thinking about heading up there? Weather's about to break today and it's going to get real bad. I can see the signs." Loot looked up at the ceiling as he said this, as if he could gauge the weather through the roof and walls of the shack, then returned his gaze to Sam and continued, "That would be good for you, 'cause the goons will be back in their holes, but it would be bad for hiking. Not too much to say about that ...except that, well, you'd probably slip and fall and freeze your ass off out there."

"Yeah, I know that. So no, not today. Maybe in a month. I need a bunch of days to look."

Loot nodded. "Diablo Rim ain't gonna be no picnic, and if'n you follow it around a ways, stopping to look around and shit, it could take you quite a while."

Sam decided to share a tidbit. "Follow the devil ... that's what Slim said."

Loot's bloodshot eyes seemed to clear by at least a shade. "Hot damn," he said, slapping his hands together.

For the first time Loot seemed to be impressed.

"You *do* know something," he said. Then the old man smiled and sat back in his chair. "Damn you, Slim, you old son of a bitch..." he muttered, staring off into space.

Loot broke out of his trance and sat up again.

"December? Crazy time. Weather is hit or miss in December. Where you coming from?" he asked.

"Austin."

"She-it. That's a long drive, partner. You figure on good weather and by the time you get here it'll change on you. Look at today," he said, pointing vaguely out toward the outer wall. "Did you know about this storm?"

Sam shook his head and said, "There's a risk. I know."

"Risk nothing. You hear what I'm saying, son? You screw this up and you will die.

"If the ranch goons don't get you, some starving old mountain cat will creep up behind you and take you down ... either that or you'll fall off some ledge and break your damn fool neck."

"I know, Loot. I've been out here a bunch of times already, maybe seven."

"That many?"

"Yeah," he said. "And I've been caught by the weather, too. I know what to expect."

"Hell, boy, you've got it bad. I can see it in your eyes. The fever..." Loot said. "Say, what did you say your name was? If we're going to be partners, I should know."

"Sam," he said, somewhat amused that here he was, telling Loot his secrets and the old man didn't even know his name. It was ironic since Loot's name was etched so firmly into his own mind.

Loot sat back. "Okay. This here's what I think you should do. A month, you said? After Christmas?"

"Yeah," he said, "I have that entire week off from my job."

"Oh," Loot said with a knowing tone in his voice, "I get it. Okay, what day do ya think you'll git here?"

"Christmas is on Thursday, so probably the next day, Friday. That gives me until at least Wednesday to poke around. I figure I'll drive back on New Year's Day, the next Thursday."

"Okay. If the weather holds, it might just work. They'll all be fat with holiday stuffing and lazy. But not too lazy, mind you. Ranching ain't no regular job. There ain't hardly no days off ... chores got to be done, you know?"

Sam nodded.

"But, well, during the holidays, most people's got some inclination to just do the basics, if you know what I mean. Even on the ranches, and sometimes they hire old Loot to fill in the cracks. Hell, they think, 'old Loot's got no family to speak of, so we'll throw him a few bucks and he can shovel the manure and hay and whatnot so's we can relax.'"

"And how does that help?"

"Good time for me to be out and about so I don't draw no suspicion. Hell, sometimes them ranch hands will even pay me to come feed their goddamned cat while they're off in Odessa or Mexico with their family."

"And...?"

"Okay, here's my deal ...it'll take you all day to drive here, right?"

"Pretty much," he said.

"Right. When you get here that Friday night, I'll clear a space in that garage out yonder," he said, pointing in a general direction Sam guessed was toward the garage. "We'll stash your little car in there, then I'll drive you up in my old clunker and let you off. I'll have figured out a good place by then. That'll be where you'd need to get back to ...we'll work out a time for me to pick you up."

"So, I hide my car here and you just drop me off in the middle of nowhere."

"Ain't no other way, Sam."

The younger man let out a hard breath, almost whistling. "Right. I can't leave my car up there that long."

"Nope. Way out there, somebody will grab that car and sell it down in Mexico for scrap. Some ne'er-do-well will look at it and say 'hey, free car!' I'm surprised you've gotten away with that as long as you have."

Sam nodded.

Loot stood up with a loud slap on both knees. "That should do it, but you need to get the hell out of here. When this 'Norther hits, you'll wish you'd never left Austin." Loot stuck out his hand as he continued, "See you the day after Christmas?"

Sam shook the hand, sealing the deal. "Day after Christmas," he said. Then he added, "But what if my plans change? I mean, like the weather."

"Okay, here's the deal. Call Ranch Feed and Supply in town ...you can get their number from information. Ask for Gillet Osmond. Gil's an old buddy of mine. He'll take a message for me and he'll be sure I get it ...especially around then. Usually his missus fixes me a little something for Christmas, fruitcake and whatnot."

Sam took out his pen and fumbled in his pocket until he found the card from The Mossback Café. He turned it over and under Smidgeon's number he wrote 'Ranch Feed and Supply– Gillet Osmond.'

Loot again took the lead, deftly guiding Sam back toward the front door. When Loot opened the door, Sam was temporarily blinded by the muted light. He instinctively pulled at his collar as if he had been sprayed with ice. Even though he had been inside Loot's shack for a relatively short time, what had earlier been just a chill had become a numbing cold.

"You driving back now?" Loot asked, surveying the featureless clouds.

"Yeah."

"Hoo!" Loot said, looking back down at him. "You better be careful, boy."

Loot shook his hand again saying, "I told you. I told you. I knew you'd have to look old Loot up. I told you."

"Yes, you did. I don't know how you knew it, but you were right." Then he hesitated and asked," You sure this will work?"

"Ain't nothing perfect in this life, Sam, but I'll do my best to help you. I don't know you from Adam, but now, well, I reckon I at least owe it to Slim."

Loot gave him a pat on the shoulder and Sam turned back to his car. As he made his way across the rubble in the yard to The Clunker, he glanced at the small building next to the house and wondered if it was just as full as the house.

He hesitated briefly before turning the key, like he always did, then, although the starter complained briefly, the engine caught and he revved it a couple of times. He slowly chugged the VW up Tesoro Road to the main road.

About a mile or two away, the Mossback glowed in the dimming light of the overcast and he decided to stop so he could get a cup of coffee for the road. The parking lot was empty except for a tan sedan, but the café appeared to be open.

Smidgeon looked surprised as she greeted him from the cash register, "Hey, Sam, I thought you had left already."

"Well," he stammered, "I-I had to finish a little business in town but I figured I had better get moving. I'm glad you're still open. I wanted another cup of coffee to take with me. From the looks of things, I really need to head east and see if I can stay ahead of this weather."

"Yeah, but—I don't know, you might have already pushed it too far. You need a large one?"

"Yeah, that would be great."

Smidgeon smiled and said, "Okay, it'll be just a minute," and then she headed, not to the coffee station, but to the kitchen. He was puzzled because the place was empty, and there was a full pot steaming right there. After the promised minute, she emerged with a bag in her hand. She stopped at the coffee station and poured coffee into a large Styrofoam cup. She eased her way back over to the register.

At the counter he asked, "How much?"

Smidgeon hesitated and looked down and then she turned her brown eyes to meet his. "On the house, Sam," she said, handing him the bag. "I grabbed you a couple of biscuits too and stuck some sausage in one and a hunk of brisket in the other. You know, like food for the road."

"Aww, Smidgeon, you didn't have to do that."

She took one of his hands in both of hers and he was again surprised by the warm and gentle softness. "Look, I want you to come back here again in one piece. This is just a little something to eat for the road ... so you don't have to stop. Okay?"

He had been so focused on himself for so long, he felt awkward and confused. He and Smidgeon had flirted a little, but this seemed like something more.

"I don't know quite what to say ... this is so nice of you." He smiled and lightly squeezed her hand and added, "And you're right. I'm sure it will save me some time. Thanks so much."

She returned his squeeze and smiled, her eyes lightly glistening. He grabbed the bag and the coffee and headed out the door.

"Sam," she said, "you be careful, you hear? I gave you my number ...you call if you need help. You sure you want to leave right now? Maybe you should sit this out a day."

"I really need to get back," he said. "I'll be careful, I promise and I'll call if I have any problems," he said as he turned to leave.

"Bye, Sam."

"See you soon, Smidgeon."

"I'll be here..."

He started his car and navigated the deserted Van Horn streets. Despite the small size of the town, there was almost always a bit of traffic whenever he was there, but there were no cars on the road and he wondered at the possible bad omen. When he got to Interstate 10, he mindlessly headed east and nibbled one of Smidgeon Toll's wonderful biscuits, alternating his bites with sips of coffee.

Nineteen

Sam shivered against the persistent chill in the car and nudged the Clunker up to sixty despite the danger presented by the change in weather. Five miles an hour would probably not be noticed by any state troopers, but it might save him significant time over the course of the long trip. Minor speeding had never been the big issue for him on these trips ...he was more worried about the wear and tear on the car. Still, with the bad weather threatening, he put both concerns aside because he thought even a small amount of time savings might make a difference. The overcast stretched as far as he could see in all directions and angry streaks in the clouds loomed ominously to the north.

His mind again began to wander as he drove, and for his first order of business, he reexamined the visit with Loot. The permeating unknown odors of the shack seemed to be lingering in his nose, but he could not be sure if this was real or his imagination. The smell had been a profound part of the experience and he could not begin to guess what might have been hidden under the piles of debris. He grabbed a napkin from Smidgeon's sack and blew his nose.

"I wish I had remembered to wash my hands at the diner," he mused.

Despite Smidgeon's warnings, the old man's expressed intention to help him seemed genuine. The maps did not lie, and Loot's opinion concurred with his own conclusion:

"Diablo Rim *is* going to be a tough hike," he said out loud. "Since there is no easy way in, the closer I can get, the better my chances will be."

Sam knew his usual tactic of abandoning his car would leave him vulnerable and the car itself would be a marker that something was up. The further away he parked, the more exposed he would be, walking a long way over a relatively open area and it would also seriously limit his exploration time.

He shook his head in dismay as he considered these particulars, then he considered the other part of the equation ...getting back. It was like the classic mountain climbing scenario: getting to the top of the mountain is only the halfway point of the trip. For him, getting to his search area on Diablo Rim would only be half of the problem because had to turn around and get back out.

In this case, he had to rely on someone he had only met twice, trusting them to be at a certain place and time to pick him up. He wondered about that and he also could not forget the fact this was someone he had been specifically warned about. He would have to blindly trust Loot and if that trust were violated, he'd be stranded out in the middle of nowhere.

Then another wrinkle occurred to him: "What if *I* can't make the rendezvous?"

The hiking could be rougher and take longer than he anticipated. Injury, weather, and capture were other possibilities.

Even avoiding capture could delay him. As he drove, he realized he would need to formulate a number of contingency plans.

He was shocked out of this train of thought by a shudder in the car. Then there was another and he quickly assessed the situation with some concern. His speed was fine and the engine seemed to be running normally. Then The Clunker shook again and he realized that gusty crosswinds were buffeting the car. The sky had taken on a disturbing, almost surreal hue he had never seen.

"I better stop daydreaming and concentrate on my driving."

He was thankful the traffic was light. The car was cold, but still just barely tolerable. He would be in Fort Stockton soon and he planned on topping off his gas tank there, and he decided it would be a good time to put on his long underwear, too. His head was cold and his hands were like ice.

Then he remembered he had bought gloves and a hat when he had bought the sweatshirt. He rooted around behind the passenger seat with one hand while he drove and found the bag from the little store in Fredericksburg and brought it around to the passenger seat. He pulled out the contents, keeping a wary eye on the road. He had bought thick socks, a stocking cap and some small knit gloves. He remembered he also had some work gloves in the trunk and he had thought at the time he could double these knit gloves up with those work gloves, so he filed a mental reminder to get those at his next stop as well.

He put the stocking cap on and it had an almost immediate effect. He had read somewhere that the human body lost a great deal of heat through the head and he believed that now. He fumbled with the gloves as he drove. They were small and he was barely able to squeeze them onto his hands, but once they were in place, they added another defense against the cold.

"Every little bit helps," he said.

Sam wondered if he should have tried to find somebody in Van Horn to look at his faulty heating, but remembered his meager budget and the fact that it was a holiday weekend, so he doubted he could have found a mechanic to look at it anyway. The problem would have to be fixed before his next trip, because it would likely be colder in December and this sudden weather change emphasized how unpredictable the weather could be. He smiled as he remembered the old joke he had shared with Smidgeon because it really did seem true.

When the Fort Stockton exit sign appeared, he felt a little relief at having reached a milestone. Every exit on the long Interstate 10 route was like another tick on the progress chart. After he exited the highway, he found a gas stop and topped off his tank. He then donned his insulated underwear in the restroom.

Sam knew he was as prepared as he could be, for he was wearing several layers. He got some coffee and went back out to the car where he remembered the socks, so he slipped off his shoes and slid the wool socks over his other socks and then squeezed back into his shoes. He gently stamped his feet and flexed his toes. It was a bit tight, but his feet were warmer.

There was an old man pumping gas into an ancient station wagon at the next pump and he had watched Sam's progress with great interest. Just as Sam was stamping his feet, he saw the guy go speak to someone in the car. A young girl emerged and they both approached him.

"Sir?"

"Yes?"

"My grandfather wants to know if you have an ice scraper. He saw you getting ready for the cold and he said he had a feeling you might need one for the storm."

Sam assumed they wanted to sell him something so he said, "No, I don't have one but ...I'm sure I can buy one if I need one."

"No, *señor*," she said, "We have an extra one. If you need one, he wants you to have our other one. He says there is going to be a lot of ice, he can feel it."

Sam didn't know what to say. The old man smiled and blinked at him. It was only then that he noticed the guy's wrinkled hand was holding a worn but serviceable scraper. He looked up at the sky again and meekly accepted the gift.

"*Si, gracias,*" he said.

The man smiled broadly, showing a mix of teeth and gaps, as he handed Sam the scraper. He extended his other hand and gave Sam a light squeeze on the shoulder.

At this point, the old man's eyes widened then he quickly looked back to the car and hurried over and leaned into the back seat to speak with someone else. An old woman slowly emerged, clutching the tattered shawl draped over her head. She also wielded a large cloth bag. The old man took her by the elbow and led her over, whispering in her ear so quietly that even if Sam understood Spanish, he probably would not have understood. She was tiny, and bent over with age, making her seem even smaller. Then the old man quietly spoke to the young girl.

"Sir, this is *mi tia*, uh, my aunt. She's a ...well in Spanish people call her *la bruja*. Some say that is a witch but for us it means many things. My grandfather is her brother. He says he *felt* something when he touched your shoulder. He wants her to meet you, to be sure, because although he is sensitive to many things, *she* is the *bruja*. Will you let her hold your hands and look into your eyes?"

Sam looked around nervously, anxious to get back on the road but he was strangely compelled to comply.

"Sure," he said, and with a gentle sigh, he held out his hands.

The old woman grasped each wrist firmly with a strength that was surprising, given her age and small stature. Her calloused palms were warm and in seconds seemed to get even warmer, almost hot. It appeared as if she were looking right through him, with her cold, once dark eyes, now cloudy with cataracts. He felt a shudder when his eyes made contact with hers. She gasped as she released his wrists and took a step back. Those cold eyes continued to stare at him while she fumbled in her bag. Then she dropped the bag and extended her right hand. It was closed into a fist with the fingers down and she mumbled something to the girl in Spanish.

"Reach out your hand, *señor*," she said, and he moved his left hand palm up under her fist.

The old woman let something drop into his open palm and quickly used both her hands to close his fist over a small cold object. She whispered something to the girl again.

The young girl's eyes showed some alarm as the old woman spoke and she averted her eyes before she spoke to Sam.

"*Mi tia* sees danger in your future, *señor*. Great danger. Don't look at this thing she gave you until you are down the road, far away from us. It is not a bad thing ...it should protect you and give you luck. But she says it needs a little time away from her for its power to bond to you."

The old woman whispered to the girl again and she continued, "She sees a spirit force following you, but don't be afraid of it. The power of the thing in your hand will enhance the protection of the spirit."

The woman whispered again. "There is something else, *señor*, something evil. Beware of it."

The old woman turned away without another word and made her way back to the other car and into the back seat.

The old man patted Sam on both shoulders and said, "*Vaya con Dios*."

The girl continued to avoid Sam's eyes and meekly said, "Good luck, *señor*, God bless you."

Sam smiled, thanked them both again and got back in his car. He put the plastic windshield scraper on the passenger seat and started the car. It seemed a little hesitant, as if warning him that this was not a good day to drive, but it started. The old man and the young girl waved at him as he drove off. He still had the object clutched tightly in his left hand.

Just up the road, he remembered the work gloves and he pulled into the parking lot of a business, put the car in neutral and set the parking brake. He opened the glove compartment and pulled the trigger to pop the trunk, got out and retrieved the gloves. He did all of this with his left fist still firmly holding onto the object. He wondered if it had been long enough to look at it, but remembered what the young girl had said and decided to get on the highway again and put a few more miles behind him before he looked.

Shortly after he got back on the interstate, he noticed something new: sleet. It was just a few grains at first, so sparse he wondered if he were imagining it, but soon he detected the delicate light sound of frozen ice nodules hitting the car. The tat-tat-tat soon became unmistakable, even over the road noise. His hands were cold and with the sleet, he started to worry about driving with one hand in a fist, so after a couple of more miles he decided to open his hand and look.

It was a piece of stone.

"A rock?" he asked himself. "All that fuss over a rock?"

Then he held it up so he could look at it more closely while he kept one eye on the road. It was shaped like a cross. At first, he thought it had been carved, but then he looked at it closer and could tell it was actually shaped like that. He had taken geology in school ...he knew a crystalline structure when he saw it. It wasn't just a rock ...it was some kind of special stone.

He wondered where or how the old woman had acquired such a piece but felt better about the little affair. He had wondered if he should humor these people from the car, wondering about their motivation.

He had heard of *brujos* and *brujas*. It was all part of a culture of folk sorcery and he knew many Mexicans were in awe of their power, but he was still confused.

Why did these people decide to help a total stranger?

Then, he remembered an old adage: it taught that a person should be compelled to help others in need because God had put them in their path.

Sam's hands were freezing so he dropped the stone into his shirt pocket and fumbled with the knit gloves again while he drove, slipping the work gloves over them. They were a bit dirty but they did add another layer over his fingers. The tat-tat-tat of the sleet increased in intensity.

"Shit," he said to himself, realizing he was losing his race with the weather.

He inched the car back up to sixty again but didn't want to chance it much more than that. He knew he would eventually have to slow down if the ice got worse, so he wanted to gain as much time as he could while the road was still fairly clear. About twenty minutes later, he became aware of dusty patches of white forming in depressions just off the side of the road. He pushed on, letting his mind wander again.

~ * ~

He had suffered through sudden changes in the weather several times in the past. Once, when he was still in college, he had gone on a camping trip to Lake Travis with Jed, a Houston friend. This was long before he had started his active search for the Sublett Mine. They had set up camp at Paleface Park on the northwest side of the lake and they pretty much had the place to themselves. At the time, Sam had a small but stout canvas tent. He didn't have a tent fly, so there was a single layer of canvas between the two campers and the world. The weather was nice and they enjoyed a wonderful time eating outside and warming themselves with a fire before zipping up the tent to go to sleep. While they snoozed, a series of violent thunderstorms moved through. The night became a nightmare, full of torrential rain, violent wind, and spectacular lightning, always punctuated by crashes of hard thunder.

A canvas tent will repel water if undisturbed, but once the canvas is saturated, all it takes is a small touch to start a capillary action and then water will readily penetrate the fabric. What they found was that with two people in the small tent, it was difficult not to touch the canvas. Then again, it was raining so hard, the rain might have done the job all by itself. Whatever the reason, water began to pool in the floor of the tent, soaking both them and their sleeping bags.

If they had been in a safe place looking out a window, it might have been a fascinating storm to watch, but they were terrified sitting unprotected in a wet tent. They were also afraid that a close lightning strike could zap them because they knew that the combination of wet trees, wet ground and wet tent would be one big circuit to a lightning bolt.

Their only option, as they saw it, was to move to the car. As they considered an action plan, they realized that before going to bed they had secured their campsite by shoving most of the camping gear into both front seats. That small attempt at convenience was an extension of their current nightmare. Sam concocted a plan.

"When there's a lull," he said, "I'll dash to the car and throw everything from the front seats to the back. You gather up the sleeping bags into a pile in the center of the tent. Then you run to the car."

Jed nodded and said, "Sounds good."

The break came and Sam unzipped the tent and raced to the car. The rain was just a sprinkle and the lightning had abated somewhat, although there were still distant, bright flashes with muted thunder echoing several seconds later. At the car, he was thankful to find that he had at least folded the camp stove, so it was a simple matter to pick it up and quickly lay it on the back seat. That served to clear the driver's seat and he dropped into the seat and closed the door.

There was a box of equipment, mostly pots and plates and such, on the passenger seat. He picked this up and shoved it into the back seat. Then he grabbed two paper grocery store bags full of camping related supplies that were on the floorboard and tossed them to the back seat as well.

He completed this operation just as lightning started to flash brightly again, quickly followed by loud rumbles of thunder. Jed swung the passenger door open and plopped down. As if on cue, the rain started pelting the car with a renewed deluge.

They were safe inside the car, but they were soaked to the skin. It was an uncomfortable night. Body heat combined with the moisture soaking their clothes to immediately steam up the windows. The spectacular lightning show was just as frightening when viewed behind fogged windows as it had been inside the confines of the canvas tent. Somehow, they both eventually fell into a fitful sleep, although they were constantly awakened by close lightning strikes and loud thunder.

The next morning, they groggily assessed their situation and decided that, with the soaked sleeping bags and tent, they had better call off the rest of the trip. This verdict was confirmed after Sam looked across the lake and in the distance spied yet another thunderstorm that was miles away but was obviously coming fast. The ominous cloud seemed like some unworldly creature, dancing across the landscape on spindly legs of lightning.

Neither one of them had any intention of weathering another lightning storm, so they rushed to break camp. They pulled out the tent stakes and extracted the poles. In their haste, they simply poured as much water as they could out of the tent and picked the whole thing up and put it in the trunk of the VW, soggy sleeping bags and all, then made a hasty retreat back to Houston.

~ * ~

Sam's attention was sparked by a rumbling sound. It was a convoy of big yellow highway department trucks inching past him in the left lane. One pulled over as they approached a small bridge over a side road and he realized they were positioning themselves to treat bridges against the buildup of ice. The "Bridge May Ice in Cold Weather" signs were being unfolded as well. These were hinged signs that most of the time said "Drive Friendly" on a yellow triangle, but once unhinged, they became diamond-shaped yellow warning signs. He knew that meant the road conditions were deteriorating and the bridges would be dangerous long before the roads would freeze. The highway crews would spread a mixture of sand and salt on the bridges to help delay that icing.

He pushed the car along at sixty as long as he felt safe, but after encountering a slight slip on a bridge, he slowed to fifty-five again. The stress of driving in these conditions was giving him a headache. Around Ozona it started sleeting harder. The staccato sound of the ice pellets was disquieting, and as he looked out the side window, he imagined this would be a torrential downpour if it were rain, but the fact that it was all sleet made the situation surreal.

Ice was actively accumulating on the side of the road and there was a dusting of ice visible in patches on the road as well. Within just a few miles, the less traveled parts of the road, over on the edge and along the lane stripes, were beginning to show more significant cover. He instinctively slowed to fifty, sometimes going back to fifty-five if the road looked clear for a few miles.

Around Sonora, as it was just starting to get dark, he also saw the first snow flurries sprinkled amidst the steady pelting of sleet. The road was passable but he was simply following a path outlined in the right lane. This was the pair of tracks left by the vehicles driving ahead of him. There were fainter tracks in the left lane but at this point most people seemed to be staying to the right.

As it got darker, it started snowing more heavily. At highway speed, this did not bother his windshield much, which was a good thing, because he had virtually no defrosting effect coming from his faulty heater. He used the windshield wipers when necessary and they managed to keep his line of vision clear because the sleet just bounced off and most of the snow flew beyond the car, caught in the airstream. The overcast and snow had caused an almost immediate transition from sunset to dark. It was like a living nightmare, enhanced of course by the relentless chill that made his bones ache.

"Snow in November ...in Texas!" he kept yelling to himself. "I can't believe this!"

The falling snow readily reflected in his headlights and the effect was almost hypnotic. His eyes would focus on a group of snowflakes dozens of yards ahead of him. They would speed toward him until they were lost from sight, only to be replaced by new targets his eyes would find, singular pinpoints of white among the blur of other white dots.

It was a struggle to maintain concentration, so he instinctively dropped his speed to forty-five. The few other vehicles on the highway had also slowed, except for a few hearty truck drivers who would speed on past in the left lane, covering his windshield with spray that would almost freeze to his windshield despite his wipers beating across the glass. A couple of times he had to augment the action with judicious use of the sprayer, but he was afraid the fluid would soon run out.

A few more miles down the road, he looked in his rear-view mirror and saw a truck quickly bearing down on him at a very high speed and it zoomed past in the left lane. He felt a wave of disgust with this driver, who was taking such a risk in these perilous conditions, but then he looked ahead and realized that this time the spray had frozen to his windshield, covering his entire field of view with ice. The wipers grated uselessly against the ice and his sprayer only seemed to add another layer. He panicked, quickly rolled down the side window and stuck his head out.

His face was suddenly engulfed in a mixture of cold air and frozen precipitation that was hitting him at forty miles an hour. Squinting against the chilly onslaught, he verified that the shoulder was clear and he maneuvered the car over to the side of the road and stopped. He stepped into ankle-deep slush and cleared his windshield with the scraper he had received as a gift back in Fort Stockton. He got back in the car and eased out onto the highway again, and kept a wary eye out for more speeding vehicles. He felt his shirt pocket and touched the outlines of the stone and silently thanked the memory of the prophetic family in Fort Stockton.

The sand trucks tried their best to keep up with the deteriorating weather situation, but they were losing the battle. Almost every substantial bridge and overpass seemed to have its own crew, but he could often feel the car slide in spite of their work. There were definite icy sections on the road surface as well. The left lane was more covered than the right, which he noticed whenever he approached vehicles going slower than he was. Rather than follow in their path, which further complicated his windshield icing situation, he carefully eased over to the left lane long before he got too close and passed them, then carefully moved back into the right lane.

Sam was freezing, in spite of the extra layers of clothing. Most of this was because of his feet, which were wet from standing in the roadside slush on his periodic windshield scraping sessions. He was miserable and exhausted from driving through the storm and needed some relief. He began to calculate the funds he had left to see if he could possibly afford a place to stay, but as he did this, he knew he also had to consider necessary expenses as well. He would still need food and gas. When he had left the state park that morning, he thought he would probably be camping somewhere another night but with the onset of the bad weather he had scrapped that idea.

He looked at his watch and saw it was about eight-thirty ...usually that meant he was about three hours from Austin, but at forty-five miles per hour, Sam knew it would be at least four, and even more if he stopped. Such a break would mean a few minutes of warmth and possibly a good meal. Food would help to warm him as well, and after hours of stressful driving in the ice, he relished the idea of some rest.

Some tail lights in the distance appeared to be on the side of the road, and he instinctively slowed to thirty. As he approached, he could see marks in the covered road that veered back and forth and then lead directly to the tail lights. Concern moved to relief when their emergency flashers suddenly began blinking, indicating that someone in the car was alive. He was past the scene almost the moment he saw it, and although he thought about stopping, he could already see that another car behind him was pulling over, so he pushed on.

"Bad sign," he muttered to himself.

After seeing that car, he judged that even forty-five was too fast. He knew one thing: the slower he drove, the longer it would take to get home.

The fuel gauge hovered over the quarter tank mark and he knew he would need to top off the tank to make it home. He was cold, tired and hungry and didn't have enough money for a room, but that likely did not matter. Judging from the sparse traffic on the highway, he assumed all the motels were fully booked. The joke about ice and snow in Texas was that people always rushed out and bought all the bread and milk from stores. As he considered his own situation, Sam assumed this could probably be extended to include motel rooms.

The first exit sign for Junction came and went and then he passed a sign advertising a truck stop, a place that would provide both food and gas all at one location. He remembered stopping there on his last trip. He slid a little in the ice as he made the shallow curve at the exit, but managed to correct and keep control.

"I've always had a good instinct about that," he said.

The approaching truck stop looked like an oasis in a sea of white. It seemed to be snowing even more heavily and his windshield wipers were making slow progress against the snow hitting his windshield. Sam figured he had about thirty-five dollars cash and knew he probably needed at least ten or twelve of that for gas and more for a good meal. Although he could get by with something cheap, these fixed costs confirmed the notion that a motel was beyond his reach.

He did have his winter sleeping bag, so he thought perhaps he could put the seat back as far as it would go and squeeze himself into the bag and wait out the storm in his car without freezing to death. His only other option was to just push on and hope the weather didn't further deteriorate. The major complication there was the fact that he was exhausted and the stress of driving in these conditions only made that worse.

The problem of no defroster further worried him, because he was not sure that he could maintain enough concentration to make it all the way to Austin. Despite his bleak situation, a hot meal seemed a welcome necessity, so he decided he would rest for a short while and see how he felt before deciding what to do.

He glanced around as he pumped his gas. The grounds of the truck stop were pretty with their fluffy white cloak of snow, but most of the pavement was covered with a dingy slush. It was quite cold, so he knew that slush would soon turn to ice. The pump stopped at 8.23, which was better than he figured. He bumped it to 8.25 and let it stand there, and he went in and paid for his gas. The adjacent restaurant was warm and quiet and it smelled good. He went back out and moved his car to a parking place in front of the restaurant. As he got out of the car again, he shivered in the damp cold. Despite his layers, he wished he had a proper coat, then he slapped his palm against his forehead when he remembered the light coat in the space behind the back seat. He shook his head, giggling to himself as he walked into the restaurant.

A waitress stopped in the midst of her duties to greet him as he came in.

"Hey there, come on in out of the cold," she said. "Just sit anywhere you like. I'll find you. Coffee?"

"Yes, please," he said, surveying the almost empty restaurant.

There were two other lone individuals sitting at tables and one couple with a child in a booth. He found a booth somewhat away from the other customers but not far enough to needlessly inconvenience the waitress, who seemed to be working alone, and was fumbling with his knit gloves when the waitress appeared again, hovering over him with a cup of steaming coffee and a tired smile.

"Awful night," she said, "where you headed?"

"Austin," he said.

She frowned. "People say it is much worse over toward the east," she said. Then she sighed, "'Course there's not much you can do about it either. People also say everything here is all full. Motels, I mean."

"Well, I needed gas and I am starving, so I figured a good hot meal would warm me up."

She handed him a menu and said, "I'd tell you about the specials but they are all sold out. Most everything else on the menu is good, though."

"Burger and fries sound good," he said. "Mayo, lettuce, tomato."

She scribbled the order down then walked back toward the kitchen.

Sam sipped the coffee. It was good and he warmed his hands on the cup as he began to contemplate his predicament. The weather was deteriorating and, according to what the waitress just told him, it would only get worse. He really *was* chilled to the bone and didn't relish the idea of continuing his cold and icy trip.

"I wonder how long I can hang out in here?" he quietly asked himself under his breath.

The other option, sleeping in his car, seemed barely workable because in a Volkswagen it would be uncomfortable and cramped at best. The sleeping bag was rated to the 20s and even if it got colder than that, with the added insulation of long underwear, sweatshirt, and wool socks, he would manage. He sighed heavily.

"Of course, my socks are wet..." he again quietly mused.

Another woman walked into the restaurant, apparently alone. She was short with dark hair and had an enormous purse. She seemed somewhat flustered as she brushed snowflakes off her coat. She came over and sat in the next booth.

The waitress moved quickly to top off Sam's coffee, then dropped off a menu and exchanged pleasantries with the newcomer. In the distance he heard a bell ding and the waitress hurried into the kitchen.

"Is there anything good here?" The question came from the next booth.

"I just ordered a burger and fries," he said.

"Probably a good idea," she said, "I guess it's hard to mess up a burger, right?"

Before Sam could answer, the waitress came out of the kitchen with a steaming plate of food.

"Here you go," she said as she placed it on the table.

"This smells really good."

"Yeah, you're lucky ...one of the better cooks is stuck here tonight." Having said that, the waitress went over to the adjacent booth.

He heard the woman order the same thing, a burger and fries.

After the waitress left, the woman in the next booth asked him, "How is it?"

"Pretty good, he said. "I think the fries are fresh cut."

"Hey, you want some company? It seems silly to talk across the back of a booth like this."

"Sure, come on over."

The massive handbag came first followed by the diminutive owner. She was young and pretty, and had an easy smile that was intensified by her brown smiling eyes. There was something about that smile that immediately warmed him.

"I guess she'll find me okay," she said, laughing.

Sam nodded, "Probably a safe bet."

"My name is Loretta," she said and flashed another one of her infectious smiles. "But I never much liked it. What's your name?"

"I never much liked my name either, but I guess I got used to it. I'm Sam," he said, adding, "What's wrong with Loretta? I love that name."

"I don't know, but, well, Loretta just always seemed like weird, sorta sounds like a nun, you know? Kids in school would make fun of it. Could be it sounds too country, you know, like Loretta Lynn."

"Well, they're nuts. It's a good name."

She smiled. "Thanks. I like Sam, too. It suits you. Glad to meet you," she said, extending a hand.

He returned the handshake, which was firm, but the hands were soft and warm. His hands were a stark contrast to that warmth.

"Honey, your hand is ice cold!"

"Yeah," he said, "the heater in my car isn't working very well."

She took both of his hands and wrapped them around the coffee cup. "You warm up your hands on that cup," she said, adding, "so the weather brought you in here too?"

He nodded. "Of course. I needed gas and I was hungry, but freezing to death sure didn't help."

She said, "I just couldn't take the ice anymore. I made the mistake of going to Ozona to spend Thanksgiving with my boyfriend's family. Double mistake."

"How so?"

"Well, we just broke up. I was planning on staying with him the whole weekend. We were going to camp out tonight. I have my dad's tent and a sleeping bag and everything."

"Oh, that's really too bad. I'm sorry."

Loretta's eyes were glistening. "Oh, it's okay, I guess. All we did was fight about nothing."

"He just let you go out into this storm alone?"

"Oh, he and his parents tried to stop me, but I just couldn't bear to stay there any longer."

Sam took her hand in his to comfort her a little.

"I can understand that. You're a little crazy, though, to leave a safe place and drive in the middle of an ice storm, but at least you're safe right now."

"It was just a bad scene. I never thought his parents liked me. I mean, I've gone out there a bunch of times and I still felt that way. And he's just a jerk. I had to get out of there. I don't know what I'll do now. Even if I had enough money for a motel, I figure they are probably already all full."

"Yeah, the waitress already told me that."

"See? Shit."

The waitress brought the second plate of food. She didn't even mention Loretta's change of scene.

As Loretta started in on her burger, Sam asked her, "So how far do you have to go?"

Through a partial mouthful of food she mumbled, "San Antonio. You?"

"Austin."

"A lot farther than me. Maybe we could try to piggyback down to my parents' house. They'd probably take pity on you and let you sleep on the couch."

Sam shook his head. "I'm too tired for that. I've got my own sleeping bag, so I think I'm just going to try to keep as warm as I can and try to catch some sleep in my car."

"What kind of car?"

"VW," he said. "It will be tight."

Loretta's eyes brightened. "Say, I have a really big car. Maybe we could sleep in that. I'd never try it alone but with you there..."

She stopped and eyed him suspiciously. "Wait a minute, did you say I'm crazy? You were out driving in this storm too ...with NO HEAT! What were you doing out here?"

He laughed nervously. "I had something I had to take care of farther west, in Van Horn."

169

"Van Horn? And you called *me* crazy." She laughed out loud. "I don't know what I was thinking ...I'm not sure I can trust somebody as nutzoid as you."

"Yeah. You've got a point there, but I guess we have similar problems ...we both needed to get home. What kind of car do you have anyway?"

"Oh, it's a monster. 1963 Chevy Impala. Used to be my uncle's."

"Want to know something weird? My uncle had one of those too. Huge inside. Of course, I was a little kid when he had it, so I probably remember it as bigger."

"I know I can stretch out in it. Anyway, is that a stupid idea? I mean trying to sleep in it? I'd never try it alone. It's funny, I really feel like I can trust you. Can I?"

"Hey, it's an emergency. No funny business."

She laughed. "Right. No funny business. I can't deal with any more emotional baggage right now."

"I understand, Loretta. Sleep. It's got to be better than cramming into that damned VW and with both of us in there and in sleeping bags it should be no worse than a tent. Maybe better. But aren't your parents expecting you?"

"Not really, not until Sunday. Unless that idiot calls them. He or his parents might just do that because of the weather. So I better call him."

After they both finished eating, Loretta went to a pay phone to make the call. When she returned, she said, "Okay. He said he hadn't called to check on me. Big surprise. Jerk!" She sighed. "I told him I was safe and had found a place to wait out the storm."

"Trying to make him a little jealous?"

She laughed. "Maybe, just a little."

"Listen, Loretta, you really can trust me. No funny business. I promise."

"I think it will be fun. Just like camping out."

"Hey," he said, "I've camped out in bad weather. It really isn't any fun."

Twenty

The waitress was doing double duty by also acting as the cashier and when Sam paid for his meal he asked, "Would it be okay if I try to wait out the storm in my car in the parking lot?"

"Sure," she said, "but you can stay in here to stay warm, as long as it doesn't get too busy. Usually starts picking up about five every morning."

"Thanks, I might do that if it gets too cold, but I just need some quiet to get some rest."

He used the restroom while Loretta paid her bill, then suggested she do the same.

He waited outside until she rejoined him. It was bitterly cold.

Her eyes glistened in the reflections of the bright lights of the parking area as she said, "Brrrrrr, it's cold, but I think the snow is slacking off."

He pointed to his car and said, "This one is mine. Let me get my sleeping bag." His breath billowed in clouds as he spoke.

Loretta pointed. "That's mine," she said. It was about three spaces to the right of The Clunker. She walked over and brushed the accumulated snow from the driver's side windshield. "I might as well get it started. Maybe we could park it over there." She indicated a parking area to the side that was in the shadows. Sam looked over and nodded. Before starting the car, she opened the trunk and pulled out her sleeping bag.

He opened the back door of Loretta's car and tossed his sleeping bag on the seat, then got in and sat in the passenger seat. The engine idled a little roughly and the heater was pumping some semblance of warm air into the compartment. She drove over to the darker area and parked the car, letting it idle a few minutes. The air coming out of the vents was already warmer.

"Maybe we could just leave the engine running," she said.

"Not a good idea. There is always a possibility of carbon monoxide in an old car like this. How's your exhaust system?"

"I have no idea."

"Exactly. Best just to let it heat us up for a few minutes that will at least warm up our bags."

She turned to him and stared at him for a few seconds. "I must be crazy to do this. I think you're crazy, too, driving all that way in this storm. At least I only drove about a hundred miles, but you ...all the way from Van Horn!"

"Well, I drove for a long time in sleet but the roads were pretty good most of the way. We both probably shared the worst part."

"What on earth were you doing in Van Horn?"

Sam hesitated for a moment.

"Oh, you have some dark hidden secret out there, huh?"

He looked her in the eye, "You might say that. It's not really something I can talk about right now."

Loretta feigned a pout by sticking out her bottom lip. "With all that I'm doing for you and you don't trust me."

"It's not that, not really, but, well..." Sam sighed. "Shit. You know, you're right. Okay, It's about a ...a... lost gold mine."

"You've got to be kidding. A lost gold mine?" She laughed.

Then Sam started in on the jail story while the car idled. It got quite warm as he related his long trips to the Van Horn area and the trespassing, then concluded with his latest trip to see Loot Meldings. Loretta took it all in without a word. When he was finished, he realized he had never related the whole story in such detail to anyone, including Sally or Godson.

Loretta's voice cracked as she responded. "So it's true?"

He nodded.

"But, well, you don't really know where it is, or if it is really there at all, right?"

"No. It's just a feeling I have. I guess I'm a little obsessed with it."

She laughed so deeply it made her cough. "A little? So little you risk your life driving across the state in an ice storm!" She chuckled again. "You're nuts, you know that? I've got an insane person in the car with me!"

"You're out driving in the ice storm, too."

She stopped laughing. "Well, maybe we are both a little nuts. I guess a person does what they need to do, right?"

"Right," he said. "And I'm really tired ...think we need to get some sleep."

She reached up to turn off the ignition and he said, "Leave it on for just a minute more. We've got to stretch out our bags and that probably means I need to get out to do mine ...leave the heat on full until I do that."

Sam quickly got out of the car, then opened the back door and unfurled his bag, unzipping it before he quickly jumped in the back seat. The heat in the car was only slightly diminished.

"You need to get out to unfold your bag?"

"No," she said, "I'm a lot smaller than you, I think I can manage." She scooted toward the passenger side of the seat, unrolled her bag and spread it out toward the driver's seat while the heat continued to pour into the car. After a few more minutes, she cut the ignition and extracted the keys, depositing them into her large bag.

"Say, Sam, do you want a nightcap?"

"What?"

"You know, a nightcap, like a drink?" She pulled out a pint bottle from her purse. "Peppermint Schnapps."

"Not sure I've ever had it," he said.

"It's sort of a sweet booze," she said. "It should warm us up a little."

"I'll give it a try," he said as he heard the sound of a twist top turning against glass.

Loretta tipped the bottle to her lips. "Sorry, I didn't remember to put some glasses in my purse." She laughed.

"I'm surprised you don't have a full bar in that thing," he said as he accepted the bottle from her. He tilted it upwards and tasted a sweet burning sensation as the liquid ran over his tongue and continued down from his throat to his stomach. He took another good-sized gulp.

"Good, huh?" she asked as he handed the bottle back to her and she took another swig herself, then replaced the cap.

He smiled back at her. "Yeah, I like it."

She locked both of the front doors then maneuvered back and forth as she slipped into her sleeping bag. "Can you get the back locks?"

"Sure, good idea. We're sort of out here in the open. But we should be okay. The windows are already starting to fog."

He swung his legs into the bag and zipped it up, boots and all. His feet were wet and he was afraid his socks would smell if he took his shoes off.

A voice came from the front seat. "This is really pretty shitty. But I'm glad you're here. I feel safe."

Sam was just settling into the cramped space. "Yeah, we should be okay. I hope we can snag some sleep."

"The schnapps should take care of that."

Sam smiled. He could already feel the glow of the booze fogging his brain. "Yeah."

They both drifted off to an uneasy sleep. The night was punctuated by creaks and cracks as the cold night air affected the accumulated ice on the metal body of the car. Large trucks drove into the truck stop, their wheels spinning in the ice as they fought for traction. Sam drifted in and out of consciousness, fighting the instinct to continually check the time whenever some noise woke him up. A combination of interior fogged windows and a haze of frozen moisture on the outside meant they were completely blind. He hoped nobody would speed into the parking lot and slide into their refuge. He worried about that all night but finally managed to get a few long snatches of sleep. The bag helped, but there was an undercurrent of chill that crept up on him and settled into his feet.

His eyes snapped open at the long blast of a truck horn. The sun was up, illuminating the frozen windows like some kind of reflector. He had long since stopped hearing the cracks and creaks of the ice outside the car, but the sounds were back, intensified by the warming effect of the sunlight. Sam looked at his watch. Seven A.M.

"You awake?"

Loretta's voice cracked, "Yeah."

"Did you get any sleep?"

"Some. What did I say before? Shitty?"

"I'd say that is a pretty accurate assessment," he said, his breath visible.

"Damn, it is really cold," she said, "but I think the sun is starting to warm things up a little."

Sam reached up at the window behind him and touched at the apparent fog on the inside. It was cold, not wet. He scratched at it with his fingernail and brought his hand down for closer inspection.

"Even the inside is frosted," he said.

He saw a hand reach up from the other seat and touch the window and quickly withdraw. "Shit."

"Maybe we should head out and see what's going on. Maybe get some coffee."

He could hear Loretta yawn, "Yeah, okay." She yawned again. "I need to find my shoes."

"I never took mine off. My feet are frozen," he said.

"What?"

"My feet were really wet. Still are. I was afraid I'd stink us out."

She laughed. "You idiot. You need to put on some dry socks."

"I think I have some in my car. I hope I do."

She sat up and looked down at him. "I must look a mess," she said, "but let's go. I'm hungry, too. A little breakfast will warm us up."

"You're fine, pretty as ever," he said, fumbling with the zipper on his bag. His entire body was sore from battling with twenty-year-old upholstery springs. He sat up and unlocked the door, then tried the handle. It did not budge. "Uh-oh," he said.

"Frozen?"

"Yeah."

He pulled on the handle while giving the door a hard shove with the other hand. There was a pronounced crack.

"One more time, I think," he said then repeated the operation. The door slowly creaked open, the encasing ice cracking with a sound that echoed within the compartment.

"You're not breaking my car, are you?"

"No, there's just a shell of ice on the outside."

He pivoted on the seat and put his feet onto the uneven frozen ground of the parking lot. The glare was blinding but he squinted and looked around. The sky was a deep blue. Large geyser-like plumes rose above some idling trucks nearby. He tested the ground with his feet then got out of the car. His feet ached but the air seemed warmer than the air inside the car.

"Nice day," he said. "Still a lot of ice on the ground, though."

He took a few tentative steps. It was a little slippery but he was able to walk. He tested the ice on the windshield. It was frozen solid. He went back to the front passenger door. Some of the cracks in the ice from the back door were stretching over to the front door frame. He leaned down and asked, "Is the door unlocked?"

He heard an "Oops, now it is," from inside the car, and heard her pop the lock. He thumped the door frame with his fist near one of the cracks and the cracks extended. He knocked on the door all around the frame and hit the handle, then tried to operate the handle. He hit it again. He was finally able to depress the button and pull on the handle and heard another loud crack.

As he began to try again, he called out, "Push!" and the door cracked again and slowly opened. Loretta peeked out.

"Hi," she said.

"Do you have a scraper?" She nodded and fumbled in the glove compartment. "We'll get a little of the ice off the windshield in a patch and that should help the rest start to clear."

Sam worked until he had scraped a hole about a foot across over the driver's side. "That should do it."

They made their way over toward the restaurant. "You were going to get some dry socks," she said.

"Right."

His car had been out in the full sun and the driver's side was already almost ice free. In fact, close to the building, all of the ice seemed to be melting fairly quickly. Sam opened the car door with no difficulty, rummaged around in his knapsack and produced a clean pair of socks. He grabbed one of the rummaged to-go sacks from behind the seat too. "To put my wet dirty socks in," he said.

In the restroom, Sam slid off his wet shoes and peeled the double layer of socks from his feet. The socks reeked like a wet dog so he put them in the bag and rolled the top down tightly. He dried his wrinkled feet with a couple of paper towels and put on the dry socks. His feet felt much warmer, even when he put them in the damp shoes. He went outside and put the sack in the trunk of The Clunker, then returned and found Loretta in the little store. "Let's go," he said.

He pulled out his wallet and reviewed his funds, "I'd love to treat, but I don't think I have enough money."

"Sam, it's not like this is a date. I can buy my own meal."

He smiled. The sign still said seat yourself, so they found a quiet booth and a new waitress soon brought them menus.

"Coffee?" she asked.

They both answered in unison, "yes!"

As they warmed their hands on their cups of coffee, they lamented their miseries of the previous night.

"Did you get *any* sleep last night?"

Sam smirked and said, "Maybe just a little. Every time I thought I was drifting off, some truck would be revving its engine or something."

"I know! And that car, creaking and popping all night. Creepy!" she laughed. "But I guess it was still better than trying to drive. I was so tired."

"And," Sam added, "today's a beautiful day!"

After they ordered and started eating, the conversation turned back to Sam's quest.

"So, basically, you go out and trespass, just hoping you get lucky," she said.

"Pretty much." He thought about Slim's riddle as he answered. He hadn't related that specific detail but wondered if he should go that far. He decided to skip it. Then he remembered the small rock the old woman had given him back in Fort Stockton.

"Ah," he said, "but I think I might have the luck thing beaten." He showed her the rock and related his recent encounter with the *bruja*.

A sly smile spread across Loretta's face. "You know, I really believe in that stuff. She said she saw something in you. That's big. Really big."

"You think? It really is a cool rock, and it was an interesting experience but I figure..."

"No, no, no," Loretta interrupted, "it's special, you can tell. You ever seen a rock like that?"

As Sam shook his head, a burly truck driver was walking past their table and he smiled as he was walking past, then stopped.

"Say," he said, "I couldn't help but notice. I'm something of a rock hound. I haven't seen one of those in a long time. You know what that is?"

Sam said, "No."

"It's a Staurolite, but most people call them fairy stones ...they mostly come from a specific area in Virginia. They are supposed to be lucky."

"Really?" Sam cast a glance at Loretta.

The truck driver was an imposing figure looking down at Sam. "Want to sell it?"

"I don't think so," Sam replied. "It is something of a good luck piece."

"Nice specimen. I guess in my line of work I'll get up past that area of Virginia one day. Well, you two have a great day."

After the truck driver left, Loretta said, "See? I don't know how that woman got it but, well, I would never doubt anything a *bruja* told me. Sam, there is magic in objects like that. I know it. I mean, look at how somebody just walking by knew all about it, right when we were wondering what it was. It was given to you to protect you and give you luck. I know about this stuff. It's real!"

"You think?"

"Let me show you something," she said and she again dove into the depths of that massive purse. Her hand emerged holding a tattered jewelry box, the kind a ring might come in.

"I have a little good luck charm of my own."

She opened the box and Sam could see it was a small jagged piece of metal. "What is that?"

Loretta looked around and turned her body slightly away from the general area of the restaurant. Sam could see she was fumbling with a couple of buttons on her top. She turned slightly back toward him and he could see that she had spread the top open with a couple of fingers and had inched up her bra a little with a finger on her other hand to reveal what looked like a scar, just along the lower contours of her breast.

"See?" she said, "That chunk of metal came from there." She was pointing at the scar. She quickly re-buttoned her top.

"Oh," he said, "how did it happen?"

She seemed almost embarrassed. "I never tell *anyone* this story." She took a deep breath and continued, "I was about three, playing in the yard while my dad was cutting the grass. We never knew where it came from, but he hit something with the lawnmower and a piece of metal went flying and hit me… there," she said, again pointing at her chest.

"You remember this?"

"A little, it is one of my earliest memories," she said. "I mostly remember the commotion. I think it was more traumatic for my parents."

"I can imagine," he said. "Why are you embarrassed?"

"I don't know. It is hard to tell people you almost died. It is sort of like I'll jinx it or something … if I tell."

"You almost died?"

"Yes. This piece stopped just outside my heart. They said if I had been even one step closer to the lawnmower, I probably would have died at the scene."

"Damn," he said. "Like a gunshot wound or something."

She nodded, then continued, "Plus, they were worried about infection. I was in the hospital for a while."

"And you keep the chunk of metal they took out of your body in your purse."

"My dad kept it and gave it to me when I was about twelve," she said, "when he thought I'd better appreciate the importance. He told me to always keep it as my good luck charm. He felt it was a bit like lightning, you know?"

"Oh, I get it," he said. "Lightning doesn't strike twice in the same place. I have an uncle who built his farmhouse right next to a tree that had been struck by lightning. I guess it worked. The house is still there."

"I believe in this stuff, Sam. It's real." She picked up the rock again. "*This* is real. It's not some cool story. I grew up in San Antonio and have heard stories …these *brujas* are scary in what they can see, what they can do. Don't take this lightly."

181

She opened his palm and put the stone in it and closed his fist over it just the way the old woman had done when she had first given it to him. "This is going to give you luck, I know it."

Sam's heart was beating rapidly. He let out a muted sigh. "I– I–I hope so. This is all a bit overwhelming, Loretta."

"I know, right?" she said. "That's the power of it, Sam. Feel it?"

He nodded and started to carefully wrap the stone in a napkin and she stopped him and said, "Wait!"

Again, she dove into her purse and she pulled out another small jewelry case. "I just remembered I had this. I don't even know why I kept it. Fate, I guess."

"Fate?"

"I don't know how else to explain it." She opened the case and put the fairy stone into it. "That will help you keep it safe."

"Gee, Loretta, I don't know what else to say. I thought this was really just some goofy trinket, but now you got me thinking." He picked up the box and put it in his shirt pocket. "I'll keep it safe."

"And it will help to keep you safe. I know it."

They both had another cup of coffee and discussed their future plans.

"So what are you going to do, Loretta?"

"I wish I knew. I thought I loved Michael, you know?"

"The guy from Ozona?"

"Yeah, but he was such a jerk. I guess when I get home, I'll try to figure out what's going on with him. I hope it isn't over but if it is, I might just take off and try something new, someplace new, maybe find somebody new. What about you?"

"Christmas," he said. "I'm heading west again the day after Christmas." He pointed outside. "That is, if the weather cooperates. If not then, I'll have to wait until spring."

"You be careful, Sam."

"I always am."

Outside in the parking lot, Sam's car looked ready to go. He walked with Loretta over to her car. It was still chilly but was well above freezing, so the Impala was also almost clear of ice. There were still icy slick spots in the parking lot but everything was rapidly clearing. Sam loosely rolled up his sleeping bag and helped Loretta roll hers up as well.

"You should start your car ...make sure it starts before I leave. Just to be safe."

"That's a really good idea," she said. She grabbed her sleeping bag and stored it in her trunk. "Hop in and I'll drive you back to your car."

Her car started right up and she backed out and drove him back over to his car.

"Sam?"

"Yes."

Loretta had a tear rolling down her cheek. "Thanks for being such a gentleman last night and thanks for helping to keep me safe."

He smiled. "Hey, thank *you*! I am thankful you suggested we share your car. As shitty as it was, it was the Taj Mahal compared to my car. And I appreciate all of the support about, well, that other thing. Most of my friends think I'm pretty much a lost cause these days."

"Well," she said, "let's keep things in perspective. I think you're nuts too, but I like nuts."

She kissed him on the cheek and gave him a hug, then rummaged in that bottomless bag and brought out a small notepad that had a pen stuck into the spiral binding. She scribbled her name and number on the pad, tore the page out and handed it to him.

"That's my number in San Antonio. If you come to town, give me a call, okay? Oh, and give me your number and address," she said. "I do get to Austin every now and then."

He told her the details and she jotted them down.

"Oh, and Sam?"

"Yes?"

"You WILL find it. I know it. Just keep that good luck charm safe."

"The talisman?"

She looked a little confused. "Talisman?"

"Another word for lucky charm ...actually it is more like a magical charm with special powers."

"Oh ...that's cool, I like that word. Yes. Keep your talisman with you. I'll be thinking about you."

She pushed him toward the door. "Now, go," she said, "before I decide to kidnap you and take you back to San Antonio with me."

He returned to his car and the engine cranked right up. His eyes watered a little as he pulled out of the parking spot and headed toward the road, almost hitting a truck pulling in while he watched Loretta's car following him in his rear-view mirror. They paced each other on the interstate until he came up to the exit to 290 and they both waved as they went their separate paths. He rubbed the cheek where she had kissed him.

Twenty-one

The rest of the drive to Austin was relatively short and uneventful. The bright sunlight warmed the interior of the car and the remaining patches of ice he encountered posed no problem. Sam was in good spirits. Once back home, he called Sally to let her know he was back.

"Sally?"

"Sam! You're back! Did you hit the ice?"

"Heh, nice choice of words." He laughed. "Yeah, I drove through that storm almost all day. The roads were okay for a while but it got worse and worse. I finally stopped in Junction and decided to wait it out."

"Well, at least you're safe. How'd the rest of the trip go?"

"Good. It seemed so anyway. I think I can safely get to Diablo Rim now. I have a contact out there who's going to help me."

"What? You always said you wanted to be completely anonymous."

"Yeah, that's always been the idea, but when you pop in and out like I do," he said, "people start to notice. I ran across this guy on my last trip. He said he had seen me and had a good idea about what I was doing. Turns out he's just an old trapper who has done a little prospecting himself. He says he just wants to help."

"I don't know, it sounds like you may be making a huge mistake," Sally said, her voice wavering with concern.

"I think it will be okay. Seriously, it's the only way ... there is no easy way to get to Diablo Rim without help from somebody who knows their way around out there."

"Well, rest up. I need you at work tomorrow," she said.

He winced at the prospect of returning to his job.

"Yeah, okay," he said with a dejected tone in his voice, "I'll be there. Bye."

"Bye, Sam," Sally said, "Thanks for calling. It is a big relief."

He decided to unload his car before calling Godson and trudged down the stone steps to the little garage. He was busily stowing some of his camping gear when he heard a car on the gravel of the alley. He looked out and saw Godson's car pulling up the short driveway. His friend parked behind The Clunker and got out.

"Hey, buddy. You sure know how to cause your friends a lot of grief. I thought you were supposed to be back last night?"

"Aw, I'm sorry, Godson, I got ambushed by the weather. I ended up spending the night in Junction," Sam said. "It was just a bunch of odd circumstances."

"A phone call would have been nice."

"Yeah. Sorry about that. I just got in and was going to call you after unloading my car. I didn't have cash for a room so I just hunkered down in a car for the night."

"You hunkered in the VW?"

"No," Sam said, "another car. Some woman's. She was stranded, too."

Godson's face lit up. "A woman? Awesome!"

"Nothing like that," Sam said. "She was travelling too. We were both stranded at the truck stop. She had a much bigger car than mine. Nice girl. Nothing happened."

"Sam, Sam, Sam..." Godson started, chuckling.

"Don't Sam, Sam, Sam me," he snapped back.

He grabbed the box of camping utensils and started for the stairs, gesturing with his chin for Godson to follow. "Come on up," he said, "and I'll make us some coffee."

Godson nodded, grabbed the sleeping bag from the trunk and followed him up the stairs. Sam fiddled with hot water and mugs while he told Godson about his trip.

"I got a late start Friday, so I stopped in Balmorhea to camp. I had no clue how bad the storm was going to be until I got to Van Horn. By then it was really too late."

"Did you find that guy? What was his name? Loot?" Godson asked.

"Yes. I had a good long talk with him."

"What's the deal with him?" Godson asked.

"Turns out he knew Slim back in the good old days," Sam said. "That was a revelation."

"Seriously. He knew the wino from jail?"

"Yeah. And he'd noticed my car on the side of the road too, and knew it wasn't broken down. He's a weird guy. Old trapper." Sam laughed as he continued, "He's a real pack rat too. His house is full to the brim with random crap. You have to almost walk sideways through the pathways of junk that are stacked up, weaving your way through the house. And it smells. Hell, he smells."

"Sounds lovely," Godson said. "So, what's going to happen?"

"I told him what I thought I could tell him."

"Like Diablo Rim?"

"Yeah, and he knows where it is. He had me pegged pretty well, knows it's about gold, but I didn't give him too many details. But what he told me about Diablo Rim was worth the trip."

"Seriously? Why?"

"It will be a tough hike without help, almost impossible. I need somebody to drop me off and pick me up, otherwise I'll be hiking too far and he doesn't think I would be able to get away with it. After looking at it countless times on the Geologic Survey maps, I tend to agree with him. He said that ranch in particular, the one where I'd need to hike, is owned by the nastiest rancher in the area and, according to Loot, the ranch hands are just a bunch of cowboy hoodlums."

"You know I could come and help you with that kind of stuff. I just have to plan it out with Moll."

"Yeah, like Moll would ever let you, but getting this Loot guy to help makes sense: I need a local who is familiar with the area and his truck is already well-known out there. He often does odd jobs for a lot of the ranches and if anybody sees him driving his truck around, they will assume he has a reason to be driving through. That means he can get me in close to where I need to go and save me a lot of time. That will reduce the risk of detection, too. Hiking in from far away has always been the riskiest part of my hike."

At this point Godson asked the big question. "What's he get out of it?"

"He says he wants a "taste" but I think he also relishes a chance to put one over on this rancher and his hands. He really hates those guys."

Godson frowned. "Sounds fishy."

"I know. But this guy Loot, well, I don't know why, but after talking with him, I trust him. I didn't at first, but it all changed after I found out he knew Slim. I know we made a strong connection there."

Sam handed Godson a cup of steaming coffee.

"So," he said, "what about this lady friend?"

Sam frowned. "Not much to tell. The road was horrendous and getting worse by the minute and my heater wasn't working right."

"Yeah, I was worried because you said you'd be back, but there was no answer when I called and the weather guy on TV said it was really bad from about Johnson City westward. Here we only got cold and rain, with maybe just a few flurries. What's this about your heater?"

"Just delivering part of what it should, mostly on the passenger side."

Godson said, "I'll take a look. Probably just the control cable got fouled up or snagged or something."

"Thanks, that would be great," Sam said. "Anyway, I drove for hours through sleet and then snow, and the road kept getting worse the further east I drove. With almost no heat, I basically had no defroster either. I had to pull over if my windshield got sprayed when a truck or car passed. It would freeze and I would have to stop to scrape off the ice. By the time I got to Junction, I knew I needed some gas so I stopped. At that point I was driving like thirty-five on the interstate and had just seen a car veer off into a field. That scared me silly, and I knew I was starting to get really tired."

"Wow. Thirty-five? That will cut into your driving time."

"Yeah. And don't forget I drove an extra hour in the morning after camping, just to get to Van Horn. I also spent a while talking with Loot. I had a long day."

Godson laughed, "I still love that name. Loot."

"Old trapper nickname, I figure," Sam said.

"Loot, Slim ...I'll say this, you are meeting some interesting people."

"And Loretta," Sam added.

"Loretta?"

"That's the woman's name."

"So, what was she like?"

"She was pretty. Very petite, with eyes that cut right through you like a knife through butter."

"But ...nothing?" Godson said, fishing.

"Nope. For one thing I was exhausted but, I don't know, Godson. She was in a bind. She took a big chance even trusting me. I mean, there I was, a total stranger. Besides, we were in a car parked at a truck stop. How am I going to try to make a move in a situation like that?"

"I've never seen you make a move."

Sam looked down, almost embarrassed. "You have a point there. Look, she was a nice girl. I liked her."

Godson laughed, "I'm just yanking yer chain, buddy. I would have probably done the same thing."

"You would have checked the weather before going out across the state."

"Yeah, there's that, too." He laughed that easy laugh of his again. Then he asked, "So, what now?"

"I'm heading back there after Christmas."

"Wait, what? Geez, buddy, are you crazy? Another winter trip? After what you just went through?"

"Well, of course, only *if* the weather allows. You know as well as I do that the weather can swing good or bad on a whim this time of year. But I have that week off and I need that much time. And even Loot said it would be a good week if the weather was okay, because during the holidays people are off their guard. Snakes and insects and predators are less of a problem too."

"Oh, didn't think about that."

"Right. So, I'll just save my money, make my preparations, and if the cards fall just right, I'll go the day after Christmas."

They finished their coffee and Godson mumbled something about an errand, but before he left, Sam stretched an old blanket on the dirt floor of the garage and Godson crawled down to take a look under The Clunker. He got up and grabbed a pair of pliers and a screwdriver from a toolbox in the trunk of his car and then stretched out again and fiddled with the engine some more, first on one side and then on the other. He had Sam move the controls a couple of times.

Finally, he got back up, and said, "The connecting pins were messed up on both of them. I took them apart and put them back on. I wonder if somebody was maybe messing with your car or something when it was parked out there. Driver's side was completely loose, but the passenger side was slipping a little less ...sounds like what you had going on. I think they'll work okay now, but you should get it checked by someone who actually knows what they're doing before you head back out there in cold weather again."

"Okay, Godson, thanks. I appreciate it," Sam said, handing his friend a dampened hand towel he had retrieved from his apartment.

Godson stowed his tools then wiped his hands, inspected them and decided they were clean enough. After shaking hands, he left, waving to Sam as he backed out of the driveway.

Sam retrieved his knapsack and the sack of kitchen sundries from the car and slowly walked back up the ragged stairs. He dropped his pack on the floor before he deposited the sack in the kitchen.

Back in the other room, he sat on one of his big pillows, rooted around in his shirt pocket and pulled out the tattered box

Loretta had given him. He opened it but didn't touch the small cross-shaped rock.

"Fairy stone," he said mindlessly.

As he looked at it, he conjured up mental images of Loretta's own good luck charm and then remembered what she had said about the power of the *brujas*. Images of the old woman's cloudy, penetrating gaze came back to him and his heart began to race. He closed the box and returned it to his knapsack.

Twenty-two

Monday morning, with the long Thanksgiving ordeal over, Sam returned to work. It was their busiest time of year, which meant he had plenty to keep his mind occupied. Sally was busy too and there was no mention of the trip, or of Van Horn, or of gold mines. The days were a blur of paperwork, keypunching, and filing.

At home, he ate simple meals to save money, and each night he pored over his maps and made lists of things he needed to do. Sometimes he just sat and mused for long hours, nursing one beer after another as he speculated about specific details of the upcoming trip.

The following Tuesday his clock radio popped on, as it did every day, and he heard, "...survived by his widow, Yoko Ono...."

Former Beatle John Lennon had been senselessly shot by some lunatic in New York City. Growing up in the sixties and seventies, the Beatles had been a major influence on Sam and

Lennon had always been a sort of personal hero. The crime was sudden and shocking and all thoughts of the trip, of the quest, of the mine, were for a short time diverted. It was all over the news; the radio station played a constant stream of Lennon's music and everywhere he went it was a constant focus of most conversations. It was a distraction for Sam, but he had a mission and he knew that even the death of a personal hero could not disrupt his planning at this stage.

Later that evening the phone rang.

"Hello?"

"Sam? It's Loretta."

"Hey, this is a surprise," he said.

"I'm in town. I wanted to see you but I can't find your place. I'm up at a convenience store on Riverside."

"Yeah, it's a little tricky, why don't I pop over and lead you back? You're really close," he said.

Sam hurried over to the store, which was about a half mile away. Loretta was sitting in her car. She got out when she saw his VW pull into the parking lot and when he got out of his car, she hugged him tightly.

"Sam! It is so good to see you again," she said.

"What are you doing here?" he asked.

"Let's get to your house," she said, "and I'll explain."

"Okay, but let me tell you where we're going. Turn left out of this parking lot, then watch where I turn right. It's just past a bridge, okay?"

"I saw that before," she said. "I got messed up after that."

"Okay, just follow close when we get on that road."

They made the short trip back to Sam's apartment with Loretta following closely and soon the '63 Chevy was parked behind his car at his garage.

"Oh, I see ...you're over off this other road."

"Yeah," he said, "the address is up at the house but I'm back here."

She smiled and said, "I wanted to surprise you."

"Trust me, you did," he chuckled. "So what's going on? Why are you here?"

"Things didn't go well when Michael came back. I know it's completely over now. He was so patronizing and overbearing I just lost it. I was so upset and depressed, I didn't go to work and got fired. Then with all this John Lennon stuff..." She started to cry. "My parents don't understand any of this, the combination of Michael and John Lennon and hell, just my life ...I just had to get away for a while, you know?"

"Yeah, I understand," he said. Loretta leaned into him as she tried to stifle the sobs and Sam hugged her and gently patted her on the back as she cried.

"I just needed some random place where I could go, then I remembered I had your number and address. I like you, Sam, and Austin is a pretty short drive, so here I am."

"So I'm just a random interlude in your crazy life?" he said as he went into the kitchen. "Beer?"

Loretta nodded and Sam returned with two. They sat on his big pillows on the floor.

"Sorry, I guess that didn't come out quite right," she said. Then she changed the subject. "This is primitive," she said. "Bachelor funky. I like it."

"Yeah, well, I don't have that many visitors."

Loretta reached out and touched his arm, "Sam? Can I stay here for a while?"

It had been a long time since he had heard anything along those lines from a woman. "Uh, well, sure, I guess. I'm busy making plans, preparing for that trip, but..."

She interrupted, "Yeah, maybe I can help you with that, you know?"

"The accommodations are a bit sparse, as you can see," he said, waving his arm across the room.

"Sam, I don't mind sharing a bed with you," Loretta said as she took his hand in hers. "I really, really need a place to stay."

Sam's face flushed.

"Oh, you're blushing," she said, giggling.

He smiled. "Of course, you can stay here for a while," he said, adding, "where's your stuff?"

"Down in the trunk. Just a suitcase. It's heavy ...can you help me with it?"

"Sure, I'll just get it for you."

Sam lugged the suitcase up the stairs and as he negotiated the crumbling steps, for some reason he remembered the 'no funny business' protocol of that night in Junction. Loretta met him at the doorway and after he set the suitcase on the floor, she gave him another light hug.

"You're so sweet. Thanks. Hey, it's getting late," Loretta said. "Can I freshen up?"

"Of course. Look, I've got to go to work in the morning. You do what you need to do. I'll go clean up a little in the kitchen while you're doing that."

The sink was a mess of dirty dishes so Sam busied himself with a quick wash of the easiest items, and soon Loretta appeared at the door in an oversized long-sleeved Tee-shirt with Scooby-Doo on the front. "I'm done," she said.

He went in the bathroom to brush his teeth and saw a new toothbrush on the counter. Then he noticed a round package of little pills as well. He usually just slept in his underwear, but he found a pair of gym shorts and slipped those on.

When he emerged, Loretta was already under the covers of the bed. Sam adjusted the heater control on the space heater. "I know it's a little chilly tonight but I don't like to leave this piece of junk on all night. It's either too hot or too cold, not much in between."

"That's okay," she said, "I love keeping warm under the covers." Then she added, "As long as you turn it on again in the morning."

"Yep, I'll do it. I'm used to it."

He turned off the overhead light and slipped into the bed with Loretta and said, "You know, like you said, maybe you can help me with some of my trip preparations."

"I know I can," she said.

Sam stretched out on his back under the covers and Loretta moved closer and put her head on his shoulder. It had been a while since anyone had shared his bed, but as she cuddled next to him, he knew she felt good.

"This is nice," she murmured quietly.

"Mmm-hmm," he answered.

The room was quiet except for their breathing as they lay there for several awkward minutes, then Loretta began to caress his toes with her own bare toes. Sam responded by gently rubbing her shoulder and lightly massaging her neck. As the evening progressed, the question of the 'no funny business' protocol was resolved.

In the morning, Sam took Loretta to a nearby coffee shop for breakfast before he left for work.

"I have no guest supplies," he said, and laughed. "I guess I need to do some shopping. But I didn't want to go to work and just leave you there hungry with almost nothing but random ingredients to eat."

She smiled. "Sam, I want you to know something. You know, I don't just sleep with anybody. I'm not a slut."

"I know that," he said.

"Look, I like you. But please understand I'm not looking for a relationship right now. I'm, well, I guess you'd call it emotionally fractured, you know?"

"I understand. Look, I try never to be presumptuous."

"I knew that. It's one reason I came here. I was impressed that you didn't try to foist yourself on me. I may be only twenty-two but it seems like I've already lived a lifetime of asshole males. You. You're different. I feel like I can trust you. It was natural, a natural thing. Let's keep it that way, okay? Let's just go slow, go with the flow."

"Hey, Loretta, you can stay as long as you need to, no strings attached."

"Oh, don't get me wrong, I loved being with you. I don't know ...I kind of expected that to happen."

"I was taken aback when I saw your pills in the bathroom."

"Subtle, huh?"

Sam laughed. "Well..."

"I just need a place to be for a while where I don't need to worry about anything."

"I get that. I do. You don't want to replace one set of worries with another set of worries."

"Exactly." She smiled and took his hand in hers. "Besides, I know you're already taken."

"Huh?"

"Look, I'm no fool. I know I'll never be able to compete with that damned gold mine of yours. I'd be an idiot to try."

Sam took a deep breath and let it out slowly. "You're probably right," he said, "you're probably right."

After he dropped her back at the apartment and left for work, he considered this new situation. For one thing, he knew she was pretty much on the rebound, and he had a working theory about that: it almost never works. And he knew she had been highly astute in her assessment of him: her arrival was not going to deter him from his mission, and the fact of the matter was that almost nothing could stop him from going to Van Horn.

When he got home, though, he decided that her presence was proving helpful. For one thing, she was helping out by straightening up his place. For another thing, it was nice to discuss things with another person. In the past he had sometimes bounced ideas off Godson and occasionally Moll or Sally, but for the most part, he just worked things out on his own. For supper, she had dipped into his supplies and made them both some tuna sandwiches and as they ate, he shared one of the primary concerns about his trip.

"I worry a lot about my trail food. In the past it has been easy to just make do with convenient junky items on the one- or two-night trips, but I know that this time, my food needs will be more substantial."

"Well," Loretta countered, "I know some hikers. They use freeze-dried stuff."

"Expensive," he said, "but I could probably afford a pack or two. Of course, the main thing with freeze-dried food is heating it."

"Oh, and you can't have a fire out there, can you."

"No," Sam said. "I might as well plug in a blinking neon sign."

Loretta laughed and he marveled at how pretty she was as she laughed. He liked having her around, but in accordance with their coffee shop conversation, he was keeping his feelings in check. And of course, she had been right ...he had bigger things on his mind.

"Another problem with heating the food," he continued, "is that December means colder weather and the colder it is, the more difficult it is to heat things."

"I've seen those little backpack stoves. They use small propane tanks."

"Yeah, that's an obvious solution, and once, I even met up with some hikers who used one and saw how cool it was, but a really good one is pretty expensive and to depend on a cheap one..."

"The same as not having one at all, right?"

"Right," he answered. "And I just don't have the cash to spare right now."

The very next day at work, he was getting something out of one of his desk drawers and spotted the corner of a book poking out from under a pile of envelopes. It had been a gift from an old friend in Houston who had mailed it to him at work. He had thumbed through it that day then got interrupted and put it in the drawer, intending to take it home. He picked it up and read the title:

Roughing It Easy by Dian Thomas.

This sparked his memory and he flicked through the pages until he found what he was looking for: tin can stoves. The author called them buddy burners and explained how to make the little stoves out of two tin cans, usually an old tuna can for the burner and a larger can for the stove. As he read, he remembered that when he first got the book, he had liked the idea and had thought about making one. Then, of course, he had let the notion slip away, replaced by other more immediate concerns, but he was pretty sure he had stashed a couple of cans for that purpose under the kitchen sink. He put the book on the corner of his desk so he wouldn't forget it when he left for the day.

When Sam got home, he marveled at the transformation of his kitchen. Loretta was still busy, standing at the sink washing more dishes.

"Hey, sweetie," she said. "You're a pig, you know that?"

He bent forward and she gave him a quick kiss on the cheek.

"Yeah, I know," he said. "Sorry. The place looks great." Then he spotted the very cans he was getting ready to look for poking from under some trash in the garbage can.

"Whoa," he said, gingerly picking them up. "I need these."

"What, that trash from under the sink? They're starting to rust," Loretta said.

Sam showed her the book and opened it to show her the tin can stoves, "I had forgotten I had this book at work. See? This could be the answer to my heating problem."

Loretta looked at the book and her eyes brightened. "It's so simple," she said. "I'm sorry, I had no idea."

"Hey, Loretta, they *look* like trash ...I picked those up sometime last year to make one of these then got sidetracked and forgot all about it."

Loretta giggled. "You saved them just in time."

Sam fumbled around in his tool box, found his tin snips and while Loretta worked in the kitchen, he proceeded to transform the trash into treasure. First, he cut a flap slightly larger than the tuna can on one side of the big can, then he punched a series of air holes in the top of the big can using a standard church-key style beer opener.

Loretta came in and admired his work. "Hey, that looks just like the one in the book!"

"Thanks," he said as he tested the opening for size by pushing the tuna can into the interior.

"Now I need to make the fuel pods," he said.

He had brought some old cardboard boxes from the limitless supplies of old cardboard in the warehouse at work. Following instructions in the book, he cut part of the perforated cardboard into a long strip to match the depth of the tuna can and tightly rolled one of the strips to make a disk that would fit into the can.

Loretta frowned at him as he rummaged in one of the lower cabinets looking for one of his more beat-up pots.

"Hey, I just cleaned in there," she said.

"Just need one of my junkier pans," he said.

"Good luck with *that*," she laughed.

He had bought some packages of paraffin wax on the way home. He put the wax in the pan and turned the stove on low to melt the wax.

Loretta came over and snuggled with him as he stood watch over the wax.

"Hey," he said, "no funny business while I'm melting wax. We'll burn the house down!"

She laughed and said, "Then what am I supposed to do, Mr. Spoilsport?"

"You could watch the wax or cut some more cardboard strips the same size as the ones in that can."

"I'll cut," she said, grabbing his belt buckle and pulling him to her to give him a kiss, "but I want to get back to this funny business later."

Loretta busied herself with the cardboard while Sam poured enough wax into the can to completely cover the rolled cardboard.

"This is going to be too slow. I need to make several of these but the wax has to harden."

Loretta jumped up and said, "You know, you have more tuna," she said. "And you have noodles and cream of mushroom soup and even a big can of mixed veggies, I'll make a tuna casserole for supper, and that will give you two more cans."

Sam smiled. "Cute *and* resourceful too. I like it."

She smiled as she opened two cans of tuna and drained them, then emptied them into a bowl. She put that in the refrigerator and proceeded to wash and dry the empty cans.

"First things first," she said.

Sam opened the mixed vegetables too, and put the lid aside before putting that can next to the bowl of tuna. He did a quick rinse of that lid.

"I've got an idea about that," he said in response to Loretta's questioning look.

Loretta rolled the cardboard she had cut to fit the new tuna cans, and Sam poured more wax into those cans. The wax in the first can was already hardened, and with some careful tapping on the back of the can, the entire disk popped out and Sam stored it in a small plastic sandwich bag.

"Neat," Loretta said.

They followed this process with a regular production line and together they made a number of the fuel disks, storing each as they were ready in a larger zip lock plastic bag.

Sam used the larger lid from the vegetables to form a damper for the burner can by twisting a piece of coat hanger into a handle and then bending the edges of the lid with pliers, until they were snug around the two open ends of the coat hanger.

"See? Now I'll crimp it tight with the pliers."

"Now that is cool" Loretta said, admiring Sam's handiwork.

"It's in the book," he said. "I hope it works. I guess we could test it with the noodles."

Loretta went to the cabinet and found the package of noodles and Sam retrieved one of the fuel disks.

"Outside, though," he said.

On the back steps, he assembled the stove and lit the fuel disk. It burned like a fat candle and he moistened his finger in his mouth and gingerly touched the top of the big can. He heard a sizzle and pulled his hand away.

"It's getting hot already," he said.

Loretta handed Sam a saucepan full of water and Sam put the pan on the hot burner.

It only took about ten minutes for the water to start simmering. The bubbles from the boil reminded him of something else he needed to take care of.

"This is going to work great," he said. "The next problem I'll have to solve is water."

During their dinner, Loretta said, "So, you said something about water. Is water a problem?"

Sam explained, "It's always a huge problem out in west Texas. You have to carry every drop you need and it's heavy, about eight pounds to the gallon."

"How much do you need?"

"There is no set answer to that. I usually take two gallons on weekend trips and that isn't nearly enough. I drink a lot before I go in and always have some stashed in my car so I can rehydrate when I get back. For this trip? I don't know. That's what I need to figure out.

"The thing some people forget is that water is not just for drinking; it is essential for hygiene as well. With some recreational packing, there are streams or other water sources and those will make do for hygiene, but out there I need to reserve some for cleaning my hands and utensils. Even a moderate bout of diarrhea can dehydrate a person faster than a day in the hot sun."

"Oh, wow," she said, "I never thought of that. What about some of those moistened 'towelettes' in the little packs, like you sometimes get with take-out food?"

"You know, I've never even thought about that. What a great idea."

With that, he got up and found a notepad he was using to help compile lists and added an entry to one of the pages.

"It isn't a one hundred percent solution but it helps. I'll still need more than two gallons, though," he said. "I need to see if I can cache some water out there somewhere. I'll have to ask Loot, that guy out in Van Horn about it."

"Do you think that will work?"

"It will have to," he said. "Of course, that won't help me if it gets down to freezing. A container of ice would be pretty much the same thing as no water because plastic bottles can't be heated."

"What can you do about that?" Loretta asked.

"I could probably partially thaw one in my sleeping bag with me," he said, but he shivered at the thought. "I will just have to hope that for the several days of this trip the weather stays above freezing."

"I just thought," Loretta said, "what about snow?"

"Well, snow can be melted for water, so that is a good thing. At least if there is enough snow and I have enough fuel pods. But that raises another question. Camouflage."

"Camouflage?"

"On my usual spring and fall hikes, all my clothes are drab, earthy colors. They blend into the background pretty well. I figured this will work in the winter as well unless it snows. I actually wondered about that while looking at the sleet and snow right before we met."

"What can you do?"

"Surely, I would abort the trip if ice and snow were in the forecast, but if I was already out there, I'd probably still have to walk out. Hopefully any ranchers would be snug in their houses but you never know with ranchers ... they could be out looking for missing livestock or something. I would stand out like a sore thumb against a snowy backdrop."

Loretta looked scared, "Do you think that might happen?"

"Depends on the weather, Loretta," Sam said, "but probably not. Just keep hoping for milder weather. I don't have room for special winter camouflage anyway."

Loretta reached out and put her hand on Sam's arm, "I just thought of something else. What if bad weather prevents that guy from picking you up?"

"That's another thing I need to ask him. It's a valid concern, but he does drive a Jeep, ancient but it runs." Sam patted

Loretta's hand. "Don't worry. I'm sure I won't even go out there if there is even the slightest chance of ice or snow."

The next day when he came home, he saw that Loretta had busied herself with working to make some sense of his general living area. His apartment was looking less cluttered and was much more organized. It seemed to Sam to be quite a domestic turn for someone who had stated she didn't want a relationship.

"Wow, you've been busy," he said. "You're sure making yourself at home."

"Well, this place *needs* some attention. I can't believe some of the crap you have lying around but I'm just putting it in bags and boxes for you to go through. I put all that stuff in the garage."

"I appreciate it, Loretta, but you don't have to do so much ...really, you don't."

"Hey, I'm bored and I enjoy doing it, and like I said, it *needs* it. Besides, I found something I think you will be interested in."

"What?"

"This cookbook," she said, handing him a book.

"Oh, I remember that," he said. "A Christmas present from a few years ago."

"Open it where I stuck that paper clip," she said.

He opened it and saw a recipe on the facing page and read it out loud.

"Logan bread."

"Right," Loretta said. "I was just taking a break and picked that up, looking at the recipes for something to maybe cook. As I thumbed through it, I saw something about survival bread."

"I see," he said reading. "It was developed as part of a Canadian expedition to climb Mount Logan. Interesting."

"It's full of whole grains and nuts and fruits," Loretta pointed out. "It's designed to be a full nutrition hiking food."

"It doesn't look hard to make either, but it might be a bit expensive," he said. "Still, that isn't a problem if it's part of my food supply."

Loretta handed Sam a note. "I already made a shopping list of the ingredients."

He read out loud, "Whole wheat flour, rye flour, oats, wheat germ, powdered milk, brown sugar, baking powder, salt, oil, honey, molasses, dried cherries, walnuts, dried cranberries, and eggs. I think I have some of those things, but looks like I'll have to go to the natural foods store too."

Sam dropped the paper and hugged Loretta tightly.

"I never would have thought of this," he said. "This is exactly what I need."

"I kinda thought you'd like it," she said. "I guess we better go shopping."

Twenty-three

At work, Sally had seen the signs before and could tell Sam was planning something but she kept quiet. This was a good thing, because Sam was quietly focused on what he needed to do at work, processing the stacks of subscription renewals. She missed the general banter, but knew he was always like this when planning a trip. Her suspicions were aroused when she took a call for him one day.

A female voice on the other end of the phone had said, "Hi. Could I speak to Sam, please?"

"I'm sorry, he's away from his desk. Can I give him a message?"

"Just tell him Loretta called. Nothing important, I'll call back."

Sally knew Sam had been on a long romantic dry spell. She had even chastised him for letting his obsession get in the way of a normal life. Now she wondered if perhaps she had misdiagnosed the reason for his quiet demeanor.

When he came back to his desk, she gave him the message.

"So," she asked, "who is this *Loretta*?"

Sam blushed. "I met her in Junction on that last trip. She showed up last week needing a place to stay."

"Is this serious? I mean, like are you guys a couple?"

Sam blushed again, "Quit. She's just a friend, you know?"

Sally laughed. "Oh, I think I know ... okay, I'll quit. Just nice to think maybe you're doing something more normal for a change."

Sam smirked and returned to his work.

Back at the apartment, Sam found the new domestic angle was starting to constrain his usual patterns. Some nights, when he tried to pore over his maps with a magnifying glass, trying to glean details in the Diablo Rim area, Loretta would get down next to him and look as well, breaking his concentration with questions.

"What's that?"

"Oh, that's a jeep trail. Not a real road but a rough path you need a four-wheel drive to get through."

"So you couldn't drive up there?"

"No, it's private land, remember? I'd be seen. And, anyway, my VW isn't four-wheel drive."

Then she said, "You know, I could probably help you more if I knew what you are looking for. All you told me was that some wino gave you some clues. What clues?"

Sam sighed. "I guess I just told you the short version of the story," he said. "Okay, now this is my secret, right? It doesn't make much sense, but it's all I have to go on."

Loretta nodded sheepishly.

"When he told me about the mine, he said this: 'you have to

follow the devil until you see the table, then turn around and you'll see the why of it.'"

"Wow. A riddle. I love riddles," she said, looking down at the map. "Diablo Rim! That's the devil, right?"

Sam was impressed. "That's pretty good. Yes, that's what I'm hoping. But this 'table' clue is still a mystery. If the riddle is right, I'll probably never understand 'the why of it' until I can make some sense of the table reference."

"Oh, and that's why you are so focused on getting out there to look. To find this table thing," she said.

"Yeah. For me the 'table' clue has always been the key. I've just hoped I would stumble across something that made sense. The old guy in jail said it wouldn't make sense until I found it. Even this Diablo Rim thing is just a hunch, but it does seem to fit. Could be just a coincidence, I guess but, well, when I just stumbled across it on the map, I thought maybe it was what I was looking for. Well, I didn't stumble across it, Sally did."

"Sally?"

"A woman I work with," he said.

"She the one who answered the phone when I called?

"Yeah, I suppose."

"Did you tell her about me?"

"Just that you are here."

Loretta laughed. "Hope I didn't make her jealous."

"I doubt it. She has a boyfriend."

Loretta laughed again, this time harder, "Hah, like *that* matters. You're so naïve. So, I'm not breaking up some office romance or something?"

Sam laughed. "No... although in the past people *thought* we were dating. We weren't."

"Hmm, why would they think that?"

"We go to lunch a lot. Why all these questions. Are *you* jealous?"

Loretta stuck out her lower lip. "A little. Maybe. And I thought I detected a little tone in her voice when I talked to her too. How'd she find it?"

"Same way you did. She wanted to see the map after my last camping trip, the one before the ice storm. I'd never noticed it. She didn't even know about the clue."

"Oh, you never told her that?"

"No. I've tried to keep the details pretty quiet. A secret isn't a secret if you tell everybody."

"Well, you told me," Loretta said and gave Sam a kiss on the cheek. "I like that you trust me, but I wish I'd found it for you first." She stuck out her lip again.

"Don't be jealous of that. If she hadn't spotted it, I never would have made that trip out to Van Horn Thanksgiving weekend."

"We never would have met."

"That's right," Sam said, "Now let's fold up these maps. I've got to go to work in the morning and we haven't even eaten yet."

"That's right. I made us some chicken salad for sandwiches," she said.

While they were munching their late dinner, Loretta asked Sam, "So you're really going to go?"

"That's why I'm preparing stuff and reading maps, Loretta."

"I know that. But it's December! What about the weather?"

"That's one of my biggest worries," he said.

"There any newsstands in Austin?"

"I think there is one downtown," he said.

"I'm going out tomorrow and am going to check it out. This is the state capital, they probably have papers from all over. I wonder if they carry one from El Paso. That would at least have the weather closer to where you need to go, right?"

Sam's eyes fluttered, surprised and impressed at her ingenuity. "I never thought ...geez, that's a great idea!"

"I'm not letting you go if there is even a hint of ice or snow," she said.

"Well, that's the thing. I wouldn't go."

"I wish I knew more about the other dangers you face. Trespassing is bad enough, but you're out with wild animals and such."

"I know. I keep on my toes."

"You ever see anything out there, something dangerous?"

"You mean like a big cat? A mountain lion?"

"They have *those* out there?"

"Of course," he said, "but I've never seen one. I thought something big was stalking me once on a night hike but I just hunkered down and waited it out."

"I know you explained to me why you don't carry a gun, but I think it's stupid."

"I think it's stupider to carry one, at least the way I hike. A rancher would probably shoot me if he saw me with a gun. They're the most dangerous predator I face, really, but in the spring and fall, I worry more about rattlesnakes. They shouldn't be a problem in December unless it is a really warm day."

"You've seen them?"

"A couple of times, but it's the ones you hear but don't see that are worrisome."

"Oh, the rattles. You've had them rattling at you? That's scary."

"I always pack a snake kit but the best defense is just to be wary of them. I've heard rattling three different times. That means they're sizing you up, you know."

"What does that mean?"

"They are pit vipers. The 'pits' under their eyes are heat sensors that can sense mass as well as distance. They should realize that we are too big to eat so they hesitate and go into defensive mode."

"But they're still dangerous."

"Oh yes, but they know we aren't food, so they get defensive. The best bet is to just back away the same way you came. That's what I did, until the rattling stopped. I only saw one of the snakes slithering away in the opposite direction. Then I kind of adjusted my course away from where I thought they might be. That one snake was huge, though."

"I've seen some pretty big ones on the highway but they were dead."

"This was the biggest snake I'd ever seen, alive or dead. Just caught a glimpse of it slithering away before it disappeared."

"Wow. I still worry about the weather. What if it changes while you are out there?"

"I could probably deal with a little rain or some minor ice, but it is a worry. Storms in the area can be severe and I'm aware of the danger of flash floods and lightning. I just know the basic rules of both: avoid places that might flood and try to find some safe cover, like stay away from trees. Can't do much more about lightning. My safest bet is to just abort if the weather changes and get back to my car. I need to talk with that guy out there about contingencies if the weather changes."

"You think they are worried that much about trespassing?"

"Yes. Listen, some people see the wide open spaces and think it's the Wild West and they can just go anywhere. I know some people here in Austin who went camping in Big Bend National Park. They drove all day from Austin and arrived at the park right at sundown. They paid their fee and drove into the park. In the failing light, they spied some inviting hills about a mile off the road, so they just pulled over in their four-wheel drive and headed that way. They found themselves what looked like a nice spot and parked. They set up their tent and built a roaring fire to enjoy while they camped out under the stars. Their joy was short-lived because they soon found themselves surrounded by park rangers. Hefty fines and a lifetime ban from the park was a hard lesson learned. They had somehow missed the sign that says, "Camp in designated areas only," when they checked in at the gate."

"Seriously? But this isn't a national park."

"No, but still, that's why I sneak in and stay quiet, and try to live on crap food like crackers and potted meat. The days and the nights are long and lonely and the ground is hard and the bug bites itch. This will be the longest trip I've attempted and I have to be extra careful."

"I guess you are careful—you've never been caught."

"I had one really close call about a year ago."

"Really?"

"Yeah. I was hiking up a hill and was trying to find a gully I wanted to investigate. I had just crossed a jeep trail that wrapped around the hill. It was about noon and the weather was good. A jeep suddenly lurched around the hill from behind me, making quite a racket as it careened around the curve. It caught me off guard. The two men in it were driving pretty fast, considering the rugged conditions."

Loretta was wide-eyed. "Wow."

"I was really lucky that time because I had just decided to take a short break and had stooped down to rest in the shade of a mesquite tree that was surrounded by prickly pear cactus and boulders. Luckily, I had already put my pack next to the tree, so it had some cover. I immediately dropped to the ground and spread out in a small space that was thankfully just big enough between the cactus patch and the tree. I could only hope I had enough cover. I held my breath as the jeep drove past. At the closest point, it was only about forty feet away from me, but they seemed intent on making progress toward some specific destination and the passenger was desperately holding onto his cowboy hat as the driver gunned the engine and sped on."

"Did you get out of there after that?"

"No, I couldn't remember this particular jeep trail from studying my maps. I didn't know if it looped around or what, and I didn't want to open my map to check because it was too reflective and would have been a hassle if it was unfolded and they suddenly returned. I know jeep trails sometimes intersect and sometimes end in a loop, so I had no idea what to expect."

"What did you do?" Loretta seemed transfixed.

"I quickly got up and found a better hiding place a little further away from the road and waited. The jeep never returned and after about an hour, I relaxed and eased out of my hiding place to continue that weekend's quest."

"Sam, I really don't like this. It's too dangerous."

"I've been out there seven times. That was the closest call I've had."

"If someone did find you, what would happen to you?"

"Most of the time I figure I'm looking at a trespassing charge and a lot of hassle. Trips out west for court and that sort of thing. Probably fines and probation."

~ * ~

The next evening after work, he returned to his garage-apartment filled with a hearty aroma of sweet baked goodness.

"Hey," Loretta said, "I baked your Logan bread."

"Really? How was it?"

"Not bad. A bit hard to mix, just because it makes so much, and you don't have a pan big enough so I had to bake it in several batches."

"Aw, you should have waited for me."

"I didn't have anything to do and I got tired of cleaning this pigsty. It was fun."

"Did you taste it?"

Loretta shook her head. "It's supposed to cool. I have one batch I've cut and it might be cool enough to taste."

In the kitchen, Sam saw the squares of cut bread in a huge stack, with some pieces already wrapped in plastic wrap.

"Wow, Loretta, that is a lot of work. Thank you. You do too much for me."

"Aw, come on, I like helping you."

She picked up one of the squares, broke it in two, offered him one of the pieces and he nibbled a corner of it and was pleasantly surprised.

"Hey, it's a bit dense but it is sweet and chewy. I like it."

"I made it just like the recipe said," she replied, looking down as if she might have done something wrong.

Sam grabbed her hand. "No, I didn't mean dense as a criticism. It's survival bread. It's supposed to be dense. It's good. It's really good." He gobbled down the rest of his piece.

He reached out to give her a hug but she pulled back while she nibbled her piece.

"You're right, it's good. A bit like fruitcake but without the spices."

"You done good, kiddo," he said as he put his arm around her. She kissed him on the cheek.

"I'm glad you like it. It was a lot of work."

"And it's a big help," he said. "It really is. I think this is going to be my main food out there. Now, let's go out to eat to celebrate."

"Sure, let me go get cleaned up," she said and she went into the bathroom.

She didn't seem as upbeat as she usually was, and he realized she had seemed a bit reserved since that conversation the previous night. They had never mentioned relationships, or love, or the future at all since that first night and it was easy to just go with the flow, as Loretta had said back then, but now Sam wondered if she was starting to change her mind about a relationship.

She *had* seemed quite worried when she questioned him about danger. At this point, he realized he wouldn't mind moving into a relationship at all. She was pretty, funny, smart, and a passionate lover. But he also knew it wasn't a good time for him, because he was so intent on making this trip, and after this trip there would be the next trip and then the one after that. Sam did know he liked her a lot and loved coming home to her smiling face every night, and the little things she did, like finding and making the Logan Bread, certainly enhanced his trip preparations in ways he had never even imagined. He figured that once he got this trip behind him, they might be able to clarify this non-relationship relationship they seemed to be forging.

Twenty-four

December seemed to pass like a blur ...job duties, trip preparations and the non-relationship relationship with Loretta completely filled his life, but with Christmas looming, Sam realized he had done no Christmas shopping.

Loretta had continued to remain a bit distant and Sam thought that perhaps a bit of Christmas spirit might help.

"Hey, I was thinking about going to do a little Christmas shopping," he said one night.

"Really?" She seemed to brighten up at the suggestion.

"Yeah, they have a pretty cool bazaar over at The Armadillo. It's not far, why don't we go over there?"

"I don't have much money for shopping this year," she said, "but it doesn't hurt to look."

"I know. Even with this trip looming, I've managed to budget in a little shopping money."

Something about this last statement hit a nerve and her mood seemed to drop a bit again.

"Come on, Loretta, it will be fun."

"I thought The Armadillo was a music place."

"It is, but they open it up for vendors and crafts people every year. They call it The Twelve Days of Armadillo Christmas."

"Weird. I always wanted to go there."

"Here's your chance. It's closing, you know."

"What?"

"Yes, developers have bought the land and are tearing it down. For me it's a last chance to see the place. New Year's Eve is the last night."

On the way to the venue, they continued chatting about Christmas.

"Thanks, Sam. I need a bit of normalcy. I know I've been a little standoffish. I'm sorry," she said.

"It's okay. I understand," he said. "Do you want to talk about it?"

"Yes and no. Part of it is like what we're doing right now, doing something about Christmas. I love Christmas and I know it's coming. I mean, you're going to see your family, right?"

"Well, I skipped Thanksgiving. I pretty much feel I have to go."

"Right. I'm kind of in the same boat. But I left so suddenly, it's awkward. I mean, you don't live with your folks. I was living there, then I just sort of bolted. With Christmas coming, I don't know, I'm a bit worried about what I'm going to do. Then you have this big trip planned and, well, after that talk about the dangers of it, I don't know..."

"Don't know what?"

"I'm just worried about you going out there, especially now, in December. I have ... well, I guess you'd call it a premonition. I don't like it. It's why I've pulled back a bit from you. I mean..."

"I've noticed. I've just been giving you your space."

"I know. You're sweet. And I know I'm intruding, but I can't bear the thought of you going out there. I know something is going to happen to you and I can't get over that."

They pulled into the parking lot. Sam grabbed Loretta's hand and kissed the back of it.

"Look, we're here. Let's go check the bazaar out. We'll talk some more about this later, okay?"

She nodded and they went in.

Sam explained as they went in, "This has been a tradition for several years. Where all these booths are set up—that's where the floor seats usually are. I've found a lot of good things here. There is big stuff, but a lot of cool small stuff too."

Loretta smiled at the lights and decorations. There were a lot of people there and there was live acoustic music playing in the background.

"It's smaller than I imagined," she said. "But not *too* small. It must be cool to see music here."

"Yeah, it's big enough to attract good bands, but small enough to still be intimate. Plus, they have food and there's a beer garden out back. I used to love sitting under this huge overflowing wisteria they have … a beer out there on a hot Texas summer afternoon seems to make the heat almost tolerable."

"It's a shame," she said as she grabbed his hand and reached up and kissed him on the cheek. "Thanks for bringing me. I like this. Let's look around."

Most of the vendors seemed to be remnant denizens of the late sixties and the aroma of patchouli was quite evident as he walked around. Everywhere they went, they could hear snatches of conversation about the impending last days of the place. Sam looked around and fondly remembered some of the concerts he had seen there.

"It is sad to think of this place closing," he finally said.

"Aw, you probably don't remember half of what you did here," she said, laughing.

"Yeah, you may be right."

They both managed to find some good bargains. Sam picked up a random assortment of smaller things he found attractive. He even bought Loretta a small bracelet, paying more than he could really afford, but she had obviously admired it and he took the hint. When they were several booths down, he excused himself for a restroom break and went around and bought the bracelet without her seeing him.

She bought a few small items too.

"This is neat," she said. "Some of the stuff here is so expensive, but you were right, there is a lot of cool, small stuff. I mean really unique things. Good gifts. I don't have many people to buy for. Do you?"

"Several," he said. "I don't ever buy big things. I just get a smattering of things that I think are nice, then divvy them up."

Loretta laughed at that. "Really?"

"Well, for me, a Christmas present doesn't have to outshine any previous present, or be the best and most glorious thing anyone ever got. I've always seen Christmas gifts as tokens. I think there are two aspects to Christmas—the most important thing is children, because there is that whole Santa thing and all—it is hard to beat that magic."

"Oh, I love that," she said.

"The other aspect for me is a basic appreciation of family and friends. I mean, I never have much money to spend on the holiday, even when I'm not saving for a trip out west, but to me it isn't about spending myself to the brink of poverty. I mean, that's not the point of Christmas."

"Oh, I agree, Sam. I have friends who spend way more than they have, always trying to impress people. I've never been like that."

He smiled. "Me either. I just like to make simple expressions of gratitude, love, and respect. To me, it really *is* the thought that counts."

Even as he said this, inwardly he was remembering that he really did need to cut as many corners as he could to save his money for the Diablo Rim trip. That was a reality he could not rationalize away, and deep inside he knew it.

After they had walked through all of the many aisles, Loretta said, "Thanks for bringing me here, Sam. I've had a good time."

"I don't know what I'll do for shopping next year."

"You idiot, let's go. This is so cool, I'm sure they'll figure out a way to keep this going."

"I hope you're right."

After they exited with their bags of goodies, he turned around one more time. "It will be hard to imagine this being gone. Too bad I'll be far away for the last show."

"You could always suffer a sudden bout of good sense and stay."

He leaned over and kissed her cheek. "Come on," he said.

In the car, Loretta said, "I was watching you shop. You have a very clinical approach to shopping, sort of the same way I've seen you work on your trip."

"Huh? What do you mean?"

"Let me put it this way. Did you buy anything specific for any one person?"

"Well, sure, but not totally."

"Everything I saw you buy was fairly generic. I bought a few things but they were all for specific people. You just bought..."

"A bunch of crap?"

"Exactly."

"I guess you're right. I buy a random assortment of gifts and then just sort of make arbitrary assignments when I wrap them. I was planning on wrapping them tonight, just to get it done and out of the way."

"Right. That's exactly how you prepare for your trip."

Sam had never thought of that before but he realized that Loretta had made a very astute observation. It was just another problem facing him and he had figured out a simple and efficient way to solve it.

"I guess you're right," he said as he parked his car at the apartment. "That's not a bad thing, is it?"

"No. It's just *you!*" She laughed as she got out of the car and Sam hoped she was maybe coming out of her funk.

He wondered about the bracelet, whether he should give it to her right away or wait; waiting seemed a normal Christmas thing to do, but then he worried that if he waited, he might not have a chance to give it to her at all. Perhaps he was having a flash of a premonition himself.

Upstairs, she was visibly shocked when he pulled several rolls of wrapping paper from the closet.

"When did you buy that?"

"Last year at seventy-five percent off."

"I'm impressed, Sam."

"I never spend too much trouble wrapping presents. One year I even used the comics from the Sunday paper."

"I can see you doing that. I really can." She laughed.

She laughed more as he made gift assignments on the fly, filling in the labels at random as he completed wrapping presents. He sneakily wrapped the bracelet when she was busy on one of her own presents. She noticed when he placed several unlabeled items including the bracelet in a separate plastic bag.

"Who are those for?"

"Spares. I always forget somebody," he said.

"Damn, Sam. Have I told you how crazy you are?"

"Yes, you reminded me earlier."

"Well, I have to say this was a good plan, though. You might be crazy but, well..."

"What?"

"I can't believe I have these presents wrapped already," she said, pointing at her own bag. "Usually, I'd be up late Christmas Eve wrapping these. It is a relief to have it done."

"Right, I'm the one who's crazy..."

As they got ready for bed, he thought about the bracelet. After brushing his teeth, he rummaged around in his bag of unmarked presents before joining her in the bed.

"Here, Loretta," he said. "I don't know what we're doing on Christmas, or if we'll be together for the big day. It's all a mess, I know, and I'm sorry. But I want to be sure I give you this."

She blinked at the small wrapped present. Tears formed in her eyes.

"Sam, you ...I'm sorry, when ...how..." she reached out and pulled him onto the bed and kissed him. "You..."

"Open it."

She carefully started to slit the tape on the bottom with a fingernail.

"You don't have to be careful ...wrapping paper is basically trash even before you buy it."

"You nut," she said as she finished tearing the paper to reveal a small box. She opened it and tears ran down her face as she realized it was the bracelet she had been admiring at the Armadillo.

"How did you know I liked this?"

"I saw you trying it on. You looked at it and tried it on twice."

"I didn't think you noticed. Hey! You lied! You said you needed to go to the bathroom."

Sam smiled. "Well, in the interest of full disclosure, I have to say I did indeed go to the bathroom. *Then* I dropped back by that booth and got this."

She dropped the box, pulled him to her and kissed him passionately, then told him to go turn off the overhead light and come back to bed.

"Come on, you..." she said. She had slipped her Scooby Doo Tee-shirt off by the time he returned.

The next day, over morning coffee, she told him, "I have to admit, Sam, you are a mixed bag of sweet and crazy. I mean, we go shopping for Christmas and you are nuts the way you do it. Almost clinical. Then you sweetly sneak *this* in." She held up the bracelet on her wrist.

Sam looked down sheepishly.

"And look at this place. Not one decoration. Not one! Camping equipment, that's your Christmas decoration. Crazy, right?"

"I haven't done that for years," he said.

"Really?"

"Just never much been into the whole Christmas lights and tree and all that. The last time I had one was when I first moved here and was sharing a place with an old college friend. I bought the tree and I don't know where he got the decorations, but he decorated it."

"It's so strange. I know you have *some* Christmas spirit."

Sam just shrugged, "A little, I guess."

On the way to work, Sam thought a lot about that conversation. Even when he had lived with Godson, it seemed like he had one overbearing purpose in his life, deciphering Slim's clues and finding that damned mine. Even if he didn't have the slightest notion of how to find it, he knew it was there. It was not wrapped in pretty paper or colorful lights and it didn't hug him or give him presents, but it was the one thing he thought about most of the time. He didn't know how he could reconcile those feelings with having Loretta in his life. She was mixing things up for him and he couldn't decide if he liked it or if it was an obstacle, but he smiled when he remembered walking arm-in-arm with her at the Armadillo.

Back at work, as things were winding down for the end of the year, Sam kept a low profile. He was quite aware that the annual Christmas party was coming up in a few days, on the twenty-third. His drunken behavior at the party a few years before was still an embarrassment, but he probably didn't need to feel that way because it was no doubt a bigger event for him than it was for most of the other people in the office, except the warehouse crew, but even Manny rarely mentioned it anymore.

His plan for this party was to eat, socialize a minimal amount, and then get away from work as soon as possible. Leaving early would allow him plenty of time to double-check his equipment and supplies and pack his car. He was planning on heading to Houston early on the twenty-fourth. He hadn't talked to Loretta about the actual holiday, but assumed she would probably do the same so she could be with her family. Beyond that, if the weather out west looked acceptable, he would get up early on the twenty-sixth and drive straight through to Van Horn. He was vigilant about watching the weather but so far it had been mild and stable throughout the state. He made another note to stop by the newsstand Loretta had found to get an *El Paso Times* on his way out of town.

Driving home he thought about Loretta. He hadn't asked her about the holidays, but it was a question that would need to be resolved. In fact, he'd be gone for over a week after that. He knew he didn't have any problem with her staying there, but he knew it was wrong to assume anything. He smiled when he thought about her. He had liked her easy way when they had first met and shared her car for that fitful night's sleep in Junction. It had been a surprise when she later showed up. Their intimacy had been relaxed and non-committal, but in the short time she had been there she had made a lasting impression. His place had never looked so good and she had made an enormous impact on his trip preparations, helping him with major details like the Logan bread and the tin can stove. He realized he didn't like the loneliness of his life and he liked having her with him, helping him, loving him. As he made the turn toward the park, he realized he was falling for her.

When he got to the apartment, he immediately saw that Loretta's car was gone. She had been squeezing it into the tiny garage, but the garage sat empty. Inside the empty apartment he could see she had straightened up the last part of his shelf, what he called his archives. There was a stack of papers and a tattered Bible on his bed and he saw two notes next to the phone.

One simply said "Godson called."

The other was more substantial.

Sam,

I cannot begin to tell you how grateful I am that you took me in. You've been patient and loving and I've enjoyed helping you. I really have.

I found a Bible with some papers in it while I was tidying the shelf. I'm nosy. I admit it. I read the letters and they must have belonged to the guy from jail. At first, I was just curious, you know? But I have to wonder, have you read the letters recently? The first two are just the feelings of someone concerned for her alcoholic father, but do you remember what the last letter said? Probably not or you would have known. Or you knew and never said a thing.

The last letter mentions a serious accident involving the woman's daughter. She pled with her father to come home and clean up, telling him that life was too short to live it away from family. Then it dawned on me—well, I should have recognized the handwriting, but the paper was wrinkled and faded. That was my mother writing about me, and that old man you only called Slim, was my grandfather, Ted Longo.

I called my mother and she verified. She told me to come home. I still didn't want to. I mean, I was planning on going at Christmas anyway, but I cried and hung up on her.

I never knew my grandfather, and although my mother never directly said bad things about him to me, she never much said good things either, I mean, if she talked about him at all. Mostly what I heard was her crying about him sometimes late at night talking to my father. She would say *it* was what had ruined his life, just like *it* had ruined his father's life and his grandfather's. I always assumed she was talking about alcohol. I called my mother back and she said the same thing. "Don't let *it* ruin your life, Loretta," and then I realized she wasn't ever just talking about alcohol.

Sam, I'm afraid I've been falling for you and that's another part of the problem. I never knew my grandfather, but you, even though it was brief, you had an intimacy with him that I can only imagine. I don't know. It's weird now when I think about the tender moments we shared ...now it seems like it was all wrong, like it was incest or something. Like I said, weird.

Sam, I'm going home. Not just for Christmas but forever. I love you, Sam, but I can't be with you anymore. Sam, this thing is CURSED and I know in my heart you'll never let it go, not for me, not for anything. Good-bye, Sam.

Love,
Loretta

Sam stood staring at the letter for a few minutes, then glanced over at the letters on the bed. He picked up the one on top and confirmed what Loretta had said about it. He could see it now. He had barely glanced at the letters those many years ago. They were personal and he had just scanned for anything that might give him a clue of how to find the family. Slim hadn't saved the envelopes, only the letters, and Sam had decided that finding them was hopeless. He folded Loretta's note in half and placed it and the other letters inside the Bible and sat on the bed, his eyes brimming with tears.

Twenty-five

Several hours later, the phone rang. It was Godson and Sam remembered the note.

"Sorry, I meant to call but I've been..."

"Forget about that. I about dropped my jaw when a woman answered. Loretta? You've been holding out on me, boy."

"Oh, she was the woman from, well, from the truck stop. You know, the ice storm."

"Way to go, Sam!"

"Knock it off, man, she's gone."

Godson could tell from Sam's tone that he was upset.

"Hey, buddy, what happened?"

"She was just cooling her heels here for a few days ... we weren't serious or anything," Sam lied, "but with Christmas coming, she decided to head back home. I doubt she'll be back. It was just an interlude, I guess." He took a deep breath, then added, "I'm trying to get done with work so I can get out of here Wednesday."

"So, even after last time, you are hell bent on trying this stunt during the winter?"

"Yeah. Godson, I *have* to try it while I have a bunch of days off," he said. "I've been checking the weather religiously. I have even been buying copies of the El Paso paper to get a more local report. It's looking good. Oh, and I had a mechanic double check my heater controls and he said you did a good job on it. The car gets toasty warm again, so I don't have to worry about that."

"The heater isn't the point, Sam. It's you," Godson said. "Look, Moll and I are thinking about going down to the coast for a few days after Christmas. Why don't you come along with us? You always liked the beach in the winter."

It was true. When he lived in Houston, he would often drive to the beach and watch the sun rise in the dark, cold days of winter. It was deserted and quiet, with just the sounds of the wind and the waves and the gulls. Without the hustle and bustle of the crowds of people, it gave him a chance to reflect on his life. It was a tempting notion, but he had already made his plans.

"We'll see," Sam said, "but if the weather holds, I don't see it happening."

"Well, then, what about Tuesday night, the twenty-third? Are you doing anything?" Godson asked.

"The twenty-third?"

"Yeah, you know, that's our special holiday. Trotsky's? The fire? Christmas Eve-Eve? Right? We usually do something. Only time we missed was that time you got blotto at that office Christmas party."

"Don't remind me about that ...I still feel bad about standing you guys up."

"All in the past, buddy, so what about this year? It really is a special day."

"Yeah, I've been so busy with preparations I haven't even thought about the anniversary. Having Loretta around didn't help either." Sam looked around the room at his pack and the pile of gear and sighed.

"I'll bet," Godson laughed, "I can't believe you forgot. I'm worried about you," Godson said. "Look, just come on over here that night ...you know we always just do something simple, so it's no big deal. You need to break out of this stupid trip mode and do some normal holiday shit or you'll go crazy. It's *our* thing, you know, the three of us."

Sam couldn't think of an excuse that would work. "Okay, sure, I'll come over. Thanks. It had just slipped my mind this year. You're right, we've got to do it ...we almost died together. It will be just like the old days, just the three of us."

"Damn right. Oh, man, it *was* close, wasn't it?" They both laughed. "Don't forget. It will be just what it's supposed to be, a night with friends on Christmas Eve-Eve."

Sam smiled. "Okay, I'll see you on the twenty-third."

After he hung up, he looked at all of his gear again.

"That messes up my plans," he said to himself, "First Loretta, now this, but I guess I can work it in. Maybe Godson is right—it will be a relief to do something normal."

Sam sighed one more time and went back to work on his gear and supplies with renewed energy because he *had* to complete his preparations in time to accommodate the new deadline.

~ * ~

Sam arrived at work a few minutes late on the twenty-third, but he was in a good mood because he expected an easy day. After doing a little more work,-all he had to do was get through the office party in one piece.

Sally greeted him as he came into their shared office. "Merry Christmas!"

"Merry Christmas," he said, handing her a small wrapped package, part of the booty he had acquired at the Armadillo.

"You didn't come through the warehouse?" Sally seemed just a bit tipsy.

"Nope, I came in through the front door," he said.

"They are forcing eggnog down everybody. Stronger than usual this year, I think."

"So I figured," he laughed.

"Seriously," Sally said. "Maybe you should steer clear."

The mood was festive throughout the office because everyone was ready to kick off for the holiday break. He had signed up to bring a dessert to the luncheon potluck and to that end he had bought a couple of pies at the grocery store. He felt a bit guilty, thinking he should have baked something, but he knew he wasn't the only person to bring store-bought food.

He visited the warehouse to check on one of his orders and of course he accepted a cup from Manny and nursed the eggnog while Manny recounted the Christmas party incident. Sam smiled and endured the jokes with a laugh. After he checked on his order, he went back upstairs to return to his desk, but first stopped in the restroom to dump out the eggnog.

At some point during the morning, he decided to sneak a long-distance call on the office phone. Following Loot's advice, he called information and got the number of Ranch Feed and Supply in Van Horn. The weather forecast seemed to be holding with mild weather, so he wanted to send Loot a message via the mentioned friend, Gillet Osmond.

"Ranch Feed & Supply, Merry Christmas."

"Gillet Osmond, please."

"Speaking, can I help you?"

"A guy named Meldings gave me your name," he started.

"Loot? Yeah, I've known Loot for years."

"He said you might be able to get him a message."

"Sure. I was going to drop off some fruitcake my missus made for Christmas. I'll see him then."

"He was going to do some work for me next week. Just tell him Sam called and said the plans are still good. No change."

"Okay. I'll be sure he gets the message. He'll be a good worker for you."

"I know. I just hope the weather is good."

"Oh, they say we'll have a really mild spell all the way until at least New Year's."

Sam smiled. That was good news.

"That should work out for us then. Thanks, Mr. Osmond. Merry Christmas."

"Merry Christmas to you, Sam," he said.

With that chore complete, he turned toward the pile of papers on his desk and finished what work he could. At noon, the entire office shut down. The party had grown too big for the conference room, so it had been moved to the warehouse where there was more space. After Sam had left that morning, Manny and his crew had moved the big shipping tables into the warehouse proper, the shipping room had been swept and large tables had been set up to accommodate the food and diners.

Although the food all looked wonderful, he ate sparingly and spent most of his time politely socializing. As usual there was a lot of alcohol, but he did not drink because he wanted to keep his mind focused on what was to come. After about an hour of nibbling and chatting, he was ready to make an early escape.

Sally spotted him as he was moving toward the door and realized what he was doing.

"Sam! You leaving already?" She was obviously feeling the effects of the party.

"Yeah, I need to go. I've still got things I need to fix up before I head west."

"Let me walk you out to your car," she said, "I need to clear my head a little anyway."

"Sure," he said, and they headed out the back door to the loading dock. It was a little chilly. He asked her, "How much have you had to drink? You going to be okay to drive?"

"Whew, I hope so," she started, "but I think I'm okay. This cool air helps. I'll eat a little more and hang out for a while before I leave. Maybe drink a couple of Cokes or some coffee. At least I think there's some coffee. So, are you heading out to west Texas right now?"

"Not right now," he said. "Gonna hit Houston and the folks first. I'll leave from there the day after Christmas."

"Oh, right, I remember now. What about the weather?"

"The long-range forecast looks good so far. I was even just talking to a guy out there who said the same thing."

"That's great. You be sure to keep an eye on that," she said.

"Yeah, I'll be watching it pretty closely."

"What about that woman who called? What was her name? Loretta?"

"She's gone back to San Antonio. She..." Sam didn't want to tell the real story, "... never planned to stay long. She went back home—I mean to her folks' house."

"Oh. That's too bad. Are you still sure about this trip?" Sally asked.

"I know it sounds crazy, but it is something I just *have* to do, Sally," he said.

"I know, I know," she said, her voice trailing off.

"You realize, of course, this is basically your fault." He chuckled, adding, "...and the last trip too."

"My fault?" She blinked innocently.

"Yeah, you are the one who found Diablo Rim on the map. Like I told you then, I'm pretty sure it is one of the clues I've been looking for all this time. That's why I can't wait to get out there to check it out."

"I just thought it was a cool name."

"I know," he said, "and that's true, it *is* a cool name. It is also a pain to get to, farther from the road, so it will take longer ...that's why I'm going over Christmas when I have a bunch of time off. I need that time."

They found themselves standing next to The Clunker.

"Well, Merry Christmas," Sally said, "thanks for the gift. Sorry I didn't get you anything."

"You already gave me a gift, remember? Diablo Rim," he said.

Sally smiled and hugged him tight and said, "BE CAREFUL!"

He smiled. "Always am. Thanks for everything, Sally. Really. I mean it. I know you probably think this is all pretty stupid, but you've never said it out loud and I really do appreciate all the support you've given me."

He got in his car and as he drove off, he saw Sally in his rear-view mirror, waving at him. He returned the wave and headed home, hoping she would drink some coffee and sober up a little before she tried to drive. The chilly air seemed to have a good effect on her, so he thought she'd probably be okay.

Once at his house, he ran down his last checklist. His pack was ready to go. He had even managed a few special touches. Loretta had suggested he could slip some small items into the aluminum tubes of the pack frame and showed him a tiny toy compass she bought at the bazaar that was small enough to fit inside one of the aluminum tubes of the frame. Toy or not, he had checked it against his bigger compass and it seemed to work. To stow it, they had pulled off one of the end caps and slid it inside. Taking her suggestion further, he had found a small pen knife that just barely fit in there too. A few days later, he did the same thing in the opposite tube with slim penlight he had found.

These items added minimal weight but gave him some options in case of an emergency.

She had not been with him for a very long time, but he'd be reminded of her every time those tiny items rattled inside the tubes. Heck, she had found and made the Logan bread and had found a place to stow it as well.

She had brushed out his pack one day and noticed an extra space between the upper and lower compartments. It was about an inch deep with a Velcro panel on top. Sam assumed it was for stashing dirty clothes or trash or something like that, to keep them away from everything else. At least that was what he used it for. But when Loretta found it, she had an idea. The individually wrapped squares of Logan bread fit in there like a jigsaw puzzle.

"See?" she had said. "It's like it was made to hold the Logan bread."

"What's this?" he said, pointing to one item that seemed out of place.

She had pulled it out. "Your good luck charm," she said. "What did you call it, a talisman? I noticed that I could just squeeze it in there."

It seemed to be a perfect fit, nestled in one corner with the squares of bread. When she reclosed the compartment, he tested it by pressing on it with the palm of his hand. It was snug and tight and like she said, it gave the impression that top compartment of his pack had a hard floor.

He smiled as he remembered her ingenuity.

Sam lifted the pack. It was heavier than he was used to, but he thought it would still be manageable and it would get lighter every day. Early attempts at backpacking had taught him that it should as light as possible, but this time he needed to carry more water and more food. To keep the heavier weight closer to his center of gravity, the bottom compartment had mostly water in collapsible plastic containers and spare clothes. Overall, he was carrying only three and a half gallons plus a quart canteen on his belt. He knew it was a minimal amount, really, but he still hoped he would be able to set up a water cache when Loot dropped him off.

The Logan bread was going to be a big part of his food supply, but he had also splurged on some freeze-dried foods in packets. He filled out his food list with some of his other staples like potted meat and peanut butter crackers. He had made a number of fuel pods for his tin can stove and he had a good supply of waterproof matches. He had also stuffed several of those into another tube of his pack frame.

Although the weather reports were calling for moderate temperatures during the day, Sam knew it would be chilly at night, so he was taking his good sleeping bag for warmth. As usual, he wasn't taking a tent because it would be too visible and added too much weight. He had a good, oversized plastic poncho, big enough to cover both his upper body and his pack, and he hoped it would give him at least some protection if it did happen to rain.

Sam had promised Godson he would come over for dinner that night and by the time he had finished doing his final prep work, it was time to leave. Prior to leaving, he picked up the phone and called Godson and Moll.

"Hello?" It was Moll.

"Hey, Moll."

"Oh, Sam! Happy Christmas Eve-Eve!"

He laughed and said, "...and a Happy Christmas Eve-Eve to you, too!"

"You aren't calling to cancel or anything, are you?" she said, a slight concern in her voice.

"Oh, no," he said, "I just wanted to know if I should bring anything."

"No," she said, "just you. We just wanted to share the anniversary with you. I didn't make anything particularly special, just lasagna. I hope that's okay."

"Sounds really good," he said. "I'm on my way. See you in a bit."

"Okay. Drive careful. I imagine there were a lot of Christmas parties today, so there are probably a lot of drunks out on the road. Bye."

"Bye," he said.

He paused before he headed out the door.

"I'm an idiot ...I do need to bring something," he said to himself.

He realized he had forgotten to earmark presents for Godson and Moll so he went over to his bag of gifts and fished around trying to find a couple of his spare presents. He had no idea what he was grabbing, but all of his gifts had been generic, so hoped they would be fitting gifts for the occasion. It was the best he could do under the circumstances; he didn't have time to do anything else.

When he arrived at the house, Godson opened the door just as he reached up to knock.

"Hah! Saw you coming. Merry Christmas!" he said.

"Merry Christmas," Sam said, adding, "and happy Christmas Eve-Eve."

"Yeah, that too. You want a beer?"

Sam winced because he really wanted one but he knew he needed to be good.

"Naw, I think I'll pass. I've got some long drives the next couple of days, so, maybe just some tea?"

"Oh, a teetotaler, huh? Okay, tea it is."

They walked into the kitchen and Godson said, "Moll, the boy is drinking tea."

She blinked at him. "Tea? This sounds serious."

Godson added, "This is a far cry from the original Christmas Eve-Eve."

Sam laughed as he said, "We were pretty wasted, weren't we ...then that fire?"

"Well, it *was* one for the history books," Godson said.

"That it was," Moll said, adding for effect, "...that it was. I love the fact that we still celebrate it like a holiday, though. We all came out okay, that is the important thing, so it's worth celebrating." Then she said, "Well, boys, we'll be ready to eat in just a few minutes. Why don't you both go set the table?"

Sam went into the small dining room while Godson followed Moll into the kitchen. He glanced over to the adjacent living room and admired the tree, then remembered he had the two wrapped gifts in his hands and he put them on a small shelf, figuring there would be an opportunity to deal with them after dinner.

Godson came into the dining room with plates and silverware and they both set the table. Godson went back into the kitchen and returned with a salad bowl and bottled dressing and Moll walked into the room bearing a huge steaming dish of lasagna. After the heavy dish had been safely placed on the table, she lit some candles and turned off the overhead light.

"Isn't this nice?" she said. "It almost reminds me a little of the night of the fire."

Godson looked over toward the picture window.

"Godson, what are you doing?"

"Waiting for the explosion and fire," he said.

She feigned a blow and he ducked and all three of them had a good laugh in the festive candlelight. Moll bowed her head and added a short expression of thanks before they began eating. Sam had barely touched the food at the party so he was hungry and his appetite was bolstered by the taste of Moll's great lasagna.

"I thought pasta was a good choice," Moll said, "since you are going out hiking, I figured you would need to load up on carbohydrates."

Sam, his mouth full, nodded in agreement. Then he managed a meek, "Yeah, that was a good idea..." before swallowing his bite. He added, "It's really good, Moll."

"Thank you, kind sir," she said.

Then she put her fork down on her plate and stared at him.

"So, Sam, tell me about this young woman Godson talked to on the phone."

"Her name was Loretta," he said.

"Did you say *was*?" Moll had always been concerned with Sam's love life, even back in the bar. Sam assumed she thought that the love of a good woman could turn him away from his silly obsession.

"Yeah. I met her at the truck stop after Thanksgiving when I got stranded in the ice storm. She was stranded too. She had a bigger car, so we camped out in it."

"Camped out?"

"Hey, we slept in the car, her in the front seat and me in the back. It was an emergency. She had just broken up with her boyfriend and had left his parents' ranch near Ozona. Then when she got home, I guess she just got a little emotional and was uncomfortable even at home. She lives with her parents. So she took off for a couple of weeks and needed a place to crash. She just showed up."

Moll smiled. "So did something happen to make her leave so suddenly?"

"Well, for one thing I think she was leaving anyway, you know, for Christmas. We were getting along okay but she said up front she wasn't looking for a relationship. I just came home and she was gone. She *was* worried about the trip, though." Sam pointedly skipped the details about the letter. That revelation was still too raw.

"Sounds like a smart girl. That reminds me, are you really going to do it? I mean go back out there after Christmas?"

He nodded.

Moll's blue eyes began to glisten and her voice wavered as she said, "I worry about you going up into those mountains in the winter. I still think it is too late in the year."

"The forecast is mild and clear all next week," he said. "I know you both are against this idea and I get that, but you need to understand this: after all of these years I finally have a solid clue and I just can't wait until the spring to check it out ...I *have* to go take a look."

"You're wasting your time, Moll," Godson said. "I've tried to talk sense into the boy for weeks. I even offered to go with him, to run interference, but he refused."

Moll shot Godson a withering glare, as the blue in her eyes seemed to intensify. "What the hell? You aren't doing that!"

Godson laughed nervously. "Well, there's that as well."

Sam decided to intervene. "It's okay, Moll, really. Although he did offer to help, I never accepted, so there never was a reason to run anything past you." He let the subject drop but Moll shot them each another murderous glance, then relaxed into a smile.

"All right then." Moll followed with a deep breath then asked, "So what is this clue, Sam?"

He told them both about the part of Slim's clue that said to 'follow the devil' and about his discovery of Diablo Rim on the map. He still kept other details to himself.

"That's interesting, but don't you think that's stretching things a bit?" Godson said with a skeptical tone.

"Maybe," he said, "but up to now, everything I've done has been pure guesswork. This time, well, I won't know for sure until

I take a close look." Godson and Moll shared a knowing glance and shook their heads slightly, unconvinced.

The three friends ate and chatted a while longer, and then Moll cleared the table and returned with a cake she had baked for the occasion. She had written "Happy Xmas Eve-Eve" with the last "Eve" stretching over the edge of the cake even including an ellipse extending down to the plate. Using red and yellow icing she had also created some 'flames' above the words. After dessert, they exchanged gifts. Like Sam, they had given him something simple, some interesting handmade wool mittens that had an outer layer that folded over the fingers. He tried them on, modeling them by folding the mitten part back and showing how he could still use his fingers. It was a thoughtful gift and he appreciated it.

It made him wish he had spent more time and effort on their gifts, but he had been lucky. The gift for Moll was a framed vintage magazine ad photo of a cat that said "Tom's Gin" with a mirror on the other side. He had bought a few of these with different images. The frames were made with some sort of burnished copper and had a hanging loop soldered at the top. Moll was a cat person so she had no idea this had not been picked out specifically for her. Godson opened his to find a piece of hand-carved bark depicting some sort of mountaintop retreat carved into a hillside. Sam had noted it was made in India and he had been amazed at how intricate the carvings were. He knew his friend liked stuff like that and he saw Godson examining it carefully, admiring the details, so he knew this gift selection had been successful as well.

Finally, he yawned and stretched and said, "Guess I had better get going. I have to drive to Houston tomorrow and then, well, I'll be heading west the day after Christmas."

As he stood, he pulled a slip of paper out of his wallet. "Let me give you a couple of contacts. The guy who is helping me out there is named Loot Melding..."

"Loot?" Moll laughed.

"Yeah, he is a town character, an old trapper. It's his nickname, I guess. He doesn't have a phone, but you can get in touch with this other guy, Gillet Osmond at Ranch Feed and Supply in Van Horn. Here's their number."

"I thought you never got involved with the locals," she said.

"Well, this guy, Loot, just sort of crossed my path. He's a good contact, has done some prospecting. He's the guy I went out to see at Thanksgiving. He's been a great resource. I trust him."

She nodded and began writing down the names and the number. He spied the card for The Mossback in his wallet.

"Oh, and if I am totally overdue, you could call this woman. She doesn't know anything about any of this, but she's friendly and she knows I camp a lot in the area and could probably be some help in a pinch."

He handed Moll the card and she started to record the information but stopped and looked up from her writing.

She smiled at him and said, "Oh, another woman? And this one out in Van Horn? This is now starting to make more sense."

"Yeah, right, I drive four hundred and fifty miles for a woman."

"I would," Godson said, pretending to duck as Moll raised her arm again.

"She owns a coffee shop I like to go to after I come out of the hills. It's a nice place and she's nice. She's helpful. That's one of her cards."

Moll flipped the card over and said, "Smidgeon. Does everybody in Van Horn have such interesting names?"

Sam shrugged and after she finished writing, they walked to the front door and all three hugged on the porch.

"Merry Christmas, Sam," Moll said, "and please, please, please, be careful? Ever since that night at Trotsky's I feel, I don't know, I feel as if we three were all bonded by the fire. We three together survived, but it was together. I really do worry about you being out there doing all this by yourself." She sighed and added, "...and really, I *do* understand why you feel like you have to do this. Just be careful. I have an odd feeling about this. Be extra careful." She kissed him on the cheek.

"Yeah," Godson added, extending his hand, "and don't let yourself get in over your head. Come back in one piece. Call if you need anything."

"Sure, you know I will. Don't worry, I know what I'm doing. I'll be fine. I'll be back here in a little over a week. Okay?"

They group-hugged one more time and he slowly walked to his car. As he was driving off, he saw Godson and Moll wave from the porch and he waved back as he headed down the street.

Once back at his apartment, the stack of supplies was right where he had left it. He thought about loading the car but decided to leave that for the morning. Then the phone rang.

"Hello?"

"Sam, sorry it is so late. It's Sally."

"Hey, Sally. This is a surprise."

"I just wanted to tell you a final Merry Christmas... and I wanted to remind you again to be careful. I wish you'd just let this go right now. I have a funny feeling about this trip."

"I think it will be okay."

"I don't know. Ever since you said this was my fault, I have had this bad feeling."

"I was joking. Look, Sally, it was just the kind of clue I had been trying to find for years. You did me a favor ... I have a *good* feeling about this. It's going to be fine. I know it."

"Well, just be careful. Don't get overconfident."

"I won't. I've done this a bunch of times. I know the dangers and I know how to get in and out. And I've got help this time. I'm sure it will be fine."

"Okay ...Sam? I want to know something. I've been thinking about this."

"What?"

"That woman, Loretta. Did she know about all this? The mine, the trip, you know, all that stuff."

"Yeah, she did."

"Seems so strange her leaving so suddenly and right now. What did she think about it?"

"She didn't like it either. Not a big surprise," he said. "Nobody does."

"Is that why she left?"

"It was a lot of things, Sally. A lot of things. Mostly, though, she wasn't planning on staying for very long anyway."

"Okay. I was just curious. Sam ...Merry Christmas again. Call me if you get in trouble, and call when you get back to let me know you're okay."

"I will, and Merry Christmas to you, too," he said.

After he hung up, he yawned as he moved the phone to a nearby shelf. It had been a long day and he was tired. He undressed and slid under the covers. The bed felt particularly lonely with Loretta gone. In the dark apartment, a muted, ghostly glow came through the window from a streetlight outside. At times like this, he almost thought he was being watched. A faint breeze outside sounded somewhat like a muffled wheezing. He stared at the darkened outlines of his stacked equipment and thought about the concern of his three friends before drifting off to sleep.

Twenty-six

His dream was flooded with sound and Sam lifted his head to squint at the face of the clock radio. It sounded like a slow news day.

"Oh, man..." he moaned to himself.

The snooze bar was a temptation because he really wanted more sleep, but he turned off the clock radio and blinked in the early morning light for a minute before he dragged himself out of bed. Coffee was his first priority, then he watched the weather on TV. The national weather map showed good weather in the western half of the country for the next several days. The best he could hope for was that this trend would hold, because once he was up in the mountains he would be committed for the long haul.

After he drained the last of his coffee, Sam began the task of loading The Clunker and followed that up with a quick shower.

247

As he buttoned his shirt, he laughed out loud and said to himself, "I might still be wearing these same clothes in a week."

He'd stashed a spare shirt and some pants in his pack, but in both cases, he doubted he'd use them unless he somehow soiled the clothes he was wearing. He had another change of clothes in an overnight bag, too. If history were any indication, he knew he would probably get another shirt or two as gifts in Houston.

The drive was uneventful and he pulled in front of his parents' house in the mid-afternoon. Sam sat in the car for a few minutes and tried to mentally prepare himself for the imminent seasonal ordeal. The family holiday routine had not changed for as long as he could remember, but despite a great deal of boredom, there was a certain comfort in tradition.

"Here we go," he said under his breath as he entered the house.

There was the usual clamor of greetings and his grandmother, who everybody called Granny, sat in her favorite chair in the kitchen, observing everyone with a smile on her face. He shared cursory greetings and salutations with everyone. Even though he thought he was being normal and friendly, his mother noticed he was a bit aloof through all of it and she thought she knew why. She caught him alone in the hall when he was coming back from the bathroom.

"Hey, I wanted a quiet word with you. Did you know I called last week?" she asked.

"Last week?"

"Had a conversation with a very nice young woman. Loretta. She didn't tell you I called?"

"No, she didn't," Sam replied nervously. "She was just a friend staying with me for a few days."

"That's what she said, too. I was just wondering about it. New girlfriend?"

"Not really. She just came to Austin for a few days and needed a place to stay. Does it matter?"

"Sam, you're a grown man. Of course not. You just seem preoccupied," she said, "and I wondered if that was why."

"Well," he said with a short hesitation, "I've got a hiking trip planned after Christmas," he said. "I guess I'm just thinking about that a bit. I'm okay, though."

"Again?" His mother's tone encompassed a range of emotion from surprise to concern to contempt.

"Yes, again," he said. "Mom, I'm just thinking about everything I packed and where I'm going. It's something I like to do. I'll be fine."

She smiled and said, "I never knew a son of mine would be such a nut for the out of doors."

She hugged him and he hugged her back.

"I love you," she said.

"I love you too, Mom."

"Just be careful," she added.

"I always am." As he said this, he had a brief flash of *déjà vu* because it seemed to him that particular turn of a phrase had been repeated a lot in the last few days.

The family never went in much for celebrating Christmas Eve, except maybe for midnight Mass, but he skipped that and fell asleep on the couch in the living room. He woke up when he heard his mother in the kitchen making coffee, and got up to help her. Holiday or not, she rarely varied her routine and woke up at the same time every day.

"Merry Christmas, honey," she whispered.

"Merry Christmas, Mom."

"You're up early."

"Well, thought I'd ease into the holiday a little with you before Christmas really starts rolling," he said.

As she cleaned and started the coffee pot, he went out and got the morning paper. He scanned the sky as he scooted out the door in his bare feet. It was chilly but the sky was clear. Christmas in Houston could be twenty or eighty, depending on the whims of nature. Sam and his mother sat quietly at the kitchen table as they read the paper and sipped their coffee. It was a comfortable, well-practiced ritual that hearkened back to the days when he still lived at home.

Eventually his dad came in and his sisters started to wake up, and by the time Granny and Aunt Dot emerged from their bedroom, it was time for another pot of coffee. One of Granny's morning customs was to heat a pastry in her immaculate little toaster oven. It was her pride and joy and she would rarely let anyone else use it. Sam was always amused when she did this because he could never figure out why she seemed so obsessed with that simple little appliance.

"Do you want me to heat you a kolache, sweetie?" she asked.

"Sure, Granny, just whatever filling is handy."

Granny and Aunt Dot were sisters and they had moved in with his parents when they sold the old family place across town. They shared a bedroom next to the den. Aunt Dot was technically Sam's great-aunt, but everybody called her Aunt Dot.

It was not long before the Christmas morning experience began with gusto and soon there was sea of wrapping paper littering the living room. Everyone graciously thanked him for his miscellaneous gifts. Maybe they were just being polite, but all-in-all those things weren't that different from the gifts he received. As he predicted, he got two new shirts along with an assortment of books and other nondescript bric-a-brac.

When they were kids, they also had stockings and every Christmas morning he fondly remembered the first time his older sister had asked him about his stocking. He was barely four years old and didn't know what she was talking about. She took him back to his room to show him, and there it was, stretched out at the foot of the bed. He had been so excited about Christmas he completely overlooked it when he jumped out of bed. In those days it really *was* a stocking, one of his dad's old army socks, stuffed to overflowing with all manner of small toys and candy, along with nuts and an apple and orange stuffed into the toe. It was a tender memory because for him there really was magic in that moment.

As for the rest of the day, there was a lot of what he called family-feast food. He knew Thanksgiving had been pretty much the same. Turkey and dressing was the focal point and there was an array of vegetables and festive congealed salads. He had seconds, and thirds in a couple of instances. Fruitcake and pie filled out the dinner.

The fruitcake was a decades-old family recipe that Granny and Aunt Dot labored over early in December, mixing huge batches of the stuff in a large tub they used only for fruitcake. They had done this every year for as long as he could remember. They made a lot because they handed out small loaves of it to everyone they knew, especially the nuns at the convent. It was associated with the Catholic school where Aunt Dot worked. Sam remembered Sunday visits to their old house after Thanksgiving when he was a kid. The place would be permeated with the distinctive aroma of clove and cinnamon. For him, that was when things started to smell like Christmas. As he munched on a piece of fruitcake, he mentally compared it with his Logan bread because they had a similar texture.

Late in the afternoon, as things settled down after Christmas dinner, he felt a wave of anxiety sweep over him. He sat by himself in the living room, away from the football games and conversation in the den, and thought about heading out west, perhaps dividing his trip into two shorter legs, just to get moving toward his goal. Then that thought was replaced by a flicker of common sense.

"Stick to the plan," he muttered to himself as he realized he might not be able to find someplace to camp on Christmas day and food and gas might be a problem as well. "Besides," he quietly whispered, "what would I tell Mom?"

He knew she would have balked at him suddenly changing plans, so he ignored the impulse to leave and just sat tight and made small talk with his family and watched television. He would not gain anything by leaving early and he knew he needed to rest.

That evening, he helped himself to a couple of turkey sandwiches and another piece of fruitcake. He continued talking with his father and sisters about nothing in particular, usually just commenting on their conversations. About nine-thirty, he hugged his mother and grandmother, excused himself, went back to the living room and stretched out on the couch. He was soon sleeping soundly.

The next morning, he woke when he heard his mother in the kitchen. He blinked and looked around the dark room. He had fallen asleep in his clothes. He got up and groggily walked into the kitchen where his mother was fumbling with the coffee pot.

"Good morning," she whispered.

"Good morning, Mom," he returned.

They followed their routine. She made the coffee and he got the paper and then they sat and quietly let the new day progress.

When he got up to get them both a second cup, his mother asked, "So you're leaving today?"

"Yep."

She asked him a few more questions about his trip. His parents knew nothing about his long quest for the gold mine, so he avoided direct answers. As far as they knew, he was just an outdoors freak who enjoyed hiking and camping. He hated being evasive, but he also knew his mother and father would not understand his obsession. They were pragmatic people who thought everything had to be clear-cut and logical, so there was a fear they would tell him the entire idea was preposterous and, even worse, they might at least try to compel him to abandon his plans. He knew his best course of action was to continue the evasion and let them enjoy the parental bliss of ignorance, at least as far as this subject was concerned.

After finishing his second cup of coffee, he started loading The Clunker. His Christmas booty was minimal, so it didn't take long. Granny was up by the time he had finished.

"So, you're going already?" Granny was smiling as she asked him this question.

"Yes, Granny. I'm afraid so."

"Make yourself a couple of turkey sandwiches," she said, then she added, "oh, and take a couple of kolaches." She pointed to the countertop near her precious toaster oven.

He followed both of her suggestions and wrapped up a couple of slices of fruitcake as well.

When these chores were complete, he said, "Well, I guess I had better hit the road."

He hugged his mother and shook his father's hand and then he went over to hug his grandmother. As he bent down to hug her, she slipped something green into his hand. Another holiday routine, he thought to himself, and he discretely slipped the folded bills into the watch pocket of his jeans.

He turned and waved from the side door, "I'll call y'all when I get back."

"Be careful," his mother returned.

"Always am. Bye."

He drove down the familiar streets of his old neighborhood, then navigated the nearby freeway and its serpentine interchanges until he got to Interstate 10. From there, it was a straight shot to Van Horn, a little over six hundred miles away.

Once he was heading west, he relaxed a little. He had left at his planned time and he didn't have any major route adjustments to make. It was a longer drive than it would have been from Austin, but it was the same highway all the way. He did have to negotiate through a large city, San Antonio, but he hoped the day after Christmas would be a light traffic day. He looked at the road ahead of him and thought that if the Houston traffic was any indication, he might be right. As the outskirts of Houston rushed past him, he wished he had gotten an earlier start because there never seemed to be enough time on these long trips.

"But I was sticking to the plan," he reminded himself.

When he was safely beyond the city, he inched his speed up to sixty and scanned the highway for the police. He knew that five mph over the speed limit was generally safe unless some aggressive local cop was on patrol. He didn't want to get a ticket and he also didn't want to push The Clunker too hard, but he also knew a little extra speed would trim away part of his driving time. The car seemed to be handling the speed just fine and the weather was good, although it was still a bit chilly. He adjusted the heater controls and relished the heat pumping into the car.

"I just might have made it home in the ice storm if the heat had been working," he said. Thinking about that also reminded him of Loretta and he sighed.

As he drove, he slipped the bills his grandmother had given him out of his jeans watch pocket and smiled.

"God bless her," he said to himself as he counted the three, crisp twenty dollar bills. That sixty dollars would help a lot.

He bought some gas in San Antonio, mostly because he needed to stop anyway to stretch his legs and get some coffee, but he spotted a pay phone and fingered a note in his shirt pocket. It was Loretta's number. He decided to call her.

"Hello?" It was not Loretta.

"Hi. Could I speak to Loretta, please?"

"May I ask who is calling?"

"Uh, Sam."

"The boy from Austin."

"Yes, I'm from Austin, may I speak with her?"

"Listen, young man, Loretta told me about you and I know she doesn't want to speak with you, but I do. Is it true you knew my father, Ted Longo?"

"I was with him when he died."

There was a pause. Obviously, Loretta had not told her that detail.

"Is that when he put that fool notion about that *damned* gold mine into your head?"

"Loretta told you that?"

"No, but I knew my father and I knew what he was all about. She kept your secret, but I know more than you do about that foolishness. Listen to me. What he gave you was a *curse*. It certainly was a curse to him ...for me it was the family curse. I fought against it for years and hoped I had gotten away from it, but now, like any true curse, it came back to haunt our family yet again. I mean, is there any other explanation for you and Loretta getting together? I don't know you, but that foolish notion of finding the Sublett Mine ruined my father's life. It ruined his father's life too ...and his grandfather's. It just doesn't exist. Sam, put it aside... it really *is* a curse and I don't want it infecting my family any more than it already has. So please stay away from Loretta and from all of us."

Sam was standing holding the receiver and staring at the keypad on the phone, blood flushing his face. "But..."

"If it doesn't kill you outright, it will ruin you. You were with my father, so you know he was a homeless drunk. Did you ever ask yourself why? It was because if we took him in, he would have just tried to figure out a way to build a grubstake and go right back out there again, that's why! We couldn't live like that anymore and even he understood it ...do *you* understand what I'm saying?"

"Okay, I've got it," he said, "but I want you to know, your father gave me his Bible and some letters. I've got them with me. Don't you want those? He said he wanted Loretta to have them."

"Burn them. The letters, well, I wrote the letters so I know what is in them and that Bible means nothing to me—there is nothing holy about this situation. Young man, I know Loretta really liked you, yet once she learned the truth, she instinctively *knew* the rest of it ...that what I'm telling you is the other part of the truth. Sadly, the curse has been passed on to you and this family needs to leave it there. I'd tell you good luck but there isn't any, not in this case anyway. Good-bye!"

The phone clicked dead and Sam stared at the handset for a few seconds before hanging up. He turned slowly, walked to his car, and continued his trip. The phone call had unnerved him, but he got back on the freeway and drove.

"Keep to the plan," he muttered.

He was thankful the traffic continued to be light. The woman's words reverberated in his head while he negotiated the freeways. He was making good time. He finally just sighed and accepted the fact that he'd probably never see Loretta again. He couldn't blame her mother after all she had been through.

"Curse?" he asked himself. "I've never seen this as a curse..."

Yet, the astounding coincidence of him connecting with Slim's granddaughter in the midst of the ice storm haunted his thoughts as he drove. He struggled to put it out of his mind and on the other side of San Antonio, he inched his speed up to sixty-five for a while. As he approached Junction, he decided to top off his tank. He didn't need the gas, but he had an ulterior motive. He stopped at the same truck stop where he had met Loretta. He scanned the parking lot while he was pumping gas but didn't see her car. He knew it was stupid, and he didn't really expect to see it, but coincidences abounded in his life.

"Or would that be part of the curse," he quietly muttered as he headed back toward the interstate.

His mind wandered again as he drove and he thought about the tatty jewelry box, safely tucked into his pack with the Logan bread and he began to wonder if the good luck charm had failed him.

Eventually his random musings turned to the upcoming hike and he ran through mental lists of equipment and food supplies, then he concentrated on formulating contingency plans with Loot. A quick review of his hiking plans followed, as he tried to remember details gleaned from hours of research, crawling over his maps on the floor. He ran all of those things through his mind again and again, thinking about different types of problems and working out theoretical solutions to them in the hope that he might cover as many possibilities as he could. When he tired of these exercises, he tried to let his mind wander to other things as he drove the long lonely miles of west Texas, but he kept returning to the recent exchange.

"So, I'm cursed," he said, as he reflected on the comments made by Loretta's mother.

All he had wanted to do was say good-bye, but the woman had ripped into him like he had stolen her parking place at the mall. But then he remembered that he had referred to this notion of a lost gold mine as being a curse himself. The fate of the old man's father and grandfather were only mentioned in passing by Slim, but Loretta's mother obviously knew more about that family history than he did. For just a moment, Sam considered the woman's comments in a new light. Here he was driving off on a clandestine mission into a forbidding landscape based on vague information he got from a broken down drunk.

A scream pierced through the road noise: "What am I doing?"

The sudden scream left him shaking but at that point, those feelings dissolved and his mind was flooded with vivid memories of the old man whispering, "follow the devil ...look for the table ...you'll see the why of it."

Sam thought he felt a tickle and reached up and touched his ear, rubbing it the way a person would if someone had leaned in close enough to almost touch him with a whisper. A chill ran down his spine and he instinctively checked the heater vents again, but the car was quite warm. A looming exit sign for Fort Stockton broke the spell and he welcomed the chance to take a break, so he took the exit.

There was probably enough gas in his tank to make it to Van Horn, but he decided to top it off. Coffee was a priority as well. Sam splashed several double handfuls of cold water on his face in the restroom and tried to shake off any aftereffects of the disquieting thoughts he had just experienced.

When he paid for his coffee, he asked the clerk, "What's the weather supposed to do?"

"Dunno, same as this, I think."

Sam got back on the highway and nudged The Clunker toward the approaching sunset, speeding a little as he sipped coffee and munched on the last of Granny's kolaches. Thankfully a few wispy clouds lingering around the horizon muted the sun just enough to allow him to see.

The Van Horn exit appeared just as the final glow of dusk was fading. As he drove past the darkened Mossback Café, he muttered under his breath, "I hope the old guy is still on board."

It was a valid concern because they had made their vague plans over a month ago. He also thought about Smidgeon as he drove past the restaurant and smiled as he wondered what she would think if she knew he was conspiring with Loot Meldings to go off trespassing in the middle of the night. A brief image of her smiling eyes flashed in his brain and Sam realized his heart was racing.

"Why am I so nervous?" he asked himself as he found the faded Tesoro Road sign and turned.

At the end of the road, he could see Loot's rusty truck was parked on the street, not in the driveway, so Sam slowly pulled onto the gravel driveway. It looked like there was even more debris in the yard and he smiled because he knew this probably meant Loot had cleared out the small garage as he had promised.

A lanky figure emerged from the shack. It was Loot, who waved and pointed to the garage where he swung the double doors open. Sam eased his car into the garage. He looked in the rearview mirror and saw Loot standing at the entrance with a cigarette dangling from his lips, waiting for him to emerge.

As Sam got out of his car, Loot said, "So, you made it."

"Yep. Long drive, but I made it."

"You still want to head out tonight?"

The question gave him a mild shock and he pondered the intent for a moment. The only alternative that might be implied by such a comment was staying the night in Loot's house.

"That was the plan. I'm a little tired, but if you can get me close enough, I can get up onto the rim and into a good hiding place in time to get a fair night's sleep."

"Then let's get yer stuff into my truck. We're burning moonlight."

"Think I can cache a jug or two of water where you drop me off? I might need them."

"Way ahead of you, chief. I've been driving around up there all week to check things out and so people will get used to seeing my truck. I know right where I want to drop you off. A couple of nights ago, I buried you a cache of water. I'll show you when we get up there."

Sam smiled. He had put his trust in Loot and this seemed to be a validation of that trust. He pulled his pack out of the back seat, then stuck his wallet under the driver's seat and placed his keys on top of the front left tire. He thought for a second about his pack and wondered if he should pull anything else out of the overnight bag in the trunk, but decided he was good to go with what he had in the pack.

When he emerged from the garage and Loot closed the doors, entombing The Clunker, Sam carried the backpack down to the roadside and laid it in the bed of the truck. Loot opened the driver's side door.

"Hop in!"

Sam slid into the passenger seat and adjusted himself to avoid several poking springs. He had a hard time finding a place to fit his feet because the floorboard was littered with Coke cans and tools and wrappers, not unlike the inside of Loot's house, but he realized his car was pretty much the same. The ancient truck struggled as Loot turned the key but it finally coughed to life.

"Okay, partner, let's go," Loot said as he gunned the engine and they bounced down Tesoro Road. Loot turned right and drove down the main road a short distance to the west and then turned right again, proceeding down a graded road that was unfamiliar to Sam. There were long stretches of straightaway, then turns to the left and right and then more long sections of straightaway. In the maze of turns and variations of speed, the younger man quickly lost his bearings, but Loot seemed to know exactly what he was doing. The night was clear, showing a blaze of stars and a half-moon. Loot drove for what seemed like a long time, meandering closer to a particular stand of prominences barely visible in the darkness.

Loot expertly moved the column shift up and down as the truck bounced along the graded roads, sometimes speeding up, sometimes slowing down. In the side mirror, Sam could see clouds of dust kicked up by the old truck, billowing light gray in the moonlight, and he was glad it was night because he knew from experience that such plumes could be visible miles away, alerting anyone to a vehicle on the roads.

Eventually Loot slowed and the truck crept down a particular road. When Loot finally seemed to find the spot he was looking for, he stopped quickly enough to cause Sam to lurch forward in his seat. Road dust settling around the truck was visible in the headlights.

"Here we are," Loot said, "At night this time of year, people might think I'm out doing illegal hunting. That could attract attention, so we better hurry it up."

"Right. You said you cached some water?" Sam asked as he got out of the truck.

Loot had brought a flashlight from the truck and shined it upward, revealing a crudely made sign indicating that three paths converged at this point. Sam could barely make out the words in the dim light: Apache - Comanchero -Crockett.

"Those are made up street names, just so the mail man don't get confused. I picked this spot because it should be pretty easy to peg on one of yer maps. Now, let me show you where I stashed that water," Loot whispered.

He trotted directly across the intersection from the sign and into the underbrush. There was a mound of rocks piled next to some scrub.

"I dug a big hole and put in two gallon jugs of water and piled them rocks over it. Another one over there," he said pointing.

Sam looked over and could see another pile of rocks about twenty feet away.

"Not real hidden, but it's not likely somebody will be out here on the side of the road looking for it, 'cepting maybe you."

Sam nodded, and took a few steps around, more closely examining the caches and the surroundings. He was satisfied he could find them if he needed to.

"Looks good," Sam said.

They went back to the truck and Loot whispered, "Now this here is Comanchero," his hoarse voice barely audible. He waved a hand back and forth in the darkness to indicate one of the roads. Then he pointed down the road in one direction and said, "You head up this way about a mile, then head off to the left about another mile or so and you should be able to start climbing up to the rim."

Sam listened to the instructions, trying to equate them to his memory of the map. He knew he would have to get up on the rim, find a good spot to bed down and then check his map in the morning.

"What if the weather changes?" he asked.

"Hunker yerself down and get out here. I'll just drive through here every night about this time, especially if the weather turns."

Sam checked his watch.

"Okay, so you'll come through around eleven every night. Got it. I guess you had better run," Sam said. Then he added, "Loot, if all goes well, I will definitely be here Tuesday night. Okay? I guess repeat again Wednesday and Thursday nights. After that, well, you can figure that I'm in some kind of trouble."

Loot stuck out his hand and said, "Okay. If you are a no-show, I'll figure out something. You just find the damned thing. I better skedaddle."

They shook hands and Loot scampered back to the idling truck, then turned and said, "...and be careful, chief."

Sam nodded and waved as Loot got into the idling Jeep pickup. The old man gunned it and bounced back down what Sam thought was probably Apache Road.

He slipped on his pack and headed in the direction Loot had pointed and tried to remember his maps, but that was useless without getting a firm bearing on his location, so he had to totally trust Loot's instructions. The road was rough for driving, but was okay for hiking so it was easy to judge distance. After he had walked about twenty minutes, he stopped and looked around.

The darkness kept its secrets well hidden but he could just barely make out a looming shape rising on the left. He gingerly stepped off the graded road and walked in that direction. It was hard going, and he had to avoid trees, scrub, and small boulders, obstacles that would suddenly appear out of the darkness, but after about twenty-five minutes of hiking, he stopped and looked and listened. All he heard was the night. He felt he had been going up a slight rise, but a little to his right, the land rose appreciably. In the darkness, it was just a big, dark bump that was gradual at first then jutted up and leveled off and continued as far as he could discern in the distance to his right. He knew this *had* to be Diablo Rim.

Sam adjusted his pack and began to pick his way up the rocky slope, at times struggling to find handholds and footholds in the dark. Because of the slope, he scrambled with his hands as much as his feet and he often winced and withdrew his hand quickly when it brushed something sharp. The moon was bright enough to give him some visibility but many details of the terrain eluded him, causing him to stumble or slip. The exertion winded him and he was already a bit battered, but this did not deter him as he kept moving steadily upward and toward the right.

"It's nothing I haven't done before," he panted to himself. "Just like every other time."

He scrambled over an outcrop and was surprised to find level footing. After just a few steps, he squinted in the moonlight and could see that the incline was gone. It was the top of the ridge.

"Finally."

The minor scrapes and bruises had been worth it. After he caught his breath, he glanced around, but could see only vague shapes in the darkness. The moon was still rising in the east, so he started walking to his right, assuming it was northeast. Moonlight provided enough of a glow to help him avoid stumbling off the edge as he hiked along the rugged rim for about another twenty minutes or so.

Eventually some vague shapes loomed to his left and as he approached the shapes, he could see that it was a small grove of mesquite, about a hundred feet from the edge of the rim. As he entered the patch of trees, he fanned out with his foot, looking for obstructions. In the dim light he could see there were about a dozen trees clumped together, and near one of the trees he found a spot that seemed smooth enough for him to stretch out. He untied his sleeping bag from the pack frame and left the pack lying on the ground. If it were a normal kind of hiking trip, he would have found an obliging branch where he could hang the pack on one of the trees to protect it from animals, but out here he had to keep it out of sight so he would use it as a pillow. It was chilly, in the upper forties, but he was glad it was not bitterly cold.

He spread out his bag, taking care to dust the larger pebbles and sharp bits of twig out of the way as he laid it down, then took off his boots and slipped into the bag fully clothed. He opened a packet of peanut butter crackers and enjoyed his first meal on Diablo Rim, washing it down with a swig from his canteen. After he finished eating, he fell into a light sleep.

Twenty-seven

Sam blinked himself awake and, unsure of his whereabouts, he followed his first impulse, reaching to his side, expecting the warmth of Loretta but then he looked up to the cloudless blue sky and he remembered.

"Geez," he said, rubbing his face with his hands.

He slowly crawled from his sleeping bag and got his first good look at the stark landscape of Diablo Rim. The craggy branches of the small grove of mesquite trees stood guard over him, aided by a patch of prickly pear cactus that bordered one side of the clutch of trees. After a quick shake to check his boots, he put them on.

"I guess scorpions or other unwelcome visitors are not too likely this time of year," he muttered to himself, his breath faintly visible in the chill.

Once he was in his boots, he rolled up his bag, then stood and looked around again. His eyes were crusty from a combination of trail dust and sleep, so he reached into an outer pocket of his pack, pulled out some eye drops and put two drops in each eye, blinking rapidly against the momentary sting.

It was chilly but it was a beautiful day. He judged that the temperature was in the mid-forties. He fumbled with another one of the side pockets on his pack until he found a packet of caffeine pills.

"Ah, my morning coffee," he said so loud it startled him, and he instinctively stifled his voice because the outburst seemed almost profane in the quiet of the desert morning.

He swallowed one of the pills with a swish of water to clear the bad taste out of his mouth.

"Bleh," he said, again speaking out loud, and he looked around, feeling a bit guilty at another vocal intrusion.

He felt a transient flash of the same feeling of being watched he always experienced out in the mountains alone. The only other sound was the chatter of unseen birds. He reached into the upper chamber of his pack, snaked his hand down to the inner compartment, felt around until he found a way in from the side, and he pulled out one of the individually wrapped pieces of Logan bread. As he munched on it, he decided it was both satisfying and unsatisfying at the same time. It tasted pretty good, sweet and salty, but it was a bit disappointing as a meal because it lacked the hearty satisfaction of a good hot breakfast.

"What I wouldn't give for an 'Especial' at the Mossback right now."

He pushed that thought out of his mind, reasoning that this was no vacation and he had work to do. Still munching on the bread, he walked the short distance to the edge of the rim and looked up and down. There was a steep drop-off with a sloping hill below that and he could see the ridge gradually rising away from him toward the left. He looked back to his protective grove of trees and marveled at his luck in finding such a good spot in the dark.

He downed the last bite of the bread and considered getting another piece, then decided he did not want to squander his supplies. Breakfast was finished with a swig of water from his canteen and the plastic wrapping was stowed in another pocket he had earmarked for trash.

He retrieved his compass and oriented himself. At this point, the rim seemed to run to the northeast, just as he had presumed in the dark. He pulled out his map and tried to determine his location based on what landmarks he could see. He followed the contours of Diablo Rim and scanned the map until he found what he thought was the place where Loot had dropped him off.

"Loot was pretty crafty choosing that spot," he said to himself, "because that triple intersection is easy to spot on the map."

He scanned the area in the distance beyond the rim and spotted several landmarks, then he reoriented himself with the compass and the map. When he was satisfied that he had fixed the location, he pulled a small pencil out of his pack and placed a light '1' at what he judged was the location of his camp, then he added a small circle where the trio of roads intersected.

He smiled and said, "If I can find this camp again, I know I can find the rendezvous spot," as he put the map away.

Sam walked up the rim about a hundred yards or so. There was no trail along this rocky ledge and, as he walked along, he could see it was going to be rough hiking because of the frequent steep drop-offs.

"An injury here would probably be fatal," he muttered.

As he returned to his temporary camp, he again marveled at the good cover he had found. He pulled a small ball of white cotton cord from a pocket on his pack and used his knife to cut a piece a few inches long. He tied this to a branch on one of the mesquite trees closest to the rim to serve as a small marker.

"That shouldn't be too noticeable unless someone is looking for it ...like me."

A bird chirped in agreement and Sam laughed and replied, "Hey, buddy, it's not just a good camping spot, it is where I need to start thinking about heading down to the rendezvous."

After nervously looking around, he attached his sleeping bag to his pack frame and surveyed the campsite. He wanted to leave no evidence of his visit except for that tiny scrap of string. Once he had his pack on, he walked over to the rim again and turned around to take a mental picture of the spot. Then he arranged three rocks in a line pointed toward the string. Satisfied, he turned up the rim and started hiking toward the northeast.

"Look for the table," was all Slim had said, then "turn around and you'll see the why of it."

He had always assumed that "table" was the key reference, but it was a vexing clue because there were many meanings to the word. Sam had looked it up in a thesaurus once, hoping to discern some hidden logic in the use of that word and he was astounded by the complexities he found. It could refer to a slab, a bench, a mountaintop, a chart, an agenda, a proposal, or even a postponement. Some of those meanings were out of place in the wilderness, but since it was couched it in a riddle, he assumed it could be *anything.*

He had long believed that a mountaintop was the most obvious choice and he had spent an inordinate amount of time searching for flat topped mesas. Some of his earlier searches had focused specifically on areas that might have such a feature, but eventually, as he became convinced the mine had to be somewhere between the national park and Van Horn, he had to accept the reality that there were no such recognizable landmarks in that particular area. His efforts were redoubled when he decided to search Diablo Rim and he again spent hours looking at his maps, trying to figure out something that might relate to the table clue. That was one reason he had been so intent on getting out here as soon as possible, so he could see the actual landscape for himself.

"Slow going," he whispered as he walked along.

This was a bad thing because he could not cover as much ground as he would have preferred, but it was also a good thing because it gave him a chance to take a better look around.

"Of course, I'll probably see all of this again on the way back," he quipped.

He knew that would give him a second glance with a new perspective, probably in different light. So far all he was seeing was the same type of landscape he always saw on these trips.

"Rocks and trees and cactus and scrub..." he muttered, his voice breaking the eerie winter silence.

About midday, he stopped abruptly because he heard a twig snap. He froze and listened. The sound had enveloped him like a rifle shot then immediately dissipated, making it hard to determine where it had come from. Finally, after a tense minute, he detected a slight ruffling off to the left and he focused his attention there. Then he saw it, a huge mule deer with a marvelous rack of antlers, standing next to a small tree. Any hunter would have prized this buck as a trophy. The deer was obviously quite wary, uneasily moving its head as it glanced around.

Sam was transfixed by the natural beauty of the animal but he absentmindedly reached up to scratch his nose and the spell was broken. The deer turned and looked right at him, then it pivoted and bolted away in a number of graceful, bounding leaps. It was out of sight in seconds.

"How cool was that?" he whispered.

Except for that encounter and a couple of small breaks to munch Logan bread and drink water, the entire day was a grueling hike along the long rim to nowhere. He had mixed feelings about the bread ... sometimes it seemed to linger at the bottom of his stomach like a rock. But he knew it was loaded with calories and protein and he appreciated its convenience as a trail food.

"It's not *that* bad and it saves me the bother of fixing something else," he rationalized to himself. Every time he talked out loud, he instinctively looked around.

The relentless search for the elusive table clue was exhausting and as the shadows began to stretch, he saw another small grove of trees that vaguely resembled the spot he had found the night before, so he decided to stop and make camp. There was not much to the term "make camp" in this case. He dropped his pack and briefly surveyed the area, but did not range too far because he was weary from the hike and it was all the same rough-and-tumble terrain. He was tired and wanted to eat something hot, so he decided to postpone pinpointing his location on the map until the morning.

It had been breezy all day, but as the sun dipped low in the sky the wind had died down. He set up the tin can stove on an adjacent rock and lit one of the rolled cardboard and wax fuel disks he had made. He retrieved the small camping pot from his gear, filled it with water, and put it on the top of the little stove, intent on boiling some water. The stove worked well and it did not take long. He picked through his limited assortment of freeze-dried meal packets and selected a stroganoff stew, mostly because it had some vegetables. It was a hearty meal, designed, it said, for two. At the time he bought it, he had assumed that the portioning, especially for a hiker, was either way off, or maybe the manufacturers thought it would be combined with two or three other things. Of course, that usage didn't correspond to his concept of trail food. In his opinion, a one-dish meal that was quick and easy to prepare was ideal.

Since these freeze-dried packets were designed to be reconstituted inside the container, he always figured that it was just easier to eat them out of the packet as well, something that would save him the worry of dirtying anything more than a spoon. Everything that was used for food consumption had to be washed, and washing required water and water supplies were limited.

He saw that the pan of water was beginning to steam, so he opened the top of the packet and using a washcloth as a pot holder, he gingerly lifted the little pot by the edge and tipped it over to pour the steaming water into the open packet, releasing a savory aroma in the cloud of vapor that drifted out of it.

"Hot, hot, hot," he whispered as he poured.

The comforting smell of the food made him realize just how hungry he was. He used the snuffer he had fashioned to smother the flame on the burner, preserving the fuel for another meal. He reserved some water in the pot to clean his spoon.

He held the corner of the steaming packet with his left hand and used his spoon to stir the contents. After a few minutes, it had cooled enough to allow him to pick it up. Although it was still quite warm, he found he could more easily steady it with his hand while he stirred it again. He tasted it.

"Not great but not bad either."

He ate it with a coming appetite and soon he was scraping the last vestiges of gravy from the packet as if this were going to be his last meal. A deep swig from his canteen washed it all down.

"Two portions!" he said out loud, laughing.

The night was clear and the stars were intense, but the waning moon was less bright than the night before.

He yawned and realized that anxiety and stress added to his weariness because as he searched for clues, he had to constantly scan for predators, large and small, animal and human, always ready to scramble to find some type of cover. Today, except for that marvelous buck, he had seen nothing, but every time he hiked and heard something he could not identify, he had to wonder if it was just the sound of the wind coming down the ridge, or one of the other eerie sounds he frequently thought he heard. He would often think of that first trip to the Guadalupe Mountains, when he had been confused by the wind blowing up the mountainside.

He unrolled his sleeping bag and laid it out on a smooth spot under the trees. This time, since he was further back into the ridge, he decided to hang his pack on a branch. He knew the pack was more visible in a tree but hanging kept it away from scavengers. At night he wasn't as concerned with it being seen and he figured taking it down would be the first thing he did in the morning. Then he thought he heard a muffled raspy murmur in the dark.

"Big mistake..."

Sam looked around and shook his head.

"It had to have been a bird or something," he whispered to himself, unconvinced, but he was never sure what he heard out here in the wild.

The episode had rattled him, but he shook the feeling off and decided to get some sleep. It was noticeably cooler so he opted to leave his boots on because his feet always got cold first, even inside the bag. This was a convenience too, because if he had to get up in the night, he wouldn't have to go through the trouble of first checking his boots then struggling to slip them on and off in the dark. He decided the minor inconvenience of negotiating the twists and folds of the bag with the heavier mass of his boots was worth the trouble.

Once he was in the bag, he looked up and marveled at the stars in the crisp cool night.

"So I'm cursed? If this is a curse, then so be it."

He was soon sound asleep. He stirred once before his alarm was set to go off and noted a reddish glow as the dawn rose to the east but fell back asleep, content to wait for the alarm.

Twenty-eight

THUNK!

Sam had been dreaming about Smidgeon, something regarding her and a motel, but an abrupt impact on the side of his head shocked him awake. He could see only star-speckled black at first but as the black faded and he struggled to understand what was going on, he tried to get up, only to be pushed back down. He blinked repeatedly and shook his head in confusion. Figures started to rise out of the black and he began to perceive his new reality. There was someone in his camp. Then as his vision cleared, he saw another, then another. The three figures were a blur of straw cowboy hats and denim. He blinked rapidly, adrenalin flushing his face, and he looked up again, trying to narrow his focus on the interlopers. They all had rifles pointed directly at him.

¿Qué pasó, amigo?"

Sam did not understand much Spanish but that was a common phrase and he shuddered at the ominous and sarcastic tone in the final word of the sentence. He said nothing and remained entombed in his sleeping bag.

The three men started chattering among themselves, talking so quickly in Spanish that any hope of him understanding what they were saying was quickly lost in a blur of unfamiliar words. Then one of the three broke away and yanked the pack down from the tree and began to rummage through it on the ground.

Their western attire resembled a makeshift uniform of sorts, with straw cowboy hats, plaid flannel shirts, boots, denim jackets, and jeans and based on their dress, he assumed they were hands from the local ranch. Judging from the rough treatment he had already received, they were likely some of the lowlife ranch hands Loot had warned him about. He assumed that if they had been migrating illegals, they would have likely avoided him. He had seen similarly dressed ranch hands in stores in the Sierra Blanca and Van Horn areas, so he felt sure his guess was valid. The man looking through his pack had placed his gun on the ground. He remembered the deer he had seen the day before and realized they must have been out hunting and stumbled across his camp.

The real or imagined phrase, "Bad idea," replayed in his head.

Their chatter sounded more like an argument than a discussion and while they were talking in Spanish, his mind began to race as he tried to understand his situation. He heard familiar words more than once, usually the curse words that comprised a good percentage of his Spanish, but one man called the other what sounded like *hef-feh* several times. He knew that word: *El Jefe*, which was roughly 'the boss,' so he assumed this must be the foreman Loot had mentioned.

Sam continued to lie there, not moving or talking but trying to remain calm although his heart was in his throat. He hoped they would just take him in and hand him over to the authorities. At this point, that was a best case scenario and he tried not to think of other, possibly worse, probabilities.

The boss returned to Sam and screamed another obscenity at him in Spanish, then kicked him hard in the side. It almost knocked the wind out of him. The boss gestured, indicating he wanted Sam to get out of the sleeping bag. He complied, and was soon standing before his captor, disheveled and still blinking in the bright early morning light, but he was thankful he still had his boots on. The two men were both somewhat smaller than he was, but they stood at angles away from him and were both still armed. The third man continued to rummage through the pack. Sam could see that many of his belongings were scattered around, but he noted that the guy was hasty and had not found all of the pockets.

Sam's attention shifted again as the boss snarled something new at him in Spanish and spat on him, then backhanded him. He stood and took it. If he had learned one thing in karate it was patience. He had the advantage in size, but he also knew that despite the impression given in movies, there was no way three guys would stand in turn waiting for him to fight each one individually. If he resisted them, they would likely jump him *en masse* and, of course, he could not ignore the fact that they were armed, certainly with guns, but possibly with knives as well.

He glanced at his belongings in an attempt to avoid the steely glare of the boss and saw his freeze-dried food packets spread out along with assorted clothes and equipment. The man who had stood with the boss began stuffing small items like the compass into his pockets. The third man, the smallest, had his own small knapsack, and he began to place various food items in that.

The boss began to interrogate him, or so he thought based on the tone, but he didn't understand what was being asked of him, so he said nothing. Finally, the boss spat out words in broken English, words he knew must have been previously peppered in the Spanish. He brought his face so close Sam could smell whiskey on the man's breath.

"You trespass, *amigo*. It no good *por* you. Why you here?"

Then the boss lashed out again with a backhanded swipe across Sam's face and he could taste blood in his mouth. The boss made another swing with the other hand, but this time Sam reacted with a roundhouse block with one arm. He hadn't consciously intended to resist but it was a move he had practiced so many times in karate, his reaction was almost automatic. The boss almost lost his balance as the force of his blow was redirected, but he recovered quickly. He smiled, revealing a silver front tooth, and hit Sam in the abdomen with his other hand. The guy was strong and Sam doubled over, gasping for breath. He regretted making the block because it was ineffective without an offensive counter-move, but in his situation, he knew it was pointless to try to go toe-to-toe with these guys.

Sam slowly raised his head to face the boss, not intending to resist any more, but as he did, he felt the crack of a rifle butt against the back of his skull and crumbled to the ground. Though dazed, he struggled through the pain and shock, wavering at the edge of consciousness for a few seconds. He stayed motionless on the ground with his eyes closed, trying to give the impression he had been knocked out. He listened while the three men continued to argue in Spanish.

He heard words like *policia* and *asesinato* from one of them. *Policia* was easy to understand and he seemed to remember *asesinato* was something like murder. The shortest one of the three, the one who had looked through his pack, seemed to be very upset and used that word in a very negative way. The other two vigorously argued with that one, all of them talking fast and loud. Then they stopped and he heard them poking through his belongings again. They had already taken all of his easy food, like the freeze-dried food packets and tins of potted meat, and crackers. He heard them pour out his water. Periodically one would come and give his seemingly lifeless body a kick while yelling something he perceived as an obscenity.

He decided his best bet was to continue to feign unconsciousness. They took his watch and poked through his pockets, which were for the most part empty, but one of them did grab his knife. He guessed they were probably disappointed that there was almost nothing in his pockets but he had hidden his wallet in his car prior to leaving Loot's place and he had stashed his keys in Loot's garage.

They began chattering again in a staccato of excited Spanish, the boss emphatically spitting out some words, but after only a little more discussion, they appeared to reach some sort of consensus. He heard them stuffing the items they had not stolen back into his pack. Then, two of them lifted him by the arms and shoulders and started dragging him.

It was a short trip. He had apparently picked a bad spot for a camp because it was just around a slight rise from a jeep trail. He regretted his decision to defer pinpointing his location the night before or he would have seen that. The close proximity to any kind of road was a serious mistake, especially since he had used bad judgment in hanging his pack.

They didn't seem concerned that he was apparently still unconscious and pushed him into the back of some kind of vehicle. He risked a quick peek when he heard one of them trot off, probably to retrieve something they had left at the camp. It looked like he was in the back of an old and battered open jeep. His mind for some reason conjured up a comical memory of *Nellybelle* from the old Roy Rogers TV show, but this thought was squelched by his pack being unceremoniously dumped on top of him. About that time, he heard the man who had left come trotting back, laughingly saying something in Spanish. He guessed the man had left his rifle at the camp.

He peeked when he could, but for the most part he kept his eyes calmly closed, choosing to depend on his hearing to keep track of his captors. His head was throbbing but his thoughts were clear, so he resolved to continue this gambit. They obviously weren't going to just kill him outright or they would have simply done so. At least that was what he assumed, and he also speculated that they were probably going to take him back to the ranch house which no doubt meant he was going to be jailed for trespassing.

It kindled the memories of imaginary conversations he had rehearsed before, something he did to kill time on his long drives.

"Why are you out trespassing on my land?"

"I'm a photographer. I wanted to take some pictures. You have some really interesting topography here."

"You didn't think to ask permission?"

"I wasn't hurting anything. I didn't think a short trip would matter."

"If you're a photographer, why don't you have a camera?"

"Probably the same reason I don't have any food or all of my camping equipment..."

He hastily appended that last part to reflect his current situation ... it seemed a logical chance to imply the theft by his current captors. Sam had read somewhere that redirection could be an effective defense.

His fantasies were interrupted when the three men suddenly jumped into the jeep and he heard the engine start. They lurched away in a spray of gravel, and he risked a quick glance and saw one of the men looming over him with a rifle casually pointed in his direction. The guard was looking forward while holding his hat with his other hand and didn't notice the occasional peek. The jeep bounced violently on the rocky trail and the guard struggled to maintain his balance.

He found it impossible to track their progress with his eyes closed because the driver alternated jarring speed bursts with quick slowdowns as the jeep negotiated the many turns and switchbacks. The throbbing in his head further complicated matters and this pain was amplified by repeated shocks as the jeep bounced and swerved on the unpaved road.

Sam struggled to remain still but his legs were beginning to cramp because the tiny area in the back of the jeep didn't have room for his body, the pack, and the guard. Some minor flexing of his muscles helped, but he knew he'd have to move before too long. That didn't matter anymore because the cramps immediately ended with the rush of adrenalin he felt as the jeep skidded to a halt. The pack was lifted from the back of the jeep, and in a few seconds, he heard faint metallic tumbling sounds a short distance away, as if the frame and its contents were hitting rocks in several places.

Two sets of hands then lifted him and he tried to maintain his composure as he was dragged along, but he was alarmed by the implication of this action. He seriously considered suddenly coming alive to take his captors by surprise, figuring it would give him a good chance to stage one last stand. He squinted, trying to see as best as he could, and saw a looming precipice just ahead.

He quickly considered his options. First, he assumed that since two men were dragging him, one of the men was probably following, still armed, so he knew that if he struggled, he'd probably be shot. Second, from the sounds he had heard, he thought the pack had been tossed off some sort of cliff, so Sam figured he was going to suffer the same fate as his pack. His best guess was that his assailants thought he was seriously injured and they hoped he would break his neck. The fall would nicely explain any other injuries. Then they could return later to 'find' his body and announce to the world they had discovered a trespassing hiker who had sustained a fatal injury. At least that was his current working theory.

His mind raced with those thoughts as they dragged him to the edge. He concluded that resistance was riskier than taking his chances with the fall, since his only other option was probably a gunshot wound. He prayed that the unseen abyss was not too high. The previous day he had seen a good part of Diablo Rim and if his observations along the rim had shown him anything, he thought it might be worth the risk.

Those thoughts were interrupted as he was awkwardly launched forward. He felt air rushing and tried to stay loose to soften the impacts. Just as he had hoped, it was not a long drop, more of a steep incline than a stark cliff. He opened his eyes as he began to tumble, and tried to anticipate the impacts. Sam assumed they wouldn't notice his open eyes due to the rapid action of the fall. He glanced off a boulder and brushed past scrubby vegetation, narrowly missed a cactus and ended up rolling down the rest of the way, coming to a stop in small cloud of dust.

From his point of view, it had been a lucky fall but he hoped it had been impressive enough from the top of the cliff. He had been pummeled by the drop but at least it had been more of a tumble than a long fall with a single hard impact. It was a miracle he hadn't hit his head and he was relieved because that had been his primary worry in opting for the fall, because his head was already tender.

Although he was bruised and battered, he was conscious and he had landed face up. He remained motionless, trying to inconspicuously squint up at the three figures on top of the short cliff.

He heard one of them yell something, *"Estúpido gringo, almuerzo de un puma!"* followed by a cruel laugh.

Even with Sam's very limited Spanish, he recognized several of the words. Stupid gringo was an easy translation of the first part and he seemed to remember that *almuerzo* was lunch. Obviously, they thought he was either already dead, or was seriously injured and so his best guess was that the guy said he was going to be lunch for a mountain lion.

He continued to lie there. Seconds ticked by but he did not move. He waited and listened and heard distant birds chirping and gentle winds rustling through the bare branches of nearby trees. The bright early winter sun was warm and he began to sweat. As the seconds moved into minutes, he could still feel their eyes looking down at him, probably waiting for the slightest motion. He tried to discreetly monitor the men, but he was not in a good position to clearly see their vague shapes above him without moving his head. He decided to close his eyes to better maintain the façade of unconsciousness. Finally, he heard an engine revving and then he heard wheels spinning in loose gravel.

After those sounds had faded, he continued to lie motionless, quietly assessing his situation. He was battered but he did not think he was seriously injured. He knew he still had a pack nearby but he didn't know what equipment they had left him. He was pretty sure he had no water and no food. He wondered why they had left him his pack, but he realized it was probably to give credence to what he imagined their story was going to be. They would come back later and find a lost hiker, trespassing out on his own, who was injured by a fall off a cliff. They no doubt assumed he was either already dead, or would eventually succumb to injuries and the elements. Even though they were employed by the ranch, they were probably undocumented workers, illegal aliens, and he doubted they were inclined to contact the authorities themselves. He had definitely smelled whiskey on the breath of the foreman, so he assumed they had all been drinking. That was likely why they had acted so rashly without thinking things through.

He ran those thoughts through his mind for several minutes, biding his time. Although he could imagine no other reason they had left him like this, if it were true, he knew they would eventually sober up and realize it was a stupid plan. That meant they would likely be back. It was also possible they might report back to the owner and he would want to come back and find him. That would eventually mean some sort of legal involvement. In either case, it meant they would soon be back, so he didn't have much time to waste.

He risked a slight movement of his head to take a better glance up the hill. All he could see besides rocks, grass, scrub, and sky was a lone stubby mesquite struggling against the rocky outcrop along the edge of the rim. Sam slowly moved his arms and legs, which were stiff and sore.

"At least nothing seems to be broken," he rasped through dry lips.

His head was pointed slightly downhill, so as he slowly lifted his upper body and moved to support himself on one elbow, he found he was dizzy and he paused to clear his head before he slowly got to his feet. Beyond the scrapes and bruises he had a bad headache but he generally felt intact. He looked around and saw his pack on the ground about twenty feet away with a few items scattered around it. As he approached the pack, he paused to pick up a small object that had obviously been ejected as the pack bounced around. It was the jewelry box. He opened it and saw the small cross-shaped rock glistening in the sunlight. They had missed it in their search because it had been tucked into the hidden compartment.

"Good luck piece, hah!" he said out loud and he almost threw it away.

At that moment he realized ...he *had* been lucky. His present situation was bad but he was alive. Things could be much worse.

He closed the box and picked up his pack and was surprised at the weight, expecting it to be completely empty. When he opened the pack to stow the box, he realized something: the layer of Logan bread was still intact. He had food. The man had searched his pack in a hurry and he must have assumed the hard layer was part of the pack. The jewelry box was lighter than the bread and had managed to dislodge itself during the tumble, but the bread had stayed put.

He searched and found the few items that had fallen out of his pack during the tumble down the embankment. These were mostly clothes, including his plastic poncho.

I'm surprised they didn't take that!

He also found his canteen and opened it and lifted it over his mouth. One drop struggled out of the opening.

"Water is going to be my biggest problem," he said.

He did not find any other water containers, or his sleeping bag, so he presumed they must have stolen them. He could have sworn he had heard metallic clangs of his pots or possibly his tin can stove rattling around as the pack fell, but he could not find them.

He poked around until he was satisfied that he had retrieved most of what had fallen out of his pack. He then fiddled with the stopper at the end of one of the frame tubes and pulled it out. He shook the pack and out came the little pen knife and the tiny compass. Then he flipped the pack and opened the Velcro panel on the back where he kept his maps. The small man had missed these as well.

"Okay," he said to himself, "I've got maps and a compass and food. Water is the biggest problem ... as is exposure."

He poked through his pack again. He had been mindlessly retrieving his few belongings without really noting what he had grabbed, but then he saw he still had his long underwear and enough other clothes to give him another layer or two.

"Enough for a couple of layers ...it's way better than nothing."

He looked around again, this time attempting to gauge his surroundings. He was in a gully with steep sides up to the top of the ridge. The more he thought about it, the more certain he was that someone would come back to look for him.

"I've got to get away from this spot as quickly as possible," he said. "The best option would be to find a better place to hide for a while."

It would give him more time to get his bearings so he could figure out a way to escape. He didn't know when they would return and wasn't sure what to expect from them when they did, but if they thought he was just some idiot hiker, he was pretty sure they would want to make an example of him, alive or dead, to scare off future interlopers. One thing they did not know, though, was that he was still alive and mobile. They also did not know he still had food, a compass, and maps.

He checked his tiny compass and hiked south out of the gully, then around to the left, generally east, around the long finger of the ridge. He continued on toward the east, skirting several smaller gullies but he soon approached another deeper ravine that cut back toward, he assumed, Diablo Rim again. He hiked up this crease, squinting through the pain in his head to try to remember what details he could of his hike. He judged he had walked at least a couple of miles or more from where he had been abandoned, which wasn't a huge distance, but he thought it was far enough to at least give him some time to rest and consult his map.

He dropped his pack on a flat rock jutting close to another sharp incline and leaned against it while he looked around. There were a few scrappy trees and a bit of scrub and a lot of rocks of all sizes. He spied a nearby patch of prickly-pear cactus so he walked over to it and carefully removed a lobe from one of the plants with his penknife. He cut off the spines and sliced into it then sucked at the pulpy flesh. It was just barely moist but he did manage to get a little relief from it. He walked toward the exit of the arroyo, still sucking at the cactus. He looked into the distance, trying to discern any landmarks because he knew he had to figure out exactly where he was if he was going to get away in one piece. When he turned to walk back to his pack, he stopped and stared.

"It can't be!"

The flat rock underneath his pack looked just like some kind of *table*. Sam walked over to it and placed his hand against the flat surface. It was so subtle he hadn't noticed it even when he was leaning on it, but it was so obvious. Then he turned around. On the opposite wall there was evidence of two ancient fault lines intersecting in the limestone. He blinked in disbelief. It looked like a giant "Y" in the cliff face.

Near the base of the Y, there was a boulder lying flat against the cliff like it had broken off and just come to rest there. It was weathered and had obviously been sitting in that spot for a long time, but there was something odd about the way it was positioned. It blended in well enough but it didn't look quite natural. This piece of rock was only about four or five inches thick and it was roughly three feet across. He dusted around the top and sides of the rock. Then he grabbed it and tugged it. It was heavy, but it moved slightly. He decided to pivot it outwards to try to lay the rock straight down, perpendicular to the cliff. It dropped with a thump. There was a deep depression behind it.

"I'll be..." he whispered.

He examined the walls of the depression and could see that this hole had obviously been excavated by hand and it was just big enough for a person to crawl into. His head was no longer throbbing at this point, but his heart was racing as he peered into the depression, squinting because of the transition between daylight and shadow. From what he could see, the depression was only clear for about five or six feet. Beyond that, he could see it had collapsed into rubble and small boulders. He scanned the walls and floor in the entrance then went back to his pack, remembering he had hidden a tiny flashlight in the frame. He pulled the stopper from the end of another of the tubes and shook the frame and the small light slid out. He smiled ...the men had missed this as well, but how would they have known? Loretta had suggested he place this light, the knife, and the small compass as a whim, mostly as a hedge against, well, he hadn't known what, but the plan had come in handy.

Armed with his light, he returned to the depression and examined it more closely. He got on all fours and inched his way as far as he could go until he was stopped by the obstructions. With the help of the light, he squinted farther down into the darkness. He was wary of the possibility of a cave-in, so he carefully avoided touching the walls or ceiling. The light didn't shine far, but it looked as if the depression might extend dozens of yards into the collapsed region. The obstructions were more pronounced the farther he looked. As he moved his dim light, something caught his eye. It was a tiny reflection rendering into a slight flicker as the position of the light shifted.

He shoved some of the rubble aside and with great difficulty dragged a couple of the larger rocks toward the opening. This allowed him to squeeze his way further into the depression, wincing when he brushed the ceiling and was dusted with a trickle of debris and gravel. With all of this effort, he managed to advance maybe another three or four feet. He lay there, squinting deeper into the opening, trying to find the sparkle he thought he had seen before.

He tried rapidly moving his light back and forth until he again saw the refection. It was much closer. He stretched his hand out and it was just out of his reach. He took a deep breath and carefully moved more rocks, sliding them over to the side. In the close quarters of the depression, he touched the ceiling again and ducked as more dust sprinkled down over his head and shoulders. He inched forward and reoriented himself with the sparkle he had seen. He reached out and touched the rock, scratching it with his fingernails.

He examined his fingertips and the edge of his nails with his small light and could clearly see yellowish specs. His heart was pounding. He looked toward the source again, shining his weak light around. There were a number of glints from the same area. He knew it would have to be tested, because other rocks and minerals could mimic gold, but he also knew that ancient veins of tracer gold could have accumulated eons ago into the fault lines that had formed the "Y" he had observed on the surface. He reached out again and tried to dislodge one of the rocks that reflected most readily but it wouldn't budge

"Crap!"

He pushed his way back out of the depression and when he emerged, he blinked in the daylight. He looked at his fingers again and marveled at the yellowish reflection. He needed more of it to be sure. He wished he had thought to include a streak plate in his kit. That would show him immediately if it was gold or pyrite, fool's gold. He remembered from his geology lab in college that gold would leave a yellow streak and pyrite would leave a greenish-black streak.

He returned to his pack to look for something that would help him break off a piece of that rock.

"Why didn't I think to include a rock hammer or streak plate in my kit?" he asked himself.

But of course, it likely didn't matter at this point, since any such items might or might not have survived the interlopers. He remembered his small knife and pulled it out of his pocket. It was tiny and not sturdy at all, so it was certainly not a tool that could be used to chip away at a rock. He fumbled in the pack and finally found something else the men had missed, a spoon. It was a poor mining tool, but it was sturdier than the little knife. He also found a wrinkled bandana. He stuffed the bandana and the spoon in his shirt pocket.

Suddenly he was startled to hear what sounded like a distant engine and he looked up. He didn't see anything but he assumed it had to be an airplane flying close by.

"Sound can carry pretty far out in this terrain," he reminded himself.

If it *was* an airplane, he knew he would need to hide. He looked around his makeshift camp. His pack was pretty obvious sitting on the table rock. He looked back toward the depression and decided that without its cover, the hole was pretty obvious too. He noticed a piece of scrub nearby, thick and round and dry. When he tested the branches with a slight tug, the entire plant broke readily from its base. He dropped this by the hole and then went over and grabbed his pack. He shoved it into the hole, then backed in, carefully pulling the scrub over the opening. He had eyeballed the piece of scrub correctly because it fully blocked the opening.

He finished just in time because the sound became louder and a small plane came into view, just barely visible through the dry branches covering the opening. He saw it circle just beyond the ridge in a slow arc that he thought was probably near the spot where he had been thrown down the cliff. It was obviously looking for something, probably him, but he didn't know if it was the law, or the rancher. It circled for about fifteen minutes, in gradually expanding circles, then it disappeared.

When the plane was gone, he pushed the scraggly bush out of the way and emerged from the hole, pulling his pack out behind him. He shoved it under the table rock and arranged the bush next to it to provide some additional cover, then he headed back into the depression. Working his way in as far as he could, he spied the glinting material again. He put the light in his mouth then pulled out the spoon, which was a sturdy soup-sized stainless steel kitchen spoon, and using the thick, blunted point on the handle end, he tapped at the rock. With some effort he managed to dislodge a few pebbles from the edge. He used the spoon to scoop up the material, brought it close to the light and examined it. The shiny grains embedded in the rock gleamed yellow. He pulled out the bandana and, cupping it in his hand, he emptied the contents of the spoon into the makeshift indentation. He bunched up the bandana like a small bag and placed it back in his shirt pocket.

He moved what rocks he could and tried to extend his reach. He began to work with the spoon again and managed to chip out a couple of more pieces. He again saved these samples in the bandana. Sweat beaded on his brow from the exertion and began to drip into his eyes. He decided he had enough material for some testing so he stopped this work. He was also worried about the battery on his little light. He carefully folded the bandana around the last batch of material and this time he slid the package into his pants pocket. As he prepared to exit, he spied another glint and saw a pebble he had apparently dropped. It was about the size of a nickel. He picked it up and slid it into his shirt pocket, then continued backing out.

After he slithered out of the hole, he could see that some clouds were moving in. He frowned because that could mean that the weather was changing. He vaguely remembered the red glow he had seen before dawn and thought of the old adage: red sky at morning, sailor take warning. There was a certain darkness to the clouds that probably indicated rain.

"Great," he said to himself, "another challenge."

He wasn't sure of the time, but figured he didn't have that much daylight left and the clouds would make it get dark really quickly.

"But if it *rains*..." he said and he quickly went back to his pack.

He smiled when he pulled out his folded plastic poncho.

"I can't believe they didn't take this! If it rains, I can use it to catch some water!"

He shoved the pack back into the depression and as darker clouds moved in, he gathered a few rocks in a wide circle about eighteen inches in diameter and about five or six inches deep next to the table rock. Although the top was flat, it was not level and had a slight slope toward one side. He spread part of the poncho over the table rock, anchoring it with more rocks, then he rigged a sort of chute down to the ring he had made with rocks. He spread the rest of the poncho in this ring, flattening it against the ground and forming it around the ring of rocks to make a small bowl-shaped area. He anchored the edges with more rocks in case of wind. He stood and examined his work. It looked like it might catch at least some water and any water was better than none.

It soon began to rain and he retreated to the small depression and watched his rain catcher. Water collected on the poncho and trickled down the chute into the small enclosure he had made. The rain shower lasted maybe thirty minutes but it was a downpour at one point. During the rain, he reached back to his pack and fumbled around until he found a piece of the Logan bread and pulled it out. He was parched and the bread was dry, but he felt he needed a little nourishment so he munched on a corner of the bread and savored the sweet and chewy goodness. He stuck his hand out the opening and let it get wet and sucked a little moisture from his skin. When he was satisfied the rain had stopped, he exited the hole and approached his construction project. He carefully dislodged the upper anchors from the poncho and lifted that section from the table rock, releasing a few more precious drops. The bowl-shaped depression was almost full.

"Better than nothing," he said.

Sam lowered his face to the water and relished a deep drink. It smelled of dust and rubberized plastic but it tasted wonderful. He got his canteen and pushed it into the small pool and he could see some of the water bubbling into the canteen and then repeated the steps, gradually narrowing the pool. Finally, he lifted the poncho and tried to funnel as much of the remaining precious water as he could into the canteen. When he was finished, he lifted the canteen again, pleased that it was almost full. He shook out his poncho and folded it.

He retrieved his pack and stowed the poncho and pulled out another piece of the Logan bread. As he nibbled on it, he considered the hole in the side of the cliff. It had obviously been dug to follow right down the fault line. There must have been an exposed vein of material there that had been scratched and clawed out of the rock for perhaps hundreds of years. He looked at his hands. They were red and raw and he knew he would need better tools to explore further. For now, he was satisfied he had found something significant and it didn't really matter if it was *the* Sublett mine or not, but he knew he never would have noticed the depression without Slim's cryptic riddle and there was no way this hole was a natural formation.

He shivered and looked at the sky again and saw it was becoming more overcast. Although that rain shower had passed, it had brought a renewed chill to the air. The temperature was sure to drop after the sun set, so he decided to put on his long underwear. He had been blessed with fairly mild weather so far, but he assumed the brief rainstorm and the increasing cloudiness probably indicated more to come.

He stripped down to put on the insulated undergarments and gently touched the tender discolored bruising that covered his torso. As he dressed, the wind whistled up the little arroyo and the extra warmth felt good against the renewed chill.

"Not bad for a man who had been left to die."

Deep down, he knew the ranch hands had most likely reported back to the owner and there was little doubt that cooler heads had prevailed. That would easily explain the sudden appearance of the plane and, judging from the area it was circling, he was certain that someone was looking for him and they would be back. The change in weather or the coming of the night might cause some delay, but he assumed the search would resume, most likely with more men and with jeeps and horses. A second capture was not an option he wanted to contemplate.

Arrest was one thing, but given the beating he had already received, he thought jail was the least of his worries. Plus he was holding some evidence that pointed to the true nature of his mission and that likely would be a game changer if he were found and searched. For that reason, Sam briefly considered abandoning his samples but vetoed the idea. He decided he would have to take the chance because *that* was why he had come out here in the first place.

The first order of business was to figure out exactly where he was, because he had limited time to get to his rendezvous with Loot. He had another deadline too. One canteen of water would not sustain him for a long time. He fumbled in the flat pocket on the back of the pack and pulled out the map that detailed Diablo Rim. He found the pencil mark where he had camped the first night. He followed the rim, retracing the steps he had taken, pulling details from his memory to cement his location. He was pretty sure he knew where he had camped the second night, because he saw the jeep trail that he hadn't realized was too close to his campsite. He lamented the mistake of not pinpointing his location prior to camping that second night. He *should* have known about that stupid trail and camped elsewhere. He rubbed the bruises on his face and winced. He couldn't find his pencil, so he poked a small hole at that second campsite location with his small knife.

As he read the map, he tried to remember the movements of the jeep. The trail that ran near the campsite paralleled this part of the rim, sometimes meandering away but it always curved back again. Finally, squinting in the muted light, he found a likely spot where there was a steeper drop-off and figured that it must have been where they dumped him.

He remembered he had hiked out the first gully and proceeded to the left around a wide spit of land. Then he traversed some smaller gullies and eventually moved into another deep cut and after hiking up that gap, he had found this spot. He looked up and examined the hills on all sides. He looked toward the open end and scanned for other landmarks on the horizon. He pulled out the little compass to gauge directions, placing the compass on the map itself, moving the map slightly to better judge the alignment. He was pretty sure the distant landmarks he could see, several low hills, were a match for what he saw on his map. Bingo. He pricked another small hole in the map with the point of his little knife and smiled.

"I know where I am!" he laughed. "Now to find a way out."

While he examined the map for potential escape routes, he shook his head.

"I doubt I would have ever hiked this far on this trip," he said. "It looks like at least three nights back, maybe four with searchers looking for me, and with a single canteen of water."

Sam knew that in his current situation, he would have to do most of his hiking in the dark, so he continued to mutter to himself as he considered the possibilities.

"It will be slow going, and I could get lost and lose my way. At the worst, I might trip and fall off the rim and really injure myself. I might be able to risk the jeep trails in the dark, but if the ranchers think I'm on the move ... they just might drive up and down those trails, even at night." He shook his head again. The scheduled rendezvous toward the west seemed to be an impossible option.

Then he looked to the east, toward highway 54, which was tantalizingly close, across relatively flat ground. It was maybe a long night's hike to that road and, realistically, that was something he had easily done before.

"But what do I do when I get there?" he whispered. "I've got no vehicle and no way to contact Loot ...and people, maybe even the law, might be looking for me out there as well."

He examined the map closely, wondering if he could possibly hike cross-country south to Van Horn, roughly paralleling the road.

"That would be a long, tough hike and I'd be out in the open and I would probably still be visible from the road." He thought for a moment and added, "And again, on one canteen of water."

Then he had another thought. "Time might be on my side if I can get down to the road tonight and hide until a car comes along. Pickups would be out, because they might be connected to the rancher, but a car might be safe enough to try to wave down. But the longer I wait, the more chance there will be that someone will be looking for me on that road. I've got to go down there tonight."

He looked at the map for a second time and again considered his two options. If he went west, it would take him at least three nights to hike to a late meeting with Loot and he would have to hide during daylight hours with pursuers actively looking for him, something that was an added disadvantage. And even when he got to the rendezvous point, he would have to hunker down and hide there as well while he waited for the rendezvous. There was another problem with that option: He had no way of warning Loot about the uncertain situation. Despite the fact that he was a local, the old man had been wary of too much scrutiny.

"It's one thing when he's just a solitary truck driving down those roads on some random night, but with the ranch on the alert, there is certainly a greater risk to Loot."

Sam folded the map.

"East it is," he decided. "If all goes well, I'll meet up with Loot before he even tries to rendezvous with me."

He rubbed his lumps and bruises again, wincing at certain spots. Although they had indeed hurt him, his captors had also underestimated him.

He laughed. "They've watched too many movies, I guess ...they assumed they had easily knocked me out, but I fooled them. They probably think I'm lost, hungry, confused, and without water, aimlessly wandering."

He had outdone them on all counts because he had food, a map, a compass, and he even had water. He also had something else they could not know. He had a plan.

"It's going to take a lot of luck," he said nervously, but deep down he knew he had that option covered as well.

Twenty-nine

It was quickly getting dark, so Sam worked to refine specific details of his plan by studying his map while he still had enough light to see.

Once I walk beyond the ridge to the left, I just need to head directly to the east toward the highway. It won't be an easy hike, but at least it looks generally flat.

Then he noticed a small feature on the map.

"That looks like a small culvert!" He laughed. "That is perfect. It will give me a little cover on the side of the road. That's my target."

He knew it would provide a hiding place near the road, which would augment his ability to pick and choose ride prospects.

Then he turned his attention to the gaping hole in the side of the cliff.

"That does sort of stick out like a sore thumb, doesn't it?" he said and then he was startled by what sounded like a faint hoarse laugh.

Sam glanced around again and felt as if someone were watching him. He shook the feeling and looked into the depression, trying to see if he had left anything. Satisfied he had all of his belongings, he strained with the flat rock and managed to pivot it upright, then rocked it gently and with some difficulty worked it back into its place in front of the opening. He spread some dirt and gravel around the edges, then, using the piece of scrub that had earlier been his cover, he tried to blend his tracks into the background. He stepped back. The "Y" in the short cliff still pointed at the rock but the scene looked pretty much the same as it had when he first found it. The threat of rain loomed above him, something that might complicate his hike but even a short rain would almost completely cover any evidence anyone had been there. He rested against the table rock and chewed on another piece of his Logan bread and waited while the dusk enveloped him.

When it was completely dark, he started hiking, following the path he had tried to memorize from his map. It was the same dangerous night hiking routine he always followed, trying not to trip, trying not to fall, trying not to bump into cactus. He did not want to use his light unless he felt it was absolutely necessary because he didn't want to risk the chance someone might spot him in the dark. He also had no faith in the batteries because he had used the light so much when he was examining the depression.

Once he worked his way around the long lobe of the ridge to his left, he did a very quick check with his light and compass just to satisfy himself that he was going in the right direction and he headed directly east. It seemed farther than he expected and he sometimes struggled to find a clear way in the dark. At one point, the overcast broke long enough for him to see his old friend Orion rising in the east. That was another good indicator that he was on the right track. It was soon covered by clouds and he was on his own again.

He occasionally tripped over rocks and small clumps of desert undergrowth hidden in the darkness. After a couple of hours of hiking, he could see occasional moving specks of white and red lights in the distance. He knew those were vehicles driving down the highway.

"There it is," he whispered when he first saw the lights.

They were like beacons to him, keeping him in the right direction. As he walked, he became transfixed by the white lights appearing far to one side, gradually approaching his imaginary destination point where they would fade to red and move on, disappearing down the road in the other direction. For him, those points of light bolstered the hope that he could make it to the highway by daybreak. He kept plodding and tripping and stumbling slowly toward the east.

A light rain began to fall as he hiked, so he stopped and pulled out his poncho. It was big, designed to provide cover for a hiker with a backpack. It was a cool night, probably in the mid-forties. The exertion of walking and the extra layers, including the poncho, helped to warm him. It was a long and lonely hike and in the dark it seemed even longer. Several times, he stopped at the sound of something nearby and stood still. He looked around, but it was so dark he didn't see anything. Several times he stumbled, falling forward. His hands were scratched and scuffed and on one of these falls he almost slammed his face into the ground. Each time he dusted the embedded bits of gravel off of his palms and slowly got up and continued walking toward his distant goal.

Finally, just as the first hints of the coming dawn began to stretch across the sky, he could see the dark ribbon of the highway. The rain had been short but he had kept the poncho on because it warmed him. He was exhausted from the hike and hadn't realized the overcast had been clearing from the east. It was slowly getting lighter and that emboldened him, so he increased his pace. As he approached the road, he spotted the culvert and was elated because his dead reckoning had kept him right on course.

He hiked toward it and then said, "Damn, it's really shallow."

That was one detail that eluded him on the map. Still, Sam decided to be thankful for even a four-foot depression and when he examined it, he decided it would likely provide just enough cover to duck into it if he needed to. At the culvert, he removed his poncho and then slid the backpack from his aching shoulders. After shaking any remaining moisture from the poncho, he stuffed it into the upper compartment, then he placed the pack below the level of the highway. The concrete was damp from the overnight rain but there was no standing water.

He originally thought he would only try to flag down a car because most trucks would probably be ranchers, but now he figured he might risk an eighteen-wheeler if one came along.

"Big trucks would probably be okay," he croaked. He took a swig of water.

He was only interested in traffic heading south toward Van Horn, so when he heard a vehicle coming from the south, he ducked down into the culvert. It was a pickup truck and it sped on past, paying him no notice at all while it headed north. Although the sky was beginning to brighten, it was still more dark than light.

After about five minutes, another set of headlights appeared from the north. He squinted at the twin lights and although he could not be sure, he was pretty sure it was a car. He decided to make his move, and emerged from the culvert. He put his pack on the ground in front of him and waved with both hands. It *was* a car and it slowed. As he squinted in the glare of the headlights, he could barely see only one person in the car and as it rolled toward him, he could see the features of a woman. He held his breath, fearful that a woman might speed away at the sight of a lone male. As the car slowly pulled alongside him, the driver reached over and rolled down the passenger window about two inches. Then the car suddenly lurched to a stop. Sam and the driver exchanged stunned looks.

It was Smidgeon Toll.

"Sam?" She was visibly shocked.

"Smidgeon?" He mirrored her shock.

"What is going on? Did you have a wreck?"

"Well, no wreck, but I'm stranded. Can you take me to town?"

Smidgeon eyed him carefully. From the look on her face, it was obvious to him that she noticed his cuts and bruises, even in the dim early morning light.

"What happened to you?"

"I was beaten up—I'm okay, but I really need your help."

Smidgeon reached over and unlocked the door.

"Get in." she said.

He opened the door and reached around to unlock the back door so he could put his pack on the back seat. He sat in the car's passenger seat. After hours in the moist chilly air, the warm car was a relief but as he sat he was within range of Smidgeon's frosty glare. She stared at him for what he thought must have been a full minute. He said nothing, trying to avoid her gaze by looking out the windshield or down at his feet. Finally, she broke the silence.

"Before I move this car, you need to tell me what the hell is going on."

As the light of dawn rose around them and the car idled impatiently on the side of the road, Sam sighed deeply, then began to outline the story for her. Her piercing dark eyes were intensely set on him as she listened and he was drawn to them as they seemed to pull the story right out of him. He told her about Slim and Ben Sublett and the clues to the mine. Then he told her about his trespassing and touched on his recent association with Loot Meldings. Finally, he recounted the latest outing, and told her about the escape and the night hike that landed him in her car. She sat in silence for another full minute after he had finished.

Smidgeon finally said, "So you've been lying to me all this time about camping up in the park. Every time you've come into my place you've been out trespassing?"

"Well, not *every* time, but that's about the size of it. Believe me, I didn't want to lie, but I was afraid to tell you the real reason. Not then."

Smidgeon frowned, but put the car in gear and slowly pulled onto the highway and headed south, toward Van Horn.

"Loot Meldings!" she growled, with obvious disdain in her voice. "I should have known that old fool was mixed up in this."

Sam knew there was some sort of history between Smidgeon and Loot, but he felt compelled to defend the old man.

"Listen, he helped me," Sam said. "He might be an old coot and a fool, but he helped me. I left my car at his place."

"Shit. Did he strip it and sell it in the meantime?"

"Well..." Sam started.

"Listen to me. This place where I picked you up ...do you know that it is at the edge of the MacGregg place? They are mean and nasty, all of them, from old man MacGregg right on down to the dog. Just look at the state you're in. When I saw you and saw where you were, I didn't doubt for a second that you had been beaten and left for dead. And understand this, Sam: they are like stink on a pig ...you can bet they'll be looking for you. You need to lay low."

"Yeah, but my car and wallet and money are all stashed out at Loot's."

"We'll figure that out later. I've got a good friend, Marcy, who owns a motel in town not far from the café. Dolings Motel. It's not a fancy place but you've probably seen it."

Sam nodded. "Yeah, so?"

"I'll talk to her and see if we can stick you in there for today. You look like you need to take it easy for a while anyway. You look awful." She sniffed and made a face. "And you need a bath."

At this, her eyes softened and she laughed that easy Smidgeon laugh of hers and continued. "I was out taking some food to a shut-in from my church but I'm running late and need to get back to the café. Marcy should already be at the motel, so we'll stop off there and I'll talk to her. I'm sure it won't be a problem and, believe me, she can keep her mouth shut. I'll bring you some food after we're done with the morning crowd."

"Smidgeon, I appreciate the help."

She looked at him and smiled. "When I saw somebody waving me down, with no car or nothing, I was thinking, 'who the heck is this all alone out in the middle of nowhere'...I was really wary, but out here we help each other, you know? Most of us, anyways. Then, when I saw it was you, and, well, there was no way I was leaving you. I was just in shock. You were the last person in the world I was expecting."

"Same here. I was worried about getting a ride in case it might be them, but I was almost speechless when I saw it was you. You were the last person I expected, but I was relieved, too."

She laughed again. "Yeah, I can say the same. A woman alone on the road shouldn't be stopping for a lone man, but there's something about you, Sam." She smiled. "I was glad it was you."

"One more thing, Smidgeon," Sam said, reaching into the top pocket of his shirt. He extracted the nickel-sized, yellow speckled pebble and placed it on the dashboard. "I think I might just have found it."

She almost lost control of her car when she glanced over and saw the sparkles on the small pebble, then regained her composure and concentrated on the highway again.

"Damn!" she said, smiling.

"Not sure how this will play out and I need to test this sample, but if this really is gold, well, who knows? I guess it doesn't matter if it is *the* Ben Sublett mine, it is surely something. The clues fit and it sure looks like *some* kind of mine, but it has collapsed and it is pretty dangerous."

"Don't worry, I won't tell nobody nothing," she said.

When they got into town, they drove past the Mossback and soon pulled into the driveway of the Dolings Motel. Smidgeon disappeared into the office and Sam couldn't help but feel a tinge of *déjà vu* ...he had a vague recollection of something about Smidgeon and a motel. She soon emerged with a key in hand, then they drove around the back, away from the main road.

"Here you go ...room one-thirteen. I'll be back by in a bit."

He took the key, and looking down at Smidgeon's feet he said, "I don't know how to thank you, Smidgeon."

"You needed help, Sam. It's what I do." She put her palm against his cheek and added, "There was no way I was leaving you out there."

He looked up and she winked and smiled again. He grabbed his pack. As he unlocked the motel door, he turned around and waved at Smidgeon. She raised her hand in response as she sped off.

The room was typical of a lower-end motel with two double beds, a dresser, and an end table between the beds. A small dining table with two chairs, and a TV completed the setup. The scene was augmented by some generic artwork on the walls, most notably line drawings of characters from The Wizard of Oz.

"Pretty strange for a motel," he remarked.

He went to the sink in the back of the room and unwrapped one of the plastic cups and filled it with water, then drained the cup. He was thirstier than he thought, and the sudden flush of liquid into his system refreshed him. He repeated this three times, savoring the sweet, clean water. The rainwater he had collected had tasted of plastic and dust and grit. He rooted around in the mess of items stuffed in his pack and found he had one pair of clean underwear. Thankful at the find, he dusted them off. He pulled out a piece of Logan bread and nibbled at it, washing down each bite with more water as he slowly undressed.

When he looked in the mirror, he thought the mottled bruises on his body looked like some kind of camouflage. He started the water running in the shower and let it flow until it ran hot and stepped in. Sam relished the soothing sensation as the hot water ran over his skin, but he had to be careful because several deeper bruises on his torso hurt when the streams of water touched them. He used the tiny bar of hotel soap to wash away several days of trail dirt, even lathering it up in his hands to use it as shampoo.

After lingering in the shower for several minutes, he turned off the water and grabbed a towel to dry himself. As he did this, he began to think about what he needed to do when Smidgeon returned. Sam knew he would need to get to Loot's place to retrieve his car and he needed her help to do that because he had only a vague idea where he was. If he went out and started wandering around on foot trying to find it, he would be vulnerable. He assumed Smidgeon would probably balk at taking him out to Loot's, but he hoped maybe she'd at least point him in the right direction.

The fact that he had been viciously assaulted, almost murdered, was a side issue, because he figured he had no legal recourse. To pursue the one crime, he would have to admit his own crime, and of course, he didn't want to reveal his secret. It was all tied together.

He pulled out the wadded-up bandana and unfolded it, laying it on the dresser top under a lamp. Some of the pebbles were more speckled than others and he could tell that some of the glitter was from a few smatterings of quartz, but there was a distinct yellowish tinge to the rocks. He was impressed, since this was just a random sample of the rock, found in a collapsed portion of the hole. He could only imagine what might lie at the end of the passage and he wondered how he could clear it out and shore it up so he could effectively explore it. He had never seen anything like this. He had been so focused on finding Slim's clues he had barely imagined what he would do if he actually found something. Back in Austin, both Godson and Sally had emphasized this simple fact to him several times in their protests but he had ignored them. Now he knew it was an important consideration, an obvious issue that never should have been disregarded.

Even under ideal conditions, an excavation would be difficult and he knew it really might be impossible for him to get in there and find out what might be at the end of that ragged hole. If it were *the* mine, meaning the Sublett mine, it had obviously been worked along the fault, most likely by someone digging along a pay streak. He had no idea how far that recess stretched into that cliff side. When he got back, he knew he would have to do a lot more research, especially about mining.

He took out his wrinkled and dirty map.

"Gonna have to order a new one," he said as he unfolded it.

He carefully scanned the contours and he could see the faint pencil markings and the small holes he had punched, especially the one at the location of his little secret. He smiled. He knew he could find that spot again ...and he thought it was fortunate that it was somewhat accessible from the highway too. He opened a drawer on the little motel desk and found a cheap ballpoint pen and instinctively scribbled on the note paper to make sure it worked. He made some small marks in ink to augment his other markings on the map, then folded it and stowed it in the map pocket of his pack. He slipped into his clean underwear and dirty jeans and stretched out on top of the bedspread and soon fell sound asleep.

Thirty

Sam was startled out of his sleep by a light tapping at the door. He quietly got up from the bed and looked through the peephole, but at first didn't see a thing. Then, straining, he barely made out the top of a head and as he squinted through sleepy eyes, he recognized Smidgeon. He opened the door and she came in, bearing a large Styrofoam cup and a food container. He immediately recognized a familiar smell.

"Geez, look at you," she said, placing the containers on the small table by the window. She reached out and gently touched one of the bruises on his side.

He retracted slightly, not so much from pain, but from the realization that he had forgotten he wasn't wearing a shirt. He was glad he had fallen asleep wearing his pants.

Smidgeon frowned and said, "They beat the ever-loving crap out of you, didn't they?"

"Yeah, but I don't know if that is from them hitting me or from them throwing me down that embankment." He fumbled with a T-shirt from his pack. It was the last of his clean clothes.

Smidgeon shook her head in disgust. "Not sure that matters, honey. Well, look, I brought you some coffee and an 'Especial' ...I remembered you liked it and, well, I know just by looking at you that you need some warm food in you."

He smiled. "I *knew* that was what I smelled! Smidgeon, you've been just super, I can't tell you how much you've helped me."

"You don't know the half of it, hon. I've heard things, people talking in my place," she said.

"What?"

"Well, it ain't regular old gossip or nothing like that, but I think some other hands from that ranch, the white ones, were in today. I heard a lot of muttering about "looking for him" and such. I don't think they were talking about missing steers."

"I need to get out of here."

Smidgeon shook her head. "You best lay low, at least the rest of the day. Marcy says you can stay here as long as you need to. This isn't her busy season and nobody stays on the back side when her business is slack."

"I need to talk to Loot, or at least contact him."

Smidgeon smirked. "I don't like the sound of that. He may be the reason you're in trouble."

"No, I don't think so, and anyway, I need to get my car and other stuff. And he's supposedly going to be out prowling around late tonight, looking for me. We had planned a rendezvous to pick me up. He might get involved in something he's not expecting and I don't want him getting hurt. I could try to walk out there after dark. It's on Tesoro Road."

"I know his place," Smidgeon said. "And I know his truck. I imagine he's got no phone. I don't think you should be out walking around. Strangers attract attention and you've already attracted enough."

"You're right, he doesn't have a phone, but he told me I could get word to him through Gillet Osmond."

"Gil? From the feed store?"

Sam nodded.

Smidgeon seemed surprised. "Gil's a good man. He knows that coot?"

"Yeah, I don't know the connection, but before I came out here Loot told me to use Gillet to get word to him that I was coming and Loot was ready for me, so I guess it worked."

"Okay, I'll try to talk to Gil. What should I say?"

He thought for a second. "Just tell him to let Loot know that Sam says the plan has changed. He should sit tight tonight. And tell Gillet to be discreet, right?"

Smidgeon shrugged. "Okay, I'll do that on the way back to the Mossback. I know Gil, he can keep his mouth shut. You stay in here and be quiet. Get some more rest."

"People will think you're keeping a man out here."

She reached out and squeezed his upper arm with a gentle touch and said with a nervous laugh, "Wouldn't be the first time they thought that about me."

Her dark eyes were quite inviting and he fought off an impulse to give her a kiss.

He locked the door behind Smidgeon as she left, sat at the little table by the window and opened the container, savoring the inviting aroma for a few seconds and then he almost inhaled the first real food he had eaten in days. The dish was a bit soggy from steaming itself in the container but he wolfed it down nonetheless, savoring each layer of spicy goodness. Satisfied, he stretched out on the bed and soon fell asleep again.

It was dark outside when there was another sound at the door, again startling him out of a sound sleep. It was pitch black and a dark figure was entering the room. He smelled food and as his eyes adjusted, he could just make out a familiar, short shape outlined in the darkness.

"Smidgeon?"

She turned on the light by the table. "Yeah. I hope you don't mind that Marcy gave me the other key. It's so dark I didn't want to linger out there alone."

"No, that's fine."

"I brought you a burger, fries and a Coke," she said.

He smiled. "I could do a lot worse than you for a savior," he said.

She laughed. "Aw, sweetie, you'd do the same for me, wouldn't you?"

He smiled and nodded sheepishly.

She set the sacks down and said, "Okay, I talked to Gil right after I left here. He was just leaving for a late lunch and said he'd drop by Loot's and deliver your message."

"Good. Thanks for that."

He looked in one of the bags. "Dinner for two?"

"Why not," she said. "I have to eat, too."

"Then let's eat," he said.

He smiled and pulled out a chair and gestured for Smidgeon to sit, which she did and then he sat in the other chair.

"You are quite the gentleman."

He laughed and said with a pronounced drawl, "Aw, shucks, ma'am."

She chuckled as she pulled burgers, fries and drinks out of the bags.

"So, what do you want to do?" she asked.

"I figure now that it's dark, we pull out of here and you drop me off close to Loot's place," he said.

"I still can't believe you trust him, but Gil did say that at least he was off the booze."

"Smidgeon, all I know is that Loot came through for me. He didn't know me from Adam, but he seemed to know what I was doing and went out of his way to seek me out and warn me. Then he gave me some really sound advice and good help. He didn't need to. Turns out he knew that Slim guy from way back. You know, the guy from the jail? They were old buddies from years ago."

"What was his name again?"

"Ted 'Slim' Longo."

"Slim Longo," Smidgeon said thoughtfully, "seems I've heard that name once or twice. You hear all sorts of snatches of conversation working in a café and Van Horn is sort of a way station for all types of people." She sighed and asked, "Well, when you want to do this?"

"I think I need to get out of town immediately, like tonight. So, right after we finish eating?"

"Really? So soon?" Sam detected a tone of regret in her voice. "I thought maybe you'd stay an extra day, rest up." She reached out and touched his arm as she said this. Then she retracted it. "Silly, I don't know what I was thinking." She seemed flustered.

"Look, you've been great. I really don't know what I would have done without you. You're an angel, you know that?"

She shook her head, "No, I'm no angel."

"Well, you are to me."

"Sam, I have had guys coming on to me all day every day for years. When I was younger, my dad scared most of them off, but I've had me my flings. It's a small town with no secrets, you know? Nothing much ever came of most of them except a couple of bad marriages. Now I've changed my reputation around here ...when I quit thinking of myself as damaged goods, everybody else stopped thinking of me like that too. I've sort of settled into my own routine and there isn't much time for romance. And I'm a respected business owner, one with an attitude. Still, I guess I get lonely sometimes. I like you, Sam."

"You are awesome. I like you, too."

She smiled. "Now here comes the *but,* right?"

He laughed. "You got me. But I have a job in Austin and I do have to go back."

"I know, I know," she said. "I don't know what I was thinking."

"Natural stuff," Sam said, "and hey, we're adults. We're attracted to each other. What's wrong with that? I do know this: I'll be back, but I have to make plans. I don't know how long I can keep this a secret, but I need to figure out if I can get anything out of that hole I found while the secret holds."

"Is there another *but* here?"

"No, more like an *and* ...and you'll be a part of that. You are a partner. As is Loot. I owe you both."

"You don't owe me nothing, sweetie," she said as she reached out and squeezed his hand.

"Nevertheless," he said. "That is a promise. I'll have to see what I can do. Old Ben Sublett, he just pulled out enough to get him by for a while and then he'd go back and pull out a little more. Maybe that's the way to handle it."

"Could be. Otherwise, if old man MacGregg ever finds it, he'll just knock the whole mountain down to get it all for himself."

When they finished eating, he gathered the few things he had pulled out of his pack and stuffed them back into it. As he did this, he noticed that the small jewelry box had worked its way around to the main compartment again. As he replaced it in the middle section, he thought about his luck. Some of it had been bad, but most of it had been good. Smidgeon gathered up the wrappers and cups. "Guess I'll have to help Marcy clean up this room now," she laughed.

He smoothed the covers on the bed and Smidgeon added, "I wouldn't bother with that. Looks like you've left a layer of dirt on them."

He laughed.

Smidgeon picked up the keys as they walked out the door. "I'll drop these off with Marcy in the morning."

"How much do I owe her for the room?"

"It was a favor for me," she said. "Don't worry about it."

When they got in the car she asked, "You sure you want to do this now? You could get another night's sleep. Hell, I could take you back to my place. You'd be even safer there."

"No, I think I need to put Van Horn behind me for a while," he said. "What's the saying, get while the getting's good? And I feel fine ...I slept almost all day."

Smidgeon smiled. "Okay. I don't like it but, well, it's your decision."

As they pulled around the motel, he saw the entire place was dark.

"Is it closed?"

"Yeah, you were the only one here, so I guess she decided to just shut down for the night. The holidays are like that sometime and this is part of the holiday week, right?"

"Right."

The roads were deserted as they pulled out and drove toward Tesoro Road. Smidgeon turned at the battered sign and headed toward Loot's shack.

"Stop here," he said after just a few yards. "Might be best to just let me walk down the road," he said, "An unfamiliar car on the dead-end road might freak him out."

"Maybe you're right," she said. "Do you still have my number? I remember I gave it to you before that ice storm."

He shook his head, saying, "I still have the card, but it's back at my house in Austin."

She pulled a card and pen from a cubbyhole on her dashboard and scribbled on the back. "Okay, here's my home number again, just to be sure. You let me know you got back safe. I mean, call me, okay? Like, right when you get back. I'm going to worry until I hear from you."

He accepted the card and put it in his shirt pocket. "I will," he said, "I promise."

As he opened the car door, Smidgeon reached out and pulled his head over and surprised him with a very passionate kiss and then she shoved him toward the open door. "Now, git! Before I hogtie you and keep you."

He touched the side of her face with his palm, "I owe you my life, Smidgeon. You *are* an angel."

She reached up and touched his hand with hers. He took a deep breath, let out a pronounced sigh before he got out of the car. He exchanged another long look with Smidgeon as he grabbed his pack and walked down the road. After Sam disappeared into the darkness of Tesoro Road, Smidgeon turned around in a driveway and drove off.

At the end of the road, Sam saw Loot's rusty pickup parked in the driveway. He dropped his pack outside the garage, walked up to the door and knocked. He knocked again. He could hear the television blaring. He knocked louder. The door swung open and he was looking down the double barrels of an ancient shotgun.

"Loot! It's me!"

Loot squinted down the long metal tubes in the darkness then his eyes flashed in recognition.

"Sam! How the hell did you get back? Gil told me the plans had changed, so I was just sitting pretty, watching me some TV. Otherwise, I'd be on my way up there right now to look for you."

"Long story," Sam said.

Loot lead Sam back through the piles of wreckage inside the house to the little room at the back. He was surprised to find that this second trip back into the dark confines of the house seemed much shorter than the first. It really was just a tiny shack, but like any trip in unfamiliar territory, the first excursion had seemed endless. Once they were in the little den, Loot cleared the usual spot and they both sat.

"So what happened?"

"They found me. Ranch hands. They were out drunk, hunting I think, and found me sleeping. Beat the hell out of me. Left me for dead," Sam said.

"I told you they was some mean ones. Owner's mean too. Hell, everybody is mean up on that ranch, even the goats."

"I think they're looking for me."

"So I heard. Scuttlebutt around town is that MacGregg was looking for a trespasser. I figured maybe it was you, I mean, you were out on his place, but deep down I hoped it wasn't. I was going to go up there and look for you, though. I knew it was a risk, but people don't pay much attention to old Loot. So what's the new plan? You leaving?"

"Yeah, I think I had better, but first I wanted to show you this." Sam pulled the glittery pebble out of his pocket and handed it to Loot. It sparkled in the light from the blaring TV.

"Shit! Does it scratch yellow?"

"I don't have a scratch plate. I'll have to test it when I get back."

Loot glanced around and laughed. "Got me one somewhere but might take a while to find it. So you think it's old Ben's mine?" Loot continued to examine the rock.

"I found something. It pretty much fits all the clues Slim gave me. Going to be tricky, though."

"Sneak in and sneak out, just like old Ben. That's what you'll have to do."

"That's what I figure. It won't be easy. If it is Ben's mine, it's collapsed."

"Makes sense after a hunnert years or more," Loot said, then added, "...but if you find anything, you'll give me a taste?"

"If I can figure out a way to get anything out of it, you'll get a share. I couldn't have done it without you."

Loot Melding, the old, grizzled trapper, stood there with his eyes glistening. "I don't need a share, just a taste. Probably wouldn't know what to do with a share."

"Well, we can talk about that later. I have to figure out how to get it out of the ground first. But, you know, it is more convenient to the main road than it is to that back way you took me. That's the way I came out."

"Well, that could be good or bad, but I can help you with that, too."

"I hope so. I think I'll have to let things cool down a bit."

"Hell, after a couple of days those assholes will probably figure a cougar, or a pack of coyotes snagged you."

"Yeah, I was pretty sure that was what they were planning at the time. I figured they thought they had finished me off, but I had a lot of luck on my side."

They both laughed at that, but Sam stifled his laugh and said, "Loot, I really need to get out of town, like right now."

"Yep, that's probably a good idea," Loot agreed. "Car's there where you left it," he said, pointing vaguely like he had done the first time Sam had visited.

They again traversed the debris canyons inside Loot's house and walked out to the garage. Loot opened the latch, holding the two doors and swung them open revealing The Clunker.

Loot turned and asked, "So they don't know you found it?"

"Nope. I found it *after* they beat me. Heh. They practically threw me on top of it."

"No shit," Loot repeated with half a laugh, then asked, "...and they don't know who you are?"

"Nope. I left my wallet and driver's license here with my car," he said, smiling.

Loot smiled. "That was a good plan."

Sam fumbled around on top of the front tire and found his keys. He got in the car and opened the glove compartment to pop the trunk latch. He jammed his pack in in the trunk, then found his wallet under the driver's seat and stuffed it in his pocket. Then he turned to Loot.

"You need a little cash, like for gas or something?" Sam asked.

Loot was still admiring the small rock in the dim light. "Nope, "Loot laughed, "I got me everything I ever wanted right here."

Loot fumbled in his pockets and pulled out a ring with an astounding number of keys and trotted over to his truck. "Guess I better move the old clunker out of the way." Sam smiled at the irony of that reference and turned to get into his own Clunker.

Behind him, Loot started the old truck with a mild roar. Sam hesitated as he turned his own key, suffering his usual bout of starter anxiety. He didn't know if it was real or if he imagined it, but there seemed to be a slight pause as he turned the key, but then the starter kicked and the engine sputtered to life. He backed out of the driveway, and then slowly rolled past Loot in his idling truck. The old trapper was still holding the rock at the end of his nose, looking at it while the truck idled. Loot looked up and smiled broadly and rolled down his window. He yelled, "You drive careful, partner!"

Sam waved and smiled, then hesitated. He put the car in neutral and set the parking brake. He got out and approached the truck and stuck out his hand and Loot shook it through the open window.

"Thanks again, Loot."

"See you next time!" Loot said, as he slammed his truck in gear and lurched back up his driveway.

Sam got into The Clunker and headed down Tesoro Road. He turned onto the deserted main street and thought of Smidgeon as he drove past the dark Mossback and was soon back on the interstate, heading east.

He drove through the night, drinking what seemed like a gallon of coffee along the way and kept thinking of little else but the gold mine and his experiences of this trip. He kept running everything through his mind, thinking about Smidgeon, Loot, Diablo Rim, the ranch hands, the plane, and, of course, the elusive 'table' and the collapsed cave-like structure at the bottom of the "Y" in the side of the hill. He repeatedly contemplated the curse and the talisman, counterpoints of his failures and his successes.

He again stopped for gas at the truck stop in Junction, half hoping he'd see Loretta's '63 Chevy Impala waiting for him in the parking lot, but deep down he knew she wouldn't be there. As he pulled back on the highway, he again considered all that talk of the curse and wondered at the coincidence, and wondered if he'd ever see Loretta again. Then, he remembered Smidgeon's dark eyes and the warmth of her parting kiss and realized she was the one he wanted to see again.

"I mean, she saved my life but, there's more to it than that," he said as he drove along.

Between Fredericksburg and Stonewall, he was delayed by herds of deer blocking the road. It slowed him to a crawl for a few miles as the deer aimlessly wandered across the highway, not caring about some puny car. He flashed his lights and honked his horn to no effect, so he had to creep along. He had to stop once when a disinterested buck just stood there looking at him until the stubborn animal finally sauntered out of the way. It was frustrating, like one last ironic twist to be endured at the end of a maddening week.

"The curse again?" he muttered.

Finally, he passed the last of the loitering deer and was able to get back up to highway speed. He was still running on a combination of coffee and adrenalin when he topped a hill and could see the glow of Austin reflecting on the night sky with just a few highlights of dawn beginning to show. Sam smiled because he knew he would soon be trudging up those crumbling old steps to his dark and silent garage-apartment outpost at the edge of the park. He was usually elated at the prospect of a safe ending to one of these trips, but somehow, this time, it didn't seem like the end of anything. It felt different, more like a new beginning.

Meet Thomas Fenske

Thomas Fenske is originally from Texas but currently lives in central North Carolina. When he wrote *The Fever*, he worked as an IT professional, but he is now retired, living a quiet life with his wife and an assortment of pets.

Other Works from the Pen of

Thomas Fenske

Traces of Treasure Series:

Book One – The Fever - When a chance encounter provides some clues that supposedly point to the location of a lost gold mine, Sam Milton's life is forever changed.

Book Two – A Curse That Bites Deep - People are dying; suspicions run high, and Sam seems to be at the center of it all. Can he unravel the mystery before it sweeps him and everyone he cares about into oblivion?

Book Three - Lucky Strike A bitter, decades-old grudge surfaces with a vengeance in a small west Texas town.

Book Four – Penumbra - Reluctant treasure hunter Sam Milton and his girlfriend Smidgeon Toll find themselves immersed in the search for a missing man they have never met and end up on the trail of a cache of ancient gold in the desert southwest.

The Hag Rider - This Civil War memoir explores a fifteen-year-old cavalryman's transition to manhood, complicated by the spectral manipulations of a hoodoo witch sworn to protect him.

Harmon Creek - Harmon Creek is crafted around several known facts of a 1930 Texas incident, effectively bridging the gap between crime fiction and true-crime.

Dear reader,

I hope you've enjoyed reading the first in the Traces of Treasure series that was first published in 2015.

Your opinion is valuable to other
readers like you,
who may be looking for books like mine.

Please consider taking a few minutes to post a review,
however brief,
on the site where you purchased this book.

You may also want to visit my author page
where you can obtain all the other books in the series
as well as two other standalone novels of mine.

Thank you!

Thomas Fenske

www.ingramcontent.com/pod-product-compliance
Lightning Source LLC
Chambersburg PA
CBHW071530110726
47908CB00007B/1822